THE PATSY

THE PATSY

JAY FITZPATRICK

Hard Pressed Publishing
New York

Hard Pressed Publishing

ISBN: 069292471X
ISBN 13: 9780692924716
Library of Congress Control Number: 2017914419
Hard Pressed, Southampton, NY

ALSO BY JAY FITZPATRICK

FEAR ITSELF

BEST SERVED ICY

For
Marge and Johnny
& 2nd Street

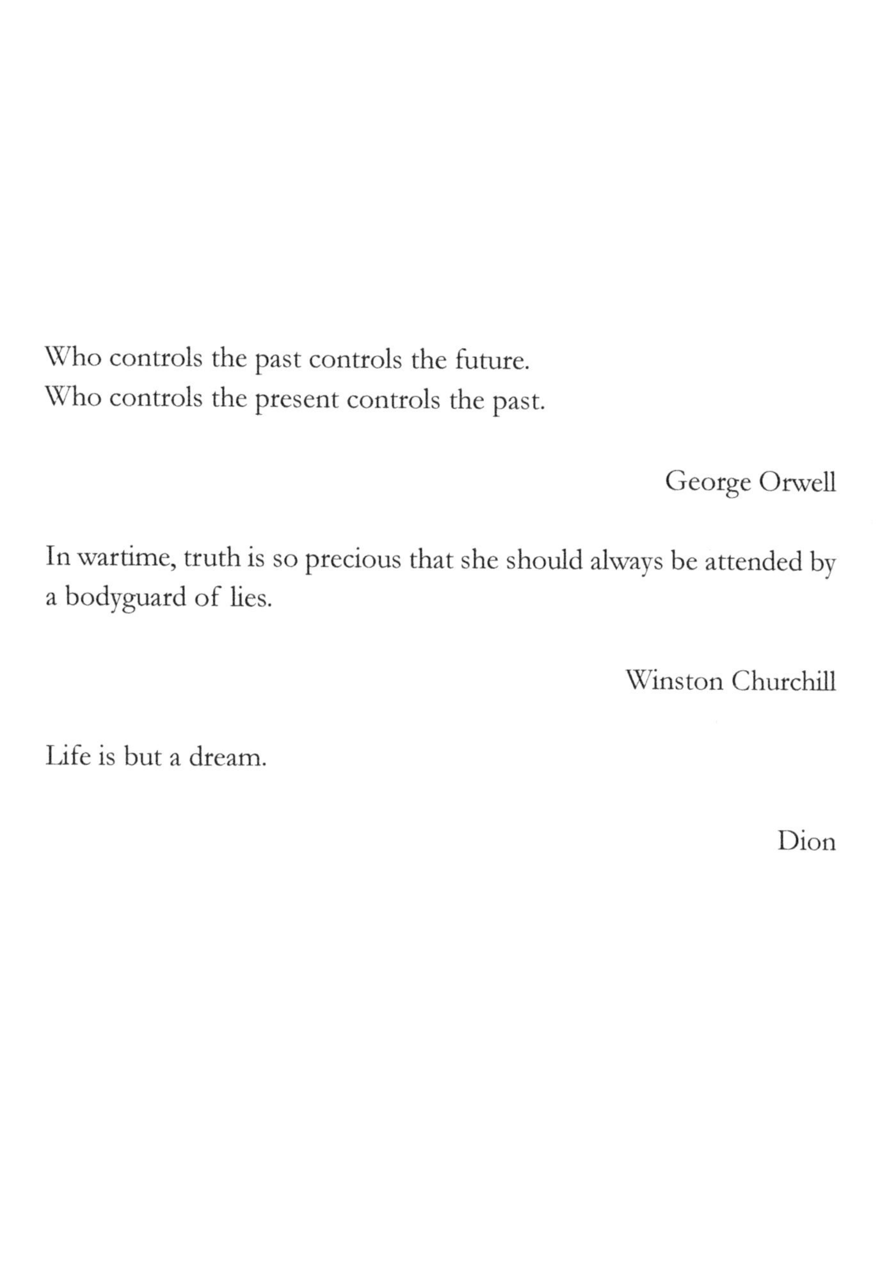

Who controls the past controls the future.
Who controls the present controls the past.

George Orwell

In wartime, truth is so precious that she should always be attended by a bodyguard of lies.

Winston Churchill

Life is but a dream.

Dion

PROLOGUE

DALLAS, TEXAS
NOVEMBER 22-24, 1963

My name is Lee Oswald, not Lee Harvey Oswald. It seems that the newspapers like to add middle names: John Wilkes Booth, James Earl Ray, and Thomas Arthur Vallee. Who? More on Vallee in a minute. In the Marines, they called me Osvaldovich, because of my Marxist leanings, while others called me Ozzie, after the TV show, but my family and friends call me Lee.

I'm going to tell you a short story, not the whole story but the whole truth, at least that which can be corroborated. I liked President Kennedy. I even tipped-off the FBI about 'Plan A', the Chicago assassination plot to kill the president. Oh, you didn't hear about that one?

On November 1, 1963, in Chicago, the Secret Service detained and questioned two members of a four-man sniper team suspected of planning to assassinate President Kennedy during his visit to Chicago the following day. Two of the team members escaped and one was released after questioning. The fourth team member, Thomas Arthur Vallee, a mentally damaged ex-Marine, worked in a building overlooking Kennedy's motorcade route.

On the day Kennedy was supposed to be in Chicago, November 2, 1963, South Vietnam President Diem and his brother Ngo were assassinated by a Vietnamese Army/CIA backed coup, sanctioned by President Kennedy.

Kennedy approved the coup but not the assassination. White House Press Secretary Pierre Salinger announced President Kennedy's trip to Chicago had been canceled, thanks to my tip. While the two suspected snipers were questioned at the Chicago Secret Service headquarters, only potential assassin scapegoat Thomas Arthur Vallee was arrested. The other two alleged snipers remained at large in Chicago. Only Vallee was ever identified publicly.

Had 'Plan A' succeeded, the press would have spun the story that Kennedy got what he deserved for sanctioning the Diem coup and assassination; I would probably still be alive but unknown and forgotten, while Thomas Arthur Vallee would be forever remembered as the 'Lone-Nut Assassin'.

Thomas Vallee and I were both former Marines. We both served at Marine bases in Japan that hosted the U–2 spy plane: me at Atsugi, Vallee at Camp Otsu. We were both involved in training anti–Castro Cubans: me in New Orleans, Vallee in New York. We both had then recently started working at premises that overlooked the routes of presidential parades: me at the Texas School Book Depository on Elm Street in Dallas, Vallee at IPP Litho–Plate building on West Jackson Boulevard in Chicago.

Does any of this sound familiar or coincidental?

Here's the truth about what happened the moment our president was assassinated and the truth about what happened to me.

At 12:30 p.m., CST, I was in the 2nd-floor lunch room taking my lunch break. Two colored boys, Junior and Harold, were also there with me but we were not sitting together.

At 12:30 p.m., the same time I was having my lunch break, President John F. Kennedy was shot.

Also at 12:30 p.m., police officer Marion Baker, riding his motorcycle in the motorcade, heard the shots coming from the upper floor of the Texas School Book Depository (TSBD), dismounted, and headed to the TSBD where he believed the shots originated.

At 12:31 p.m., police officer Marion Baker accidentally bumped into building superintendent Roy Truly at the TSBD entrance and together they headed across the floor to the elevators. The elevators were stuck on an upper floor, so they took the stairs.

At 12:32 p.m., police officer Baker and Roy Truly reached the second floor and saw me in the lunch room. Junior and Harold had just left. Officer Baker, with his revolver drawn, called to me, "Come here." I walked towards him. Officer Baker turned to Truly and asked, "Do you know this man, and does he work for you?" "That's okay. He works here, that's Lee Oswald," answered Truly.

At 12:34 p.m., as I was leaving the building, a young man identifying himself as a Secret Service agent, asked me where the nearest pay phone was. I pointed the phone out to the agent then left the building. I went outside and stood around for five minutes with foreman Bill Shelly, and after hearing what had occurred, meaning the president had been shot, I knew I had to leave.

At 12:40 p.m., I left the book depository wearing a long-sleeve brown shirt, walked east on Elm Street and saw a city bus stopped in traffic as I was approaching Griffin St. I think I am being followed. I walked to the bus and began pounding on the door. The driver, later identified as Cecil McWatters, opened the door and allowed me, and a blond woman, to board the bus. I think the blond woman is a tail.

By 12:44 p.m., the bus was soon stalled in traffic and I got up from my seat, obtained a bus transfer, and left the bus via the front door. The blond woman left the bus at the same time via the rear door. I walked three blocks south on Lamar St. toward the Greyhound Bus station and got into William Whaley's taxi. Whaley later said of me, "He wasn't in any hurry. He wasn't nervous or anything. He was wearing a dark brown button-up shirt, over a white t-shirt."

At 12:54 p.m., I get out of the cab at Beckley and Neely Street, one block from my rooming house. No one seemed to be following me. I lost the tail.

At 1:00 p.m., I walked to my rooming house at 1026 Beckley Street. The housekeeper, Earlene Roberts, saw me come in and go to my room. She and I both heard a car horn toot and she said later that she looked out the window and saw Dallas police patrol car number 10.

At 1:05 p.m., I walked out of my rooming house and went to the bus stop. A police car pulled up and the officer slid over and opened the passenger door for me to get in. I am vaguely familiar with the officer from the Carousel Club and the coffee shop so I get in. Then, according to a pre-arranged plan, I'm driven to the Texas Theatre. The police officer, whose name I later found out was J. D. Tippit was sent to drive me because I don't drive. I suspected my handlers arranged this.

1:07 p.m., Instead of driving directly to the Texas Theatre we pull over at 10th. and Patton. Two men get out of a gray car, approached our car, say something to Tippit and motioned for me to get out. Now the hair on the back of my neck stood up and I suspected trouble. I opened the door to get out but instead of going towards the two men I ran and dove into some bushes. I heard a gunshot and felt a round go over my head. I ran like hell between the houses into a backyard, over a fence, and onto the next street. I heard more shots but they didn't seem to be coming in my direction. I later found out that Tippit was shot four times in the chest and stomach and a 'coup de grace' point-blank shot to the head. It had been said later that I was the prime target. The killing of Jefferson Davis Tippit was an unfortunate accident. He just got in the way. They pinned the killing on me to help motivate the Dallas police to kill me in the Texas Theatre, which would have in effect disposed of me, the scapegoat, before I could protest being framed.

1:13 p.m., I run as fast as I can to the theater about five blocks away. I hear police sirens in the distance. I enter the theater, take a seat and try to make contact with my cutout, a contact who I was told would be at the theater and would give me further instructions. You didn't think I was trying to pretend I was not involved in this whole mess, did you?

At 1:17 p.m., I purchase popcorn from the concession clerk, and then returned to the lower level and take a seat next to a pregnant woman. Within a few minutes, we both get up from our seats. It was uncomfortable as she was not the cutout. I then walked again into the concession area and then back into the lower level and took a seat next to a fellow (later identified as Jack Davis) in the first row on the right side. Davis remembered that I was sitting next to him, in the nearly empty theater, as the opening credits to the movie began. After sitting next to Davis for a few minutes, I got up and walked past empty seats to the small aisle on the right side of the theater and into the concession area. Davis watched me as I again re-entered the theater and took a seat next to a man on the back row, directly across the aisle from Davis. Within a few minutes, I got up and once again returned to the concession area. I returned a few minutes later and took a seat across the aisle from Mr. Davis, next to another guy, and then moved to another seat in the fourth row. It appeared to Davis, as he later testified, that I was looking for someone, perhaps a contact.

At 1:45 p.m., I'm arrested at the Texas Theatre. How that happened went something like this. About 30 minutes earlier, Mrs. Julia Postal, selling tickets at the box office of the Texas Theatre, heard police sirens and then saw a man, she later identified as me, duck into the outer lobby space of the theater near the ticket office. Attracted by the sound of the sirens, Mrs. Postal stepped out of the box office and walked to the curb. Shortly thereafter, Johnny Brewer, who had come from the nearby shoe store, asked Mrs. Postal whether the fellow that had ducked in had bought a ticket. She said, "No; by golly, he didn't." Brewer told Mrs. Postal that he had seen the man ducking into his place of business and that he had followed him to the theater. She sent Brewer into the theater to find me and check the exits, told him about the assassination news on the radio, and said, "I don't know if this is the man they want...but he is running from them for some reason." She then called the police.

The police found me, watching a movie.

I was sitting alone in the rear of the main floor of the theater near the right center aisle. Brewer pointed me out, but the police searched two other theater patrons first. Then a policeman, later identified as M.N. McDonald, reached me and told me to get on my feet. Fearing these officers would also try and kill me I rose from my seat, bringing up both hands. As McDonald started to search my waist for a gun ... I struck him between the eyes with my left fist; and with my right hand, I drew a gun from my waist. McDonald struck back with his right hand and grabbed the gun with his left hand. We both fell into the seats. Three other officers, moving toward the scuffle, grabbed me from the front, rear and side. McDonald fell into the seat with his left hand on the gun, he later claimed he felt something graze across his hand and heard what sounded like the snap of the hammer. (I found out later that the gun I was given didn't work. It had a bent firing pin.) McDonald felt the pistol scratch his cheek as he wrenched it away from me. A detective, who was standing beside McDonald, seized the gun. I was handcuffed, and led from the theater, and was, according to McDonald, "cursing a little bit and hollering police brutality." They said I rambled. I think I did. "Well, it's all over now. . . I don't know why you are treating me like this. The only thing I have done is carry a pistol into a movie. . . I don't see why you handcuffed me. . .Why should I hide my face? I haven't done anything to be ashamed of. . . I want a lawyer. . . I am not resisting arrest . . . I didn't kill anybody. . . I haven't shot anybody . . . I protest this police brutality. . . I fought back there, but I know I wasn't supposed to be carrying a gun . . .What is this all about?"

From 2:00 - 2:15 p.m., I'm driven to the police department. In the car, I'm questioned, and I ramble a bit more. "What is this all about? I know my rights. . . A police officer has been killed? I hear they burn for murder. Well, they say it just takes a second to die . . . All I did was carry a gun . . .Why are you treating me this way? ... I am not being handled right . . . I demand my rights."

At 2:15 p.m., I'm taken into the police department.

At 2:25 - 4:04 p.m., interrogation begins in the office of Captain Will Fritz. "My name is Lee Oswald; I work at the Texas School Book Depository Building."

"Have you ever been in Mexico City?"

"I was never in Mexico City. I have been in Tijuana, though." I'm asked dozens of questions and I fire back answers. "I never owned a rifle myself, but I was present in the Texas School Book Depository Building. I have been employed there since Oct. 15. My usual place of work is on the first floor. However, I frequently use the fourth, fifth, sixth, and seventh floors to get books. Because of all the confusion, I figured there would be no work performed that afternoon, so I decided to go home. I changed my clothing and went to a movie. I carried a pistol with me to the movie because I felt like it, for no other reason . . . and no I didn't shoot President Kennedy or Tippit."

From 4:45 - 6:30 p.m., the second interrogation began in Captain Fritz's office. "When I left the Texas School Book Depository, I went to my room, where I changed my trousers, got a pistol, and went to a picture show. You know how boys do when they have a gun, they carry it. The only package I brought to work was my lunch. I got the pistol in Fort Worth several months ago . . . but I refuse to tell you where the pistol was purchased. I never ordered any guns . . . I am not a malcontent. Nothing irritated me about the president. Everybody will know who I am now."

6:30 p.m., I appear in a lineup for witnesses Cecil J. McWatters, Sam Guinyard, and Ted Callaway. I have no idea who they are. On the way, reporters yell questions at me.

I answered back to reporters in the hall.

". . . giving me a hearing without legal representation or anything."

"Did you shoot the president?"

"I didn't shoot anyone. No, sir."

7:10 p.m., I'm arraigned for the murder of Officer J. D. Tippit of the Dallas Police Department.

7:55 P.M., In the hallway I responded to more questions from reporters.

"I'm asking for legal representation, but these police officers have not allowed me to have any. I don't know what this is about."

"Did you kill the president?"

"No, sir, I did not."

"Did you shoot the president? Were you there?"

"I work in that building."

"Were you in the building at the time?"

"Naturally, if I work in the building. Yes, sir."

"Did you shoot the president?"

"No. They are taking me in because I lived in the Soviet Union. I'm just a patsy."

8:55 p.m., A paraffin test is conducted in Captain Fritz's office.

"I will not sign the fingerprint card until I talk to my attorney. . .What are you trying to prove with this paraffin test, that I fired a gun? You are wasting your time. I don't know anything about what you are accusing me of." A paraffin test is applied to my hands and right cheek. While they said my hands reacted positively my cheek did not. I told them that it was probably from all the ink from the books I pack.

At 12:10 a.m. Saturday, November 23, I appear in a lineup for a press conference. As I am being led to the lineup, reporters ask me about the earlier arraignment.

"Well, I was a questioned by a judge, however, I, ah, protested at that time that I was not allowed legal representation. So, during that, very short and sweet hearing, ah, I really don't know what the situation is about. Nobody has told me anything, but I am accused of murdering a policeman. I know nothing more than that, and I do request someone to come forward to give me legal assistance."

"Did you kill the president?"

"No. I have not been charged with that. In fact, nobody has said that to me yet. The first thing I heard about it was when the newspaper reporters in the hall asked me that question."

"You have been charged."

"Sir?"

"You have been charged."

This was the moment I knew I was done for. My expression tells it all. I'm in shock and turn to leave. I've had it. As I am escorted away a reporter asked me a final question.

"What happened to your eye?"

"A policeman hit me."

From 10:30 a.m. until 1:10 p.m., I am back for more interrogation in Captain Will Fritz's office. "I never owned a rifle . . . I didn't shoot John Kennedy . . . I didn't even know Governor John Connally had been shot. I don't own a rifle . . . I don't own a rifle at all, but I did have a small rifle some years in the past."

From 1:10 - 1:30 p.m., my mother, Marguerite, and my wife, Marina, along with my daughter, are allowed in to visit. "It's a mistake. I'm not guilty," I tell them.

At 1:35 a.m., I'm arraigned for the murder of President John F. Kennedy.

From 3:30 - 3:40 p.m., my brother Robert is allowed in to see me. "I don't know what is going on. I just don't know what they are talking about," I tell him.

From 5:30 - 5:35 p.m., I'm visited by H. Louis Nichols, President of the Dallas Bar Association. "Well, I really don't know what this is all about, but I have been kept incarcerated and kept incommunicado."

6:00 - 6:30 p.m., I'm again interrogated in Captain Fritz's office. "I have no receipts for the purchase of any gun, and I have never ordered any guns. I do not own a rifle, never possessed a rifle."

Around 10:15 p.m., I try to make a phone call to my cut-out John Hurt in Raleigh, but I'm told there was no answer.

9:30 - 11:15 a.m., Sunday, November 24, I am back in Fritz's office. Fritz asked me what happened after the assassination and he and the other detectives just keep firing questions at me. I told them, "After all the commotion, a police officer stopped me, and my superintendent of the place stepped up and told the officer that I am one of the employees in the building. A Secret Service agent came rushing into the School Book Depository Building and asked me, 'Where is your telephone?' He showed me some kind of credential and identified himself. 'Right there,'" I answered, pointing to the phone ... If you ask me about the shooting of Tippit ... I don't know what you are talking about ... The only thing I am here for is because I popped a policeman in the nose in the theater on Jefferson Avenue, which I readily admit I did because I was protecting myself ... I learned about the job vacancy at the Texas School Book Depository from people in Mrs. Paine's neighborhood ... I never ordered a rifle under the name of Hidell, Oswald, or any other name ... I didn't own any rifle. I have not practiced or shot with a rifle. I subscribe to two publications from Russia, one being a hometown paper published in Minsk, where I met and married my wife ... I don't recall anything about an A. J. Hidell being on the post office card. I presume you have reference to a map I had in my room with some Xs on it. I have no automobile. I have no means of conveyance. I have to walk to where I am going most of the time. I was seeking a job, and I would put these markings on this map, so I could plan my itinerary around with less walking. Each one of these Xs represented a place where I went and interviewed for a job, you can check each one of them out if you want to…but I told you I haven't shot a rifle since the Marines, possibly a small bore, maybe a .22, but not anything larger since I have left the Marine Corps … I never received a package sent to me through the mailbox in Dallas, box number 2915, under the name of Alek Hidell, absolutely not … I did not kill President Kennedy or Officer Tippit. If you want me to cop out to hitting or plead guilty to hitting a cop in the mouth when I was arrested, yeah, I plead guilty to that. But I do deny shooting both the president and Tippit.

At 11:10 a.m., it was time for the preparation for my transfer to the county jail. I asked for a shirt from clothing that was brought to the office to wear over my T-shirt. "I don't want a hat; I will just take one of those sweaters, the black one."

At 11:15 a.m., Inspector Thomas J. Kelley of the Secret Service, has a conversation with me. Kelley approached me, out of the hearing of others, except perhaps Captain Fritz's men, and said that as a Secret Service agent, he was anxious to talk with me as soon as I secured counsel because I was charged with the assassination of the president but had denied it. I said, "I will be glad to discuss this proposition with my attorney, and that after I talk with one, we could either discuss it with him or discuss it with my attorney, if the attorney thinks it is a wise thing to do, but at the present time I have nothing more to say to you."

"I put the handcuffs on him," Leavelle said.

"In the process of doing that, I more in jest kind of said, Lee if anybody shoots at you, I hope they're as good a shot as you are, meaning, of course, that they'd hit him and not me. He kind of laughed and he said, oh, you're being melodramatic, or something to that effect. Nobody's going to shoot at me."

At 11:21 a.m., while walking to the armored car that was to take me to the county jail, we came around the corner and were surrounded by reporters and TV crews. A man rushed towards me. I recognize him and thought to myself, *Ruby? What are you….*

I was shot once in the stomach. It was very painful but I could have easily survived. However, I laid there on the floor for 30 minutes and was given no bandages or oxygen, and no medical personnel attended to me. Leavelle did remove my handcuffs. When the ambulance finally arrived, I was placed on a stretcher and put in the back. The ambulance medical assistant in the front seat, beside the driver, was not asked to attend to me on the way to the hospital. Leavelle, Graves, and Detective Charles Dhority rode in the back with me, but neither made any attempt to stop the bleeding, or help me in any way. It's as though they wanted me to die.

I was pronounced dead at Parkland Hospital at 1:07 p.m. local time.

CHAPTER 1

The Oval Office Washington, DC November 2016

It was Saturday evening and President Thomas Dean Burk and his guest had just finished dinner in the West Wing dining room and retired to the Oval Office for after dinner drinks and conversation. His guests included some of his staff who also happened to be his closest friends: FBI Director Raymond Riley, Chief of Staff Bill Nicholas, White House Press Secretary Kelly Sullivan Burk, and another old friend, Dr. Tony Provenzano.

It was an easy night following a hectic day, but as tomorrow was Sunday the five friends felt they could loosen up a bit and enjoy themselves. Coffee and drinks were available on the sidebar and everyone helped themselves. They sat on the two couches: FBI Director Raymond Riley, and Chief of Staff Bill Nicholas were on one couch while White House Press Secretary Kelly Sullivan Burk sat on the other. Dr. Provenzano sat in one of the two chairs closest to the fireplace while the president sat in the other. Next to the president sat Max, his young German Shepherd.

Tommy Burk and Tony Provenzano worked together in Manhattan, many years ago, building many projects together. Before Tommy Burk was president he was an architect in New York City, and Tony, before he received his

Doctorate in Physics and Engineering from MIT, was one of New York's biggest electrical contractors. President Burk and Dr. Provenzano both started life as tough guys. Burk in Southwest Philly, Tony in Brooklyn. President Burk was now 70, stood 6' tall and about 200 lbs. Not fat, not muscle; he was just a big guy. He had blue eyes, dirty blond hair, an infectious smile that let you in but not for long. In other words, you had to earn his respect and friendship. President Burk didn't suffer fools and didn't take shit from anyone. He never started anything but when he felt he was right he went in with his left. Dr. Provenzano at 72 years old looked every bit like a younger Richard Gere. Tommy Burk and Tony Provenzano may not have been princes of the city back in the eighties, but they helped build the kingdom.

President Burk had dismissed the steward for the evening and rose from his chair to stoke the fire. With the fire now awake, the president put the poker back in the stand and returned to his chair. President Burk seemed to be reflecting on something, then said, "Now that we have won reelection and are about to start our second term, I have been thinking about my legacy. Just look at the presidents in our lifetime. Kelly, a few of these fellow's pre-date you so please indulge me. Our previous president's two terms pulled us out of a bad recession but doubled our debt. Some say she created a racial divide and signed a ridiculous nuclear deal with Iran; a decent president, yes, but..."

"A decent president? Have you forgotten how we got here? As for the nuclear deal with Iran, your executive order reversed it," said Riley.

"Yes, that's true, but we digress. Bush, the son, dropped the ball on 9/11, and yes you could argue that the Bill Clinton administration also fumbled that ball, but Bush's biggest mistake was that bloody revenge war in Iraq. He, Rumsfeld and his vice president, the one that drowned, should be charged as war criminals. Then as he leaves office he gives us the worst financial meltdown ever. Clinton rode the good times, but if he only could have kept his pecker zippered... Bush the father restarted the crusades, but he and Carter were both just one-timers. Fords legacy was giving Nixon a pardon. Johnson gave us Vietnam, and then gave Nixon the currency to end it, but Nixon instead made it his war. Eisenhower gave us the Cold War. Truman gave us the nuclear bomb, despite the protest of his two top generals, MacArthur and LeMay. Both generals said the atomic bombs dropped on Hiroshima and Nagasaki were unnecessary for victory in World War II, and were used primarily as a tool to impress and contain the Russians. Truman also gave us the CIA, the Korean War, and the first use of political correctness. He called the Korean War a 'Police Action'. Over three Million were killed and he called it a fucking 'Police Action'. He then gave Vietnam back to the French for which America would later pay the price. Truman was possibly the worst president ever. Regan did a respectable job with the economy, but he will mostly be remembered for his famous challenge to Russia: 'Mr. Gorbachev, tear down that wall…'"

"Want to take a breath, Sarge?" asked Riley.

President Thomas Dean Burk and FBI Director Raymond Riley had a long history and had been through a couple of wars together, one in a far-off country, and another closer to home. In the far-off war, Riley had been Captain Riley, commanding officer of Golf Company 2nd Battalion 7th Marines. Burk had been Sergeant Burk, 2nd platoon sargeant. President Burk sometimes addressed Riley by his former title of Captain, while FBI Director Riley would sometimes refer to the president as Sarge. In the war, closer to home, Burk took command, and together they fought evil, won, and Burk was propelled from darkness into POTUS, and Riley, then NYC Police Commissioner, to Director of the Federal Bureau of Investigation. Riley at 71 was just under 6' and 170 lbs. and was in great shape. His face was chiseled and he still sported a regulation high and tight.

"Yeah, I do tend to go on, but there is one more president that did more in less time than all the others put together."

"Kennedy," answered Kelly.

White House Press Secretary Kelly Sullivan Burk was also the president's wife and the country's first lady. She was half her husband's age, blond hair, tall, thin and quite attractive. Kelly was the reporter who tried to bring

Tommy Burk down before the election, and before she learned the truth and joined his side. She helped launch and run Tommy's presidential 'Live and Let Live Party' along with FBI Director Riley. The three of them were thick as thieves.

"Yes, Kennedy. I am not going to get into everything he had to deal with because I just want to stick with legacy, and his was the greatest."

"His womanizing or his assassination?" asked Nicholas.

Chief of Staff Bill Nicholas was the president's oldest friend. From sixth grade on the two were almost inseparable. Bill was a big guy with a big laugh and a big personality. He had a mop of red hair, fair skin and a mind of his own. He was easy to get along with until he wasn't.

"Neither, and don't be cheeky. I am talking about the greatest, most fantastic, impossible journey ever taken. President Kennedy took us to the Moon."

CHAPTER 2

THE PENTAGON ARLINGTON, VIRGINIA

Secretary of Defense Ed Stanton sat across from NSA Director Roger Michaels, CIA Deputy Director Prescott Cabell, and newly installed National Security Adviser, General Michael (Mickey) Finn.

"Are we sure?" asked SecDef Stanton.

"Positive," replied NSA Director Michaels. "We have excellent voice prints that are 99.9% positive. It's ISIL's Abu Bakr al-Baghdadi."

"He not talking directly to him, is he?" asked SecDef Stanton.

"Of course, not. They both had translators."

"Just give me the main gist again."

"They were discussing a proposed meeting."

"Where? Not in AL-Raqqah or Pyongyang?"

"Bulgaria. In Sofia, sometime in the next couple of weeks."

"But Bulgaria is part of NATO."

"Correct. But the two countries, North Korea and Bulgaria, established diplomatic relations back in 1948 and signed a bilateral cooperation agreement in 1970. Bulgaria is one of the few countries officially visited more than once by Kim Jong-un," advised NSA Director Michaels.

"But why? What could those two see in each other, aside from both wanting to destroy the U.S?" asked Stanton.

Quiet until now, General Finn murmured, "The coming storm."

"What was that Mickey? Go on," said Stanton.

"North Korea is an agnostic state and is definitely not looking for religion. Radical Islam, ISIL, The Islamic State of Iraq and the Levant, is a state in name only. ISIL is looking for a state. If the North Korean and Islam stars align, we will be looking into the face of pure evil."

"You know something, Mickey?" asked Stanton.

"I did my thesis on North Korea at the War College and fought ISIL in Iraq. Yeah, I know something. Look. Kim Jong-un and Baghdadi talking or even thinking about each other is never a good thing."

"Why wouldn't ISIL align with Somalia, Iran, or Seria?" asked Stanton.

"They have. And I believe it's with Iran."

"But it's Baghdadi talking with Kim Jong-un, not the Ayatollah."

"It's Baghdadi's voice print but it's Iran's fingerprints all over this thing. Iran doesn't have the bomb but desperately wants to send one to America. North Korea has the bomb but no conventional way to deliver it; regardless of all the media hype. Think of ISIL as their delivery service - you know: 'When it absolutely, positively has to be there overnight.'"

"We need to get more information and then inform the president," Stanton declared.

CHAPTER 3

THE OVAL OFFICE WASHINGTON, DC

President Burk and his guest FBI Director Riley, Chief of Staff Nicholas, White House Press Secretary Kelly Sullivan Burk, and Dr. Tony Provenzano continued the discussion about the president's legacy.

"So, you want to go back to the Moon? Mars perhaps?" asked Chief of Staff Nicholas a bit sarcastically.

"No. Been there, done that. I think entrepreneur outfits like Jeff Bezos' Blue Origin, and Elon Musk's SpaceX have that under control. After fifty years of human activity in space, we have produced societal benefits that improve the quality of life on Earth. The first satellites, satellite telecommunications, global positioning, and advances in weather forecasting, solar panels, implantable heart monitors, cancer therapy, light-weight materials, water-purification systems, improved computing systems, global search-and-rescue, and cell phones. All great stuff came from JFK taking us to the Moon, but I'm thinking something a little different."

Scratching Max's head, the president looked at Chief of Staff Nicholas and asked, "Have you ever thought about time travel?"

"You mean like H. G. Wells' *The Time Machine*?"

"Yes, that, but any kind of time travel."

"I love history, so I would go back in time," said Nicholas.

"Kelly?"

"If the future would make me look older and the past younger, I'm guessing..."

"I don't have to ask Tony and Ray since we have discussed Newton's, Einstein's and Tesla's theories, paradoxes and possibilities many times. Tony, as you know, is a consultant for NASA and is studying new methods of propulsion that will allow the building of a warp drive ship. This ship, the IXS Enterprise, will be our ride into the future."

"I always thought time travel was a fantasy," suggested Kelly.

"If it is, we are all living a fantasy," Dr. Provenzano chimed in.

"How so?" asked Kelly.

"Because we are all time travelers. We are all traveling into the future as we speak. Admittedly it is kind of slow but forward nevertheless. I started traveling into the future seventy-two years ago and just got here now. It seems like only yesterday I started my journey, and in just a few hours we will all travel together into tomorrow," stated Dr. Provenzano.

Everyone just kind of sat there and contemplated the doctor's revelation.

CHAPTER 4

Pyongyang, North Korea and Tehran, Iran

Pyongyang is the capital and largest city of North Korea. It is located on the Taedong River about 110 kilometers (68 miles) upstream from the West Korea Sea and, according to preliminary results from the 2008 population census, has a population of 3,255,388.

Inside Room 39 located inside the ruling Workers' Party building in Pyongyang, sat 34-year old Kim Jong-un, Chairman of the Workers' Party of Korea and Supreme Leader of the Democratic People's Republic of Korea (DPRK), commonly referred to as North Korea. Kim is also Marshal and Supreme Commander of the Korean People's Army. With him was 72-year-old General Kim Yong Chol, Director of the Reconnaissance General Bureau. Kim is one of the DPRK's most senior intelligence community's managers, and he has been a member of the DPRK intelligence community for over two decades.

Reconnaissance General Bureau (RGB) is responsible for clandestine operations. The RGB includes six bureaus charged with operations, reconnaissance, technology, cyber, overseas intelligence, and service support which includes Room 39. Room 39 is a secretive North Korean party organization that seeks ways to maintain the foreign currency slush fund for the country's Supreme Leader Kim Jong-un.

"I will not be going to Bulgaria to meet with Abu Bakr al-Baghdadi. It may well be a CIA trap to draw me out, and I'm sure they are, at this moment, attempting to decrypt our encrypted phone conversation with Baghdadi," said Supreme Leader Kim Jong-un.

"But he is offering 5 Billion US dollars for a nuclear bomb, of which we have many," answered General Kim Yong Chol.

"You are not paying attention general. I said I will not be going but I intend to be there. Do you understand now, general?"

Fearing retribution and not having any idea what the supreme leader was talking about, he put on his best look of amazement and nodded politely in deference to his leader.

"We will send my double, my doppelgänger, I believe you in the intelligence world call him. You, general, will accompany him."

"What is your direction, my leader?"

"Show him samples of our nuclear offerings: bombs, devices, and warheads, that can be dropped from a plane, packed in a suitcase or launched from a submarine or other platform. Let him decide which meets his needs and let him have two."

"And when he decides?"

"Inform him that we require half now in cash and the balance upon receipt."

"And how will we deliver the bombs to him?"

"We won't. He must steal them from us. And the cash, all of it will be deposited into Room 39."

General Kim Yong Chol again nodded and wondered to himself, *will my devoted service to the supreme leader keep me alive or am I a liability? I must think on this soon.*

Tehran, Iran

Tehran is the capital of Iran and Tehran Province. With a population of around 9 million in the city and 16 million in the wider metropolitan area, Iran is situated primarily between Iraq to the west, Afghanistan, and

Pakistan to the East, the Caspian Sea to the North and the Persian Gulf to the South.

In the office of The Ministry of Intelligence of the Islamic Republic of Iran (MOIS), sat: 62-year-old Mahmoud Alavi, an Iranian cleric, politician and the minister of intelligence, 77-year-old Sayyed Ali Khamenei, Supreme Leader of Iran, and Abu Bakr al-Baghdadi, the leader of ISIL.

"What our-our terms?" asked Baghdadi in Arabic.

"Give them whatever they want. We are close, and I do not want any stumbling blocks," replied Khamenei.

"So, I will have all the money with me?" asked Baghdadi.

"Of course not. Do you have any idea how much 5 billion in cash weighs? You will agree to the two nuclear weapons we desire, and they will ask for half the money. You ask when we can take possession of the weapon and if it falls within our schedule, you proceed."

"Why not wire the money?" asked Baghdadi.

"I do not believe the monkey leader wants to leave a trail."

"And if they can't meet our schedule, I walk away?"

"Of course not. You simply offer them, as they say in the West, a carrot."

"And what is this carrot?"

"Come my friends and I will tell you."

CHAPTER 5

The Oval Office Washington, DC

The five friends, President Burk, Riley, Nicholas, Kelly, and Dr. Tony Provenzano watched the wall clock ease them into tomorrow as time travelers.

"My dear friends. We have just boldly gone where no man, or woman, has gone before," announced President Burk.

Putting aside the president's attempt at humor, Kelly said, "If we were able to travel into the future or back into the past, wouldn't it create an opportunity to be used for nefarious reasons?"

"Yes. If we could go back in time, someone somewhere would find a way to use it to their advantage. For example, a get rich scheme by getting sports or stock information from the future, and taking it into the past and placing sure bets," said Nicholas.

"Like *Back to the Future,"* suggested Riley.

"Yes. And then there is the grandfather paradox of time travel in which we change the past. A person who travels to the past and kills their own grandfather, preventing the existence of their father or mother and therefore their own existence," added Nicholas.

"Are we done having fun? Can't any of you see the potential of time travel? Going back in time to find out the real 'history' of the world, not 'his-story'.

History has been written by the victor and we all know how that goes. I think humanity would like to know, deserves to know the truth. We will observe and report the truth. We will not be changing history, only changing history books," declared the president.

"So we're going to go back to the origins of Christianity and rewrite the Bible? I'm sure that will go over big in Rome," replied Kelly.

"I am not suggesting that."

"No, but if you find a truth that disrupts common belief but withhold it, are you no better than the victor that wrote a lie in the first place?"

"Whoa. Everybody calm down and take a deep breath. Aren't we putting the cart before the horse? We don't have a time machine, and unless I missed something, I haven't seen any time travelers from the future hanging around Washington snapping selfies to show to their friends the Jetsons when they get back to Orbit City," Nicholas commented.

"Very good point, Mr. Nicholas," pointed out Dr. Provenzano, "but because we have not seen travelers from the future doesn't mean they are not here or never visited. The similarities between the Mayan and Egyptian pyramids are so striking as not to be related or at least singularly influenced. And that's not to mention the Bosnian Pyramid of the Sun. What about the Peruvian Nazca landing lines that are visible only from space? I could go on and I will later, but suffice to say time travel is not only possible but that I have done it and so has President Burk."

CoS Nicholas and Kelly pondered that revelation.

Kelly looked at her husband, rolled her eyes and mouthed, "*Really?*"

The group broke up but promised to continue the discussion later. CoS Nicholas headed home, Kelly retired to her bedroom, while the president, Riley, and Dr. Provanzano took Max out for a walk in the Rose Garden.

"How much can we tell them, Tommy?" asked Dr. Provenzano.

"Well TP, (How the president referred to Dr. Provanzano when they were alone or in close company), now that you outed us as 'jumpers', I don't see any reason to hold back."

"I couldn't help myself. Sorry, but we have to get this going. Not only do we have to get Kelly and your friend Nicholas on board, we need to get your Cabinet on board. Then Congress, then the American people, and then the world."

"I am not sure we shouldn't keep this between friends and those that need to know. Keep it as a secret project until we have some success, then get Congress to bless and fund it. Then we can announce it to the world; you know, in case we have a failure. It's 'better to beg for forgiveness than to ask for permission.'"

"Every country in the world will want in on this," cautioned Riley."

"That's not going to happen. We do the research and development and take the jump. This whole project will be proprietary. We'll share information but not technology. I don't want this getting away from us like the 'Manhattan Project,'" advised the president.

"What do we call it?"

"How about 'Project Christopher', after the patron saint of travelers," suggested Riley.

Max finished his business and the three of them headed back in and up to the second level while Riley headed home. The president and Max joined the first lady in their bedroom, while Dr. Provenzano retired down the hall to the Lincoln Bedroom.

The White House
Sunday Morning

The president rose early and took a short two-mile run accompanied by about a dozen Secret Service agents. He was breaking Max in for longer runs. Max, a German Shepherd, was almost two years old but already big for his age. After a shower, the president joined Kelly and Dr. Provenzano in the dining room for breakfast. Max sat under the table, and to Kelly's consternation, was sneaking bacon out of the president's hand.

"Sleep well, doctor?" asked Kelly.

"I did. I have always dreamed about what it would be like sleeping in President Lincoln's bedroom and I must say it lived up to my expectations."

"How so?" asked Kelly.

"Don't encourage him," interrupted the president.

"Why? Did you two fly away together or did Lincoln come for a visit?"

"Neither," said Dr. Provenzano, "I just had a wonderful, peaceful sleep. It was the best I have had in a long time. I did have some rather lucid dreams, though."

"Kelly, the doctor and I are very serious about this. Time travel and all of the historical, preventive and technology residual benefits will become my legacy, my 'Moon Shot', so to speak. We need and want your and Nicholas' support."

"I am sorry, Tommy. I know you're serious but it's just so out there. If the media gets ahold of this prematurely they could destroy you. I can just see the Tweets: # Captain Burk, or worst, # President Marty McBurk."

"Thanks for that optic, Kelly. But what do you think the media and people said when Kennedy announced he wanted to land a man on the Moon by the end of the decade? That was 1963; they thought he was nuts. The only people to go near the moon till then were Flash Gordon and Alice Kramden," joked the president. Then in his best Ralph Kramden from the *Honeymooners* said, "'One of these days, Alice. One of these days, pow, zoom to the Moon.' But you know that's where you, as my number one press secretary, come in. You, Bill, and my speech writers will put it together in a way that will win Congress, the media, and the people over. Kennedy's Rice Stadium Moon speech comes to mind and I paraphrase: 'We choose to go to the Moon in this decade … not because it's easy, but because it's hard … because that challenge is one that we are willing to accept, one we are unwilling to postpone, and one which we intend to win…' You need to write something of that caliber."

"Can you raise the bar any higher? And if that's what you want you better win me over first. Is it really possible to travel into the future and go back into the past? And if so, what would you do with it?"

The president was about to answer when Dr. Provenzano held up a finger implying indulgence. The president acquiesced, "Kelly, don't believe anyone who tells you that humans can never acquire efficient technology for backward and forward time travel. Accurately predicting future technology is nearly impossible, and history is filled with underestimates of technology:

"'Heavier-than-air flying machines are impossible.' Lord Kelvin, President, Royal Society, 1895."

"'I think there is a world market for maybe five computers.' Thomas Watson, chairman of IBM, 1943."

"'There is no reason for any individual to have a computer in their home.' Ken Olsen, President, Chairman, and founder of Digital Equipment Corp., 1977."

"'The telephone has too many shortcomings to be seriously considered as a means of communication. The device is inherently of no value to us.' Western Union internal memo, 1876."

"'Airplanes are interesting toys but of no military value.' Marshal Ferdinand Foch, French commander of Allied forces during the closing months of World War I, 1918."

"'Who the hell wants to hear actors talk?' Harry M. Warner, Warner Brothers, 1927."

"Okay, I get it," said Kelly. "The world is full of naysayers, but how does it work and what will you do with it?"

Dr. Provenzano was about to answer when a soft knock on the door stopped him. The steward opened the door and the president waved him in. He whispered something to the president and the president excused himself and walked out into the west sitting hall. After a minute he returned and said, "You'll have to excuse me; something has come up and I have to go. We'll pick this back up later."

CHAPTER 6

The Situation Room Washington, DC

A Secret Service agent opened the door to the Situation Room for the president. Secretary of Defense Ed Stanton, NSA Director Roger Michaels, CIA Director John Bader, CIA Deputy Director Prescott Cabell, National Security Adviser, General Mickey Finn, FBI Director Ray Riley and Deputy Secretary of Homeland Security Lucia Borras were already seated. Bader and Cabell were seated on the left side of the conference table.

The White House Situation Room is a 5,525 square foot conference room and intelligence management center in the basement of the West Wing of the White House. It is run by the National Security Council staff for the use of the Presidents of the United States and their advisors (including the National Security Advisor, the Homeland Security Advisor and the White House Chief of Staff) to monitor and deal with crises at home and abroad, and to conduct secure communications with outside (often overseas) persons. The Situation Room is equipped with secure, advanced communications equipment for the president to maintain command and control of U.S. forces around the world.

The president sat down at the head of the table. Riley, Borras, Stanton, Michaels, and Finn were already seated to his right. The president began,

"Okay ladies and gentlemen, based on your sense of urgency and the nature of this meeting, I asked Director Riley and Deputy Secretary Borras to join us. Let's hear it."

SecDef Ed Stanton took the lead. "We have positive voice prints of ISIL's Abu Bakr al-Baghdadi and DPRK's Kim Jong-un discussing what we believe is a weapons deal with a meeting in Sofia, Bulgaria to finalize it."

"When?" asked the president.

"A little over three weeks from today, December 7."

"December 7? Interesting. 'A date which will live in infamy'-again," offered FBI Director Riley.

"Bulgaria is a NATO country," reminded the president.

"Yes, but the two countries, North Korea and Bulgaria, established diplomatic relations back in 1948 and signed a bilateral cooperation agreement in 1970. One of the few places Kim Jong-un likes to visit," added NSA Director Michaels.

"Why?" asked the president.

"Why Bulgaria or why what are they up to?" asked Stanton.

"Why what are they up to," replied the president.

"Mickey called it 'The coming storm', so I'll let him tell you what he thinks."

"I did my thesis on North Korea at the War College and fought ISIL in Iraq. Look. If Kim Jong-un and Baghdadi are talking, it's not a good thing. If the North Korean and Islam stars align, we will be looking into the face of pure evil," declared Finn.

"Why wouldn't ISIL align with Iran?" asked the president.

"They did. It's Baghdadi voice print but it's Iran's fingerprints all over this thing. Iran doesn't have the bomb but wants to send one to America. North Korea has the bomb but no way to deliver it. Think of ISIL as their delivery service - you know, 'When it absolutely, positively has to be there overnight'. Think of ISIL as their FedEx."

"So, they are getting together in Bulgaria December 7, to finalize the deal. Money for the bomb. Sort of cash and carry. Sneaky Jap bastards," cursed Riley.

Everyone looked at Riley with a kind of WTF expression. President Burk knew better.

"We think they will agree on the actual device. Bombs of some sort, devices, missiles or warheads, that can be delivered by plane, packed in a suitcase or launched from a submarine or fishing boat. Baghdadi will decide on what he wants. They will agree on a delivery date and Baghdadi will give him a cash deposit," said Stanton.

"So, you think it's more than one device?" asked the president.

"Yes."

"So sometime after 12/7 Baghdadi and Iran will take possession of nuclear bombs?" asked the president.

"Yes."

"So, what's your best guess as to how, where and when they will deliver it?"

"There is no limit to how they will come at us. We're completely open. They can fly in, boat in or just walk in," advised Stanton.

"We have the no-fly list and we can profile the hell out of them. Anybody that even looks, talks or smells Arab will be arrested," offered FBI Director Riley.

"This is their big one and they are on to our methods. Whoever delivers the bomb will not be the 'Usual Suspect'. Not Arab - no beards or hijabs. They probably have already recruited homegrown blond hair, blue eyed radicalized San Diego surfers. We are going to have to approach this in a completely different manner," Stanton warned.

"Where?" asked the president.

"East Coast, West Coast, Chicago, Miami or Dallas. Take your pick," said Stanton.

"Do we have any idea of when?" asked the president.

"Yes. We think this December," answered Stanton.

"Jesus Christ! What day?"

"His birthday," said Stanton.

"Who's birthday?"

"His birthday. December 25, Christmas Day," Stanton grimaced.

"Jesus Christ," said the president.

"Exactly," said Stanton.

"Why don't we just take them out in Bulgaria when they're both together? You know, like in the *Godfather*," suggested Riley.

Oh, no, thought the president, *here it comes.*

"They wanna to have a meeting, right? It will be me, Kim Jong-un and Abu Bakr al-Baghdadi. Let's set the meeting. Get our informers to find out where it's gonna be held. Now, we insist it's a public place … a bar, a restaurant … some place where there's people so I feel safe. They're gonna search me when I first meet them, right? So, I can't have a weapon on me then. But if Bader can figure a way to have a weapon planted there for me, then I'll kill 'em both. Where does it say that you can't kill a supreme leader?" asked Riley doing his best Pacino impression.

Finn, Michales, Borras, and Cabell looked a bit surprised and confused by Director Riley's response, but the president, Stanton, and Bader heard it all before.

"We are considering that option and that's on the table, but there will be consequences if we get caught or are somehow associated," admonished Stanton.

"Then give it to the Israelis," offered Bader.

"I am not too sure they would want their fingerprints on this. Killing Baghdadi is one thing but having North Korea up your ass is another," said Stanton.

"Like I said," continued Riley, "I want somebody good – and I mean very good – to plant that gun. I don't want to be coming out of that toilet with just my dick in my hands."

CHAPTER 7

THE OVAL OFFICE WASHINGTON, DC

After the secretary of defense and his group left the Situation Room, the president and Riley headed upstairs to the Oval Office where Kelly, Nicholas and Dr. Provenzano were waiting. The president and Riley entered and reclaimed their previous seats.

"Ray, how can you channel Michael Corleone in the middle of an important national security meeting? Michaels, Finn, Borras, and Cabell didn't get it. Did you see the look on their faces?" asked the president.

"Yeah, but they got the point didn't they. And why did Bader bring Prescott Cabell to the meeting?" asked Riley.

"He is one scary guy. He must be 6'-5". He reminds me of Lurch from the *Addams Family*, a shambling, gloomy butler who somewhat resembles a cross between Frankenstein and a zombie. He really creeps me out," said Kelly.

"You don't know about Cabell?" asked Nicholas.

"Know? Whats to know?" probed Kelly.

"Charles Cabell, Prescott's grandfather, was deputy director of the CIA under Allan Dulles. Both were shit-canned by Kennedy, after the Bay of Pigs. On top of that, Charles Cabell's brother, Earle, was mayor of Dallas at the time of Kennedys assassination. Just saying," said Nicholas.

"Isn't that a coincidence. Now I really know he's a scary guy," Kelly reiterated.

Everyone just kind of sat there for a moment.

Turning to Kelly and Dr. Provenzano the president said, " We just had some terrifying news. I really can't go into it with you now, but suffice to say, I believe Saint Christopher may have to appear sooner than later."

"I'm not even going to ask," said Kelly, "but when we left off, Dr. Provenzano was about to explain how time travel works and what we'll do with it."

"Have you ever read any of Finney's novels on time travel?" Kelly nodded no. "Well, according to Einstein, says Finney, time is more like a river that flows along, and the only reason we sense it passing is that we're like being in a boat on that river. So, you pass a tree and then it's behind you, and unless you get off the boat or find some other method to do so, you can't go back to that tree you saw a while ago. But, and this is the trick, everything you've passed in time is still back there, still just like it was. Finney goes on to describe a method of time travel that he believed would actually work."

"First, you must disconnect yourself from the millions of little threads of reality that grasp you and hold you in your boat in your present time, moving forward. These threads are all realities in the time you belong in, not in the time way back before they existed. Next, you have to immerse yourself in the time you want to be in. Everything must be perfect. It all must be just right. Now, even if you can do these things, and even if you can get your mind convinced completely, only a tiny percentage of the population could ever do it. If the person's mind isn't suggestible enough to make the leap, they won't ever go. The tiny threads of the mobile now in their minds will hold them in the boat, so to speak. But if someone can do these things … if someone can totally immerse themselves in the time they want to visit, and they can really believe they are sometime else … then they can do it. That and our NASA team introducing into the 'Jump Rooms' a way of opening a vortex or wormhole to send them through the space-time continuum and then bring them back," finished Dr. Provenzano.

"You lost me at the bend in the river," said Nicholas.

"Look. Astral projection is the technique of the spirit leaving the body and traveling any distance. It commonly happens accidentally in dreams to everyone and is a part of life. However, there are many ways to induce this practice, and many studies reveal it can even take us back in time. This is called astral time travel. How astral time travel works is like focusing a memory. It is a practice that should be done very carefully. By theory, time is like that river Einstein described, it flows down, but a memory with the aid of astral projection can go back to certain times in that river and look at a memory. Out-of-body experience or OBE and the NASA vortex will get them there and back. We just need to be careful."

"How so," asked Kelly.

"Have you ever heard of The Time Travel and Teleportation Experiments of Project Pegasus?" asked Dr. Provenzano.

"I don't believe so," said Kelly.

"Project Pegasus was the classified, defense-related research and development program under the Defense Advanced Research Projects Agency (DARPA) in which the US defense-technical community achieved time travel on behalf of the US government – the real Philadelphia Experiment."

"The mission of Project Pegasus was to study the effects of time travel and teleportation on children, as well as to relay essential information about past and future events to the US President, the intelligence community, and military. According to Dr. Basiago, the project director, children were recruited specifically for their ability to adapt 'to the strains of moving between the past, present and future.'"

"Documents, Dr. Provenzano continued, allegedly retrieved from Tesla's New York City apartment after his death January 1943, revealed the schematic for a teleportation machine. Using something Basiago calls 'radiant energy', the machine would form a 'shimmering curtain' between two elliptical booms.

Passing through this curtain of energy, Basiago would enter a 'vortal tunnel' that would send him to his destination. The other teleportation devices included a plasma confinement chamber in New Jersey and a jump room in El Segundo, California. There was also some kind of holographic technology which allowed them to travel both physically and virtually."

"That sounds horrible. Children? Why can't you just climb into a time machine or a DeLorean and set off for an adventure?" asked Kelly.

"We do have a time machine in the works but it's decades away from going online," said the doctor. "It's called the IXS Enterprise ship and will be the spaceship of the future. Harold White, a physicist working for NASA, is studying new methods of propulsion that can allow the building of a warp drive ship, A warp ship such as the IXS Enterprise could allow travel to interstellar space in a matter of weeks rather than, say, centuries. And the science behind why it might be possible is truly mind-boggling. An oversimplified explanation is that the concept seeks to exploit a 'loophole' in Albert Einstein's theory of relativity that allows travel faster than the speed of light by expanding space-time behind the object and contracting space-time in front of it. Essentially, the empty space behind a starship would be made to expand rapidly, pushing the craft in a forward direction. Passengers would perceive it as movement despite the complete lack of acceleration."

"I think we should stick with astral projection. I remember a movie I saw as a little girl starring Christopher Reeve and Jane Seymour. Reeve's character becomes obsessed with the idea of traveling back to 1912 and meeting the Jane Seymour character, with whom he had has fallen in love with. I remember it as a wonderful love story," said Kelly.

"Do you remember how he managed to do it? Go back in time, I mean," asked the president.

"Yes, I do. He purchased an early 20th-century suit and some vintage money; he cut his hair in a time-appropriate style. He dressed in a time-appropriate suit, and removes all modern objects from his hotel room and attempted to will himself into the year 1912. He succeeds and finds his lost love."

"Bingo," said the president, "I think you just nailed in a few sentences what we have been belaboring about for two days. Now get your team to put it together in a way that will win over Congress, the media, and the people. In other words, 'Make it so number one.'"

CHAPTER 8

Tehran, Iran

Iran Minister Mahmoud Alavi, Supreme Leader Sayyed Ali Khamenei, and ISIL leader Abu Bakr al-Baghdadi walked out of the ministry building and under a trellis which provided relief from the Arabian sun and American drones.

"We need their bombs, but we also require them to meet our schedule. So, the carrot my friend, which is to be offered only if necessary, is that we offer a gift to Kim Jong-un. We will board Thae Young Ho upon Air Koryo for a direct one-way flight from Bangkok International Airport to Pyongyang Sunan International Airport," said Khamenei.

"I have heard of this Thae Young Ho. He defected from the North Korean embassy in London and is likely the highest-ranking North Korean official to ever defect. But I was led to believe he was in South Korea. How did you get him?" asked Baghdadi.

"He has an affection for the type of forbidden sex that was not available in South Korea and took leave of his handlers to visit Bangkok. Our Mahmoud Alavi knew of this and was there waiting. After he was repatriated by us, Pyongyang called him human scum and accused him of embezzling official funds and committing other crimes."

"I will save this gift for a special occasion," said Baghdadi.

"What type of bombs are you going to request?" asked Alavi.

"I desire two devices. Both will be nuclear. One will be able to fit in a suitcase, while the other will be in the form of a warhead attached to a SAM, surface to air missile," said Baghdadi.

"Ah. You are going to bring down a commercial jet while it lands in New York City and you are going to launch a missile into the White House. I am correct, yes?"

"Allahu Akbar! I congratulate your perception, supreme leader" answered Baghdadi. *He could not be more wrong. I trust him to supply the money for the bombs but not to know how the bombs will be delivered,* thought Baghdadi.

Flying back to ar-Raqqah, Syria, Baghdadi, and his Military Chief Abu Saleh al-Obaidi sat in the lap of luxury within a Gulfstream V, on loan from a Saudi benefactor. They enjoyed coffee served by the aircraft male steward. The 1,000 kilometers passed uneventfully as both men keep their conversations to a minimum and guarded. In less than two hours they arrived back in Syria and were met at Deir ez-Zur airport by a single car and driver for the less than hour drive to ar-Raqqah. As soon as the car door closed serious interaction between the two began.

"I don't trust that Khamenei. He is Shia and will send us to Satan when he is through with us," complained al-Obaidi.

"Yes, my brother. But until then he needs us, and we need his money. We must finalize everything before our meeting with the Korean monkey. Have our scientists determined our exact needs?" asked Baghdadi.

"Yes. For the Tun…"

"Stop you dog! Do not say another word." nodding towards the driver, "We will never discuss where or when, but if we must we will always refer to one as the below and the other as the above."

"Yes. I understand and agree, but the driver is my wife's cousin and a trusted aid," whispered al-Obaidi.

Baghdadi nodded in agreement and continued, "For the below, we must have enough power to implode the entire structure and for the above, we must shut down the entire northeast coast."

"For the below, we will ask them for the American W54 or the Russian RA-115. Both were developed in the 60's-70's, weigh from fifty to sixty pounds, and are small enough to fit into a large roll-on suitcase. Both have the equivalent of six kilotons. Not much by the normal standards of the 16-kiloton nuclear bomb dropped on Hiroshima, but will more than do the job we require," confided al-Obaidi.

"Go with the American W54. The Russian stuff is shit. And for the above?"

"For the above, we want the HEMP and have been told they have what we want."

"This is what they call the High-Altitude Nuclear Electromagnetic Pulse Bomb?"

"Yes. I am told that a HEMP warhead is designed to be detonated far above the Earth's surface. The explosion releases a blast of gamma rays into the mid-stratosphere, which ionizes, and the resultant energetic free electrons interact with the Earth's magnetic field to produce a much stronger EMP than is normally produced in the denser air at lower altitudes," said al-Obaidi.

"English please," begged Baghdadi.

"But I do not speak English," replied al-Obaidi.

"I know my friend. It is a figure of speech Americans use to keep an explanation simple."

"Yes. I see. The missile with a nuclear warhead will be launched from a platform mounted on a large fishing ship that we will move within range of our target. The missile, when fired, will detonate about ten miles above our target cities and will destroy unprotected military and civilian electronics nationwide, blacking out the electric grid and other critical infrastructure for many months if not years. All the modern conveniences upon which American life depends will suddenly and completely vanish. All of them. The electromagnetic pulse will destroy the chips that are at the heart of every electronic device. Passenger jets will fall from the sky. It will disable communications, fuel manufacturing and production, hospitals, and medicines, and will disable 911 call centers. Everything will shut down. Water treatment facilities, food storage facilities, everything will be gone. Financial records will be wiped out. American investments will be gone. Their medical records and prescriptions will be zapped. Their computers and the internet, heating and air conditioning, supermarkets, cell phones, telephones, and radio and television, banks and ATMs will shut down; credit cards will become useless. All vehicles made after 1970 will be useless. The vast majority of Americans will die from starvation or disease or will freeze to death. We will bomb them back to the 14th century," snarled al-Obaidi.

"Aha, my friend! Now you have finally spoken English. Bomb them back to the 14th century. That I understand. We will take them back to the time of the Crusades, but this time we will fight on the infidel's soil."

Their car stopped in front of a safe house and both Baghdadi and al-Obaidi got out and walked towards the front door. Baghdadi whispered to al-Obaidi, "Too bad you didn't speak English sooner; we might have been able to spare your wife's cousin's life."

Had al-Obaidi any regret of the grief his wife would put him through when her cousin did not return home tonight, he didn't show it.

CHAPTER 9

The Oval Office Washington, DC

Chief of Staff Nicholas and FBI Director Riley had previous appointments and the president asked Noreen Ward, his private secretary to have them both join in when they concluded their business.

Noreen at 72 was the gate-keeper and was both lovely and loyal. By the way she presented herself every day for work you could tell she had a good upbringing and had once been a very attractive young woman.

The president, White House Press Secretary, Kelly Sullivan Burk, and Dr. Provenzano continued the meeting while waiting for Nicholas and Riley. When Riley and Nicholas finally arrived and were seated, Kelly asked her husband, "Earlier you mentioned the benefits of going back in time to find out the real history of the world, not 'his-story'. What then do you perceive the benefits will be going forward in time?"

"Good question and very germane to what I am about to tell you," said the president. "Time travel into the future will allow us to see natural disasters, such as earthquakes and tsunamis, hurricanes, tornados and make arrangements to evacuate before they occur and prevent massive loss of lives. Forest fires and floods may also be prevented. We may be able to prevent epidemics and save thousands of lives. We can also get a peek at how we're doing, how mankind and the environment are progressing together. We may also see wrong and right it."

"That's a lofty aspiration, especially the last bit, 'see wrong and right it,'" said Bill Nicholas.

"But aren't natural disasters nature's way of controlling the population?" asked Kelly.

"The fact that natural disasters lower populations in some areas is simply one of the many side effects of the disaster. I for one am for helping get innocent people out of Dodge. Time travel is a technology induced tool which will enable us to accurately predict the future," remarked Dr. Provenzano.

"As I was saying before we broke up earlier, something terrible had come across our radar screen and we need to move Project Christopher up. Just so you know, the good doctor, Riley and I have assigned Project Christopher as the code name for our time travel project," advised the president.

"Let me guess, said Kelly, the patron saint of time travel?"

"Ingenious. No one will ever break that code," mumbled Nicholas sarcastically. "But besides us, who else knows about Project Christopher?"

"Dr. Provenzano's NASA team assigned to Project Christopher, the jumpers, SecDef Stanton, Attorney General Fare, Secret Service Director Chris Bounty and us. I don't want it to get out to anyone else yet. Democrats and Republicans have become the best of friends since my reelection. If my barometer is correct they are going to be coming after me soon. If they find out about Project Christopher before we have tangible results they might join together to certify me or impeach me," answered the president.

"Jumpers?" asked Kelly.

"The two 3-man time travel teams we assembled. One team back and one forward," added Dr. Provenzano.

"Who are the jumpers and where did you find these brave souls," asked Kelly.

"You know a couple of them. Our old friends Tom Sweeney of the *Hedghampton Press* and Ron Todd of the *New York Post* will be the reporters. Sweeney will go forward along with an a/v tech, Kathleen Felton and FBI

Agent Rob Ceretti as security. Ron Todd will go back in time with Adrian Flatly as the a/v tech, and Secret Service Agent Bob Scales."

"I thought we saw the last of Sweeney and Todd?" asked Kelly.

"They turned out to be pretty square shooters, so we invited them to join Project Christopher. They both jumped, no pun intended, at the chance. Surprisingly, they tested extremely well and were accepted," Riley explained.

"How far along are you? I mean, you sound so sure about everything," offered Kelly.

"We've done several tests, baby steps if you will. We call them hops and skips and they were all successful. Now we're ready to jump," said Dr. Provenzano.

"For the jump into the past, we are going to go back to November 22, 1963, to the JFK's assassination," declared the president.

"You're not going to try and prevent it, are you?" asked Nicholas.

"No. As I stated before, we are just going back to find out the truth. I never believed Oswald shot Kennedy. I believed he was involved but not a shooter. Just look at the film. After he was arrested, when a reporter told him he was being charged with killing the president, Oswald's expression is priceless. Oswald knew at that moment he had been set up, and there was nothing he could do about it. He was a patsy," said the president.

"You couldn't have gone back and prevented the assassination anyway. If you did, we wouldn't all be here today talking about preventing it, would we," stated Nicholas.

"Correct-I think," said the president.

"So how are you going to prove he's not the shooter?" asked Nicholas.

"Simple. We are going to have two cameras pointed directly at the Texas School Book Depository buildings six-floor window as the assassination takes place," said Riley. "One will be a period Bell & Howell 414 PD Zoomatic, the same model Zapruder used for his famous film of the assassination, and the other will be a concealed digital GoPro Hero."

"Why use an old B&H camera when there are better cameras today and why hide the GoPro?" asked Nicholas.

"We don't want to stand out or have our picture appear in *Life Magazine* holding a Sony XDCAM that won't be invented for another fifty years. Can you imagine the conspiracists and apologists going on about that," said Riley, "Besides, it's all part of the legend that we will get into with you later."

"But how does that prove Oswald's not the shooter?" asked Nicholas.

"Simple," said the president, "if it's not Oswald we see in the sixth-floor window of the TSBD holding a rifle, then it's someone else. And if it's someone else then Oswald was right all along: 'I'm just a patsy.'"

The president got up and asked Noreen to send in the steward with coffee and tea. Everyone took that as a break and retired to the facilities or checked their cell phones.

When the president returned he poured himself a cup of tea and sat back down in the chair next to Dr. Provenzano. "We need to get moving on both jumps. As I said earlier, a bad situation is about to happen and we need to find out the outcome. Neither Kelly or you have the proper clearances to know the specifics but I really don't care. We have positive intel that ISIL's Abu Bakr al-Baghdadi and DPRK's Kim Jong-un will be discussing what we believe is a nuclear weapon deal in Sofia, Bulgaria on December 7. SecDef Stanton and our IC, Intelligent Community, believe Iran is behind it and we will be attacked on Christmas Day," advised the president.

"Jesus," replied Dr. Provenzano.

"Exactly," said the president. "We are working on options but unless we do a preemptive strike on that meeting we may not be able to prevent them from setting off a nuclear device somewhere in the U.S. on Christmas day."

"We're sure Iran is payrolling the operation and that NOKO is supplying the nuclear bomb or device; at least one but possibly more. We believe Baghdadi and ISIL will deliver it. It can be aboard an incoming commercial jet or they can walk it across the border or bring it in by boat. They could hit either coast, Miami, Galveston or Bangor. We have no idea. Our chances of intercepting it are 50-50. Not the kind of house odds I prefer," said the Riley.

"Nor I," acknowledged the president.

"So why don't we just take them out in Bulgaria on December 7 ?" asked Nicholas.

"Bulgaria is a NATO allied state and we would be the prime suspect. All hell would break loose on us," cautioned the president. Looking back at Riley and shaking his head remembering Rileys *Godfather* solution.

"So what are we going to do, send a time travel team to the meeting to find out where they intend to strike?" asked Kelly.

"No. Baghdadi will not be discussing tactics or possible target acquisitions with Kim Jong-un. He can't trust him. No, we are going to go January 3," said Riley.

"I thought you said the attack was planned for December 25, Christmas Day?" asked Kelly.

"We believe it is but it could also be for New Year's Eve. We want to get there after the attack not before or during," informed Riley.

"How will you know where to land the jumpers? In Washington, New York, or L.A.?" quizzed Kelly.

"None of the above. Probably somewhere in middle America. Somewhere that will probably survive the attack but will still have access to media. From there the team will find out what happened, where and when. They can then jump back to the present time and we will then have the exact details of where, when and how," added Riley.

"Why not Colorado Springs, Colorado? We have NORAD in the nearby Cheyenne Mountain complex and it has the alternate command center," suggested Nicholas.

We thought about NORAD but then we would have to bring them aboard. We just can't have three-time travelers show up after a nuclear attack and say, 'We just happened to be in the neighborhood,'" confided Riley.

"We decided on Cleveland, January 3," advised President Burk.

"Okay, so here are the three key dates. The weapons buy meeting in Sofia, Bulgaria, December 7. The assumed attack date of December 25, and the January 3, jump date to find out if the attack took place, and if so the details so we can then prevent it," finished Riley.

"This is all very confusing. If we're not sending a jump team to Cleveland till January 3, haven't we missed the opportunity to take out the weapons buy meeting in Sofia, Bulgaria on December 7 ?" asked Kelly.

"Ah! Good question," expressed Dr. Provenzano. "For the Cleveland jump or the Dallas jump for that matter, we do not have to jump on the exact same day we want to land. As long as our jump team is in Cleveland and Dallas, our NASA team will direct the vortex, the wormhole if you will, to the exact time and date we want to land. Our jump date to Cleveland will be November 28, but our landing date in Cleveland will be January 3."

"Oh, now I get it," said Kelly sarcastically.

"We have three weeks till the weapons buy meeting in Sofia, Bulgaria, Saturday, December 7. The Cleveland jump will take place Monday, November 28. If we're successful we will know how to stop the attacks. If not, we will take them out in Sofia. The Dallas jump, which we are way ahead of in planning, is set for next Monday, November 21. Even though it's a backward jump it will give us at least one full jump under our belt before we attempt Cleveland," President Burk pointed out.

"If our Cleveland jump is successful we will eliminate the threat and then eliminate them. We will ServPro them and their entire operation," said Riley.

"ServPro them?" asked Nicholas.

"Like it never even happened," explained Riley.

CHAPTER 10

The Willard Hotel Washington, DC

American author Nathaniel Hawthorne observed in the 1860s that "the Willard Hotel more justly could be called the center of Washington than either the Capitol or the White House or the State Department." The new Willard, designed by New York architect Henry Janeway Hardenbergh was hailed at its opening as Washington's first skyscraper. It is located at 1401-09 Pennsylvania Avenue and is less than 200 yards from the White House.

Four of the most important and powerful people in America were seated in a private room at the Willard Hotel on Pennsylvania Avenue. Each entered surreptitiously through different doors at different times.

"How did that clown Burk ever get reelected? Hell, how did he even get elected in the first place? How could we all get it so wrong? How could the polls be so wrong? This 'Live and Let Live Party' is going to ruin our country. He had no political or military experience. He wins as a spoiler independent third party run with the help of a talk show host, then marries his press secretary. He thinks he can just waltz into the presidency and take over," ranted Senator Schuster.

Francis "Chuck" Schuster, born November 29, 1949, is the senior United States Senator from New Jersey, and a member of the Democratic Party. On

November 16, 2014, he was unanimously elected Senate minority leader to succeed the Burk induced retirement of Harry Tweed.

"He did everything he promised. Can you believe that? We'll never be able to top what he's done," griped Speaker Bryan.

Paul Danny Bryan, born February 12, 1969, is the 53rd and current Speaker of the United States House of Representatives, and a member of the Republican Party. He has represented New York since 1997. On January 20, 2012, Bryan was elected to replace John Bonner as Speaker of the U.S. House of Representatives following Bonner's, Burk induced retirement.

"Come on Paul, you know how it works. Once we get rid of him we will inherit all the good, make it ours and own it. As for the bad, we'll make sure it follows him to Hell," encouraged Schuster.

"But now we have to suffer through four more grueling years of his kumbaya bullshit. The country, the world for that matter, is laughing at us. Everything we achieved through our last two administrations is gone. Either your party or mine must put up an unbeatable candidate to make sure Burk is out on his ass come 2020. And on top of that, we now have to deal with this new political movement; 'The Old-Timers'. They're a bunch of old fart Baby Boomers from the left, right and middle who are joining together across party lines to vote for their entitlements. All they care about is their Social Security and Medicare benefits and they're only going to vote for politicians who are pro-old. Pro-old? Add that to pro-life and pro-choice. What's this world coming to? Well, we'll have to get them back. We'll just do what we have always done. We'll tell them what they want to hear to get their votes, and then we'll cut the shit out of Social Security and Medicare," spat Speaker of the House Paul Bryan.

"Hey. I'd love to have those old-timers on my side. I'm one of them, but Burk has them bought and paid for. He even sends them dividend checks; he's running the country like a goddamn corporation. Dividend checks! Anyway, between both our parties we have the votes in both houses to block Burk every step of the way. The few of our honorable gentlemen and gentleladies that crossed the aisle are being reined back in, and we are actively pursuing Burk supporters. We'll soon be able to effectively shut him down. Paul, your side may win, or my side may win, but if either wins we both win. The enemy of my enemy and all that. Burk might be the most powerful man in the world but here in Washington, he serves at our pleasure," snapped Schuster.

"Or," said CIA Deputy Director Prescott Cabell.

"Or what?" asked Schuster.

"Or there are other alternatives," suggested Cabell.

"Such as?" asked Bryan.

"We could get rid of him now. Why wait four more years? He has already appointed one of his kumbaya buddies to the Supreme Court. With four more years, he will certainly get the chance to appoint another which will tip the balance for the foreseeable future," said Cabell.

"God help us," sighed Schuster.

"How can we get rid of him now?" questioned Bryan.

"We place him in a situation which would compromise his ability and duty to 'preserve, protect and defend the Constitution of the United States', something that would be bound to fail and beyond his ability to control. As has been said by one who unwittingly experienced such subterfuge, '*Victory has a thousand fathers, but defeat is an orphan.*' We'll make him an orphan. You two would then start impeachment proceedings, or..."

"Or what?" asked Bryan.

"Or why wait? We could have a disenfranchised lone nut sniper take him out with one shot. Worked before," suggested Cabell.

They all looked towards the fourth member of their very private and secret meeting. She would, if either of Cabell's alternatives were embraced, become the most powerful woman in the world.

CHAPTER 11

The Situation Room Washington, DC

The Secret Service agent opened the door and admitted SecDef Stanton, NSA Director Michaels, General Mickey Finn, CIA Director John Bader, and CIA Deputy Director Prescott Cabell into the Situation Room. All were summoned by the president, and seated themselves in any empty chairs around the table. The president was already seated at the head of the table with his back to the door, FBI Director Riley, Deputy Secretary of Homeland Security Lucia Borras and CoS Nicholas sat to his right.

CIA Deputy Director Prescott Cabell didn't stand on ceremonies and didn't sit and wait for the president to start. He cleared his throat and just began, "We need to take them out on 12/7, while they are meeting in Sofia, Bulgaria. Both degenerates, Kim Jong-un and al-Baghdadi need to be sent to Hell."

CIA Director John Bader looked hard at Cabell, clenched his teeth and tried hard not to smack him. Bader also felt SecDef Stanton eyes burning into the back of his neck. The president didn't respond but rather continued reading a report lying on the table. FBI Director Riley, however, had no such restraint. Riley started to get up but felt a hand on his and he eased back down into his chair. Riley didn't like Cabell and now Cabell was appropriating his idea. President Burk knew Riley could get ugly and he couldn't take that chance.

Lifting his head to look at Cabell, President Burk said, "Go on Prescott; continue with your thought."

"We send in an MQ-1 Predator with two Smart Pyron bombs and blow Kim Jong–un and Baghdadi to Hell. NATO may suspect us but they won't have a shred of evidence. For that matter, it could be the South Koreans, Israelis. Hell, even Kim's own SSD State Security Department would be suspected of taking them out. We can put out so much fake news, world opinion will be spinning all over the place."

The president stared at Cabell for a moment while everyone waited for a big slap down. "You know," said the president, "Prescott may have hit the nail on the head. If our smart bombs are sterilized and our drone doesn't get shot down we may be in the clear. We may take some heat but we can handle that considering the alternative."

General Finn coughed, and President Burk turned to him and said, "You have something to add Mickey?"

"Yes, Mr. President, I do. On the surface, a preemptive strike may solve our immediate problem but what would be the repercussions? With Kim gone a vacuum will exist, if only for a brief time. Will the South react and take advantage? The Chinese? Who will replace Kim as supreme leader? Do we know? They are telling us about the meeting: the where, when, and why. They are giving us two irresistible tempting targets. What if it's all misdirection and the actual meeting takes place at a different location and time? What if it's a trap, and instead of Kim Jung-un and Baghdadi it's their doubles, or worst, a room full of school kids?"

FBI Director Riley looked at the president and said, "General Finn offers a lot of 'What ifs' but he's spot on." Turning towards Cabell, Riley continued, "This whole thing smells to the high heaven and before we rush in and send anyone to Hell we had better get all those 'What ifs' changed to 'What is.'"

Cabell bristled at Riley's direct rebuke and was about to answer when he felt Director Bader's strong hand on his arm.

President Burk, standing to signal the meeting was coming to an end, said, "We have some thinking to do before I would give the go ahead, but we need to keep this option on the table. I would like Prescott and Mickey to work together and take this to the next level. Let's meet back here in 24 hours."

After President Burk, Nicholas and Riley left the Situation Room, SecDef Stanton, NSA Director Michaels, Homeland's Borras and CIA Director Bader, all looked at Cabell and Finn.

Although the Army, Navy, Air Force, and the Joint Chiefs all report to SecDef Stanton, the CIA along with 16 other intelligence agencies, including NSA Director Michaels, report to the Office of the Director of National Security while General Finn reports directly to the president.

SecDef Stanton cleared his throat and out of deference, everyone turned towards him. He was, after all, a Cabinet member and next to the president, the most important recipient of their intelligence. Turning towards General Finn, the SecDef said, "General Finn, as National Security Advisor you just received a direct order from the president. Deputy Director Cabell, your orders come from Director Bader, but I am sure he agrees with the president." SecDef Stanton looked towards Director Bader for approval and received a nod. Turning his attention back to Finn and Cabell he continued, "My advice to the both of you is to put your differences aside and work together and figure this out. Come up with a plan that considers every possible contingency when implemented. Do it, do it fast and be ready when and if we get the go ahead."

The SecDef rose from his seat, nodded to Directors Bader and Michaels and Secretary Borras and left the Situation Room.

Bader, Borras, and Michaels got up and followed Stanton out. NSA Director Michaels turned, looked back at the two and said, "You both have your marching orders. We'll meet back here tonight at 7 p.m. to see what you come up with. If you need anything, you know what to do and how to do it."

Cabell, an extremely tall, gaunt, devious Harvard intellectual, looked across at Finn, a six-foot hardcore Annapolis Marine. As their eyes bore into each other, General Mickey Finn felt a cold chill run up his back. The man sitting across from him had an agenda and it was one not unlike his grandfather Charles Cabell's agenda, 55-years previous when he reassured Kennedy that Operation Zapata would succeed.

With these two meeting and working together for the rest of the day, what could possibly go wrong?

CHAPTER 12

Tehran, Iran

Back in the office of the Ministry of Intelligence of the Islamic Republic of Iran (MOIS), sat Sayyed Ali Khamenei, supreme leader of Iran, and Mahmoud Alavi, the Minister of Intelligence.

"Why do we need these fools? This kafir Korean monkey Kim Jung-un and this ISIL head-hunter al-Baghdadi? I don't trust them, and we could use the 5 billion dollars for our own cyber attacks against the Jews and their Satan puppet, America. We succeeded beyond our wildest expectations against Satan's banks and Satan's dam in Rye Brook, New York," gloated Mahmoud Alavi.

On November 29, 2010, Iranian President Mahmoud Ahmadinejad stated for the first time that a computer virus had caused problems with the controller handling the centrifuges at its Natanz facilities. According to *Reuters*, he told reporters at a news conference in Tehran, "They, Israel and the United States, succeeded in creating problems for a limited number of our centrifuges with the virus software they had installed into our computers controlling the facility."

This virus designated Stuxnet was developed jointly by Israel and the United States and had a limited effect on Iran's nuclear development but managed to go viral and was captured and used in retaliation by the Iran state sponsored cyber army with remarkable success against the United States.

At least 46 major financial institutions and financial sector companies were targeted, including JPMorgan Chase, Wells Fargo, American Express, and AT&T.

The Iranian hackers were accused of hitting the banks with distributed-denial-of-service attacks on a near-weekly basis, a relatively unsophisticated way of knocking computer networks offline by overwhelming them with a flood of spammed traffic.

"These attacks were relentless, they were systematic, and they were widespread," U.S. Attorney General Loretta Lynch told a Washington news conference.

The indictment from a federal grand jury in New York City said the attacks occurred from 2011 to 2013. Washington had falsely accused military officers from China and the North Korean government of these cyber attacks against U.S. businesses.

"The attack on the Bowman Avenue Dam in Rye Brook, New York, was especially alarming," said Lynch. It represented a known intrusion on critical infrastructure. "A stroke of good fortune prevented the hackers from obtaining operational control of the floodgates because the dam had been manually disconnected for routine maintenance."

"The Bowman hack was a game-changing event for the U.S. government that prompted investigators to uncover other systems vulnerable to similar attacks," said Andre McGregor, a former FBI agent and a lead case investigator on the dam intrusion.

"Yes. You are correct, Mahmoud. We do not need these fools. They need us. More specifically, they need our money. But isn't it ironic, my dear Mahmoud, that we are using money America gave us in the so-called 'Iran Deal' to use against them and destroy them? But we must continue the charade, and while the Jews and Satan are chasing this Korean monkey Kim Jung-un and this ISIL headhunter al-Baghdadi, we will advance the real attack. Who knows? Maybe these fools will succeed and Allah will be doubly blessed. Unlike the Jews, the Americans are good Christian appeasers, but we are the crocodile."

"Is it good to be a crocodile?"

"It was Churchill who said, 'An appeaser is one who feeds a crocodile, hoping it will eat him last.' Yes. It is better to be the crocodile."

CHAPTER 13

Dallas, Texas 2016

In the center of Dallas, on Commerce Street, just a few blocks from the TSBD sits The Adolphus Hotel. The Adolphus opened on October 5, 1912, and was built by Adolphus Busch of the Anheuser-Busch company, in a Beaux Arts style. Busch's intention in constructing the hotel was to establish the first grand and posh hotel in the city of Dallas. Under the management of Otto Schubert, from 1922–1946, the hotel grew to national prominence. The building underwent a series of expansions, first in 1916, then 1926, and finally in 1950, at the time giving the hotel 21 floors with a total of 407 rooms.

Under the direction of Project Director Russell Randazza, working directly for NASA and Dr. Provenzano, the entire 14th floor had been reserved for six months, portions of which were completely restored back to 1963. Using hotel archive photographs, architects, designers, building contractors, decorators, and a period stylist replicated three connecting rooms including the hallway. The most important reason for picking the 14th floor was that the archive hotel registry showed the three dictated rooms assigned to the three jumpers, as well as most of the floor was unoccupied on November 21, and 22, 1963. The only reasonable explanation for the vacancies was that most hotel guests then, as now, will not take a room on the 13th floor because the number 13 is considered bad luck. Consequently, hotels and commercial buildings skip the 13th floor and rename it the 14th floor. Apparently, their guests were not fooled.

Matthew Weiner, the creator of *Mad Men*, was asked to consult on the renovation along with his team of art directors, set designers, and costume and wardrobe procurers and tailors. Everything had to be perfect down to the smallest detail.

Each of the adjoining three rooms looks out across South Akard Street at the Magnolia Hotel, originally the former headquarters of Mobil Oil's predecessor, the Magnolia Petroleum Co., hence the name. The windows, in each team members room, were replaced with soundproof windows and heavy curtains. It wouldn't do to have the one or all the team members concentration or mood broken by the loud irritating beep-beep-beep of a truck backing up, or modern police and fire sirens. Each room had period furniture and accouterment as well as a Zenith color television and stereo console complete with rabbit ears. A daily TV and radio schedule was programmed in including period shows such as *77 Sunset Strip*, *CBS News with Walter Cronkite*, *The Outer Limits*, *The Beverly Hillbillies*, and *Bonanza*, and hit songs such as *Sugar Shack*, *My Boyfriends Back*, and *Wipe Out.* Each TV and radio show was interrupted as now, although less often, with commercials for Oscar Myers, Pepsi, Maxwell House coffee, Ford, Chevy, and Studebaker, with an ample selection of commercials for Camel's, Lucky Strikes and Winston's, because 'Winston's taste good like a cigarette should.'

That was what one was expected to see; a 1960's hotel. However, hidden within each of the three teleportation room walls were two 3 meter diameter rotating rings. The Tesla inspired vortex rings have exceptional strength, are extremely lightweight and made of 86% magnesium, and 14% silicon carbide particles. One within the back wall closest to the bed headboard (the present) and one in the wall closest to the bed footboard (the past or future as the case may be) capable of spinning concentrically at or greater than the speed of sound. Simply put, these rings, when activated, create the wormhole or tunnel through which the jumpers will travel.

Russell Randazza was having the last team meeting in the team's training room, with the Dallas jump team; Ron Todd the reporter, Adrian Flatly, the a/v tech. and the muscle, if needed, Secret Service Agent Bob Scales. Ron

Todd, 58 years old is a reporter for the *New York Post* and a darn good one at that. With an unruly mane of red hair and beard, he looks like a short Viking. He had a run-in with the Burk administration while covering the so-called 'Revenge Murders' but ended up playing square and lived to report again. Adrian Flatly, 68 years old, is a very tall, thin audio-visual tech guy. His professor's tweed sports jacket, signature bow tie, and round silver rimmed glasses allow one to judge the book by its cover. Secret Service Agent Bob Scales op/coned for this operation was average. He was average looking, average height and weight, but he could be tough as nails and had excellent tradecraft. All three team members were picked because of their expertise, their susceptibility to OBE, and because one was in grade school, and one in high school Friday afternoon November 22, 1963 - the day John Fitzgerald Kennedy was murdered. Scales, at 32, was picked because he was in neither.

"We just got confirmation on the jump date. You leave here this Monday, November 21, 2016 at 6 a.m and arrive there Thursday, November 21, 1963 at 6:01 a.m. If all goes well you will leave Friday, November 22, 1963 at 5 p.m., and return back here in 2016 at 5:01 p.m. That gives you enough time to get from the Texas Theatre to the hotel and set up before your 5 p.m. jump back here," said Randazza.

"I wish we could stay for Oswald's murder." admitted Todd.

"We have been all through that before, Ron. After Oswald's arrest, everything is pretty well documented up to and including his murder by Ruby. We need you three to fill in the blank and gray spaces from the day before Kennedy is assassinated, the assassination, the Tippit hit and Oswald's arrest. Then we need to get you back here for the debriefing. If we pull this off there will be plenty more adventures for your team," promised Randazza.

"I'm just saying," said Todd.

"Okay. Here's how it will go down. Tonight after an early dinner, you and your team will leave this training area at 7 p.m. in full costume and with full legend, and enter the hallway to your three rooms. You will say goodnight to your teammates, place your key in the door and enter your room. You will stay isolated in your respective rooms with no contact with your teammates.

While in your room you will have access to room service, TV, and radio. Your one and only focus is obtaining total submersion into the Dallas of 1963, and your total emersion back into the past, back to the America most of you remember. You'll be going back to Dallas in November of 1963 when a gallon of milk cost 49 cents and a gallon of gas was 39 cents. Back to when Aldous Huxley died, the Beatles wanted to hold your hand and Martin Luther King Jr. had a dream."

"Before you retire you will take your Avinal. You will receive a wake-up call at exactly 5:30 a.m., thirty minutes before your 6 a.m. jump time. During those thirty minutes, you will shower, dress and get back into bed, place your Samsonites and briefcases at your lap and prepare for you OBE. Lie on your back with your pillow behind your neck so your neck is concave and your head is slightly back. Concentrate only on leaving today and going to yesterday. Close your eyes and focus up and back into your brain. Submit to your inner vibration and ringing. You do that and we'll do the rest. And one final thing. Don't get caught and don't get yourself photographed. See you all tonight for dinner in the French Room at 5:30 p.m.," finished Randazza.

CHAPTER 14

The Oval Office Washington, DC

"Do you have what I asked for?" asked the president.

"I do," answered Attorney General William Fare.

"It's possible?" asked the president.

"Yes," replied AG Fare.

"Let's have it then."

"In July of 1987, during the Iran-Contra Hearing grilling of Oliver North, the American public got a glimpse of highly sensitive emergency planning he had been involved in. Ostensibly these were emergency plans to suspend the American Constitution in the event of a nuclear attack, a legitimate concern. But press accounts alleged that the planning was for a more generalized suspension of the Constitution. This planning for 'Continuity of Government' (COG) called for the suspension of the Constitution, turning control of the government over to the Federal Emergency Management Agency, emergency appointment of military commanders to run state and local governments, and declaration of martial law. Reagan's Attorney General, William French Smith, had intervened to stop the COG plan from being presented to the president. Seven years later, in 1994, Tim Weiner reported in *The New York Times* what he called 'The Doomsday Project' – the search for "ways to keep the government running after a sustained nuclear attack on Washington – had 'less than six months to live.'"

"The two key COG planners on the secret committee were Dick Cheney and Donald Rumsfeld, the two men who implemented COG under 9/11. What they and Weiner did not report was that under Reagan the purpose of COG planning had officially changed: it was no longer for arrangements 'after a nuclear war,' but for any 'national security emergency.' This was defined in Executive Order 12656 of 1988 as: 'any occurrence, including natural disaster, military attack, technological emergency, or other emergency, that seriously degrades or seriously threatens the national security of the United States.' It is clear that the planning by Cheney, Rumsfeld, and others over the last two decades was not confined to an immediate response to 9/11. The 1000-page Patriot Act dropped on Congress, as promptly as the Tonkin Gulf Resolution had been back in 1964, is still with us; Congress has never seriously challenged it, and President Hilton, the vice president's mother, quietly extended it on February 27, of this year," declared AG Fare.

"That's amazing, Bill," said the president. "By the way, where is the vice president? I asked that she be present to hear this."

The attorney general looked at FBI Director Riley and Riley took the cue. "Tommy, we found out yesterday and just confirmed it this morning, Vice President Hilton was the fourth person present in the closed-door meeting with Schuster, Bryan, and Cabell."

"Please don't tell me she's with them," said the president.

"Looks that way, sir. I asked Ray and he agreed with me. Better to keep her at arm's length till we know her loyalties," suggested AG Fare.

"Jesus. They won't stop at anything, will they? I can't believe she's with them," said the president.

"Maybe the apple didn't fall too far from the tree," suggested Riley.

"Maybe. Anyway, that makes this discussion more timely. What other powers do I have at my disposal?" asked the president.

"Besides what President Lincoln used during the Civil war, the suspension of Habeas Corpus, we have the executive order, a presidential power not designated by the Constitution."

"Well, yes, I know that and have used it several times but..."

"But what you don't know is that there are several executive orders that are already on the books. A presidential executive order, whether Constitutional or not, becomes law simply by its publication in the Federal Registry. Congress is bypassed." Fare handed President Burk a piece of paper saying. "Here are just a few executive orders that would suspend the Constitution and the Bill of Rights. These executive orders have been on record for nearly 30 years and could be enacted by the stroke of a presidential pen."

President Burk read what was on the paper.

EXECUTIVE ORDER 10990 allows the government to take over all modes of transportation and control of highways and seaports.

EXECUTIVE ORDER 10995 allows the government to seize and control the communication media.

EXECUTIVE ORDER 10997 allows the government to take over all electrical power, gas, petroleum, fuels, and minerals.

EXECUTIVE ORDER 10998 allows the government to take over all food resources and farms.

EXECUTIVE ORDER 11000 allows the government to mobilize civilians into work brigades under government supervision.

EXECUTIVE ORDER 11001 allows the government to take over all health, education and welfare functions.

EXECUTIVE ORDER 11002 designates the Postmaster General to operate a national registration of all persons.

EXECUTIVE ORDER 11003 allows the government to take over all airports and aircraft, including commercial aircraft.

EXECUTIVE ORDER 11004 allows the Housing and Finance Authority to relocate communities, build new housing with public funds, designate areas to be abandoned, and establish new locations for populations.

EXECUTIVE ORDER 11005 allows the government to take over railroads, inland waterways, and public storage facilities.

EXECUTIVE ORDER 11051 specifies the responsibility of the Office of Emergency Planning and gives the authorization to put all executive orders into effect in times of increased international tensions and economic or financial crisis.

EXECUTIVE ORDER 11310 grants authority to the Department of Justice to enforce the plans set out in executive orders, to institute industrial support, to establish judicial and legislative liaison, to control all aliens, to operate penal and correctional institutions, and to advise and assist the president.

"So, by executive order and without Congressional approval, the president now has the power to transfer whole populations to any part of the country, the power to suspend the press and to force a national registration of all persons. The president, in essence, has dictatorial powers never provided to him under the Constitution. The president has the power to suspend the Constitution and the Bill of Rights in a real or perceived emergency. Any president faced with a similar, or lesser economic crisis now has extraordinary powers to assume dictatorial status," concluded President Burk.

"That's correct."

"But then some judge somewhere in Podunk, looking for 15 minutes, files suit alleging my executive order violates the US Constitution and blocks it," said the president.

"Yes. That can and will probably happen, but If they do try or attempt a coup d'état all we have to do is declare martial law. You as the head of the government then remove all power from the executive, legislative, and judicial branches of government, as well as civilian authorities. Get the Governors on your side and no need for tanks in the streets. It's not nice. It's not pretty but it's legal, and you, like Napoleon, could go from First Consul to Emperor with a stroke of a quill," added Attorney General Fare.

"It's good to be the king," smiled President Burk.

CHAPTER 15

The Situation Room Washington, DC

SecDef Ed Stanton, NSA Director Michaels, CIA Director Bader, and Deputy Secretary of Homeland Security Borras came back into the Situation Room precisely at 7 p.m. Several of General Finn's staff and several of DDCI Cabell's agents were getting reports together and tidying up before they all cleared the room.

National Security Adviser, Mickey Finn, and CIA Deputy Director Prescott Cabell stood as SecDef Stanton et al entered.

As soon as they were all seated SecDef Stanton said, "Okay, what do you have?"

Cabell looked at General Finn and Finn nodded.

In a precise tone and measured cadence, Cabell said, "Upon further research we have discovered that the meeting in Sofia, Bulgaria between Kim Jong-un and al-Baghdadi is hidden within a larger Bulgaria sponsored and hosted ASEAN Association of Southeast Asian Nations meeting, more specifically the ASEAN Regional Forum. The D.P.R.K. is a member of the Regional Forum Association whose objectives are to foster constructive dialogue and consultation on political and security issues of common interest and concern and to make significant contributions to efforts towards confidence-building and preventive diplomacy in the Asia-Pacific region."

"The more important and or controversial participants are Australia, Bangladesh, Brunei, Cambodia, Canada, China, Democratic People's Republic of Korea, European Union, India, Indonesia, Japan, Malaysia, Pakistan, Republic of Korea, Russia, Singapore, Thailand, Viet Nam and the United States. Kim Jong-un, or more likely his doppelgänger-double, will obviously represent the D.P.R.K and al-Baghdadi will, we believe, be passed off as a member of the Pakistani delegation. A drone strike would, we now believe, do nothing but kill a doppelgänger, a terrorist, and bunch of bureaucrats. General Finn and I feel that capturing and having al-Baghdadi alive and within our grasp a better option."

Looking at General Finn, SecDef Stanton asked, "You agree, general?"

After a slight hesitation, General Finn offered a simple, "Yes."

"Why do you think Kim Jung-un will use a double?" asked NSA Director Michaels.

"Because we believe Kim knows we know. He may have even set this whole thing up as a gift to us. Regardless, he will not be there. He will send his doppelgänger," Cabell reiterated.

"A gift?" asked Director Michaels.

"Yes, a win-win gift. He gets half of the 5 billion and gives us Baghdadi."

"And why would he want to do that?"

"An olive branch perhaps? We lift sanctions on the North or agree to begin reunification discussions between North and South Korea with China," said Cabell.

"Delta Force or Seal Team Six?" asked SecDef Stanton.

"Sir?" queried Cabell a bit confused.

"Would you send in Delta Force or Seal Team Six to abduct Baghdadi?"

"I believe a lower profile might be more prudent," advised Cabell. "We have in place our core Special Operation Group which we will augment with local embassy personnel and our German embassy assets."

"So, we just grab Baghdadi and extradite him out of Bulgaria to where?" asked Stanton.

"Incirlik Air Base in Turkey," said Cabell.

Looking back and forth between Cabell and Finn, SecDef Stanton said, "Okay. Write up the Covert Operation Order and if Director Bader approves it, he can present it to the president."

As the meeting broke up, Stanton asked General Finn to walk with him. "You were very quiet in there, Mickey. What's wrong?"

"Just a gut feeling. It's as though…"

"Come out with it, Mickey," said Stanton. "Now is not the time to stand on formalities. What's your gut telling you?"

"Cabell seems to have had a complete change of heart. He has become a team player. You should have seen him in there with the intelligence support staff. But I sense he has another agenda. He's presenting the abduction of al-Baghdadi as a fait accompli and it's anything but. It's as though he knows something the rest of us don't."

"Like what?"

"Like when his grandfather planned the CIA 'Bay of Pigs' invasion of Cuba. The CIA trained invasion group Brigade 2506 and President Kennedy were led to believe, by the CIA, that the invasion would be a complete success. The Cuban people would rise up and support the invasion but the complete opposite occurred. Somebody tipped off Castro and his 250,000 man army and militia were there waiting for the 1,500 anti-Cuban force. There were 118 killed, 360 wounded, 1,202 captured, four American B-26 bombers shot down and two supply ships sunk. CIA Director Dulles and Deputy Cabell, the Joint Chiefs and many of Kennedy's own team were pressing for Kennedy to pull out all the stops. It was found out later that Dulles and Cabell knew and wanted the small invasion force to fail, and we're betting young President Kennedy would not want the failure on his watch, and would call in the Marines for a full-scale invasion. The CIA wanted to win one for the good guys against Russia in the Cold War. Kennedy didn't take the bait and never trusted the CIA again. He shitcanned both Dulles, Cabell and a few others shortly thereafter."

"I know that story, Mickey, but why would Prescott want the al-Baghdadi abduction to fail?"

"Because I believe he wants to drag us into something bigger. Something we're not seeing yet."

"Interesting. I'll pass your observation along to the president. Better yet, why don't you come along?" added Stanton.

CHAPTER 16

The Oval Office Washington, DC

President Burk finished a grueling two-hour meeting in the Cabinet Room with his Cabinet and top advisers. The conversation centered on topics such as immigration, borders, walls, terror, terrorists, and terrorism. In addition, the meeting touched on how to deal with a do-nothing obstructionist Congress and a population that demands free college, free health care, and lower taxes. How's that supposed to work?"

As he was walking out he motioned for Vice President Hilton to walk with him back to the Oval Office. President Burk stopped and turned to look directly at the vice president. He wanted to gauge her reaction to what he was about to ask. "You know, Chelsey, everything seems to have gone to Hell since our reelection. It's like the Republicans and Democrats in both the House and Senate are teaming up against us. Are you feeling that?"

He watched her expression.

"Mr. President-Tommy, what's bothering you? You've been acting funny the last couple of days. We're doing good. You and me, we're a good team, and we have most of the country behind us. There will always be those on the other side of the aisle who will oppose you. Let me work on Schuster and the Senate, while you handle Bryan and the House. Together we'll find out if anything is going on. In the meantime, let's '*keep calm and carry on*.'"

I want to believe her but if she's lying she's good, thought the president, *real good!*

Already in the Oval Office, FBI Director Riley, and Press Secretary Kelly Sullivan were both seated and working their smart phones when the president and CoS Bill Nicholas entered. The first thing out of the president's mouth was, "I just saw a news feed of General Nicholson telling Senator McCain that after 15 years in Afghanistan we're at a stalemate. A fucking stalemate. I want to get out of there but McCain and his hawks keep wanting more. Every time I get a troop reduction he wants a surge. Another surge? We've been surging for 15 years. We've now surged to a stalemate. Outstanding!"

"Sounds like your meeting went well," offered Riley sarcastically.

"After Vietnam and the '91 collapse of the Soviet Union, we have been searching for enemies. When we couldn't find any we started a 'War on Drugs'. Then came the 'War on Terror'. If we win that we'll need to find a new enemy."

"Russia or North Korea were good runs. I bet our political opponents and the military industrial complex try for an encore. They need war to survive and we're not giving them any," said Riley. "They'll find some pretext to start a war. They always do."

"Like I said, outstanding. By the way, I confronted the vice president on the way out. I think you guys got it wrong," said the president.

"I don't think that apple fell too far from the tree. I wouldn't doubt her mother is coaching her. The Senate and House have turned against us and Schuster and Bryan could be planning a coup with your own vice president," warned Kelly.

"I think you have been reading too many of Fitzpatrick's novels," joked the president. It was a comment attributed to the author's uncanny ability to accurately chronicle his administration's rise and fall through two novels *Fear Itself* and *Best Served Icy.*

"Fitzy hasn't been too far off your last four years and he's probably still at it now. I bet he's watching and writing about everything that goes on here. I just finished reading *Best Served Icy*, and can't believe I, the director of the FBI, missed that final message on the fireplace mantle. But, I'll tell you one thing, if I ever find the leak I'll cut his balls off," boasted Riley.

"Let him be. Whatever Fitzy writes comes out long after all is said and done. What's the harm? By the way, have you heard anything from him?" asked the president.

"Fitzy?"

"No. Not Fitzy."

Riley gave the president a cold hard stare but said nothing.

Both Kelly and Nicholas noticed the difficult moment but before it could become uncomfortable CoS Nicholas interjected, "I have a feeling Fitzy's current novel is going to get a bit more interesting. SecDef Stanton and General Finn are outside and want a few minutes."

The president nodded and Nicholas went to the door and asked Noreen, the president's secretary, to bring them in and to have some coffee and tea brought in.

With the president and Kelly sitting in both chairs, Nicholas and Riley sat on one couch and Stanton and Finn on the other. The steward served coffee and tea then left and closed the door. Kelly would not necessarily sit in on a meeting like this but she was also first lady, one of his most trusted advisors, and besides, President Burk didn't care. "Okay, let's have it," demanded the president.

"Director Michaels, Bader, Borras, Finn, and Cabell along with myself reviewed the final draft for the weapons meeting in Sofia, Bulgaria. We now know that the meeting in Sofia between Kim Jong-un and al-Baghdadi is part of a larger Bulgaria sponsored and hosted ASEAN Association of Southeast Asian Nations, more specifically, the ASEAN Regional Forum," said SecDef Stanton.

"I'm familiar with ASEAN," said the president.

"We don't believe Kim Jong-un will attend, more likely he will send a double. Also, al-Baghdadi will, we believe, be passed off as a member of the Pakistani delegation. A drone strike would, we now believe, do nothing but kill a doppelgänger, a terrorist, and a bunch of bureaucrats. We feel that a surgical abduction of al-Baghdadi is the better option. Cabell feels his in place assets, 'SOG' Special Operation Group, augmented with embassy personnel and our German embassy will do the trick."

"So, we just grab Baghdadi and extradite him out of Bulgaria to where?" asked the president.

"Incirlik Air Base in Turkey," replied Stanton.

"Then to a safe house in Greece?"

"Correct."

"Why aren't Director Bader and Deputy Cabell here pitching this? It seems like a CIA operation?"

"The COO is being written up for you – they will brief you tomorrow."

"As much as I enjoy your and General Finn's company, why are you here now telling me about a briefing due tomorrow? A heads up?"

"Yes and no. There is something bothering General Finn that is now bothering me and I think it will soon be bothering you."

"Outstanding. Let's hear it."

SecDef Stanton looked at General Finn and said, "general."

"Cabell's acting funny. He's treating me like his newest best friend. He has become a team player, so that alone tells you something's wrong. I sense he has another agenda and he wants to control its outcome."

"Like what?"

"Like when his grandfather planned the CIA Bay of Pigs invasion of Cuba. The CIA trained invasion group Brigade 2506 and President Kennedy were led to believe, by the CIA, that the invasion would be a complete success. The..."

"I know the story, General Finn," interrupted the president. "I was alive and lived it. The upshot is that Kennedy began signing his own death warrant by not sending in the Marines to support CIA-sponsored anti-Castro rebels. Then Kennedy fires Dulles and his two deputies Bissell and Cabell and threatens to 'splinter the CIA into a thousand pieces and scatter it into the wind'."

"I'm sorry Mr. President, I didn't mean..."

President Burk waved his hand in a gesture to signal it's was okay.

"So you think Prescott wants the al-Baghdadi abduction to fail or escalate into something that will at the least embarrass us and at worst put us in harm's way?"

General Finn was amazed at how quickly the president grasped the situation and didn't want to flower his response and simply answered, "Precisely."

Turning to SecDef Stanton, President Burk said, "What I am about to tell you stays in this room. Only you, the others in this room, AG Fare, and Secret Service Director Chris Bounty have been read in. We have some concerns about the vice president."

"How so?" asked Stanton.

"Her loyalty. After my Cabinet meeting, I pulled Vice President Hilton aside and told her about my concerns. I told her I felt everything seemed to be going to Hell since our reelection. It's like the Republicans and Democrats in both the House and Senate are teaming up against us. All true I might add. I asked if she was feeling that. She looked me in the eye and told me I'd been acting funny the last couple of days. She said everything was fine and that we have most of the country behind us. She said she would work on Schuster and the Senate, and that I should work on Bryan and the House. Together, she said, We'll find out if anything is going on."

"So? That sounds like a perfectly good answer. She has never given me any indication of intrigue. What do you suspect her of? I think you're being a bit paranoid, Tommy," suggested SecDef Stanton.

"Maybe, Ed. I hope so, but we just confirmed two days ago that Vice President Hilton has been in a secret closed-door meeting with Schuster and Bryan," revealed the president.

Stanton rose up off the couch and said, "She's the president of the Senate for Christ sakes, Tommy. She's just doing her job."

"Preston Cabell was also in the meeting," added the president.

Stanton fell back into the sofa spilling his coffee all over himself.

CHAPTER 17

Dallas, Texas 5:59 a.m.

Todd, like his teammates Flatly and Scales, was very close to achieving his OBE, Out of Body Experience. The ringing in his ears had started and now came the vibration. The orgasm of leaving his body was occurring.

In the adjoining control room, Russell Randazza and his room full of NASA technicians and engineers watched the wall mounted a/v monitors in each room, and via Bluetooth monitored each jumper's vital signs.

"Are all three showing signs of vibration and ringing?"

"Check."

"Have all three achieved OBE?"

"Check."

"Open the vortex on my count."

"Check."

"On 5-4-3-2-..."

The 14th floor started to shake, rattle and roll, but as quickly as it began it subsided. Then complete quiet.

The rooms visible on the monitors showed three empty beds. "They're gone," said Randazza. "Have a good trip guys, I wish I could be there with you."

Todd felt himself being pulled back into his body. *No please no, I want to stay out.* Too late. He was back but then he realized where he may have returned to. He turned and looked at the clock on the nightstand, it read 6:01 a.m. A knock came on his door, not the front door but the adjoining guest room. He got up and opened the door. Bob Scales, looking very much like a current hipster, walked in.

"Did it work? Are we there?" asked Todd.

"Yeah, we're back," said Scales. "I'm not exactly sure if it's November 21, 1963, but were back."

There was another knock on the opposite adjoining guest room. Todd went to open the door for Flatly and said over his shoulder to Scales, "Everything looks the same; how can you be sure?"

"Our Zenith TV's are now Philcos, the prop guys got it wrong. I think we're in the right church, but I'm not sure about the pew," said Scales, "and I don't hear Randazza in my ear."

Looking out the window Flatly said, "The outside looks the same as yesterday. Hard to tell but I'm pretty sure we are now where we were not a couple of minutes ago."

Looking at Flatley, Todd gave a WTF look and said, "Huh?" Then, turning and looking at his disheveled bed cover said, "Okay, let's tidy up our rooms, grab our stuff and get out of here before someone stumbles on us. When we get down in the lobby we'll find out real fast if we nailed it. Then we'll check into these same three rooms, grab a cab and get over to Dobbs House Restaurant, have breakfast and see if it's true."

Todd was wearing a tweed sports coat over a white shirt and rep tie, brown slacks and brown fedora with a hidden hat cam lens. Flatly wore a cardigan sweater vest over a white button-down with bow tie and dark slacks. His cam was hidden in his belt buckle. Scales wore a brown checked shirt over a white tee-shirt with black slacks as a tribute to Oswald. His sunglasses contained a hidden cam lens.

All three with their Samsonites and briefcases exited their rooms, locked the doors and stood by the elevator. Scales pushed the down button. The door opened and to their amazement there stood a man and a young girl. The man looked about 50 and was dressed in a tan cowboy/country suit, complete with a string tie, cowboy hat, and boots. The young girl, who looked no more than 20, was quite pretty and was wearing a pleated skirt, blue and white harlequin sweater and light blue pill box hat.

Todd tipped his hat and pushed the cam recorder remote button and started recording their first encounter.

"Good morning," said the cowboy.

"Morning," replied the jumpers.

In a heavy Texan slow drawl, the man said, "My niece and I are up from Houston. We're here to have lunch with President Kennedy. Where you boys from?"

Scales wasn't buying it and didn't like the man at all. He reminded him of the TV host from *Hee Haw* and his niece. Really? He flippantly answered, "2016, and I don't think so."

The cowboy had a confused look on his face until Todd covered it up with a quick thinking retort and a glaring look towards Scales, "2016 Endi Street, SoHo."

The cowboy still looked confused until Todd added, "New York."

The cowboy then pulled out a cigar, bit off the end, and lit it. As he shook the match out and put it in the elevator ashtray, the above light indicated their arrival on the ground floor, and the doors opened. The cowboy and his niece walked past the jumpers and out into the lobby. As they began to follow he turned, blew smoke towards Scales and said, "Well, you New York City boys be careful here in Dallas. Hear."

The lobby and reception areas were pretty busy for 6:15 a.m. People were coming and going and were all dressed in suits and dresses, but there wasn't a black face in the crowd. Even the bell boys were white. Todd saw one black man, *Excuse me, colored man,* he thought, working the bootblack stand in the recess around the corner. Todd needed to have a talk with Scales but that would have to wait.

Now they just had to check in and get the exact same three rooms.

The hotel lobby was grand and gorgeous. All three approached a magnificent cherry inlaid panel reception counter and waited for the next available clerk. A very beautiful young girl with blond hair in a flip cut beckoned them forward. She looked like a blond Mary Tyler Moore and just as bubbly.

With a big smile and a wonderful southern drawl, she said, "Good morning and welcome to Dallas and the Adolphus, gentleman. How may I help you today?"

Todd answered, "Good morning. May we have three adjoining rooms for two nights?"

She smiled and asked, "Are you here to see the president?"

"We are."

"Isn't he so handsome. I would just love to meet him. He will be coming right past the hotel at noon and I will be standing right out front."

Oh, shit, we may be a day late, thought Todd. "I'm sure he will notice you, dear. The rooms?" asked Todd trying not to sound disappointed or impatient.

Behind the counter was a large wall of cherry wood cubbyholes, each containing a key. Computers were not used at the Adolphus in 1963 and not used in most places except IBM. She turned and searched the cubbyholes, removed three keys and turned back to Todd with a big smile which quickly turned into a frown.

"I hope you're not superstitious because I only have three adjoining rooms on the 14th floor if that's okay?"

Two of the room keys were correct and as planned but one was not. Todd, the fast thinker, came up with a solution. "I'm not superstitious of the floor but could you manage to switch 1407 with 1404? That would give us 4, 5 and 6. and 456 is my lucky number."

"We can do that for you. Not too much demand for the 14th floor." She turned and replaced the 1407 key in its cubby and removed key 1404. "Will that be cash, check or credit card? We take Carte Blanche and American Express."

Todd had an American Express card to be used for an emergency only and was instructed to use cash whenever possible. It was the most common form of payment in the 60's and would draw the least attention.

"Cash."

"Okay. That will be $60.00 each per night plus tax. Can I ask you to please sign the registry and then we can check you in right away. You pay when you check out and you can also charge room service, the bar, and restaurant to your room."

Todd got the rooms for two nights because check-out was 12 noon and they needed to be in the room at 5 p.m. to jump back to 2017. Still hoping it was Thursday not Friday.

She rang the little brass bell and porters showed up immediately. She handed Todd the keys saying after reading the register, "Thank you, Mr. Logan, Mr. Flatly and Mr. Scales for staying at the Adolphus and we hope y'all enjoy Dallas."

While waiting for the elevator Todd pulled Scales aside and started quietly dressing him down. "What the hell was all that about? Where do you get off telling that man we're from the future and that he's not going to have lunch with the president? Are you crazy? You're with the Secret Service and supposed to be our security. Do your job and keep your pie hole shut."

"Niece my ass. And why did she call you Logan?" mumbled Scales.

"You'll find out when we get back to the future," said Todd. He was about to get back in Scales' face until the chime alerted him that the elevator had arrived, and Flatly shoved a copy of the *Fort Worth Telegram* November 21st morning addition into his face: "City Awaits Arrival of Kennedy Party. JFK Due At Carswell Air Force Base Tonight."

"Nailed it," grinned Todd.

CHAPTER 18

THE OVAL OFFICE WASHINGTON, DC

Noreen Ward opened her door to the Oval Office and interrupted the president's meeting, "Mr. President, Dr. Provenzano is on the line."

The president picked up the phone, "Tell me something good, TP."

"As Marty McFly said, 'History gonna change.'"

The president, to the dismay of the Senators he was meeting with, let out a Marine Corp yell. "Oorah! That's great. Are they there?"

"We're pretty sure they're there. But damn sure of one thing."

"What's that?"

"They're not here."

"Get back to me on a secure line. I want to hear everything. Outstanding!" exclaimed the president.

"Good news?" asked Senator Angie Kling of Maine."

"Wonderful news, Angie," beamed the president.

Senator Kling and the fifteen other Senators in the president's office were there for an early morning breakfast meeting. All were true supporters, friends and 'Live and Let Live Party' loyalists. Another fifteen House loyalists were due in later for a lunch meeting.

The president was feeling them out to see if any were becoming weak links, loose lips or were being pursued to cross over to the dark side. Ten minutes later the president was ushering the Senators out with an admonishment to do a better job on recruitment and to keep their eyes and ears open. As they walked out the door to the corridor, SecDef Stanton, AG Fare, FBI Director Riley, CoS Nicholas, Secret Service Director Bounty, NSA Finn and Press Secretary Kelly Sullivan came into the Oval Office through the president's secretary's door and took seats on the couches and chairs around the coffee table.

"CIA Director Bader and Deputy Director Cabell were in here earlier and presented a COO for me to sign. They are advocating an extraction of al-Baghdadi and ignoring Kim or his double. If we get Baghdadi we in effect help Kim's and disappear Iran's messenger. Kim gets half the money and doesn't have to deliver the nukes. Iran gets stiffed, losing 2.5 billion with nothing in return. And they both lose because America remains safe, at least until the next time. We get Baghdadi and everything and everybody he knows. Cabell gave me a 100% guaranteed success rate and it seems like a win-win for us. I approved the mission," said the president.

"Did you get a guarantee in writing?" asked Riley.

Not taking the bait, the president continued, "I consider you all my inner circle. There may be a few more let in, but for now, this is it. All of you now know what's going on with the Sofia, Bulgaria nuclear weapons buy and the proposed abduction of Baghdadi. Some of you know the rumblings of the brewing coup d'état being hatched by leading Republicans and Democrats against me and my administration. And a few of you know about our secret project - Project Christopher. It's about time we all got on the same page because, the nuclear weapons buy, the coup d'etat and Project Christopher may all be connected."

For the next hour, the president laid out exactly what was going on and how he wanted to proceed. There were many questions about the nuclear weapons buy, a bit of skepticism and shock about the coup, but total astonishment from those who were hearing about Project Christopher for the first time, especially when the president told them a jump team was currently in 1963, what they were doing, and where and when the next jump team was heading.

Noreen opened the door and advised that Dr. Provenzano was on the secure line.

The president explain his relationship with Dr. Provenzano then put him on speaker, "TP. You're on speaker and among friends. You have more good news?"

"We are tracking the team through a rudimentary version of GPS. On July 26, 1963, NASA launched the Hughes' Syncom 2. Syncom 2 was the first communications satellite in a geosynchronous orbit. It revolves around the earth once per day at a constant speed. It's still up there and functioning. We're using it to track the team's microchip GPS implants, but we're not able to communicate with them. What we now know is the team left the Adolphus jump site rooms and went 200 feet west, which we assume was to check in, then 200 feet east which we assume is back to the elevator and their room. We tracked them leaving the hotel lobby and then we lost them. We'll pick them up again tomorrow morning. But the good news is they're there and on the job."

"But how can you be sure they are there November 21, 1963, the day before Kennedy gets assassinated?" asked the president.

"Good question. Since we can't communicate, we set up a series of codes that are keyed into geographic locations. For example, if they, we, missed the date they would have gone to the Magnolia Hotel for breakfast. They didn't, so we're sure we nailed it."

"Outfuckingstanding!" hollered the president.

CHAPTER 19

DALLAS, TEXAS NOVEMBER 21, 1963 6:57 A.M.

The morning weather was already balmy and clear when they walked out of the Adolphus and onto Commerce Street. They were greeted by provocative photos of scantily clad burlesque dancers plastered on the building façade above a Bar-B-Q joint and on the club entrance marquee.

"That's my stop tonight," said Scales, pointing across the street towards the building.

"The Bar-B-Q?" asked Flatly.

"No. The place above it. That's Ruby's place. The Carousel Club."

Most of the men they saw, as they waited for a cab, were dressed similarly in jackets and ties. The younger men were wearing tee-shirts or short sleeve shirts or trending to the new mod look. The women wore skirts or dresses, some wore scarves and a few had lightweight coats. Even though it was 53 years in the past, 1963 seemed very familiar, the irony being everyone had a cigarette in their hand instead of a cell phone.

A Dallas Yellow Cab pulled up and the three jumpers got in. Todd and Flatly sat in the back and Scales in the front. The cab was a 1951 Ford.

"My dad had this same car, black, not yellow, and he also had three on the tree," stated Flatly proudly.

"Three on the tree?" asked Scales.

"Before your time, Bob. It's a three-speed gear shift lever attached to the steering wheel. See," said Todd pointing over the front seat at the steering wheel column.

It took 15 minutes for the less than two-mile cab ride from the Adolphus Hotel in downtown Dallas across the Trinity River into the Oak Cliff section of Dallas and the Dobbs House Restaurant. Looking out the cab window they saw no banks, no nail salons, no drug stores, and no wireless cell phone stores. Only shoe stores, record stores, five & dime stores and phone booths on every other corner. The three sat quietly as they watched cars and people pass by. They were all vibrant and alive now, but very few would be tomorrow at 5:01 p.m. The three got out in the parking lot in front of the Dobbs House Restaurant and asked the cab driver to wait.

"What a dive," remarked Scales. "It looks more like a coffee shop than a restaurant."

The Dobbs House Restaurant was really just a little pancake house back in 1963, part of a regional chain on the corner of North Beckley Avenue and Colorado Boulevard. It had a very 50's modern design and decoration and looked more like a restaurant than a diner, and was a mere three blocks from Oswald's rooming house. Witnesses stated that Oswald and Tippit were regular coffee customers and that Ruby who lived about a mile away was also known to stop by. This is where Todd and his team intended to pick up Oswald and tail him to the TSBD where he had to clock in for his eight-hour shift by 8 a.m.

"Okay. Let's go in and see who's there," dared Todd.

The three walked in and found an empty table and sat down. There were about ten tables they could see and a counter. It was a very small restaurant but half the tables were occupied as was most of the counter. It was a coffee, eggs, and pancakes kind of place.

"You boys know what you want or would you like to see a menu?" asked the waitress.

"Just three coffees to start please," answered Todd.

Flatly looked at the waitress and was about to order something more substantial until he noticed that both Todd and Scales had their heads turned and were looking at something.

What they were looking at was a man's back sitting at the counter almost directly in front of them. The man they were looking at appeared to be in his early twenties, had short dark hair, and was wearing dark slacks and an untucked dark shirt. *Could this be Oswald?* thought Flatly.

They could only see his back and side. He was eating something and had his head buried in a book, but it was defintely Oswald.

"Is that really him?" whispered Flatly.

Suddenly there was a commotion at the counter. "I ordered my eggs over light. These are cooked too hard," said Oswald. The waitress offered to redo the order, but Oswald accepted them and continued eating for a minute or so until he again became agitated. He pushed the plate away, said something nasty, left some money on the counter, pocketed his paperback and got up to leave.

Out from the side dining room came a police officer. "They're going to arrest him?" whispered Flatly.

"No, it's Tippit," muttered Todd softly.

They came face to face, Tippit, and Oswald. No words were spoken but Tippit shot Oswald a hard glance. Oswald turned and left the restaurant.

Todd got up and said to Flatly, "Stay with Tippit."

He and Scales followed Oswald outside.

Todd, Flatly and Scales were each equipped with highly modified 1963 Sony nine transistor- transceiver walkie-talkies, which were nothing more than an ear receiver and lapel mic transceivers rigged to use off a single Dallas radio channel and sporting a mere six-mile range.

Outside Todd and Scales watched Oswald walk to the bus stop on the corner of Colorado Blvd.

"Did you have your cam on in there?" asked Todd.

"Got everything," said Scales. "You?"

"Yeah."

Just then Flatly came running out shouting, "He went out the back door and got in his cruiser along with a guy that looked like Ruby."

"What? Are you sure?" asked Scales.

"It was so fast and the guy had on a fedora hat like yours, Todd. I just couldn't get a good look."

"Did you have your cam on? Did you get them together?" asked Todd.

Just then the sound of screeching tires could be heard as a Dallas police car number10 pulled out from behind the restaurant onto Colorado Blvd. and headed east. There was a civilian sitting shotgun and he seemed to signal to Oswald as they sped by.

"Jesus. Did you see that?" asked Scales.

"Yeah." Turning back to Flatly, Todd asked again, "Well did you get them on cam?"

"I couldn't. My cam is in my belt buckle and I was running and all and well..."

"You're supposed to be my a/v guy. What the fuck are you doing with your cam lens in your pants? What are you going to do stop and grab your crotch and point it? Why don't you have your cam lens up where we have ours?" questioned Todd.

"How am I supposed to do that?" asked Flatly.

"I don't know? How about you take your belt off and tie it around your head like a hippie?" yelled Todd.

"I don't think the hippie movement started till '66 in San Francisco," answered Flatly, not meaning to be flippant, but it was just the way he thought.

"Well, you can be the world's first hippie right here in Dallas in 1963, and get your picture on the cover of *Life Magazine*."

"I can only dream," said Flatly.

Scales was now in tears laughing. Before Todd could respond, a city bus appeared and was less than a block away.

"Look. Here comes the bus. I'll ride in with Oswald, while you two take the cab back to Elm and Huston. You'll get there first so just wait and stay out of trouble." To Flatly he added, "Get that cam lens away from your crotch and put it somewhere useful."

Todd hustled over to the bus stop and stood behind Oswald. Scales and Flatly got in the cab and headed back to the TSBD. They would keep in contact via their walkie-talkies.

Todd switched on his hat cam and carefully watched every movement Oswald made entering the bus. Oswald paid his fare and took a seat in the third row. Todd put his twenty-three cents in the coin slot, walked past Oswald and took an empty seat two rows behind on the opposite side of the aisle. He was still recording as Oswald pulled out a paperback from his back pocket and began reading. Todd struggled to see what he was reading and saw it was appropriately, Ian Flemings James Bond, *From Russia, with Love.*

Scales and Flatly took the cab back across the Trinity River to Dallas after telling the cabbie to go by way of North Beckley Avenue past Oswald's rooming house three blocks away. They stopped out in front briefly but didn't get out. They continued down to East 9th St. and made a left then a right onto North Patton to East 10th St. where police officer Tippit would be murdered in a little over 24 hours. Scales wanted to do a little recon before they would follow Oswald there tomorrow after the assassination of the president.

Without incident, Oswald's bus finally arrived a little before 8 a.m. at the corner of Elm and Houston. Oswald got off and Todd followed. For the first time, Todd noticed Oswald was carrying a small paper bag which Todd believed to be Oswald's lunch. Oswald went to the TSBD entrance on Elm Street and disappeared into the building. He was not supposed to emerge again until a little after 5 p.m., but the jumpers would be watching just in case.

CHAPTER 20

The Oval Office Washington, DC

The president was just ushering out his fifteen loyal members of the House of Representatives with the same admonishment he had earlier given the Senators. His inner circle and stewards were coming in through Noreen Ward's door: SecDef Stanton, AG Fare, FBI Director Riley, Secret Service Director Bounty, and General Finn. CoS Nicholas and Press Secretary Sullivan were already with the president. They again all took seats on the couches and chairs around the coffee table while the stewards tidied up and brought in fresh coffee and ice tea.

"I've added two more into our inner circle and have brought them up to date: NSA Director Roger Michaels and Deputy Secretary of Homeland Security Lucia Borras," announced the president. "I'm waiting for a report from them now."

Noreen Ward stuck her head in and said that NSA Director Michaels and Deputy Secretary of Homeland Security Borras had arrived. Both came in and took whatever available seats were left. The inner circle was growing.

"By now Vice President Hilton and Minority Leader Senator Schuster will know of my breakfast meeting with my Senators and will be suspicious as to why they weren't invited. Speaker Bryan will soon know about my lunch meeting with my loyal House members," said President Burk.

"Good. Let them sweat a bit," Riley chimed in.

"This will slow them down or speed them up," advised Nicholas.

"What they are doing borders on sedition and treason," claimed AG Fare.

"That may be. All we have so far is circumstantial evidence, but no smoking gun," said the president as he looked towards NSA Director Michaels.

"We have something," hinted Director Michaels.

"What do you have Roger?" asked the president.

"A secure phone intercept between Cabell, Schuster, and Bryan."

" I thought secure phone calls were supposed to be secure?" asked the president.

"Well, yes. That's what we want people to think but we have the technology to penetrate today's secure or scrambled phones, even Smart TV's," said Michaels. "Your conversations, however, are secure Mr. President."

"Why do I have a hard time believing that, director?" asked the president. "Let's discuss that later; what do you have now?"

"Cabell knows our capabilities so I think he may want us to know what's going on, but his motives are still not clear," declared Michaels. He took out a voice recorder, placed it on the coffee table and pressed start.

> *"I'll get the elite left, the mainstream media, pro-choice, the nasty women and our protesters. The ones Burks people are calling Radical Left Anarchists. You get the Christian right, the Alt-right, Pro-life, the neoconservatives, NRA and the military, and together we'll get late night to turn the youth against him. We'll get rid of Burk and his 'Live and Let Live Party.'"*

Director Micheals stopped the voice recorder. "That, so all of you know, is Senator Schuster's voice. The next voice is that of Speaker Bryan then Schuster again. The last voice is that of CIA Deputy Director Cabell. He leaned over and pushed the resume button.

> *"Vice President Hilton will replace him and we'll get her to get rid of most of his staff. We'll also need to make some Cabinet changes. That will give us back our country and level the playing field for 2020. Then it will be just you and me, my friend. May the best man win."*

"I can just see Burk leaving the White House for the last time, just like Nixon aboard Marine One."

"Or like Kennedy aboard Air Force One."

Director Micheals pushed the stop button.

For a few seconds, everyone in the room was very quiet while they each digested the conversation, especially Cabell's unveiled threat.

CoS Nicholas was the first to speak, "That's a smoking gun."

"That's sedition and treason," advised AG Fare.

"But why? I don't understand," said Kelly. "Why? The country, despite what they are saying, is on the right track. The people gave us four more years; elections have consequences after all. There have been no homegrown terrorist attacks in the last two years. We fixed and improved the Affordable Healthcare Act. We solved immigration without mass deportation, and our borders are now secure. Crime and murder in the inner cities are down. Schools are much better, and producing bright kids for college and trade schools. We're on board with climate change. Jobs are way up, the stock market is over the top. We even helped give Vice President Hilton her pet project: college debt forgiveness. The deficit is under control, and we are nibbling at the debt. We got rid of the income tax in favor of a national sales tax for everyone making under a million, but kept it for millionaires and corporations. Medicare and Social Security are solvent. We even gave two cost of living increases to Social Security, and added dental, hearing and vision coverage to Medicare. You sent USA dividend checks to a quarter of the population. I don't get it. Why are they doing this?"

"Because they have to. Both Republican and Democratic parties are like huge dinosaurs with tiny brains, and their survival instincts are keen and have been honed since before the Civil War. If I, we, our Live and Let Live Party are allowed to continue they will perish. We're like the meteor that came out of nowhere that crashed and blocked out their sun. They have to eat us to survive. It's in their DNA," explained President Burk.

"Let's round all four of them up, take them into the Rose Garden and shoot them," barked Riley.

"No. I have a better idea," admitted President Burk.

CHAPTER 21

Dallas, Texas
November 21, 1963 12:30 p.m.

The team spent most of the morning exploring the area around the TSBD, and Dealey Plaza. Before jumping back from 2016 to 1963, many hours were spent with Randazza and his team deciding where and how to place the GoPro cameras at the Grassy Knoll, the Picket Fence and especially at the corner of Houston and Elm pointing at the TSBD sixth-floor corner window. As much time that was spent on locating the cameras more time was spent trying to find ways to retrieve them after the shooting stopped. The plaza would be crawling with cops so any attempt to shimmy up a pole and retrieve a GoPro might draw unwanted attention. Randazza and Flatly came up with a solution: a magnet mounted on the GoPro camera back that would hold the camera in place on one of the many metal poles and signs that are all over Dealey Plaza. Flatly would carry an umbrella and place the GoPro on the umbrella ferrule and place the GoPro about eight feet up a pole or sign. Each camera would automatically begin filming at 11:45 a.m. on the next day, the 22nd and stop one hour later. Then Flatly would retrieve the three GoPro's using the umbrella. When the ferrule is reinserted it will snap release the GoPro from the magnet. The GoPro will come down with the umbrella but the magnet will remain on the metal pole.

"Okay, let's recap what we have so far," suggested Todd.

"We have one GoPro placed across Elm Street which will capture Zapruder and the picket fence to the left. We have another mounted behind the picket fence on a metal pole between the railway bridge and the picket fence. Now we need to place the final one on the street lamp pole on Elm and Houston," said Flatly.

With both Scales and Todd as lookouts, and as possible diversions if needed, Flatly placed the final GoPro on his umbrella ferrule and walked over to the street sign pole. The metal pole was right next to the reflecting pool and when affixed properly would be focused on the TSBD six-floor window. There were a fair amount of pedestrians and vehicle traffic in the area, but Flatly just went up and leaned against the pole. When the moment seemed right he turned, and as practiced a hundred times, quickly and precisely raised his closed umbrella and pushed the GoPro to the pole. The magnet held, and he simply pulled the umbrella in a downward motion freeing the male ferrule from the female receptacle.

"There. It's done," said Flatly.

"Not too bad. The GoPro color blends perfectly with the pole color. If I wasn't looking for it I wouldn't notice it," admitted Scales.

Looking at Flatly, Todd said, "Okay. We all know the drill but it's worth repeating. We'll go back to the hotel and take care of our end and get ready for tonight. You stay here and make sure Oswald doesn't take a powder. Bob will be back before 5 p.m. with the rental car. When Oswald and Frazier come out at 5 p.m., you follow Frazier's car to Paine's house in Irving and sit tight. Park down the street, stay in your car and don't let anyone see you. Stay until 10 p.m., then head over to the Ritz Motel on South Walton Walker Boulevard. Check in, get something to eat, sleep and be back to Paine's house by 6:45 a.m. and follow them back here. Got it?" asked Todd.

"Got it," answered Flatly.

"And Adrian, make sure you record everything, especially the package."

Earlier, while they were exploring the train yard and the area north of the TSBD they checked that Frazier black 54 Chevy Bel Air was parked in his regular parking lot behind the state building. Buell Wesley Frazier works with Oswald and will drive him to Ruth Paine's house tonight, where Oswald's wife Marina and daughters were staying, and bring him back to the TSBD tomorrow morning. Frazier lives close to Paine and since Oswald doesn't drive he sometimes chauffeurs Oswald back and forth to work. Why tomorrow morning's trip to work is so important to the jumpers is because Frazier will be bringing Oswald to work and Oswald will allegedly be bringing a rifle.

At 5:15 p.m., after dropping off the rental car to Flatly, Scales returned to the hotel and met Todd for a drink at the bar.

"Everything go okay?" asked Todd.

"Yeah. I stayed and watched Frazier and Oswald come out, get in the car and leave. Then I watched Flatly follow. You ready to make your calls?" asked Scales.

"Ready but nervous. If I blow either one I may have to crash the party. But first things first. I'll call *The New York Post* and see if they remember me. Got a dime?"

Todd's first call would be to his mentor, Vincent Musetto, who worked at the *New York Post.* The only problem was that Todd didn't start working at the post till 1981. So here in 1963 Musetto would not know Todd. Musetto became famous in 1983 for his reporting and writing about an infamous crime story about Charles Dingle, who, in April of 1983, shot the owner of a topless bar and forced a hostage to decapitate the dead bar owner. His grisly crime which included a rape inspired Musetto to write what may be the most celebrated *Post* headline of all time: "Headless Body in Topless Bar".

Todd needed Musetto, should anyone in 1963 call to check on him, to say he knew and worked with Todd and that he, Todd, was a good solid reporter.

"Yeah?"

"Vincent Musetto," said Todd.

"Hold."

"Musetto here. Who's this?"

"You don't know me but I know you. Names Michael Logan. In a few years from now, you're gonna hire a guy named Todd and you're gonna be best friends. You're gonna marry a girl name Clair and have a beautiful daughter named Carly. You're gonna become a managing editor and go on to write the most famous *Post* headline ever."

"Say, what is this, some sort of a shakedown?"

"No. I just need you to do me a little favor, and I will do you a big favor."

"What's the little favor?"

"If Helen Thomas, the White House UPI correspondent..."

"I know who the hell Helen Thomas is."

"Right. If she calls you in a few minutes, tell her I work for you, that I'm a good reporter, a stand-up guy, and we should get together."

"What's in it for me Logan? What's the big favor?"

"Take the red eye and get down here to Dallas tomorrow morning. Be at the Texas School Book Depository on Elm and Huston by 12 noon."

"Why should I do that?"

"Because you're gonna be in the middle of the biggest story of the century."

Todd hung up. He was not sure Musetto would cover for him if Helen Thomas, Todd's next call, called Musetto to check Logan's bonafides. But he was positive Musetto would be in Dallas tomorrow because Musetto told him all about his JFK assassination scoop the first day Todd came to work at the *Post* seventeen years later in 1980.

Todd gave Scales a thumbs up.

"All good?" asked Scales. "And why do you keep calling yourself Logan?"

"So far so good and I'll explain later," said Todd as he walked past Scales towards the check-in counter. Scales followed.

The counter was busy. There were several couples and business persons waiting to check in but only two clerks. Todd got in line but Scales walked up to the counter and Todd followed. "Excuse me," he said to the hotel clerk, "what room is Helen Thomas in? She's expecting my call."

The clerk and what appeared to be a newlywed couple he was attending seemed annoyed and getting ready to object before Todd added as he smiled at the couple, "It's okay. We're from New York."

For whatever reason, that seemed to make everything acceptable, and the couple smiled back as the clerk turned to check something, turned back and said, "Room 1003. The house phone is right over there," he pointed.

Scales thanked the clerk and turned towards the house phones while Todd smiled and nodded to the clerk, bowed to the couple, then followed Scales to the phones.

It was 5:30 p.m. when Todd picked up the house phone and dialed 1003. After a few rings, Helen Thomas answered.

Helen Thomas was born on August 4, 1920, in Winchester, Kentucky. She became the first female member of the White House press corps during the John F. Kennedy administration and covered 10 presidents over five decades. Helen was always the first reporter called on to ask the first question at a presidential press conference. She was the *United Press International's* first female White House bureau chief and the first female member of Washington's historic press group, the Gridiron Club. After working for *UPI* for nearly six decades, Thomas became a syndicated columnist for *Hearst*. Thomas will die July 20, 2013, at the age of 92.

In 1963, Helen was yet the celebrity she would become but knew both Kennedy and Johnson and that got her invited to most A list parties and events. Helen is not a looker. She was short and plump, but a matter of fact-no nonsense reporter that everyone wanted to be seen with. Tonight, Helen, along with some of the richest and most powerful men in the world along with their wives, mistresses, and escorts, were invited to dine and party with oil baron Clint Murchison in Murchison's home on Preston Avenue in North Dallas. This is why Todd was calling Helen. He needed to go to the party to capture on film all those rich and powerful men together, and most importantly, capture the audio of the most chilling promise ever uttered.

"Hello."

"Miss Thomas, I'm Michael Logan from the *NewYork Post*. My boss, Vincent Musetto, said if I ever have the opportunity I should look you up. I heard you were here in Dallas and I'm also here in Dallas, at the Adolphus, to cover the Trade Mart luncheon tomorrow. I was hoping you would join me for dinner tonight. I have something important I would like to discuss with you."

"Mr. Logan, I am terribly sorry, but I have a previous commitment this evening. Perhaps we could meet tomorrow at the Mart?"

"Oh. Just my luck, all dressed up and no place to go. I'll call room service and take you up on your offer to meet tomorrow. Sorry to have bothered you, Miss Thomas. Good afternoon," said Todd.

"No bother. Goodbye, Mr. Logan," said Thomas.

Scales had been listening to the one-sided conversation and shook his head at the rejection and wondered why Todd keeps using an alias.

"Let's get up to our rooms," prompted Todd as he headed towards the elevators.

The elevator ride up to the 14th floor was crowded. Two of the passengers were the couple from the reception counter, a bit awkward, so both Scales and Todd keep quiet and kept their head and eyes down and forward. Luckily the couple and their bell boy got off on the 10th floor.

Back in Todds room Scales said, "What do we do now?"

Todd sat on the bed, looked at the phone and said, "We sit tight and pray for it to ring."

No sooner did he say that when the phone rang. Todd gave a thumbs up, waited for another ring, then picked up. "Hello, Logan here."

"Mr. Logan, Helen Thomas. I felt so bad after we hung up. I couldn't bear thinking of you all alone in your room tonight. I had a thought. Why not join me? I'm attending a dinner party, a pretty special one. Are you up for it?"

"Miss Thomas, I don't want to be a bother."

"Nothing could be further. You be my walker and we'll have a wonderful time. There will be some big boys there and who knows, you might get a story. They are sending a car. See you in the lobby at 7:30."

With that said, Thomas hung up and Todd smiled at Scales and said as he placed the phone back in the cradle, "Showtime."

CHAPTER 22

DALLAS, TEXAS NOVEMBER 21, 1963 8 P.M.

The dinner party that Todd got himself invited to was arguably the most important gathering since the Last Supper. It was more important than the November 14, 1957, Apalachin meeting where Vito Genovese invited mafia bosses, their advisers, and bodyguards, approximately one hundred men in all, to meet at Joseph "Joe the Barber" Barbara's 53-acre farm in Apalachin, New York. The purpose of that meeting was to discuss La Cosa Nostra operations such as gambling, casinos, narcotics, hits, murder, and Aniello "The Lamb" Dellacroce and Armand "Tommy" Rava's proposition to go to war against the Genovese family. Things went south when the farmhouse was raided by police sending mobsters running off in all directions. Many mafiosi escaped through the woods surrounding the Barbara farm. Police did, however, apprehend numerous mobsters, including Genovese, Gambino crime family boss Carlo Gambino, and Bonanno crime family boss Joseph Bonanno.

The dinner party that Todd aka Logan was escorting Thomas to tonight, at oil baron Clint Murchison's 40,000 square foot house on Preston Avenue in North Dallas would be attended by, among others: Richard Nixon, J. Edgar Hoover and his lover Cly Tolson, Jack Ruby, Deputy Director of the CIA

Charles Cabell (recently fired by Kennedy), Charles' brother Dallas Mayor Earle Cabell, Malcolm Wallace, Vice President Johnson's hatchet man, Carlos Marcello, boss of the New Orleans mafia, Joe Civello, boss of the Dallas mafia, Bill Decker, Sheriff of Dallas County, Larry Campbell representing Jimmy Hoffa, George Owen, Madeleine Brown, LBJ's mistress, and Helen Thomas. Also attending the party were: H. L. Hunt, Governor John Connally, former Texas Republican congressman Bruce Alger, and John J. McCloy of Chase Manhattan Bank. Oh, yes, and Vice President Lyndon Baines Johnson. These men attended with their wives, girlfriends, and escorts. The friendly press were also invited to the Big Event Pre-Party as they were calling it. But this dinner party was the best-kept secret ever. Only soul searching long after Kennedys assassination by Helen Thomas and Madeleine Brown did the party and the 'Good Old Boys' private meeting come to light. Unlike the Apalachin meeting, police and federal agents would never apprehend these conspirators and mobsters.

"Helen, I can't believe I'm here with you. This is unbelievable," blurted Todd.

"Let me introduce you to a few of the *boys*," said Helen.

As soon as they walked into the library the magnitude of the event hit Todd like a sledgehammer.

"Helen Thomas. So good to see you again. What brings you to Dallas?" asked former Vice President Nixon.

"I could ask you the same thing, Mr. Vice President."

This was a time before air kisses and man hugs. People, even famous people, just shook hands but only if the lady offered her hand first. Helen didn't.

"May I introduce a friend and colleague, Michael Logan with the *New York Post*."

Todd thought of his future interview with Nixon in 1982 when as a cub reporter he will question Nixon's thought process on Vietnam. As things would eventually unfold, Johnson and the Democrats would take America to war in Vietnam. Nixon would inherit Johnson's war, but instead of ending it immediately and leave it to history as Johnson's War, Nixon continued the war never attaining his 'Peace with Honor' pledge. Johnson's War became Nixon's War.

"Mr. Vice President," said Todd as he offered his hand. Nixon's handshake was firm but his hand like his face was moist. Nixon had just a few years earlier come off a devastating and humiliating defeat by Kennedy and had little love for Kennedy or the press.

"Mr. Logan," reciprocated Nixon while breaking off the handshake. Nixon then looked to Helen and put his hand on her elbow and guided her away while whispering something in her ear.

Todd, now alone in the middle of the library, thought he liked Nixon even less now than he would in the future. Todd had to remind himself to be careful not to do or say anything which could create an incident. It had been drummed into his team that they could do nothing that might change events and possibly alter the future. Todd thought to himself how Nixon would react if he would have said to him, *Mr. Nixion, I have some good news for you and some bad news. The good news is that you'll become president in 1969. The bad news is you will resign in disgrace in 1974.*

Todd came out of his wishful thinking to take in the who's who he was standing among in Clint Murchison's library. There were many glamorous and beautiful women but it was the men that held his attention: J. Edgar Hoover, Jack Ruby, Carlos Marcello and Governor John Connally, all together in the same room. It became a bit of a juggling act for Todd to point his fedora hat cam lens with one hand while pushing the on-off switch with a drink in the other. He knew most of the other men from the pictures Randazza had him study. Many were wealthy beyond compare and most fitted out in traditional Dallas power cowboy suits complete with Stetson and Amarillo boots. He considered wearing his fedora like the yahoos did but, for some reason a Stetson works indoors as well as outdoors. A fedora doesn't work indoors unless your Carlos Marcello.

Helen came back to rescue him and the evening progressed with more introductions, dinner, and dancing. He thought Helen was charming and a delight to be with. Towards 10:30 p.m. the party began breaking up. Helen disappeared and Todd became nervous because he was standing out with his flaming red hair and beard and the rich and powerful might begin to take notice, something Todd needed to avoid. He looked for Helen but she was otherwise engaged and instead gravitated to a lovely young girl standing alone. He recognized her immediately and moved in to make her acquaintance. She was, after all, a young raven haired beauty and the main reason he was here. The fact that she was alone was not unusual, and meant that her boyfriend was near.

"May I introduce myself? I'm Michael Logan, a friend of Helen Thomas." He purposely avoided mention of the *New York Post,* as it was not considered 'friendly press.'

"I'm Madeleine Brown from right here in Dallas. Where are you from, Mr. Logan?"

"Manhattan, and please don't hold that against me. May I freshen your drink?"

"That would be lovely. It's like you, Mr. Logan," she said as she handed him her empty glass.

"How's that, Miss Brown?" asked Todd.

"It's a Manhattan." With that, she let out a little giggle.

Todd managed without incident to fulfill her drink order and was returning to continue their conversation when a tremendous commotion occurred outside the library. Before he could reach Miss Brown, Lyndon Baines Johnson, the Vice President of the United States came bounding into the room. Clint Murchison immediately broke away from his other guest and rushed over to greet the vice president. Johnson's booming voice demanded a cold Fresca soda which was on hand and immediately brought to him. He ignored everyone else in the room and headed straight for a large conference room off the library. Murchison looked around the library and signaled for all the boys to follow him and the vice president into the conference room. When the doors of the conference room closed only the wives, girlfriends, escorts, servants and a few men including Todd remained. Todd made his way to Miss Brown and offered her the drink.

"What was that all about?" asked Todd.

"Why, Mr. Logan, as Lyndon has told me many times, little girls should keep their ears covered and their eyes closed," said Miss Brown with another little giggle.

They made small talk for a few more minutes and were soon joined by Helen Thomas and a few other guests hoping to pump Madeleine Brown for any information about what was going on in the other room. Around 11:30 p.m. the conference room door flew open and an angry, violent vice president came storming out. Madeleine broke from the group and walked towards Johnson. This is what Todd was waiting for. This is why he came. Would Johnson really say it or was it just a myth? Todd, only ten feet away from the vice president and his mistress, raised his fedora, which he kept by his side in his right hand, and aimed the lens towards the couple. Lyndon was wild with anger and grabbed Madeleine by her shoulders and in a loud voice said, "After tomorrow those son of bitches will never embarrass me again. That's not a threat. That's a promise."

Todd got it, got it all on tape. He just heard a promise made by a man who unfortunately was not known for breaking them. *"...those son of bitches... "Johnson was referring too,* thought Todd, *were John and Robert Kennedy.*

CHAPTER 23

THE OVAL OFFICE WASHINGTON, DC

"Nothing?" asked the president.

"Not until tomorrow morning, Mr. President. But we're optimistic that everything is coming together according to plan," assured Dr. Provenzano.

"Or everything is falling apart according to plan," said the president. "Look, TP, we have got to do better in the future."

"The future is not the problem. We have plenty of technology today that's compatible with tomorrow. It's the past that's the problem. At least we have this one satellite in '63 we could use. But the further back we go the less technology we have available to tap into. We have usable signals from TV in the 40's, radio in the 30's, telephones in the 20's, then the telegraph. After that it's waving flags, yelling and smoke signals. I can't send satellites, text messaging or Twitter back in time."

"You know what I mean, TP. Look, we can't send teams back in time without proper support and an ability to communicate and track. And I don't consider a 30-minute satellite pass over once a day and Hasbro toy walkie-talkies as communication."

"We'll figure something out for the next one. This is just our first jump," reminded Dr. Provenzano.

"Okay. I hope, as you said, it all comes together tomorrow. I'll be waiting for your call."

The president touched the speaker phone button and disconnected the call.

FBI Director Riley, CoS Nicholas and Press Secretary Sullivan had been sitting in the Oval Office with the president while he had Dr. Provenzano on speaker phone.

"Tommy, you sent three men back in time. That's huge. It's monumental. People have been dreaming and writing about that since H.G. Wells," said Kelly.

"Hell, since *Memories of the Twentieth Century*," said Nicholas.

"What?" asked President Burk.

"I've been reading up on time travel since you first brought it up. *Memories of the Twentieth Century* was written by Samuel Madden in 1733 about a guardian angel traveling back in time to the year 1728 with letters from 1997 and 1998."

Ignoring Nicholas' revelation, Riley said, "Come on, Sarge, chill out a little! Tomorrow morning we'll have an update from the doc, and by tomorrow afternoon the team will be back, and we'll get to see and hear what really happened in Dallas fifty-three years ago."

"What you and Dr. Provenzano are doing needs to be shared," suggested Kelly.

"I don't think so. What if it comes back that Oswald did it, acted alone, and the Warren Commission was right all along," grilled the president.

"Come on, Sarge, you don't believe that. We've studied the assassination to death. You know the facts and you know in your heart and in your gut that Oswald was not the shooter. Tomorrow we'll have three eyewitnesses and film of the actual assassination and the day leading up to it. You know as well as I do it was a conspiracy at the highest levels. 'The Unspeakable,'" said Riley.

"What they come back with tomorrow will prove none of that. If I'm correct it will prove one thing and one thing only: Oswald didn't take the shot. He was just a patsy," added President Burk.

CHAPTER 24

Dallas, Texas November 22, 1963 7:15 a.m.

At 7:15 a.m., November 22, 1963, Adrian Flatly was sitting in his rental car watching Oswald leave the Paine house. Flatly started his engine and slowly followed Oswald for about half-a-block to the residence of Mrs. Linnie Mae Randle, the sister of the man with whom Oswald drove back and forth to work-Buell Wesley Frazier.

"Flatly to base. Over," said Flatly into his collar mic.

Todd and Scales, waiting for the call responded immediately.

"Scales here. Over."

"Scales here. Over."

"Take your finger off the talk button, Flatly."

Of course, Flatly couldn't hear Scales because he had his finger on the talk button.

"Flatly to base. Over." This time he remembered to take his finger off the talk button.

"Scales here. Listen, guy, you got to remember to take your finger off the talk button. That's why you say 'over'. You can't hear me if you keep your finger on the talk button. Over."

"Sorry. Anyway, Oswald is out and over at Frazier's house. Over."

"You getting all this on your belt cam? Over."

"Roger that. Over."

Mrs. Randle, while her brother was eating breakfast, looked out the breakfast-room window and saw Oswald cross the street and walk toward the driveway where her brother parked his car near the carport.

"He's carrying a brown bag. He's got it gripped in his right hand near the top. It's tapered, and he hugged it in his hand. Oswald just opened the right rear door of Frazier's car and put the package in the back seat. The package looks about 36" long. Over."

"You just keep reporting and we'll just listen. Over," said Scales.

Frazier met Oswald at the kitchen door and together they walked to the car. After getting in the car, Frazier glanced over his shoulder and noticed a brown paper package on the back seat. He asked Oswald what was in the package. Oswald said it was curtain rods. As they sat in the car, Frazier asked Oswald where his lunch was, and Oswald replied that he was going to buy his lunch today.

"They're on the move to the TSBD. See you there. Over."

Twenty minutes later Frazier parked the car in the company parking lot about two blocks north of the depository building.

Todd and Scales watched as Oswald left the car first, picked up the brown paper bag from the back seat, and proceeded toward his place of work ahead of Frazier. Frazier stayed in the car a bit longer for some reason.

Todd walked behind Oswald while Scales positioned himself at the building entrance. One end of the package was under Oswald's armpit and the lower part was held with his right hand, so that it was carried straight and parallel to his body, sort of like old corps 'shoulder arms'.

Scales was smoking a cigarette by the door when Oswald approached the depository building. Todd was 10 feet behind and Frazier was 40 feet behind Todd. It was the first time that Oswald had not walked with Frazier from the parking lot to the building entrance. Scales smiled, nodded and opened the door for Oswald. Oswald seemed to expect the courtesy but did not acknowledge the gesture and disappeared into the bowels of the TSBD.

When Todd caught up to Scales, Scales murmured, "Smug bastard."

Scales opened the door for Frazier and Frazier said, "Thank you," and followed Oswald into history.

"At least someone has manners," hissed Scales.

"Yeah, and he's a real nice guy. Too bad, because after today the rest of his life goes down the toilet," remarked Todd.

They walked over to where Flatly was parked, and got in the rental.

"It's 8 a.m. Four and a half hours till showtime; let's have breakfast," said Flatly.

"Bob. You return the car to Hertz while Adrian and I double check the GoPro's as we walk back to the hotel. We'll meet you in the restaurant for breakfast."

They checked all three GoPro's, and everything seemed good, at least they were in place and had not been discovered.

Dealey Plaza was quiet and there were no barricades lining the route. There were also no police or Secret Service presence. No tow trucks removing parked cars were observed. This would all change after today. These few hours before the president is murdered will be the last remaining hours of American innocence. Like the December morning twenty-one years before and September morning yet to come, everything will be forever changed.

Later in the hotel restaurant, the three men sat around the table and ordered breakfast.

"Sorry about the button thing," said Flatly.

"Don't sweat it," said Todd. "But today will be crucial. We all need to stay in contact so we can't afford any fuck-ups."

"You get good film on Oswald this morning?" asked Scales.

"Yeah. I think so," said Flatly. "You?"

"Yeah. Unlike your belt cam and his hat cam I have playback on my glasses," said Scales. "Sure didn't look like curtain rods to me."

"Nor me, but we're supposed to be fair and balanced. We report, they decide," answered Todd.

Flatly, who had been out of the loop since yesterday afternoon asked, "How did it go for you guys after I left to follow Frazier and Oswald home?"

"I went to the Carousel Club across the street last night. The place was full of cops and Secret Service agents. Can you believe it?" asked Scales.

"Were they drinking?"

"Drinking? They were all two sheets to the wind when I left around midnight."

"Was Ruby there?" asked Flatly.

"No. I'll let Logan fill you on that," said Scales eyeing Todd, "but Tippit was there and I met a beautiful hostess, Tammi True."

"Logan? Tammi True? Didn't I see her name on the marquee?" asked Flatly.

"Yeah. You got a problem with that?" asked Scales.

Todd intervened to head off what was surely coming.

"Ruby was at Clint Murchison's party. I saw him. Nixon was there as well, as were: J. Edgar Hoover, Carlos Marcello, Governor John Connally, and Johnson. It was a who's who of the JFK fan club," said Todd.

"Wow. Did you get it? Is it true?" asked Flatly.

"I got it alright. That man is one angry cowboy. He opened his mouth and I got it loud and clear. He said, 'After tomorrow those sons-of-bitches will never embarrass me again. That's not a threat. That's a promise.' After he said that he looked over Madeleine Brown's shoulder and noticed me. He gave me the meanest look I ever saw, and made a gesture towards me," said Todd as he formed his index finger and thumb into a gun and pointed it at Flatly.

"What's that supposed to mean?" asked Flatly gawking at Todd's extended hand.

"That my friend, is the smoking gun."

CHAPTER 25

THE OVAL OFFICE WASHINGTON, DC

Press Secretary Kelly Sullivan, FBI Director Ray Riley and CoS Bill Nicholas were sitting on the couches discussing an upcoming presidential press conference while President Burk sat at his desk with a phone to his ear, appearing to appease Speaker Bryan for yesterday's meeting screw-up.

"Paul. Paul, listen. I don't set up the meetings," Looking over to Nicholas he continued. "I'll speak to my CoS; it's his screw up. It won't happen again. Okay? And by the way Paul, haven't you ever had a meeting where you inadvertently forgot to inform someone?" With that said the president hung up.

The president got up from his desk and moved to his chair by the couch. It was 8:15 a.m. and everyone was on their third cup of coffee while the president was on was on his third Diet Coke.

"Nice parting shot, Sarge," said Riley.

"He so self-absorbed I doubt he got it."

Noreen popped her head in and said Doctor Provenzano was on the phone.

"Morning, TP. 'What do you hear, what do you say'?" asked President Burk over the speaker phone.

As much as Riley morphed into *Godfather* characters on occasion, President Burk was known to channel James Cagney and Dr. Provenzano was quite used to it.

"They're on the move. Flatly was in Irving this morning following Oswald and Frazier back to the depository, and Todd and Scales were in the depository north parking lot to meet them. Scales took the rental back and Todd and Flatly walked back to the hotel after stopping, we presume, to check on each GoPro. All three are now in the hotel having breakfast. All's good."

"Outstanding, TP," praised the president. Riley, Kelly, and Nicholas were all up and cheering and clapping.

"The satellite has passed and we lost them again so from now on we just keep our fingers crossed. These guys have done everything by the book so far, so I'm not worried about them."

"Then what are you worried about?"

"Getting them home."

"Yeah, but when they get here they'll have one hell of a story to tell," offered Kelly.

"All right, TP, get back to work. I'll expect to hear from you by 5:30 tonight at the latest. How's Randazza holding up?"

"He's on it. Hell, he's all over it. He's already got the communication problem worked out for the next time," confirmed Dr. Provenzanno.

"Okay. Less than four hours to, as our vintage IC intelligent community friends referred to it, the 'Big Event'. Talk to you soon, TP," promised President Burk as he pushed the speaker button to disconnect the call.

"Yesterday, just before we broke up, I said that tomorrow we'll have three eyewitnesses and film of the actual assassination and the day leading up to it and that will prove conspiracy at the highest levels. 'The Unspeakable,'" reminded Riley. "You said it will prove nothing other than Oswald was or was not the shooter? What are you saying?"

"I'm saying the Bay of Pigs invasion was the Central Intelligence Agency's attempt to entrap Kennedy into a full-scale U.S. invasion of Cuba. Kennedy was the target of a CIA covert operation that collapsed when the invasion collapsed. The result of that operation was Kennedy's avowed intention 'To splinter the CIA into a thousand pieces and scatter it to the winds'. The forced resignation of CIA Director Allen Dulles, his deputies Bissell and Cabell, and several others served notice that that statement might be followed through. Kennedy's conflict with the military, including the Cuban Missile Crisis, the Partial Nuclear Test Ban Treaty, and a back-channel to Fidel Castro and Khrushchev aimed at normalizing relations, culminated with his signing of National Security Action Memorandum 263 beginning the withdrawal of US troops from Vietnam."

"Tell me something I don't know," said Riley.

"Captain, what you and I do know, as James Douglass so brilliantly researched and wrote in his book *JFK and the Unspeakable*, is that Kennedy at the height of the Cold War risked committing the greatest crime in human history: starting a nuclear war. He was so horrified by the specter of nuclear annihilation that he gradually turned away from his long-held cold warrior beliefs and toward a policy of lasting peace. But to the military and intelligence agencies in the United States, who were committed to winning the Cold War at any cost, Kennedy's change of heart was a direct threat to their power and influence. Once these dark unspeakable forces recognized that Kennedy's interests were in direct opposition to their own, they tagged him as a dangerous traitor, plotted his assassination, and orchestrated the subsequent cover-up."

"But sending our jump team back is not an indictment. It is only to show whether Oswald pulled the trigger on Kennedy and Tippit," disclosed President Burk.

"But what if Todd is able to record Johnson's threat. His promise? What if he gets film of who's who at the party? Nixon, Hoover, Cabell, Ruby? Surely that's an indictment?" asked Kelly.

"Kelly, if we go there we risk the same fate as Kennedy. I'll pick my own battles. I never had any intention of releasing to the press what we find out today from the jumpers," advised President Burk.

"What? Then why are we doing it? What about all that rewriting history crap?" asked Kelly.

"We can't risk anyone, other nation states and especially our intelligence community and political adversaries finding out about our ability to time travel."

"So what Todd and his team bring back with will remain a secret?"

"I didn't say that," corrected President Burk.

"Tommy Burk, you mischievous devil. What are you not telling us?" asked Kelly.

CHAPTER 26

Dallas, Texas November 22, 1963 11:30 a.m.

"Mr. Todd, I'm Charles Carman, bank manager, how may we be of service."

"Mr. Carman, I have a special request. I would like to open three savings accounts, in different names, and I require a safe deposit box."

"Certainly. We can certainly accommodate both for you right away, Mr. Todd; please have a seat. And just how much would you like to deposit today and how long would you be requiring the safe deposit box?"

"I would like to deposit $100,000.00 each in three different accounts and I need the box for 53 years."

The Republic National Bank of Dallas at 300 North Ervay Street in downtown Dallas, started life in 1920 as the Guaranty Bank and Trust Company. On the backs of oil baron money, it soon became The Republic National Bank and Trust of Dallas and by 1963 it was known as The Republic National Bank of Dallas. With the savings and loan scandal of the eighties, it became the Nations Bank Corporation and was finally acquired by Bank of America. But with all that said and done in 2016, the bank was still at its original location and operating under the name of Bank of America and under the protection of the National Registry of Historic Places. Although the commercial space above was converted into luxury apartments in 2007, the ground floor bank and the lower level safe deposit vaults containing hundreds of solid brass boxes would remain untouched and in service.

"It's almost noon; where is he?" asked Flatly.

"He'll be here. Don't worry," said Scales.

Crowds were already gathering in and around Dealey Plaza and the showers seemed to have stopped. Women, girls, men, and boys were beginning to line Houston Street. It seemed like most of the girls had on skirts, white bobby socks, and sweaters, and all seemed to have big hair or wore scarves. The boys all had button downs or pullovers, mostly short sleeve, jeans and Chuck Taylors. Most of the older women had on light coats and carried pocketbooks, while the men wore suits or sports coats and many wore hats. There were some blacks or coloreds as they were called then, and quite a few kids even though it was a school day.

"Here he is. Where have you been? It's almost time," asked Scales.

"I had to do a little shopping then go to the bank. On my way here I stopped around the corner on Main Street at an MG dealership. I couldn't walk by without going in; then I saw it and just had to have it. I bought a brand new two seat 1962 MG A 1600 Mark 11 convertible in British racing green with brown leather interior and spoke wheels for 2,500 bucks. I'm going to have it shipped to myself in New York," chirped Todd.

"What?" asked Scales. "Are you fucking nuts?"

"Hardly. I always wanted one but could never afford it. A pristine 1962 MGA in 2016 will fetch 70,000 bucks."

"So you brought it now to sell it when you get back home?"

"No, no. It's is a keeper. This car is definitely me and I intend to drive it all around the Hamptons. With my red hair, beard, driving cap and driving gloves, I will be a classic in a classic. We will be absolutely irresistible to the ladies."

'You'll be certifiable if Randazza finds out. I wouldn't put it past Adrian to do something like this. But you? What's going on?" asked Scales.

"Nothing. I just thought we might as well get something out of this whole thing seeing as how Randazza said our jump is going to be kept secret," said Todd.

"What? He told you that?"

Flatly, still fixated on Scales' demeaning comment said, "Buying a car is the last thing on my mind. Look at all these people. At 5:00 p.m. this afternoon they will all be alive. Sad, scared, confused by what happened, but alive nonetheless. By 5:01 when we arrive back in 2016, they will all be dead. There will be nothing left of them. Not just here in Dallas but everywhere across the country, almost 200 million souls. Sure, all the teens and kids will still be alive, at least the ones Johnson doesn't send to die in Vietnam, but the rest will all be gone. Their clothes, their pocketbooks, their combs, everything will be gone except a few vintage items on eBay."

"Jesus, Adrian. I didn't mean to make you so maudlin," said Scales.

"You didn't and I'm not. I'm just stating a fact. In less than six hours, when we're safely back in 2016, mostly everyone here will be dead, even your hostess friend Tammi True."

At 12 noon Scales took his place behind the picket fence on the Grassy Knoll. He was wearing a dark suit today, had authentic Secret Service credentials, just in case, and stood far back in order to let things play out. Besides the GoPro mounted on the metal fence post behind the wood picket fence, Scales had his cam glasses.

Flatly was positioned across Elm Street facing the Grassy Knoll, almost exactly where Kennedy would receive the fatal head shot. The GoPro was affixed to the street lamp behind him on Elm Street. He was also dressed in a dark suit and hat and he remounted his belt buckle cam to his suit lapel.

Todd was on the corner of Elm and Houston just north of the North Reflecting Pool. His GoPro was attached to the sign pole and directed on the TSBD across the street with the wide angle lens focused on the easternmost sixth-floor window. In addition to his hat cam, he was holding a Bell & Howell 414PD Director Series Double 8mm Zoomatic home-movie camera. It was just like the one Abraham Zapruder would use to capture for all time what the conspirators called the "Big Event" while history would refer to it as "The President's Commission on the Assassination of President Kennedy, aka "The Warren Commission."

"I saw the camera. Nice. Where did you get it? Over," asked Flatly.

"Neiman Marcus on Commerce Street. Over," answered Todd.

"I've got movement. Over," said Scales.

"What do you got? Over," asked Todd.

"I got four maybe five guys moving towards the picket fence from the railroad tracks. One of them looks like a cop, another a railroad worker, another a soldier. I got another guy in a suit going over to the soldier. He seems to be chasing the soldier away. Over," spoke Scales.

"Jesus. I just saw Oswald in the window. Over," gasped Todd.

"Did he have a rifle? Over," asked Scales.

"Negative. Over," replied Todd.

About ten minutes later from the distance, they could now hear the president's motorcade turning off of Main Street onto Houston. The police motorcycles and the roar of the crowd were gaining in intensity. It was 12:26 p.m.

"I've got Zapruder climbing up the wall and getting ready to film. I can see some men behind the picket fence. Over," said Flatly as he absent-mindedly practiced opening and closing his umbrella.

As the motorcade was about to turn left onto Elm Street, Todd, as scripted, focused his Bell & Howell on the motorcade but made sure to accidentally capture the sixth floor then pan back down to the motorcade then right back up to the sixth floor seemingly going back to something he saw in the sixth-floor window. Todd, looking thru the viewfinder pushed the zoom button and focused on a man with a dark complexion. He had a rifle and was aiming down towards the president then all hell broke loose.

The first shot didn't come from the TSBD but from the Dal-Tex building roof on the east side of Elm Street. Todd immediately panned right and saw smoke and movement on the Dal-Tex roof. The next shot rang out from the TSBD sixth floor and Todd swung back and captured the shooter pulling the bolt back to chamber a round for another shot. Another shot came from Dal-Tex but Todd stayed focussed on the sixth floor. Crack! The shooter fired again. Four shots were fired by now and Kennedy was just coming out from behind the highway sign almost in front of Zapruder and clutching his throat. Another two shots rang out from the TSBD and the Dal-Tex building. President Kennedy and Governor Connally have now both been hit. One more shot rang out from the Dal-Tex and simultaneously one from the picket fence. Kennedys' head explodes.

"My, God! blurted Flatly, "his brains and skull are on the back of the limo and in the street."

"My guys took one shot each and are packing up. Over," said Scales.

Nobody replied.

"Flatly, take your fuckin' finger off the talk button or I swear I'll cut it off." Scales said it so loud that Flatly must have heard it across the street because he released the button.

Scales said again, "My guys took two shots, packed up and are leaving the area. Over," said Scales.

"Roger that, Bob. I had shooters from the TSBD and the Dal-Tex building. At least nine shots in all including your two. My shooters are also gone. Over."

"Flatly, can you hear me? Over," said Scales.

"Roger, and sorry about that. Over," answered Flatly.

"You do it again and your peace sign will look like you're giving someone the finger. Over," said Scales.

"Okay, guys, knock it off. Man, can you believe what just happened? What we just witnessed? What we just filmed? Over," asked an excited Todd.

The president's limo, motorcycle escort, and Secret Service follow car were gone. The limo with Johnson, Ladybird, and Senator Yarborough were just going under the overpass.

"Where was Johnson? Over," asked Flatly.

"The chickenshit knew what was coming and ducked. Over," said Scales.

Then it was over. They were gone. Even the cars with the press were gone. But Dealey Plaza was anything but over. People were screaming, standing in shock. Some were pointing or dropped to the ground. Others were running away and some were running towards the sound of the shots from the Grassy Knoll. Some hadn't a clue that the president had even been shot. It was all sheer chaos.

"Okay, let's move and we can chat later. Adrian, you get the GoPro's and take them to your hotel room, then head to the Texas Theatre. Bob, you get over here most ricky-tick and pick up Oswald and stick with him. I've got to go to the bank and take care of something. I'll meet you at North Patton and East 10th. Let's move. Over and out," said Todd.

CHAPTER 27

DALLAS, TEXAS NOVEMBER 22, 1963 12:33 A.M.

Scales got there quickly and entered the TSBD and found Oswald just as he was coming out. He literally bumped into him and by some quick thinking identified himself as a Secret Service agent and asked where the nearest pay phone was. Oswald pointed the phone out to Scales then left the building. Scales watched him leave, linger for a while, then followed him as he began walking east on Elm Street. Oswald was wearing a white t-shirt, long-sleeved brown shirt, light gray work pants, and carrying a light blue/gray flannel jacket; he was easy to follow. Oswald wouldn't take the Beckley bus he normally did to go home, but as Scales watched, he headed to the Marsalis bus.

About 12:40 p.m., Oswald boarded the bus in the middle of an intersection instead of at a regular bus stop. Scales watched as Oswald and a blond woman boarded the bus approximately six blocks before Houston Street. Scales knew he wouldn't go far. At 12:44 p.m., Oswald and the blond woman unexpectedly exited the bus and began walking south on Lamar St. toward the Greyhound bus station. The blond-haired woman was following Oswald and Scales followed her.

Oswald walked south on Lamar where he saw a cab at a taxi stand and jumped in the front passenger's seat. Scales had to hustle to find another cab, but just then two more cabs pulled into the stand and an elderly lady grabbed the first one, and before the blond women could grab the second, Scales raced ahead and grabbed it. "Follow that cab," instructed Scales. He knew where Oswald was going but saying it and trying to follow the cab made it more exciting.

Scales' cab followed Oswald's cab out of downtown Dallas, across the Trinity River and into the Oak Clift section. Oswald's cab drove past his rooming house and stopped a couple of blocks away at Beckley and Neely where Oswald got out. Scales' cab then continued and circled around, and pulled over on Eldorado Avenue, facing the rooming house and waited. Scales watched as Oswald walked north on Beckley, and approached his rooming house at 1026 North Beckley.

Oswald entered the rooming house at 1:00 p.m. and spent about three minutes inside. Scales watched as a Dallas police patrol car slowly cruised past the rooming house and honked the horn a couple of times. Scales watched as Oswald walked out of his rooming house and head towards the bus stop just a few feet away on the corner of Zang and Beckley streets. The same patrol car from just a minute ago pulled up and Oswald opened the front passenger door and got in.

"He's in Tippit's patrol car heading to 10th and Patton. Where are you, Todd? Over," asked Scales.

"What did you say?" asked the taxi driver.

"No. Sorry. I was talking into my tape recorder. I'm a private eye. This guy is cheating on his wife and I gotta tail him. Just follow that police car and keep a lid on it," advised Scales.

"I'm at 10th and Patton. Over and out," said Todd.

'I'm at the Texas Theatre. Over and Out," announced Flatly.

Tippit's patrol car with Oswald inside pulled out onto Zang and quickly made a right onto North Crawford heading south. He made a left on Davis, a right on Patton and a left onto 10th heading east. He slowed down and pulled over in front of one of the houses.

Scales' cab followed and turned onto 10th, saw Todd but kept going. He passed the patrol car and looked in to see Tippet with Oswald sitting next to him. A gray car was parked across the street. As he passed he observed two men get out of the gray car and approach the patrol car. He had his cab drive slow while looking over his shoulder out the back cab window until he asked the cab to stop. He paid and got out.

Todd saw and began recording two men as they got out of a gray car and approach the patrol car, say something to Tippit, and motioned for Oswald to get out. Oswald opened his door to get out but instead of going towards the two men he ran and dove into some bushes. Gunshots rang out as one of the men shot at Oswald. Oswald ran between some houses into a backyard, over a fence, and onto the next street. Scales followed. Todd watched Tippit get out of his patrol car and draw his pistol. The second man, who from the back looked like Ruby, drew his pistol and shot Tippit four times in the chest and stomach and a 'coup de grace' point-blank shot to the head. Several neighbors, hearing the gunshots, came outside to investigate. Todd began to quickly back away, so not to be noticed. He ran around the corner and hid behind a tree.

"Flatly, it's 1:13 and Tippit is down. Oswald is on the run towards you. Scales is following. I'm on my way. Over and out," said Todd as he watched the two men get in the gray car and speed away.

Scales followed Oswald the six blocks from the ambush to the Texas Theatre. From across the street, he watched Oswald duck into a store front then continue into the theater. Scales watched Flatly follow Oswald into the theater. Police sirens could now be heard from where Tippit went down.

"I'm on him. Over," said Flatly into the walkie-talkie.

Around 1:16 p.m. Scales watched as a female ticket seller came out of the box office of the Texas Theatre. The sound of police sirens were getting louder and coming from many different directions. The ticket seller started talking with a man who came from the nearby shoe store, and after less than a minute the two of them went into the theater.

Todd showed up and both he and Scales entered the theater. The ticket taker was busy on the phone, presumingly calling the police, and they slipped by unnoticed.

"May I have a large popcorn, please," asked Oswald as Todd and Scales walked past the concession stand. Flatly was peeking around the corner from inside the theater, keeping an eye on Oswald.

Todd and Scales walked past Flatly and entered the theater. Scales took a seat in the back and Todd keep walking down the aisle to the front by the screen near the emergency exit that led to the rear alley behind the theater.

Oswald returned to the lower level and took a seat next to a woman. Within a few minutes, they both got up from their seats. He walked again into the concession area, followed again by Flatly, and then back into the lower level and took a seat next to a man in the first row on the right side. The theater was nearly empty, as the opening credits to the movie began. After sitting next to the man for a few minutes, he got up and walked past empty seats to the small aisle on the right side of the theater and into the concession area. He again re-entered the theater and took a seat next to a man on the back row. That man was Scales. This was unexpected, and Scales thought he may have been busted. But it was dark, so he relaxed a bit and hoped Oswald wouldn't strike up a conversation or ask for a password. Scales might have been tempted to respond. Oswald got up and once again returned to the concession area. He returned a few minutes later and took a seat across the aisle from Scales, and then moved to another seat on the third back row. He was definitely looking for someone, looking for his contact.

At 1:40 p.m., Oswald was sitting alone in the rear of the main floor of the theater near the right center aisle, the third row down, the fifth seat in. The lights came on and the gray seats became red, then the shoe store man walked onto the stage and pointed Oswald out to the police. The police started searching two other theater patrons first, including Todd. Then a policeman, named McDonald, reached Oswald and told him to get on his feet. The cop then yelled something at Oswald. Oswald rose from his seat, bringing up both hands. As McDonald started to search Oswald's waist for a gun, Oswald hit him in the face and drew his revolver. McDonald struck back with his right hand and grabbed the gun with his left hand. They both fell into the seats. Three other officers, moving toward the scuffle, grabbed Oswald from the front, rear and side. McDonald fell into the seat with his left hand on the gun. Scales could hear what sounded like the snap of the hammer. A detective, who was standing beside McDonald, seized the gun from Oswald. Oswald was handcuffed and led from the theater cursing and rambling.

Flatly followed Oswald and the cops out the front door while Todd went out the back exit into the alley and waited. Scales headed up to the balcony.

"Here's up here. Jesus, he looks just like Oswald. Over," said Scales.

There was a tussle and the cops began to drag a man down the balcony steps through the theater to the front by the screen and out the exit that Todd went out just minutes before. Todd hid as police cars began converging in the alley behind the theater. Todd filmed the cops as they brought a young white man out the back. The man was dressed in a pullover shirt and slacks. He seemed to be flushed as if he'd been in a struggle. The cops put the man in a police car and drove off. He was never heard from again.

"I got Oswald coming out the front. The cops threw him in a squad car and took him away. Over," said Flatly.

"I got the second Oswald coming out the back. The cops threw him in a squad car and took him away too," advised Todd. "Okay, guys, that's a wrap. We got what we were sent here to get, and we did what we were sent here to do. Good job. Let's meet out front. Over and out," said Todd.

Standing outside the front of the Texas Theatre, Todd, Flatly and Scales blended in well with the fifty or so other men, women, and kids gathered to see what all the fuss was about. Some Dallas police remained, and people were asking them what the man did, or "Is he the guy who shot the president?"

Scales took off his sunglasses and placed them on the roof of a Dallas police patrol car and walked back to his two team mates. He corralled them and pointed to the glasses and said, "Smile … 3-2-1." He walked back to the car, retrieved his glasses and went back to show the team their selfie. It was a great pic with the three of them and the Texas Theatre marquee in the background.

"Might as well have something to prove we were here. I'll email you a copy when we get back to the land of email," remarked Scales.

"I'm ready to get back. What about you guys?" asked Todd.

"I like it here. Not here in Dallas but here in this time. It was the best of times, at least before today," said Flatly.

"I feel sorry for Oswald. He didn't deserve all this. He had done nothing but tell the truth. 'I'm just a patsy.' This Sunday morning, he will pay the ultimate price. I'll bet he had no idea how it would all turn out seven years ago when he joined the Marines at seventeen," said Todd.

"*War is Hell*," said Flatly.

"What Adrian? Is that supposed to be the moral of the story?" asked Scales sarcastically.

"No," said Flatly. "That was the movie that was playing when the cops arrested Oswald."

"Right, said Todd. Okay, we have less than three hours to get back to the hotel before they zap us back. Let's head back now, grab some lunch, get our stuff together, get into bed, go to sleep and go home."

CHAPTER 28

Dallas, Texas, 2016

Back in the Adolphus Project Christopher control room, Russell Randazza and his NASA team were powering down the portal retrieval vortexes.

"President Burk is on line two," said Randazza.

"Yes, Mr. President," answered Dr. Provenzano.

"TP. How did it go? Are they all back in one piece?" asked the president.

"Tommy, they're not here. They never made it back," said a worried Dr. Provenzano.

There was a long pause before the president responded, "Is it them or us?"

"It's not us, Tommy. We jumped them on schedule at 5 p.m. Everything on our end worked. We tried again, as per protocol in case they got held up, at 5:30 p.m. Again, nothing. I'm sorry, Tommy."

"What went wrong?"

"Either they never made it back to the hotel, in which case we will, again according to protocol, jump them tomorrow morning at 7 a.m. if we locate them in the hotel via the satellite window."

"You said either. What's the either?"

"They could have been compromised."

Randazza held up the hotel phone to Dr. Provenzano motioning that he should take it.

Dr. Provenzano put his hand up and hunched his shoulders to express to Randazza, WTF?

"You're gonna want to take this," said Randazza, "it's the front desk. Bob Scales is in the lobby asking for you."

"Tommy, I'll call you back. One of our jumpers is down in the lobby," said Dr. Provenzano and hung up.

"Russell, I just hung up on the President of the United States; this better not be a fucking joke."

Dr. Provenzano and Russell Randazza exited the elevator and walked to the front desk while scanning the lobby for Scales. It was a pretty busy time of day and there were plenty of couples, and business people, young and old, in the seating area and hurrying this way and that, but no Scales.

"How is it just Scales made it back and how come here in the lobby and not the room?" asked Dr. Provenzano.

Randazza didn't answer but started instead to search.

Dr. Provenzano went to the front desk and the young lady behind the counter, who happened to be the hotel assistant manager greeted him with a smile. "Ms. Bush, you said you had a Mr. Scales asking for me?" She smiled again and pointed to the elderly couple in the seating area. They were looking directly at him. He made eye contact with Randazza and moved his eyes towards the couple as he walked towards them.

"I'm Dr. Provenzano. Did you want to speak with me? You have some information about Mr. Scales?"

The man looked to be in his early eighties, the woman possibly a bit younger. The man, who kept his eyes on Dr. Provenzano, stood, extended his hand and said, "Dr. Provenzano, Bob Scales. It's been 53 years but seems like only yesterday."

Dr. Provenzano began putting it all together. It was the women that threw him at first but now it was making sense. *This was the 30-year-old Bob Scales they left behind in 1963. He's what, 83 now? He didn't come back through the vortex. He came back the long way,* thought Dr. Provenzano.

Bob Scales looked healthy for his age and was dressed in a sports jacket and slacks and was wearing New Balance running shoes, presumably for comfort. He turned to Randazza, offered his hand, and said, "It was not your fault Razz." Scales then turned back to Dr. Provenzano and said, "May I introduce my wife, Nancy Myers Scales." She nodded at both but did not stand or offer her hand. She looked to be in her mid-70's, though she was still attractive with blond hair and blue eyes. She wore her hair pulled back in a bun with large hoop earrings, red lipstick and an embroidered denim jacket over a white tee-shirt with a picture of a young scantily clad woman with a name under the picture. She said hello in a raspy smoker's southern drawl.

"Is it really you, Bob?" asked Dr. Provenzano, as it all started to become clear. "Where are Todd and Flatly?"

"Dr. Provenzano, Razz, I have a story to tell you and it's a good one. I've never talked about it or said a word about it to anyone except my wife, Todd and Flatly. But I'm sure you're dying to hear it, so I'll give you the short version now and the long version later in the 14th. floor debriefing room."

"I love a good story, Bob. Let's sit down and get comfortable. Would you like something to drink?" asked Dr. Provenzano.

"Later perhaps. I just want to get on with what I came here to tell you."

Dr. Provenzano and Randazza both nodded and settled in.

"We did everything by the book. We got there early on the 21st. and found Oswald in the restaurant if you can call it that. Ruby and Tippet were there too, but they skedaddled out the back. Todd followed Oswald to work on the bus then we met up in Dealey Plaza and planted the GoPro's. Later, Flatly tailed Oswald back to Paine's house and babysitted until the next morning. I checked out the Carousel Club and the Colony Club next door. Tippit was there along with a bunch of Kennedy's Secret Service agents. That's where I met my wife Tammi."

"I thought your name was Nancy?" asked Randazza.

"Tammi was my stage name, Tammi True. I headlined for Jack at the Carousel Club back then. But that's a whole other story, sugar."

"I'll get to all that but as I was saying, I did the clubs, but Todd did the party at Clint Murchison's house. He got it all. Hoover, Nixon, Ruby, CIA's Charles Cabell, Marcello all of them. Then he gets Johnson's threat on tape. He played it for us in the cab: 'After tomorrow those son-of-bitches will never embarrass me again. That's not a threat. That's a promise.' Johnson even looked at Todd like he knew him. He made a gun with his fingers and thumb and pointed it at Todd and said, 'Bang.'"

"What? That's ridiculous. How could Johnson possibly know Todd?" asked Randazza with a smirk.

"Now you just wait a minute, young man. You may still be my boss, in which case you owe me 53 years back pay at least, but I'm now your senior so show some respect. Now, where was I? Yes, he made a direct threat to Todd and then stormed out of the party."

"The next day Flatly followed Frazier and Oswald to work. We watched and filmed Oswald walking to the TSBD and saw what he was carrying. It wasn't curtain rods. Around noon we split up and went to our post, me behind the picket fence, Flatly across Elm, and Todd at the corner of Houston and Elm. Todd saw Oswald in the six-floor window but…"

"Mother fuc…, Oh, sorry Mrs. Scales. It's just that…," began Randazza.

"Sugar, you can call me Tammi and I've heard much worse than that. The Carousel Club taught us girls how to tune out vulgar talk a long time ago. And that trash talk didn't come from the military boys, not even the from the sailors. No, sir. The vulgar talk came from the oil men and politicians."

"Thank you, Tammi. What I meant is that President Burk was certain Oswald didn't pull the trigger and that he was just a patsy. That was the primary reason for sending the guys back," explained Randazza.

"I ain't finished!" yelled Scales. "Todd saw Oswald in the window a little past noon, but when the shooting started it wasn't Oswald in the window and it wasn't Oswald pulling the trigger. In fact, Todd captured the whole thing on film and the first shot didn't even come from the TSBD; it came from the Dal-Tex building across the street. There were seven shots, not three, then the two guys behind the picket fence that I was watching opened up with one shot each including the fatal head shot. Four shooters and nine shots."

"If you don't mind, all this talking is making me thirsty. A Vesper right now would hit the spot. One for you, dear?"

"Vesper?" asked Randazza.

"Right. I forgot. You weren't born yet. James Bond was all the thing then and a Vesper was one of his favorite drinks. Three measures of Gordon's, one of vodka, and a half a measure of Kina Lillet. In a shaker filled with ice like a martini. Shake it very well until it's ice-cold, then add a large thin slice of lemon peel. Got it?"

"Got it. I'll be right back," promised Randazza.

"Make it three," said Dr. Provenzano.

"Four Vespers coming up," stated Randazza.

What was just revealed was exactly what Dr. Provenzano and President Tommy Burk always believed, but was so different from the official Warren Commission, mainstream media, and apologist version. Dr. Provenzano pulled out his phone and texted the president. *Scales is back and telling an unbelievable story. I will call you soon but we were right; Oswald was just a patsy.*

CHAPTER 29

Dallas, Texas, 2016

Bob and Tammi sat quietly and let Dr. Provenzano contemplate the story he had just told until Randazza and a waitress returned with the drinks.

They raised their glasses and brought them together in a toast. "Chin Chin," said Tammi.

"Chin Chin," joined the others.

"Now where was I?" asked Scales.

"Four shooters and nine shots," reminded Dr. Provenzano.

"Right. All hell broke loose, and we saw it all and we got it all. After the president was shot we all had jobs to do and mine was to tail Oswald from the TSBD to his rooming house, to Tippit's murder, then on to the Texas Theatre. Flatly gathered up the GoPro's and took them back to the hotel then went directly to the Texas Theatre. Todd went to the National Bank and then on to meet me at 10th and Patton where Tippit got it. Again, everything goes according to plan. I ran over to the TSBD and literally bump into Oswald as he's leaving. I froze for a minute then asked him where the phone was; I think I showed him my CIA creds. I watch him leave the building and follow him in a cab to his rooming house. I watch him go in, come out and get in Tippets patrol car. I follow them to 10th and Patton and met up with Todd. Two men get out of a parked car and approach Tippit's car, then Oswald jumps out and hightails it while one of the men shoots at him.

I follow Oswald. Todd told me later that Tippit got out to help Oswald and they shot him. Todd thought one of the shooters could have been Ruby. I followed Oswald to the theater where Flatly picked him up inside. Todd and I went in just minutes before the police swarmed in and took Oswald into custody. Flatly followed them out while Todd and I watched as another man, who looked like Oswald, was being pulled out of the balcony by the cops, and taken out the back."

"Jesus. And you got all this on film?"

"Yep. Then we got in a cab and headed back to the hotel. We had plenty of time before the jump back so we decided to have lunch at the hotel. We got out of the cab in front of the hotel then everything turned to shit. Dallas County Sheriff cars pulled up and deputies jumped out and before we knew it we were in handcuffs in the back of sheriff cars and on the way to the Dallas County Jail just a few blocks away."

"Why? Why did they arrest you?"

"We didn't know at first. We kept to our legends but they found our walkie-talkie transmitters and ear pieces and our hidden cams. We were busted. Sheriff Bill Decker, who Todd recognized from the party the night before, a real hard nose, said we were part of the assassination and worked with Oswald. He said we were gonna get the chair along with Oswald for murdering the president and Tippit. A spook was working with him. We found out later that it was Deputy Director of the CIA, Charles Cabell, who was also at the party. They figured out how to use the walkie-talkies easy enough, but couldn't get Todd and Flatly's cam to play back because they didn't have the means to download it. Mine they figured out pretty fast and when they did we were busted. They seemed to know all about us."

"How could they unless they saw you planting the GoPro's or they had a tail on Oswald and their tail picked up your tail?"

"Could be, but it was something else. Another spook we saw was talking to Cabell. Never got his name, but he seemed to know about us, where we came from, everything. He kept feeding information to Cabell, and Cabell would catch us in a lie. Finally, we had to come straight with them. They were not surprised, or shocked that we came from the future the way you would expect. They keep us Friday night and on Saturday morning gave us back our wallets and personal stuff, and said we could go. They said to keep our mouths shut, and to never go near the hotel again. They keep the walkie-talkies and the cams. They didn't tell us, but we saw the GoPro's and other equipment from our rooms laid out on an evidence desk."

"What did the other spook look like that seemed to know all about you?" asked Dr. Provenzano.

"His hair was short and combed forward. He had a very thin face, chalky complexion. His eyes were sunken and in shadow. He was tall and creepy. Very tall, very creepy, and he dressed like where we came from in 2016, not like the 60's."

This meant nothing to Bob or Tammi but it spoke volumes to Dr. Provenzano and Randazza.

"So what happened after they let you go?" asked Dr. Provenzano.

"It's funny. We all went our separate ways. Seeing as how we couldn't communicate with you and couldn't go back to the hotel, we felt abandoned. We were not sure if you would send anyone back for us. We waited a couple of weeks. But because of the contingency money you gave Todd to deposit in our names we all had a pretty good stake. A hundred grand in 1963 was a bloody fortune. Flatly loved the 60's and took his money and bought a used '59 Volkswagon bus, and had it all painted up in different colors with flowers and stuff. He said he was going to San Francisco. I asked him why and he said he wanted to find 'Gentle people with flowers in their hair'. I got a funny letter from him a few years later with a news clipping. He had been arrested with a guy named Timothy Leary for doing LSD. I heard Flatly passed some time in '83."

"Todd hung around Dallas for a few years and I saw him now and then. He was a real bon vivant and ladies man. He had a green British sports car and was seen driving to all the social events always accompanied by a lady. He went to Vietnam in '67 as a UPI correspondent, came back here then finally moved to the Hamptons in the 70's. I got a letter from his lawyer sometime in '93 telling me he died."

"What about you?"

"I used my stake to buy Ruby's Carousel Club from his sister and manager. Tammi and I kept it going through the 60's as the same kind of burlesque club. We had a regular clientele, but then we got a lot of tourists because of the Ruby connection. In the early 70's we changed to a disco and that bombed. In 1972, we lost our lease, and we sold all the stuff. We tried to open in another area, but we lost our mojo."

"What have you been doing for the last 44 years?"

"Not much. We traveled a bit, and invested in small companies wherever we landed."

"Where and in what?"

"In '76 we went to Albuquerque and bought shares in a small company and in '77 we went to Palo Alto, California and invested in another small company. That kind of thing."

1976 Albuquerque and 1977 Palo Alto? Humm? I'm guessing Microsoft and Apple?" asked Dr. Provenzano.

"Billy and Steve, God rest his soul," said Tammi. "They have been awful good to us."

"Dr. Provenzano, I am getting a little tired. Would it be okay if we came back tomorrow to do the formal debriefing?"

"Not at all. Let us put you up in the hotel for the night. Our treat," said Dr. Provenzano.

"I think I had enough of this hotel and If it's all the same to you, we'd rather go home. We bought Clint Murchison's house in '87 and did a cosmetic renovation. We put it back as it was in 1963; thought it would be a hoot. Our driver is waiting outside. Say tomorrow morning at 9 a.m.?"

"That would be fine."

As Bob and Tammi got up to leave, Bob turned to Randazza and said, "He went anyway you know."

"Who?"

"Todd. He went to see Oswald being transferred to the county jail Sunday morning. Saw the whole thing live. Just thought you would like to know."

Scales reached down and took a medium size box out of a shopping bag and handed it to Dr. Provenzano. "When the lawyer sent the letter informing me of Todd's death, he enclosed a key, a receipt and a power of attorney for the safe deposit box in the Republic National Bank. I kept an eye on the bank over the years and even had some investments there. When I saw this day was coming I visited the bank, and retrieved what was in the safe deposit box all these years. I think you know what it is."

In all the excitement Dr. Provenzano forgot about the safe deposit box and its contents. The box Bob Scales handed him was a hermetically sealed container NASA had designed to keep the B&H movie camera and film in pristine condition for a hundred years. Todd had taken the camera and film to the bank right after the assassination. He placed it along with the shopping bag and receipt in the special container which was already in the bank vault box, sealed it, and there it remained for 53 years.

"I'm going to call the president and tell him what you did. I'm sure he will want to hear the story directly from you and personally thank you."

"I don't fly anymore if I can avoid it, but he's welcome to come over to Clint's place. One more president won't hurt its provenance."

"Thank you, Bob. You, Todd and Flatly have witnessed firsthand what so many have believed but could never prove until now. This film will rewrite history.

Looking at Randazza, Scales said, "Todd said you were never going to release the film or the truth."

"We're not. I don't think our president wants our capabilities known just yet. But if some young investigative reporter we know happens to find the camera and film, well, you can imagine what will happen when they have it developed."

"Might this have something to do with a guy named Logan?" asked Scales.

Dr. Provenzano smiled and said, "See you in the morning."

CHAPTER 30

THE WHITE HOUSE WASHINGTON, DC

It was 8 p.m. when Dr. Provenzano got back up to the control room and could get a secure line back to the White House. The president and first lady were finishing a quiet dinner in their second-floor dining room where the White House operator tracked them down. The steward alerted the president of the incoming call. The president dismissed the wait and kitchen staff and took the call.

"TP. Thank God. I'm here with Kelly and we have been on pins and needles since your text. Tell us what happened."

"Good evening, Tommy, Kelly. Are you ready for a bedtime story to top all bedtime stories?"

"TP, I have been waiting 53 years to hear this story. Ever since Uncle Walter announced to the world on *CBS* that Friday afternoon that 'President Kennedy died at 1 p.m. Central Standard Time, 2:00 Eastern Standard Time, some 38 minutes ago,'" said the president.

Dr. Provenzano proceeded to retell the story that Bob Scales had told him and Russell Randazza in the lobby of the Adolphus. The president and Kelly listened as two six-year-olds would when their grandfather first read them *Peter Rabbit.* The president had so many questions but didn't want to break the spell and held them for the end.

"You've developed and watched the Bell & Howell film already?"

"Tommy, we're NASA for Christ sake. Yeah, we've seen it. Clear as day and it's not Oswald pulling the trigger. It shows Oswald by the window a little after noon but he wasn't there when the shooting started."

"I'll be damned. He didn't shoot the president and he didn't shoot Tippit. What did he say in the hallway when questioned by reporters, 'I didn't shoot anyone. No sir.' Oswald was set up. He was maneuvered and manipulated but innocent."

"He might not have pulled the trigger, Tommy, but he was not innocent. There was a rifle in that bag he carried to work Friday morning; Scales swears to it. We lost all our body cams and GoPro's, but we still have the film and an eyewitness to history. If Oswald was innocent, he would not have been with Tippit and gone to the Texas Theatre looking for his contact. He was involved."

"Well, who was the shooter on the sixth floor?"

"We may be NASA but were not the FBI. Riley will have to do a facial recognition scan using a 1963 database. This guy was dark with a swarthy complexion. I would look at the Miami Cubans."

"Email me vid-cap of his face on my secure server and bring me a thumb drive of the film when you come back tomorrow."

"Tommy, there's one thing I left out of the story."

"What was that, TP?"

"Scales said they saw another spook talking to Charles Cabell. He never got his name but he seemed to know about them, where they came from, everything. He kept feeding information to Cabell and Cabell would then catch them in a lie. Finally, our guys had to come straight with them. They were not surprised or shocked that we came from the future the way you would expect."

"What did the other spook look like?" asked the president.

"Scales said his hair was short and combed forward. He had a very thin face, chalky complexion. His eyes were sunken and in shadow. He was tall and creepy. Sounds to me like Lurch from the *Addams Family*, and like someone we know."

CHAPTER 31

The Oval Office Washington, DC Wednesday Morning

Sitting in the Oval Office before the scheduled Situation Room meeting was to begin, President Burk, Riley, Kelly, CoS Nicholas and Dr. Provenzano prepared to watch the Bell & Howell film that Ron Todd took 53 years ago. Dr. Provenzano handed Kelly a thumb drive and she inserted it into the USB port on her laptop. While it was loading, the president said, "I can't believe we're going to see this. I have been waiting 53 years for the truth and now we're going to rewrite history."

"I've watched it several times on the way here aboard Air Force Two. It's short, sweet and nothing short of amazing," said Dr. Provenzano.

Everyone watched the 23-second film in complete silence. It was just three seconds less than Zapruder's but now just as important. They watched the silent film hearing only the mechanical clicking of the 8-mm film passing through the spindle during processing. They watched the motorcade turn onto Elm Street from Houston. They watched as Todd played the part of a tourist with a new fangled camera panning around and capture the TSBD and the sixth-floor window by accident. Then they saw the man in the window with a rifle. Todd panned back down to the motorcade but then pretended to quickly realize what he just saw and pan back up to the sixth-floor window. They watched as he jerked and quickly turned to his right towards the Dal-Tex building then just as fast back to the sixth-floor easternmost window. Now he zoomed in and watched the shooter, clear as day, take two more shots before disappearing. Todd then panned back down Elm to capture the end of the motorcade and recorded the final two shots from the Dal-Tex building and the picket fence. The film then abruptly sputtered and stopped.

"Jesus," said the president. "Kelly, can you take it back to the sixth-floor shooter?"

Kelly pressed the back button until she got to the window and the man's face. She went back and forth a bit to get the clearest frame.

"Captain, did you get a match on this guy?"

"Last night when I got the vidcap from you, we went to work identifying the shooter. Using ours and the CIA's archived 1960's photos and dossiers of Cuban dissidents in Miami, we found an exact facial recognition match: a Cuban hitman named Herminio Diaz Garcia, aka Angel. He's a real piece of work. Born in Cuba in 1923, he was a member of the Cuban Restaurant Workers Union and worked as a cashier at the Hotel Habana-Rivera. Later he became involved in illegal activities and eventually became a bodyguard for Santos Trafficante."

"Diaz Garcia killed Pipi Hernandez in 1948 at the Cuban Consulate in Mexico. In 1957, he was involved with an assassination attempt against President Jose Figures of Costa Rica."

"Diaz Garcia moved to the United States in July of 1963, After the JFK hit, he was involved in an unsuccessful attempt to assassinate Fidel Castro. He was also involved in providing weapons to anti-Castro groups, where he worked for Tony Varona. Varona worked closely with organized crime leaders such as Santo Trafficante and Johnny Roselli. Varona was also involved in several attempts to kill Fidel Castro," advised Riley.

"So, if the sixth-floor window shooter was Angel, what about his partner, the one he and Oswald were with when they went to see Sylvia Odio in Dallas on September 25, Eladio del Valle?" asked the president as he gave Riley a knowing look.

"We showed Scales some photos of Angel's known associates. Of the four people Scales saw behind the picket fence he could only positively identify two. One of the two shooters was Eladio del Valle, aka Leopold. This was the same Leopold that accompanied Angel and Oswald to see Sylvia Odio two months previous to the assassination. He felt he recognized Bernardo De Torres, aka Carlos, and came close to identifying the other two from the photos, but said his memory was a bit fuzzy after 53 years," informed Provenzano.

Director Riley held his breath, looked back at the president and hoped the doctor would let it drop. President Burk and Riley used an older Carlos, Leopold, and Angel just four years previous to clean up a mess for them. It was a bad time and seeing Angel's face again, admittedly younger, brought back unpleasant memories best left buried.

"We have to get down to the Situation Room so we'll watch the Todd film again when we get through. Let's keep this to ourselves for now. TP, did you return the original undeveloped film to the camera?" asked the president.

"Yes. The original film is back in the camera with only Todd's excuse me, Logan's fingerprints on it, the camera and the case. The camera is back in its case and it has been turned over to Director Riley."

"Captain, go ahead and plant the Bell & Howell where we decided and have your forensic team make it look like it's been there for 53 years. Build Logan's legend using Todd's fingerprints. Then, as events unfold our young unsuspecting accomplice will discovers the film and make it public and make himself famous at the same time."

"Whoa, Tommy, you chicken shit. That's your plan? Have some kid find the camera and film, have it developed and give it or leak it to the media, so the media does your dirty work? I can't believe you thought this all up by yourself," Kelly was looking directly at Riley then back to the president. "All so this creep Cabell and his CIA rogue unit won't kill you?" asked Kelly.

"And you," said the president grinning. "Actually, it was set up to have this old Bell & Howell camera and film be found 53 years later so it would be believable and accepted. What? Do you think it would be more convincing if we announce to the media and the world that Oswald was not the shooter because we sent our super-secret time travelers back to 1963 to film what really happened?" asked the president.

"Good point," admitted Kelly.

CHAPTER 32

The Oval Office & the Situation Room
Washington, DC
Wednesday Morning

Members of the president's inner circle were seated around the conference table. SecDef Stanton, AG Fare, FBI Director Riley, Secret Service Director Bounty, General Finn, CoS Nicholas, Press Secretary Sullivan, NSA Director Michaels, Deputy Secretary of Homeland Security Borras, plus two others.

Everyone stuck to small talk because most of those present knew DCI, Director Central Intelligence Bader was not part of the inner circle and some did not recognize the other individual, until President Burk said, "Ladies. Gentlemen. Thank you all for coming on such short notice. In addition to those present, we have many loyal members of the House and Senate, my Cabinet, and the military, but you are the inner circle. I've officially added two more members to our inner circle, DCI John Bader and from NASA, Director of Project Christopher, Dr. Tony Provenzano. I trust both of these men as much as anyone in this room and both have been read in and are up to speed. We have several situations which are above and beyond the normal workings of government. I believe these situations are interconnected, and this group needs to address and get in front of them."

"Project Christopher has had a successful jump back in time to 1963. Everything we could have possibly hoped for was achieved above and beyond our wildest expectations. With that said, we encountered an unexpected situation. Yesterday, late afternoon as we were preparing to jump the team back, the project was hijacked and compromised by one of our own. We now know who that individual is, and suspect why he crossed to the dark side."

Most around the table looked perplexed by the president's statement.

"Mr. President, this is very alarming. One of our own disrupted the jump? Is the team back?" asked SecDef Stanton.

"The team is not back, at least not as expected. Just as the team was about to be jumped back to the present they were arrested by the Dallas County Sheriff's Department. That could be explained by good police work, like observing and detaining suspicious persons at the scene of a presidential assassination. The jumpers, after all, had walkie-talkies and body cams in their possession and were certainly at the scene and juxtaposed with Oswald. To make a long story short, the jumpers were unexpectedly released, no charges were brought against them, and they were allowed to remain in the past, grow old and die. However, one jumper, Bob Scales, the youngest of the team, is still alive and managed to make contact with Dr. Provenzano yesterday and tell the story of what happened," the president revealed.

"Amazing," declared Stanton.

"It gets better," said President Burk. He nodded to Dr. Provenzano and said, "Doctor."

"Last night Bob Scales, now into his early eighties, told me a story about what happened that day in Dallas so many years ago, the actual true events surrounding the assassination of President John F Kennedy. Believe me when I say we now have proof that the Warren Commission not only got it wrong, they purposely misled the American people and flat out lied. Why the Warren Commission and the powers behind it lied is another story, but the most disturbing point is they seem to want to continue the lie. It was not the Dallas County Sheriff's Department that initiated the arrest but the CIA. Former DCI Charles Cabell, fired by Kennedy, instigated the arrest of our jumpers. How he knew about our jump team is where the dark side comes into play," related Dr. Provenzano as he turned towards DCI John Bader, "John."

"Last night President Burk called me with some disturbing news. He told me about the Dallas jump and the CIA's involvement in the arrest and interrogation of the team back in '63. He then told me about what he called the dark side. The DDCI, Deputy Director of the CIA in the early '60s was Charles Cabell, that is until he was fired by Kennedy for the Bay of Pigs fiasco. For the CIA and not the FBI to be involved in any domestic murder investigation of a United States President is highly irregular, to say the least. My suspicions peaked with the president's description of another agent present on the scene. After a simple schedule sign-in, sign-out check, I was able to confirm my suspicion. Hard as it was for me to believe that agent was one of mine, DDCI Prescott Cabell, the grandson of Charles Cabell, and he turned to the dark side and somehow hijacked Project Christopher," said Director Bader.

"Director Bader has assigned his Inspector General's investigative staff the task of identifying and conducting a high-profile investigation into Prescott Cabell and his entire internal operation. If Prescott Cabell somehow managed to travel back in time it means he compromised and infiltrated Project Christopher and that means he had to have help, inside help," said Riley, as he and everyone around the conference table turned and looked at Dr. Provenzano.

With all eyes on him and realizing the implication of Director Riley's accusation, Dr. Provenzano continued seemingly unfazed. "We have the future jump scheduled for this Monday, our time November 28, and returning November 29. This jump, as you all know, is to Cleveland and necessary because of the proposed nuclear attack on the United States slated for Christmas Day. The jump is to land in Clevland future time January 3, 2017. The purpose is to see if the attack took place and if so collect the details and information necessary to prevent it."

"So, if the team jumps to January 3, and finds that the attacks never occurred, we don't need to abduct Baghdadi. We could still go through with the abduction, but we don't have too, right?" asked Stanton.

"Right. But by not going after and abducting Baghdadi we circumvent Cabell's plans and whatever he has in store for us. Yes?" offered CoS Nicholas.

"Yes. But conversely, if the jump team finds the attack did occur and we find out all the who, where, when and how, we can place all our assets to prevent it. And we still may circumvent Cabell's plans," said Dr. Provenzano.

"Or we could just take Cabell out back now, shoot him and be done with it," said Riley.

"All good scenarios, but if we find out the attack did not occur we might still do two of the scenarios: take out Baghdadi and take out Cabell. And as Meatloaf said, 'Two out of three ain't bad,'" offered the president.

"What is Cabell up to? If we don't take him out now he may disrupt the future jump like he did the past jump," asserted SecDef Stanton.

"He's not going to bother the future jump. He can just sit back and wait to hear the results."

"This is all so confusing. Why is Cabell doing all this?" asked Kelly.

"Cabell wants to control the Baghdadi abduction and I believe his intent is to escalate the situation," replied General Finn.

"How?" asked Stanton.

"He intends to do what he originally proposed," remarked Finn.

"You mean sending in an MQ-1 Predator with two Smart Pyron bombs and blow Kim Jong–un and Baghdadi to Hell?"

"Possibly. He may also go through with the abduction and accidentally kill Kim Jung-un's double and leave America's fingerprints all over it," said Finn.

"Why?"

"So it becomes an international incident. The United States executive order 12333 prohibits the act of state sponsor killing of foreign officials and heads of state outside the boundaries of the United States. If we kill Kim and get caught we become a world pariah," Finn explained.

"But it's not Kim Jung-un; it's his double," said Kelly.

"North Korea, China, and Russias and most of the world's comeback will be: 'You didn't know it was his double. You thought you were assassinating the supreme leader not a double.' They will have us. The United Nations, the entire world will condemn us. No matter how it plays itself out, Bryan and Schuster will ask for your head, Mr. President and they will get it," lamented Finn.

"Okay," said the president, "We'll deal with Bryan and Schuster later. This is what we're going to do now regardless of what the jumpers find. The day before the weapons meeting on December 6, Director Bader will swoop in and take out Cabell and his entire team.

Then Stanton will have his Seal Team Six abduct Baghdadi and replace him with a double. Start working on that now, Ed. If Baghdadi has the 2.5 billion, which most likely will be in $10,000.00 denominations, and if it's real, send it back here and replace it with counterfeit bills. If it's funny money let our double pass it on to Kim Jong-un's double. Let the meeting go on as planned. We won't find out more about what Baghdadi wanted or how the weapons and the balance transfer will go down, but as soon as the real Kim Jun-un gets the funny money the jig will be up. When the real Kim finds out about the double cross I wouldn't want to be Iran. Make it look like Baghdadi pulled a fast one on Iran and I also wouldn't want to be ISIL."

"Why not take out Kim's double and replace him with another double?" asked Riley.

"So we can double cross the doubles. Right?" asked Stanton.

"No. We don't touch Kim's double. We might kick ourselves for not taking him, he knows Kim first hand and studied him. But no. Let him be. And Ed, if you can get a transmitter planted on Baghdadi's double we might get to hear a lot of double talk," said the president with wink and a smirk.

CHAPTER 33

Cleveland, Ohio

In the heart of Cleveland's Little Italy, two men, one of them very tall, sat at a quiet table in the back of a restaurant on Mayfield Road.

"It's been here 97 years, the food's good, and it's a bit gaudy, but occasionally you see a wise guy or two."

"I didn't know Cleveland had wise guys."

"Yeah well, they did and do."

After the small talk, the tall guy said, "Do they know it was me? Was I recognized?"

"You weren't recognized by the jumpers, but to say you stand out would be an understatement. The one that survived, Scales, must have seen you and was able to provide a description."

"I told Charles we should have terminated them; a few more wouldn't have mattered."

"Maybe they didn't pick up on what Scales said and won't put it together."

"Are you kidding me. Everything Scales told them will be gone over with a fine-tooth comb. If they haven't already linked it to me they soon will. It's too bad we dismantled our Dallas clone jump site because we could have gone back and taken care of him."

"My Dallas jump rooms in the Adolphus are still active. It's dormant, but I received orders to keep it online for another two months."

"Why? Do they intend to go back again?"

"Your guess is as good as mine. I was told the request came from the top and to keep all three rooms ready. Do you want to take another jump? I might be able to squeeze you in, but we dismantled the retrieval portals so it's a one-way only trip."

"Thank you, but one jump was enough for me. Let's keep that open and stay in touch."

The Cleveland jump site, which will propel the team to January 3, 2017, that Dr. Provenzano and Russell Randazza established, was nothing like what they had to do for Dallas. This was mainly because they were going forward in time rather than back, and they were only jumping a little over a month into the future to see if the Christmas attack occurred or not. The three-person team consisted of investigative reporter Tom Sweeney of the *Hedghampton Press*, A/V Tech, Kathleen Felton, and on loan from the FBI as security, Rob Ceretti. The three have been in Cleveland for several days making contacts and getting the feel of the 'Land of Cleve'.

Tom Sweeney grew up in Hedgehampton, an incorporated village in the town of Southampton, New York. He was a real hometown boy. Tom was just over six feet tall, with dusty blond hair. He just turned twenty-seven and has been with *The Hedgehampton Press* for five years and became a star reporter after breaking a major terrorist attack in Hedgehampton against a local author less than two years previous. Sweeney had since had many offers to leave for the bright city lights but decided Hedgehampton was where he belonged. He was good looking, hardworking and proving to be a good, aggressive reporter.

A/V Tech, Kathleen Felton grew up in South Philadelphia and studied engineering at the University of Pennsylvania. In her late twenties, she's very tech savvy, feisty and a gorgeous redhead. To make this jump she put her engagement on hold. If she makes it back they intend to get married regardless of what they find.

Rob Ceretti is the SAC Special Agent in Charge of the Bangor, Maine field office. At 62, he is 6' tall, 180 pounds, with black hair and a chiseled face, right out of Hollywood central casting. He's bright, in great shape and well-liked by FBI Director Riley, having helped him out of a bad spot not long ago in Moscow, Maine.

The jump site was a very private house on five acres off Lakeshore Drive in Cleveland. The nondescript, one level four-bedroom house had plenty of room for the jump and support team to complete its mission of jumping into the future to witness first hand whether the nuclear attack on the United States took place or not.

Press Secretary Kelly Sullivan placed personal calls to the owners of all the major news media outlets such as *CBS, NBC, ABC, FOX*, and *CNN*, and radio station to alert their Cleveland affiliates that Tom Sweeney represented President Burk on an important fact-finding mission, and to offer him every professional courtesy and access. Tom's boss, the editor of *The Hedgehampton Press* was a personal friend of the editor of *The Plain Dealer*, aka the *Cleveland Plain Dealer*, and that guaranteed Tom all professional courtesies.

FBI Director Riley made personal contact with SAC Taylor Ross. Special Agent in Charge Ross was recently promoted from the Bangor, Maine field office to Cleveland and previously worked for Rob Ceretti. In fact, it was Ceretti who recommended Ross for promotion so professional courtesies and full access was pretty much a given. SAC Ross would also open communications with Ceretti to the local offices of Homeland, CIA, the State Police and the Cleveland PD.

A/V Tech, Kathleen Felton had letters of introduction from the Secretary of Education and the Director of National Intelligence to be used to gain access to places of higher education and priority access to any and all international civilian and military communication outlets, offices and bases. But Kathleen's top priority would be connecting with all the many shortwave and ham radio enthusiasts in the Cleveland area and setting up the jump house emergency generator and communication system including her own high-tech cell tower and low tech UHF roof antenna.

When the team lands on January 3, they will either have nothing to do but sightsee for the day or have 15 hours of sheer pressure to find out the what, where, when, how and who. They will check and verify their information with all available sources including international social and mainstream media outlets.

It was Sunday morning November 27, the day before the future jump. From the command room in the jump house, Roberta Tonk, one of Randazza's assistants announced, "I have the president."

The three jumpers, Dr. Provenzano, Russell Randazza and Ms.Tonk all looked across the conference table at the wall mounted monitor as the image of the president appeared. "Ladies and gentlemen. I thank you for your service, and for those of you who are about to travel into the future, I salute you. I and the American people are depending on you to find out if we have been attacked, by whom, where, when, how and the damages we incurred. If we are so lucky to dodge the bullet this time, then consider it as a test jump for something else in a few months. You'll get first dibs. Good luck and God speed." The screen went black.

"Well, that was your confirmation. You jump tomorrow morning. You leave here tomorrow, Monday, November 28, 2016 at 6 a.m. and arrive there in the future on January 3, 2017 at 6:01 a.m. If all goes well, you will leave that night at 9 p.m., and return back here at 9:01 p.m. That gives you an entire day to sightsee or work your asses off to find out what happened," instructed Dr. Provenzano.

"Okay, here's how it will go down. You will spend the rest of the day confirming in person your appointments for the 3rd. If the attack did occur, everyone everywhere will be in different emotional states: disbelief, denial, fear, confusion, and possible loss of loved ones. So everyone you speak with today may be in a different state on the 3rd. Tonight after dinner, you will leave this training area at 9 p.m. You will say goodnight to your teammates, go into your bedrooms, read, watch TV, email or call mom. Your one and only focus is obtaining total submersion into Cleveland on January 3, 2017: your total emersion into the future.

Before you retire you will take your Avinal. You will receive a wake-up call at exactly 5:30 a.m., thirty minutes before your 6 a.m. jump time. During those thirty minutes, you will shower, dress in business attire, get back into bed, and prepare for you OBE. Lie on your back with your pillow behind your neck so your neck is concave and your head is slightly back. Concentrate only on leaving today and going to tomorrow. Close your eyes and focus up and back into your brain. Submit to your inner vibration and ringing. You do that and we'll do the rest.

Your Recon Instrument Jet V Smart Eyewear is on your nightstand. We've added extended battery life to 13 hours. Your Recon Instrument glasses will have a constant live feed, two-way a/v, mic and cam display, text, call notifications, maps, and GPS. Everything you see and hear, we will see and hear and record. You have an open mic so everything you say will be picked up by your team members and us. Everything else you'll need is in your individual or team locker. One last thing. What's the first thing you do when you get there at 6:01 a.m.?" quizzed Randazza, looking first at Sweeney.

Having a bit of fun with Randazza, Sweeney said, "Turn on *CNN*."

"Turn on *BBC*," added Felton.

"Turn on *Al Jazeera*," uttered Ceretti.

"No! No! The first thing you do is put on your Recon smart glasses, then you turn on the TV. We here in the command center and the president in the Situation Room want to see and hear everything you see and hear, exactly when you see and hear it. Got it?"

Seeing the smiles from the team, Randazza knew he had been had. "Funny. Now go confirm your contacts and don't get in trouble and stay in constant contact with me and your teammates. See you all back here tonight for dinner in the dining room at 7:30 p.m.," said Randazza.

CHAPTER 34

The White House Washington, DC

The president, Kelly and Nicholas came back into Oval Office from the Cabinet Room, after placing the video call to the Cleveland jumpers. Riley came in and all three sat on the couches. The president sat in one of the chairs.

"Captain, I just got off the phone with the jump team. They're all set for tomorrow. Bill, I want you to have our inner circle in the Situation Room tomorrow morning by 5:30 a.m. Somewhere just after 6:00 a.m. tomorrow morning, November 28, we'll have three live feeds from the Jan 3, 2017 Cleveland jump house, and we'll know whether to shit or get off the pot," pronounced President Burk.

"Nicely put, Sarge," said Riley.

"Okay. That's tomorrow and now for today. Don't get upset but I asked the vice president to join us. I know everything points to her joining a coup against us but she came to see me earlier and convinced me otherwise. I think it's important you hear her side directly. She is outside," mentioned the president. The president pressed the buzzer and Noreen opened the door and the vice president walked in.

Chelsey Hilton, at 37, is bright, self-assured, determined, attractive and Vice President of the United States. She's all those things and more, but is she loyal? She walked into the Oval Office like she owned it. In a way she did. Her mother was president for 8 years. Now with 4 more under her belt as vice president and beginning another 4 she will have 16 years in the White House.

The president alone stood and offered the vice president a seat on the couch next to Riley and across from Nicholas and Kelly. "Go ahead, Chelsey, tell them what you told me," said President Burk.

"I was not entirely truthful with the president when he confronted me in the hallway. He asked me if I thought everything seemed to be going to Hell since our reelection and if I felt the House and Senate were teaming up against him. I told him everything was fine but that I would speak with Schuster if he spoke to Bryan. The truth is the president's suspicions were correct and I was holding back."

"Why?" asked Kelly. It was a question accompanied by an expression of suspicion and disdain.

"I was seduced by Schuster into a private meeting at his suite at the Willard. I was ambushed when Bryan and Cabell appeared. I pretended to go along but was soon drawn in by their hubris and logic. Cabell was pretty persuasive and graphic regarding his description of your treatment of my mother…"

"Treatment of you mother?" interrupted Kelly, "Chelsey, I was there. I was on your mother's … President Hilton's side until I saw what she was doing to Tommy and the country. When Tommy became president he could have had you mother thrown in jail for treason, but instead, he put her in charge of the Hilton Commission investigation herself. For God's sake, Chelsey, he brought you in as his vice president and you were enamored by their hubris? What they're proposing is a move of almost unimaginable boldness foolhardiness and treason. You want to be part of that?"

"No. I do not. That is why I'm here. I know the truth about my mother and her presidency. I love her but can see what power does to someone. 'Power corrupts. Absolute power corrupts absolutely,'" said the vice president.

"Yes. Well, we'll see about that," hissed the president, casting a knowing glance towards Riley.

"Schuster, Bryan, and Cabell have that lust for power and I want no part of it and I intend to tell them so," declared the vice president.

"No. You're in; stay in. You be our eyes and ears on what they are up to and when they intend to move. That's critical, Chelsey. I have to know when," insisted the president.

The vice president agreed to continue meeting with the conspirators and continue a very dangerous deception. After she left the Oval Office the four were left to decide whether to believe her story and accept her loyalty or not.

"Bill?" asked the president.

"I believe her. I think she was taken in but has since seen the light. She knows what side her bread is buttered," speculated Nicholas.

"What does that mean?" asked the president.

"It means I trust her," replied Nicholas.

"No, I mean, 'know what side of your bread is buttered?' I never could understand that." confided the president.

"I think it means you know who to be nice to and what to do to get an advantage for yourself," explained Nicholas.

"Yeah. That's Chelsey, alright," agreed Riley. "She knows how to butter you up, Sarge."

"So, I take it you're not a believer in redemption? You don't trust her, Captain?" asked the president.

"I do believe in redemption, and I do trust her, but as President Reagan said, 'Trust and verify.'"

"Let's give her a chance and see how she does, but let's not bring her into the inner circle just yet. Let her be our double agent and see how it goes," proposed Riley.

"We certainly seem to have a lot of doubles lately," Nicholas pointed out.

Ignoring Nicholas' bait, the president said, "I agree with the Captain. That's three votes for Vice President Hilton. That leaves you, Kelly."

"Call it a woman's intuition but I don't believe her. I will never believe her and as far as trust is concerned, I don't trust her, and listening to you three Neanderthals just verified it," sniffed Kelly.

CHAPTER 35

CLEVELAND, OHIO JUMP DAY

Sweeney, like his teammates Felton and Ceretti, was very close to achieving his OBE. The ringing in his ears had started and now the vibration. The orgasm of leaving his body was occurring.

In the adjoining control room, Dr. Provenzano and Russell Randazza and their NASA technicians and engineers watched the wall mounted a/v monitors in each room and via Bluetooth monitored each jumpers vital signs.

"Are all three showing signs of vibration and ringing?"

"Check."

"Have all three achieved OBE?"

"Check."

"Open the vortex on my count."

"Check."

"On 5-4-3-2-..."

Just like the hotel rooms a week earlier, the house started to shake, rattle and roll, but as quickly as it begun it subsided. Then there was complete silence.

The rooms visible on the monitors showed three empty beds. "They're gone," said Randazza. Randazza repeated his farewell. "Have a good trip guys, I wish I could be there with you."

Sweeney felt himself being pulled back into his body. *Wow, this feels so cool-so real*, he thought. Before he knew it he was awake and sitting up in the bed. It was 6:01 a.m. He lunged up and forward hoping the jump succeeded, a leap of faith to be sure, and reached for his Recon glasses on the nightstand and put them on. The glasses, set to motion activate, gave Cleveland Command and President Burk's Situation Room an immediate live feed on their wall mounted monitor. He reached for the remote and swung himself to the end of the bed and pushed the TV's on button. The TV came to life. It was January 3, and *CNN's* Chris Cuomo's face along with a banner stating "BREAKING NEWS" filled the screen.

Almost simultaneously, Felton's *BBC* and Ceretti's *Al Jazeera English* live feeds came up on the Cleveland and Washington monitors.

Cleveland and Washington all breathlessly watched all three monitors but focused on *CNN* because it came up first. That was until they realized Cuomo's face was replaced by a man hugging a pillow. *CNN* had gone to a commercial, and the entire inner circle was now watching a 'My Pillow' commercial. President Burk yelled, "Bring up *Al Jazeera* on the main monitor and mute the others. Goddamn fucking pillow commercial. I would like to come up behind that guy and smoother him with his own fucking pillow." Cleveland Command followed suit.

Al Jazeera London is a 24-hour no-nonsense news station with a distinct bias, and just as it came up on the big monitor, a similar BREAKING NEWS banner appeared and the face of an unknown anchor saying, "...and we have two live reports from New York. First, from Tracy Borman live in downtown Manhattan. The shot switched to Tracy. She was dressed from head to toe in a yellow Haz-Mat complete body suit with a respirator. Smoke could be seen rising from behind and above the many buildings with a slightly skewed Freedom Tower in the background. The sound quality was bad inasmuch as her microphone was competing with her respirator, sirens and the sound of a generator.

"Right. Tracy Borman here, *Al Jazeera London* live in New York City, somewhere north of Houston Street looking south. The horror story is here in downtown Manhattan and under the Hudson River. The nuclear attack during rush hour on Black Friday, December 23, has now been officially reclassified from a rescue mission to a recovery mission. A tactical nuclear bomb was hidden in a suitcase and brought aboard a PATH train heading from Newark, New Jersy to the World Trade Center Station. It was detonated just short of the World Trade Center Station imploding the Hudson River, destroying the station, flooding most of lower Manhattan and precariously underpinning the Freedom Tower. Over 5,000 are feared dead and with the nuclear fallout that may increase dramatically. This is a horrific disaster of epic proportions. There are thousands of commuters trapped and now presumed drowned in trains and cars under the Hudson River. Many more thousands are trapped and now presumed dead under the collapsed World Trade PATH Station and thousands more drowned in Lower Manhattan. My live film time allowed here is monitored, limited and controlled and I am now being told to shut it down and move further north. I will sign off now come back as soon as they give me the okay. Tracy Boman, *Al Jazeera,* in Lower Manhattan or as close to it as I can get."

Tracy's mic was still hot when Cleveland and Washington heard what sounded like a police officer or official attempting to confiscate Tracy's generator. Then the mic went cold.

"Oh, shit." "Son-of-a-bitch" and "Jesus Christ" were some of the expletives heard from both Cleveland Command and the Situation Room.

Looking at the president SecDef Stanton said, "Thank God we can stop this. Right?"

"They moved the attack to Black Friday to increase casualties. Son-of-a-bitch. And why are they trying to take her generator?" asked Nicholas.

Before anyone could answer, the *Al Jazeera* anchor in London said, "Now to Rupert Stone in front of the Trump Tower on Fifth Avenue."

The screen flashed to Rupert standing in front of dark Trump Tower on Fifth Avenue. He was wearing a blue North Face jacket; no Haz-Mat suit for Rupert. Even though it was early it was dark and eerie. You could hear a generator in the background and then floodlights lit up the tower and Rupert. There were police sirens in the background but no traffic on the avenue, vehicular or pedestrian.

"The second shoe is about to fall," said the president.

"Good Morning, Rupert Stone *Al Jazeera London* live in New York City in front of a deserted Trump Tower. In fact, I am standing in an almost deserted part of Manhattan. The lights went out in the Big Apple midnight New Year's Eve and most of the east coast from Boston to Washington, from Cape Cod west to what I'm told are the Appalachian Mountains range running north from West Virginia through to Pensylvania. Millions of people are without power, transportation, and cell phones. There are only a few TV news crews out broadcasting because they, like us, were been able to ship in uncontaminated generators. Even as we broadcast no one on the east coast is watching; all the TV's are fried. We're lucky to still have some broadcast satellites online. Hopefully, someone somewhere is watching this report. There are no radios because all the transistors, circuits and antennas have been taken out. As food and water begin to run out people are now beginning to run out. Out of the city that is. But to where? There is nowhere to run, nowhere to hide."

"Homeland Security is telling us that a missile was launched off the south coast of Long Island just before midnight New Years Eve and exploded miles above Manhattan in what they called a Pulse Bomb. They suspect a Nuclear Electromagnetic Pulse Bomb or NEMP. It is a lethal, and a highly destructive weapon that explodes high up in the atmosphere and emits an electromagnetic pulse that disables all electrical circuitry within a certain radius. After an EMP is detonated, all objects with electrical components within the radius are rendered inoperative. These objects include, but are not limited to: phone lines, power lines, computers, cars, radar and electronic warfare equipment, electronic flight controls, television/radio equipment, and most satellites. Basic systems working with batteries, such as torches, are not affected; but devices connected to main power, such as lighting systems, are. Homeland is describing it as a high-altitude explosion. I have personally seen the results of several commercial passenger jets that crashed when they lost power just after midnight. Now the radioactive fallout will begin, and your guess is as good as mine what will happen. So far, no radiation has registered on our Radex RD1212, but we have our Haz-Mat suits ready."

Rupert continued. "People are beginning to loot food stores but are passing up Best Buy and the like because nothing from those types of stores work. From what I can see in traveling here to Manhattan: hardware stores, convenient stores, gun stores, Home Depot and liquor stores are the most targeted. Bank ATM's aren't working so people are just stealing the entire machines right out of the bank and onto the back of their pre-1975 pickups. Most vehicles after '75 with electronic ignition or electronic injection will have been fried."

"And people are dying. The first wave came from within the hospitals. Doctors, nurses, and attendants all seem to have left Manhattan leaving the patients to fend for themselves, although I have seen some doctors and other medical personnel attending to injured out in the street. Next to die will be the very old then the very young."

"The Sunni militant terrorist organization known as ISIL the Islamic State of Iraq and the Syria has claimed responsibility for the attacks and have posted videos of the missile launch and the tunnel explosion on their ISIL website just hours ago. A spokesman for ISIL posted a personal message: 'The final Crusade has begun. We have joined together and now we have brought the battle to your land. We have come to destroy Satan in Hell.'"

"Back to you Sandy. Rupert Stone, *Al Jazeera* live in New York City."

"I'm gonna kill that bag of shit mother fucker, Baghdadi. You would think what Colburn did to him and his family would have taught him a lesson and kept him in line," blurted Director Riley.

"Yeah, well I guess he heard that Colburn is no longer a threat, but we still have Baghdadis family, minus his father, incarcerated at Hanger 22 in Bagram," said NSA Director Roger Michaels.

"Yeah, and with Icy out cold, so to speak, Baghdadi thinks he can resume his old habits without interference by our Luca Brasi," added Riley.

Director Michaels shook his head, puzzled by Riley's last comment.

Al Jazeera's London broadcast studio came back on the screen and the anchor, Sandy someone, took up where the reporter left off. "The United States is appealing for international assistance in the form of cars, trucks, and electrical equipment, especially cell phones, TV's and radios that have not been exposed to the effects of EMP. We're told so far, assistance has been dribbling in from Israel, Britain, France, Canada, and Mexico. The only saving grace for the United States so far is that two-thirds of the country has been spared."

The president and the inner circle continued to watch until the president had enough, got up, and nodded for Stanton, Kelly, and Riley to follow him out. He turned to the remaining who were seated and said, "I have what I need for the moment. Direct Cleveland Command to have the jump team get out into the field and get details. We'll be back shortly and I will want a full update."

Back upstairs in the Oval Office, the three flopped into the two couches, the president in his chair. Noreen had coffee and Diet Coke brought in, and Max, the presidents German Shepherd saw an opportunity and snuck through the open door. Noreen came in after him, but the president waved her away and said, "I think I need Max with me now. Thank you, Noreen."

"Yes, Ed, we can stop it and will," said the president as Max came over and sat next to him and was rewarded with a scratch on the back of his neck.

"Tommy, I'm sorry for ever doubting your time travel idea and everything I said or joked with you about time travel. What we just witnessed, only because of your vision and persistence, can now be prevented," apologized Kelly.

CHAPTER 36

Cleveland, Ohio - Washington, DC

The jump team, communicating through their microphones, placed tripod mounted transmitting cameras in front of each TV, grabbed their equipment and exited the house.

"Wow. This seems so weird. We're here in 2017, the house is here, and our equipment and cars are here, but Razz and the control room guys aren't. Why is that?" asked Ceretti.

"Remember what Randazza told us? The house, cars, and equipment were here yesterday, today and will be here tomorrow. We took the trip and the guys didn't," said Sweeney.

"Yeah, well, the guys were here yesterday and today, too, but they're not here tomorrow. I just don't get it," said a confused Ceretti.

"Why don't we let Flash Gordon and Buck Rogers figure that out while we get on with what we're here to do," coaxed Felton.

"Why? I mean, why bother now? We know what happened. We know the where, when, how and who," said Ceretti.

"We'll continue the mission because 'the devil is in the details,'" remarked Sweeney.

"Right, Tom. But Robs correct. They really don't need us now; I mean live jumpers. They can send bots, or drones to do what we're doing," protested Felton.

"You know they're listening to us, don't you," informed Sweeney.

"Yes, but they could send a bot here with a GoPro and place it in front of the TV and it would send back to them what's happening in the future. Heck, they could have a new TV channel called Future TV. You could just sit in the comfort of your home and time travel through your own Future TV station," said Felton.

"You could watch future wars or a tsunami envelope Florida," added Ceretti.

"You two are hilarious. Can we please get on with it?" begged Sweeney.

"This is Randazza in Cleveland Command Control. Knock it off and get to work."

Later, back in the Situation Room, President Burk, Stanton, Kelly, and Riley rejoined AG Fare, Secret Service Director Bounty, General Finn, CoS Nicholas, NSA's Michaels, Homeland's Borras and DCI Bader.

"What did we miss?" asked President Burk.

"Plenty. Some good news and some bad. Our jumpers are out in the field meeting with all their contacts and their live reports are streaming back. We have also been closely monitoring the three news stations still streaming live. The good news is they now determined that neither bomb, the Holland Tunnel or the EMP was nuclear. The tunnel bomb was dirty, but small and contained. They have surveillance camera film of the suspected terrorist driving into Newark, parking and wheeling a large suitcase into the PATH terminal…"

"What does he look like?" asked Riley.

"She look like," corrected Finn. She looks like a California co-ed; blond and tan." General Finn continued. "They also located a 90-foot commercial fishing boat that carried and fired the EMP off Long Island. It's registered out of Newfoundland and was reported hijacked on December 26, and not reported missing till the 30th. The original seven-man crew were all found dead in the food locker. The East Coast is still facing high casualties but it could have been much worst if the bombs had been nuclear…"

"General Finn, I don't mean to interrupt, but you said that was the good news. What's the bad?"

"The bombs were not nuclear..."

Interrupting General Finn again, the president asked, "Wait, I thought that was good the bombs were not nuclear?"

"Yes, that's good, but because the bombs were not nuclear could be bad because they may not have gotten them from North Korea. The spokesman for ISIL said they were joining together and took credit for the attack but Baghdadi is conspicuously absent, obviously, because we will have taken him out on December 7. We're not all in agreement here, but my gut tells me that even if we take Baghdadi out on December 7, we'll need to send the jump team back."

"Why?"

"To make sure we have not been led down the garden path. I think ISIL may have gotten the bombs, despite losing Baghdadi, from someone other than the North Koreans. We also just monitored a conversation between one of the jumpers. Kathleen Felton, talking with a ham radio operator in South Korea, heard that a North Korean defector, Thae Young Ho, was poisoned in Ghezel Hesar prison. He defected from the North Korean embassy in London and is likely the highest-ranking North Korean official to ever defect."

"Where is Ghezel Hesar prison?" asked the president.

"Iran. And apparently, the Ayatollah is going ape-shit for losing him. The Iranian's wanted to keep him alive as a bargaining chip for the North Korean nuclear bombs, but Kim Jung-un wanted him dead. Looks like one supreme leader double-crossed another supreme leader. I think this whole thing is a set up like the Bay of Pigs to draw us in, and I think we know the sick son-of-a-bitch who set it up."

"I think your gut is right, Mickey. This is getting out of control. Ed, we need to bring in the Marines. See if you can get the Chairman of the Joint Chief of Staff, General Ely Parker to my office for lunch and tell Dr. Provenzano to bring those jumpers back in," ordered the president.

The president, SecDef Stanton, DCI Bader and FBI Director Riley met with the Chairman of the Joint Chief of Staff, General Ely Parker in the Oval Office for lunch.

The five were sitting around the coffee table having just finished a light lunch. During lunch, Stanton filled General Parker in on the two looming situations: the possible coup d'etat being led by Speaker Bryan, Senator Schuster and DDCI Cabell, and the possible terrorist attacks on New York City and the East Coast. SecDef Stanton purposely, at the president's direction, omitted the time travel piece and attributed sorting out both to good human intelligence (HUMINT) by the CIA and FBI. The general remained silent during the entire read in and now everyone waited to hear his thoughts.

"President Burk, gentlemen, I have heard a lot of sea stories in my time but this takes the cake. If it wasn't coming from men I respect and trust implicitly I think I would show myself the hatch. But I've always prided myself on knowing what was going on in my Marine Corps, I now make it my business to know what's going on in my Army, Navy, Air Force and National Guard as well. I run a tight ship and have a great crew. They are loyal and will follow me to Hell and back as long as I'm out in front. I'll lead and they'll follow, but I have to tell you my BS needle is off the charts on this one," stressed General Parker.

General Parker was not being disrespectful; it's just the way Marines communicated with other Marines and three of the five men in the room were Marines or former Marines. The Joint Chiefs and their Chairman report directly to SecDef Stanton but President Burk answered, "General, everything the SecDef told you is true and accurate. I will add that we used some future technology, above and beyond what is currently known to exist, to assist our human and current electronic and cyber assets in acquiring information and details of the looming terrorist attacks planned for this upcoming holiday season. What happens in the next few weeks will determine the fate of our country and therefore the world. It's going to get a bit rough around here and I need to know if I can depend on you, the Joint Chiefs, and the military to help put the coup down, stand by your president and your oath to the Constitution, help us destroy ISIL and prevent the attacks."

"Sir, under my purview, I have Marine Corps Intelligence, Army Intelligence, Navy Intelligence, and Air Force Intelligence. We have not been idle. Yes, you can count on us and to put it in more current terms, we in the military 'know what side of our bread is buttered.'"

The president laughed and said, "Kudos to you and your intel community, general, and if I may put it in more familiar terms, outfuckingstanding and welcome aboard!" President Burk put his arms out as if to draw everyone in and said, "Now here's what we're going to do."

CHAPTER 37

THE WILLARD HOTEL WASHINGTON, DC

For the second time in two weeks, four of the most important and powerful people in the America met in a private room at the Willard Hotel on Pennsylvania Avenue. Senate Minority Leader Chuck Schuster, House Speaker Paul Bryan, DDCI Prescott Cabell, and Vice President Chelsey Hilton.

"We have the mainstream media, print, and broadcast including radio behind us. They will set the tone and agenda for the smaller news organizations who will parrot it. Social media is with us. Together they will sway the proletariat towards our way of thinking. We have a majority of both Houses, numerous think tanks, super-PAC's and lobbyists behind us. We have activists from both the left and right, and we have Soros and the Koch brothers. We have all the organization and support we need to bring President Burk down," assured Senator Schuster.

"Most everyone I speak with in the House, everyone at the club, and on the cocktail circuit, feels the same as I do. A public opinion poll released by Quinnipiac University on Wednesday reported decreasing levels of approval for President Burk in his attempt to save, fix and improve the Affordable Health Care Act, and his continued insistence that outside entities had no influence in his reelection," said Speaker Bryan.

"How can you say that, Paul? The American people reelected President Burk and his agenda, not the Russians or Chinese. The Russians? Really? Paul, you're living in an echo chamber. You need to get out of Washington and get real," suggested Vice President Hilton.

"Whose side are you on, Chelsey? The people reelected Burk? What do they know? They only know what we tell them and sell them. They think their vote counts but we count the votes. They only know what they hear on TV and read in the papers and that my friend comes from us," boasted Bryan.

"I'm on your side, Paul, but if everything is so bad, why is the stock market so good? American worker's 401k's are out the roof," said Hilton.

"Irrational Exuberance". The stock market is driven by headlines and we make the headlines. We can leak this or that and send the market into a nose dive. But that's all window dressing. What we now need is a reason to impeach Burk." Turning towards Cabell, Schuster continued, "Prescott, are you going to deliver us that reason?"

"In less than a week you will have your reason," promised Cabell.

"So what is this situation your planning that will give us the reason, the one that will compromise Burks ability and duty to preserve and protect?" asked Schuster.

In his soft measured cadence, Cabell said, "We have discovered that a secret nuclear weapons meeting is to occur December 7, in Sofia, Bulgaria between North Korea's Kim Jong-un and the ISIL leader al-Baghdadi. The actualization is for ISIL to attack the United States over the holidays. President Burk signed a COO Covert Operation Order that allows my assets to prevent the meeting and hence the sale," said Cabell.

"And how exactly are you going to do that, and more importantly, how exactly does Burk's administration preventing a nuclear attack against the United States give us the capital to impeach him?" asked Schuster.

"I don't think you need to know the how, plausible disability aside. What you do need to know is that I will not be allowed, or should I say my assets will not be supported in their efforts to execute our mission order and the situation will escalate beyond the president's ability and duty to preserve, protect and defend the Constitution of the United States," said Cabell.

"What can we do on our end with our assets to help you?"

"To help me? Nothing. Your OSINT-Open Source Intelligence information is your concern," advised Cabell.

"Does this operation have a code name? Doesn't the CIA assign a secret name for what you do?" asked Bryan.

"We like to refer to ourselves as the Company and the operational code name is 'Emiliano.'"

"That's a strange code name for what you're doing in Bulgaria. Spanish isn't it?"

"Mexican actually," said Cabell.

"Intentional misdirection?" said Bryan with a knowing smirk.

"If you were a student of history you might know Emiliano's last name, and understand the significance," added Cabell.

"Please indulge us."

"Zapata," answered Cabell.

As Bryan and Schuster pondered Cabell's riddle, the vice president asked, "I want to know the "how" Director Cabell, and why you and your rogue agents are doing this? I mean, what's in it for you? You're the number two man in the Company. You want the number one slot is that it?"

"No. That's not it. What I and many of my, as you call them, rogue agents believe, is that we are losing the war on terror. We believe Burk has sold us, our civilization, our way of life, our democracy, and our children to Islam. He is an appeaser. He has opened our borders to Islam and they are coming to destroy us. Islam is the fastest-growing major religion in the world with over 1.7 billion followers. Islamic extremism is any form of Islam that opposes democracy, the rule of law, individual liberty and mutual respect and tolerance of different faiths and beliefs. This Jihad, this holy war is enflamed by the Qurans explicit demand for the Muslim faith and the rule of Islamic law to be spread unceasingly across the world. There are many of us in the Company who see this as a weakness by our president, a cancer within our government that needs to be eliminated," Cabell seethed.

"Director Cabell, that's a lofty endeavor but do the ends justify the means? And by the way, Burk hasn't opened the borders to anyone, all they have to do is come through the front gate. What are your ulterior motives?" asked Hilton.

"There are none," replied Cabell.

"Really Director Cabell? I am a student of history and I'm aware of Emiliano Zapata. I also know about Operation Zapata, your grandfather's brainchild to invade Cuba. Operation Zapata aka the Bay of Pigs Invasion, your grandfather's failed military invasion of Cuba by the CIA-sponsored and trained paramilitary group Brigade 2506 in 1961. The brigade, launched from Guatemala and Nicaragua, intended to overthrow Castro's communist government but were defeated within three days. They were doomed to fail weren't they Director Cabell? Your grandfather, Charles Cabell, Dulles, Bissell, Harvey, Helms, Phillips, Angleton, Hunt, and the rest of them, the Joint Chiefs and even some of Kennedy's own staff wanted and expected Kennedy to send in the Marines, finish the job and win one for the Gipper. But he didn't, and that's what ultimately cost him his life. Is that what's this is about, carrying on CIA vendettas and wars, cold or holy? Operation Zapata failed when President Kennedy didn't take the bait. But it was supposed to fail wasn't it, so Kennedy would commit American troops. You're banking that Burk is no Kennedy, and that he will go all the way when Operation Emiliano escalates?" quizzed Hilton.

"You have it all figured out don't you Madam Vice President," intoned Cabell.

"Not all of it. I'm guessing that by preventing the nuclear weapons sale you're going to accidentally kill North Koreas Kim Jong-un."

"Why are you so concerned about the how Madam Vice President?" asked Cabell.

"I think that's a fair question, Chelsey," Schuster chimed in.

"Because when the smoke clears I'm the one holding the bag," said Hilton.

"None of us wants an operation like that. Do we? The Bay of Pigs was a real FUBAR, Fucked Up Beyond Any Recognition," implied Bryan.

"We don't have FUBAR's, Mr. Speaker. We have blowback. And I don't expect any unexpected negative consequences, at least not for us," assured Cabell.

"Regardless of what you call it, if it goes south, I own it!" blurted Vice President Hilton.

"Well, in that case, Madam Vice President, lead, follow or get out of the way," rasped Cabell.

CHAPTER 38

The Oval Office Washington, DC

The usual suspects, Kelly, Riley, and Nicholas joined President Burk on the two couches.

"Senator McCain said it just this past week; he called Kim Jong-un "the crazy, fat kid that's running North Korea." McCain said Rahn Paul is working with Vladimir Putin and that Putin is a greater threat than ISIL. Rahn Paul says McCain is unhinged. Putin says McCain is an old fart. McCain says Putin is a thug and a murderer. What the fuck is going on?" asked Nicholas.

"You need to get out there, Tommy. It's a circus and you're beginning to look like the ringmaster," interjected Kelly.

"I'll tell you what's going on. It's not a circus. It's nothing but a side show and they're a bunch of clowns. The Hawks are looking for a new enemy. With Islamic terrorism on the downswing, at least here in the US, the military industrial complex, and their proxies are looking for a new dance partner. They'll throw out threats and bullshit and see what sticks. The mainstream media then picks it up and feeds it to the public until it becomes accepted as the truth. Russia, North Korea, Niger and most of Africa all look promising," said President Burk.

"Then why did you bring the Joint Chiefs Chairman Parker into our inner circle? How can you trust him?" asked Kelly.

"Because I do trust him. The big chief and his little chiefs don't want war. They've been through too many wars as it is. It's the young bucks we must worry about: the majors, colonels and one stars. You know how greed was good for Wall Street? Well, war is good for Promotion Street. At least it's a good political tool to get everyone's mind off important things like: jobs, infrastructure, health care, global warming, education and the debt, especially the debt," said the president.

"Is that your euphemism for the Chairman and the Joint Chiefs? The big chief and the little chiefs?" asked Kelly.

"You don't know about Chief Parker?" asked Nicholas.

"I know he's the top Marine general and Chairman of the Joint Chiefs. But I have a feeling you're going to enlighten me," said Kelly.

"His great-grandfather was Ely S. Parker. Among other things, Ely was General Grant's adjutant during the Civil War and was with Grant at Appomattox to accept Lee's surrender," divulged Nicholas.

"Aren't you a fountain," said Kelly.

"It gets better," added Riley. "Ely was a real American Indian, part of the Iroquois Nation and a real Seneca Chief. So now we have his great-grandson running the entire US military. What would Custer think?"

"What would Sitting Bull think?" asked Nicholas.

"So that's why we refer to General Parker as Chief Parker," explained Riley

"They are a couple of bubbling fountains of knowledge, aren't they Kelly? But can we now get back to my ranting? We've been fighting Islamic terrorists since 2001, sixteen years and how many hardcore jihadis have we actually killed?"

"You mean all of them? Like al-Qaeda, ISIS and ISIL, the Taliban, Boko Haram, Hezbollah, Hamas; and there are a hundred more I can't remember?" asked Nicholas.

"Yes."

"Thirty thousand?"

"I'm not talking about the poor smucks that get pressed ganged out of the mosque or the kids kidnaped out of school who become cannon fodder.

I mean the hard-core guys. A little over five thousand and that's it. A trillion spent, and American boys and girls dying in the desert for what? A million Arab civilians slaughtered by them or bombed by us. Ancient cities and civilizations destroyed and for what? We killed just over five thousand hardcore jihadis since 9/11 another vitamin war," lectured the President.

"Vitamin war? You mean the Vietnam war?" asked Nicholas.

"No, I mean vitamin war: A 'One A Day' war. That's how many Jihadis we killed since 9/11, 5000 days, 5000 assholes, one a day. Pathetic. When Bush the father invaded Iraq in '91 to help his friends the Saudis, he awakened the hornet's nest. They paid us back in '93 when they tried to blow up the World Trade Center, then succeed in '01 when they brought them both down. Persistent bastards. Fifteen of the 19 hijackers were citizens of Saudi Arabia and all part of al-Qaeda, but Bush the son instead went after the Taliban in Afghanistan? But when he went after Saddam in '03 we stepped on the hornet's nest. We have been fighting, surging and nation building in Iraq for twelve years till I pulled us out. We completely destroyed the 'Cradle of Civilization'. They would have been better off under Saddam, a benevolent dictator not, but you get what you deserve. He kept them in line; Sunni and Shiites. Picture 1980's Belfast with Catholic and Protestants on steroids. We led a coalition to topple Gaddafi and succeeded in destroying another civilization. The Arab Spring? They could have toppled Assad, but they didn't want it bad enough to die for it. They just weren't ready, and I will not participate in taking Assad out and destroying another civilization. Let Putin own it."

"Jesus, Sarge," said Riley as he watched his friend getting wound up.

"If people want to be free from the shackles that bind them or delivered from a dictator they have to want it. We wanted out from under the British rule and we had a revolution. You know what the British called us? Terrorists! No one helped us, we fought and died for our own freedom. Only the French came in to help at the end when they smelled blood. No one helped us with our Civil War. Only when people have enough and are willing to fight and die can they overcome. All I see are young men of fighting age abandoning their Arab countries for the safety of Europe. If they don't want to stay and fight for their country, why should we? Unfortunately, some people need dictators to keep them in line and from killing each other," said the president giving a tense look towards Riley.

President Burk continued, "All you need is one man one shot and the dictator is gone. Yeah, the shooter will probably die but if no one has the balls to do that then they deserve what they get."

Noreen buzzed, and the president answered. "Happy for the distraction," he said, "ask her to come in please."

In walked the vice president.

"Have a seat, Chelsey. What did you find out?" asked the president.

"Plenty and it's not good. They're coming for you and they're not waiting for your term to end. They want you gone now."

"What's the plan," asked Riley.

"Schuster and Bryan have a lot of backing to take you out. They are talking impeachment but waiting for Cabell to create an incident to draw you in. It is planned to spiral out of control and escalate to a situation to make you look bad. Cabell, that's one scary guy, discussed the secret nuclear weapons buy meeting on December 7, in Sofia, Bulgaria with Schuster, Bryan and myself. He told them everything. The actualization is for ISIL to attack the United States over the holidays. He told them you signed a COO Covert Operation Order that allows his assets to take them out. He said his assets will not be supported in their efforts to execute their mission order and the situation will escalate beyond your control, beyond your ability and duty to preserve, protect and defend the Constitution of the United States," said Hilton.

"Your right about that," agreed Kelly.

"Excuse me?"

"Cabell is a scary guy."

Ignoring Kelly's remark, the vice president continued, "That will be the reason they need to force you out. Cabell called it Operation Emiliano and compared it to Operation Zapata but not with the same fate. Operation Zapata was …"

"I know what Operation Zapata was, Chelsey,"

"I know Schuster and Bryans motive so I asked Cabell what his angle was."

"I'm guessing because he's a patriot?"

"Pretty much. He said you sold us out, sold out our civilization, our way of life, our democracy, and our children to Islam. He said you're an appeaser. You opened our borders to Islam and they are coming to destroy us. I think they are beginning to question my loyalty."

Kelly gave the president a knowing look and said, "Why, Chelsey? Did you give them a reason to?"

"I think I pressed Cabell too hard. He gave me a veiled threat."

"Why? What did he say?"

"He told me to lead, follow or get out of the way."

"Chelsey, you done good and thanks for covering for me with my Cabinet and Congress. I need time to think," concluded the president.

After Vice President Hilton left the Oval Office the President said to Kelly, "She just laid out the opposition's entire plan to bring me down. Still don't trust her?"

CHAPTER 39

The Situation Room Washington, DC December 6

Back again in the Situation Room, President Burk, Stanton, Kelly, Riley, Dr. Provenzano, AG Fare, Secret Service Director Bounty, General Finn. CoS Nicholas, NSA Michaels, Homeland's Borras, DCI Bader, were now joined by Chairman of the Joint Chief of Staff General (Chief) Ely Parker.

Tomorrow, December 7, in Sofia, Bulgaria, Cabell's and his CIA assets presidentially approved rendition plan, Operation Emiliano, to prevent the weapons buy between North Korea's Kim Jong-un and ISIL's al-Baghdad is scheduled to go down at 1700 hours.

So this morning, December 6, here in Washington those sitting around the Situation Room conference table were watching the final stages of DCI Bader's counter operation to hijack Cabell's Operation Emiliano before it can turn into another Operation Zapata. If Bader's hijack is successful, General Parker will then put his operation in play to have Delta Force snatch Baghdadi and replace him with a double.

Cabell, his lieutenants, and all their assets were assembled in and around Sofia finalizing last-minute pre-launch protocol when all hell broke loose.

DCI Bader had given the order 15 minutes earlier and his agents swooped in and corraled all seven teams Cabell was planning to use for the rendition, most of whom were just good agents or soldiers following orders.

"What time is now in Sofia?" asked SecDef Stanton.

"16:20 hours," answered Bader.

"English."

"4:20 p.m. Sofia time and 9:20 a.m. here in Washington," said Bader as he took a call on his secure line.

There was no live feed because they wanted to keep the raid against Cabell low key, but they were hoping Bader was getting a good report from his operatives.

"We shut it down!" exclaimed Baker. Everyone around the table clapped and let out a sigh of relief. "Everyone is accounted for except Cabell. The SOB got away; he either got tipped or his survival instinct kicked in," lamented Bader.

Everyone around the table now had that WTF look. "Jesus, John. That's who we wanted. He's the kingpin and he got away?" asked the president.

"He was there. We had eyes on him the entire time. He just did a Houdini the moment we took them down. We know from Chelsey he was expecting interference," said Bader.

"Let's hope he doesn't resurface and interfere with the Chief's snatch team, which is what, 10 minutes out Chief?" asked the president.

"Correct. We also have eyes on al-Baghdadi, his deputy al-Anbari, their interpreter, and Kim Jong-un, General Kim Yong Chol, Director of the Reconnaissance General Bureau and their interpreter. As soon as I give the order, Delta Force will snatch them," said General Parker.

"General Parker," asked SecDef Stanton, "why didn't you use Marine Corps Forces Special Operations Command (MARSOC) instead of Delta Force for the snatch?"

"Mr. Secretary, if you have a hill to take or a hill to defend I would put my Marines up against anyone, but after that, it gets a bit tricky for Marines," conceded General Parker.

The few former Marines in the room, including President Burk, looked at each other and kinda smiled, chuckled or shook their heads at the general's depiction of Marine capabilities. Only another Marine would appreciate what the general was inferring. Marines excelled when limited to 'KISS', Keep It Simple Stupid, but only a Marine could get away with saying it.

"Are the doubles for Baghdadi and his deputy al-Anbari convincing?" continued SecDef Stanton.

"As far as optics and mannerism are concerned they're like exact twins. What we're able to extract from Baghdadi and al-Anbari today will be fed to the doubles in time for showtime tomorrow," assured General Parker.

"What about the interpreter? Will you replace him?"

"We'll talk to him to see if he'll play along. My sense is he will. Interpreters are smart guys and a dying breed. They all seem to disappear after the gig. I think he'll play ball."

"Do they have the money with them?"

"It never leaves their side. They and the money are all holed up in the same hotel as the meeting."

"2.5 billion dollars must be awful hard to move around."

"Five orange Travelers Choice Maxporter roll-ons. We purchased the exact same luggage from Overstock.com and filled them with funny money in case their's turns out to be the real thing, in which case we'll have some serious money to buy fire water and rifles," said General Parker with a grin.

"Looking at General Parker the president said, "When your team is ready, issue a 'Go.'"

Less than a half mile from the Situation Room, in the Hart Senate Office Building, Senator Chuck Schuster sat by his secure phone and waited. The phone rang directly into his office.

"Yes," said Schuster.

"It's done. They shut down all seven teams."

"Are you all right?" asked Schuster.

"Don't worry about me. Just make sure you take care of your end," said Deputy Director Cabell and disconnected.

CHAPTER 40

Sofia, Bulgaria December 6

Sofia is the capital and largest city of Bulgaria. The city has a population of 1.26 million. It's located at the foot of the Vitosha Mountain in the western part of the country, less than a 50 kilometer (31 mile) drive from the Serbian border. Its location in the center of the Balkan Peninsula means that it is the midway between the Black Sea and the Adriatic Sea.

Sofia has been an area of human habitation since at least 7000 B.C. Being Bulgaria's principal city, Sofia is the hometown of many of the major local universities, cultural institutions, and commercial companies.

The ASEAN Association of Southeast Asian Nations, Regional Forum was set to begin tomorrow morning, but most if not all of the participants have been in the city since Sunday enjoying the sites, pre-event dinners and parties.

The Lux Hotel Sofia where al-Baghdadi, his deputy al-Anbari, and their interpreter Abdullah Mansour were staying, is a nine-story neoclassical building that stops at the third floor with a six-story modern glass addition above. The selling point for Baghdadi, besides the fact that Kim Jong-un was staying in the presidential suite, was that it is only a few blocks away was the Sofia Public Minerals Bath, a temptation Baghdadi could not resist.

The 1st Special Forces Operational Detachment-Delta (1st SFOD-D), aka Delta Force, is a U.S. Army unit used for hostage rescue and counter-terrorism as well as direct action and reconnaissance against high-value targets. Delta Force is one of the United States military's primary counterterrorism units and falls under the operational control of the Joint Special Operations Command.

Lt. General Troy's Headquarters Company was based at Bagram Air Base, Afghanistan, where he releases his appropriation snatch and grab teams throughout the Mideast, Europe, and Africa. He assigned several teams to hunt Baghdadi once he arrived in Sofia.

A Team (Alpha) was responsible for hunting, abducting and swapping out al-Baghdadi, his deputy al-Anbari, and their interpreter Abdullah Mansour.

B Team (Baker) was responsible for ground and air transportation.

C Team (Charley) was comprised of operational support troops, advanced force operations, reconnaissance, and surveillance. They had eyes on Baghdadi, Kim, and company since they arrived in Sofia.

Alpha was the lead team and was commanded by Captain Mitch Beck, call sign Alpha one six actual. Beck was six-foot, 180-pounds. with short sandy blond hair and currently sporting a week's growth of stubble. He was handsome, determined and a bad-ass. His A Team consisted of eight gender integrated operatives plus Beck, in two squads. Each squad leader was a staff sergeant. The 1st. squad would perform the abduction of package one and two, Baghdadi and Mansour. The 2nd. squad would abduct package three, al-Anbari and insert the doubles and make the money switch if required.

Captain Beck and his Delta Force performed admirably in a previous terrorist's operation rounding up terrorist's family members as hostages to prevent future terrorist activities. Baghdadi's people along with other terrorist's family members were still being held at Bagram Air Base in Afghanistan. Baghdadi obviously didn't believe the United States, without their operative

Israel Colburn aka Icy would further harm any women or children as Colburn had promised.

B Team was responsible for transportation out of the city and out of the country.

C Team reconnaissance has had eyes on Baghdadi since Baghdadi and his two accomplices arrived in Sofia on Monday. They were also responsible for authenticating the 2.5 billion bucks, switching out currency if required, and providing and maintaining audio/video.

It had been difficult for the Delta operators to steer clear of Cabell's assets preparing to abduct Baghdadi and DCI Bader's CIA contractors hunting Cabell. That, fortunately, was now history and they were ready and awaiting their Go order to get Baghdadi. Most of the three teams members wore appropriate civilian attire, (jeans, backpacks, caps, and sunglasses) with concealed microphones, receivers, a compact Ingram MAC-11 SMG 9mm short with a sound suppressor and a 9mm short Makarov pistol. No matter how you dressed them, these guys and gals stood out. No matter how hard they tried, they looked, walked and had the air of military personnel; but they would try nevertheless.

Alpha team leader Captain Beck informed Colonel Robert Axelrod, his boss and General Troy's operations director in Sofia, that Baghdadi and the interpreter Mansour acting as his manservant had left the hotel. Under the guise of being members of the Pakistani delegation, and were now in the public mineral bath a few blocks away. His deputy, al-Anbari, remained in the hotel room with the money.

Colonel Robert Axelrod called General Troy, General Troy called General Parker, and the 'Go' was issued and passed back down the line to Captain Beck.

"We're good to go," said Beck in his throat mic.

Baghdadi was already in the bath submerged up to his neck in the hot natural spring water. Baghdadi at 46 had a face that was well known throughout the IC community but not so much in Sofia. Nevertheless, he allowed one minor nod to deception: sunglasses. The bath was crowded but segregated between male and female. Mansour, the interpreter, was dressed in a typical Pakistani kurta shalwar suit, nothing more than then a long beige top covering white trousers and sandals. Baghdadi's similar outfit was folded neatly beside Mansour. Men and boys, in various stages of undress, were getting in and out of the hot bath, scrubbing backs or were just sitting on the stone ledge taking in the scene.

Charley Team's recon squad verified that Baghdadi was traveling without security. Beck suspected Baghdadi assumed not having an entourage was the best option. Beck with 1st. squad were quietly and quickly surrounded Baghdadi and Mansour.

The public bath was in a very old building that had recently been renovated and modernized with among other upgrades a fire alarm system.

"Hit it," said Beck over his throat mic.

The fire alarm activated with a loud, irritating, pulsing squeal while recessed floor LED lights guided patrons towards the exits. Everyone began reacting in different ways. Some looked confused, some ran for the exits, and some just jumped up out of the hot mineral water covering their privates. Baghdadi did the latter and fell into the arms of what appeared, to anyone who cared to notice, to be his security force. He was given an injection which lightly sedated him but allowed him to remain ambulatory. His clothes were quickly applied, and he and Mansour were quickly led to the exit and the waiting Range Rover convoy. With the alarm still blaring, hundreds of confused and frighten semi-clothed bathers rushed out of the bathhouse, and the entire abduction went unnoticed.

Simultaneously, 2nd. squad entered Baghdadi's hotel room using the hotel master room key and found al-Anbari and five orange Travelers Choice Maxporter roll-ons all within one room. Anbari was watching porn on the hotel TV and was rushed, restrained and injected with the same sedative his leader received, and all before he could get his trousers up.

Two Charley team operatives accompanying 2nd. squad were US Treasury agents and quickly evaluated samples of the currency. The currency portraits, Federal Reserve and Treasury: seals, borders, paper, starch, feel and watermarks were evaluated and determined that the money was real. Over a secure connection, samples of the discontinued but still legal $500, $1,000, $5,000 and $10,000 bills were photographed and sent back to Washington for confirmation. The money was real alright responded the US Treasury Department back in Washington. In fact, Beck was informed the serial numbers coincided with those of the 100 billion the US gave to Iran as part of the nuclear agreement/prisoner swap in January 2016.

Al-Anbari and the five orange Travelers Choice Maxporter roll-ons went out the hotel room door while Baghdadi, Anbari, and five orange Travelers Choice Maxporter roll-on doppelgangers came in.

"Alpha one six actual, this is Alpha two six. The third package and luggage is secure. Over. "

"Alpha one six actual to Alpha two six, first and second packages are secure. The interpreter has decided to play ball and is being escorted to you now. We'll take package three and the luggage off your hands. Keep our guy happy and healthy till we get there. We'll feed you whatever we get from packages one, and three as soon as we get it. Over."

"Alpha one six actual, this is Alpha two six. Roger that. We'll have the package and the luggage curbside. Have a good trip. Out."

This was Delta Force at its best. No muss, no fuss, no drama.

CHAPTER 41

The Situation Room Washington, DC December 7

The usual suspects, aka the president's inner circle, including the vice president who was sort of in but not fully, sat around the Situation Room glued to the wall mounted monitors as the president entered and sat at the head of the conference table.

"Ten minutes till showtime," said SecDef Stanton.

"Everything set?" asked the president.

"Affirmative," answered General Parker. "We have a video cam contact lens's embedded in the eye of each double along with implanted transmitters in both doubles: al-Baghdadi, and al-Anbari, and the real Mansour. We'll hear and see everything that happens. Our interpreter, nodding to the Arab looking officer wearing headphones to his left, Captain Ameri, will translate Korean and Arabic for us."

"The packages?" asked the president.

"Both the real Baghdadi and Anbari were driven four miles to Sofia International Airport where they boarded a helicopter to the former Nazi airbase Graf Ignatievo, 86 miles from Sofia, then to Turkey and are now enjoying Greek hospitality in a safe house outside Almiros," said General Parker.

"Are they cooperating?" asked the president.

"As it turns out, Baghdadi is a real bad ass, but Captain Beck said his interrogators in Greece are reporting back that al-Anbari is a fish out of water and has become extremely conversant. What we now know about the buy, which is a lot, our team and doubles in Sofia know," said General Parker.

"Good job, Chief. Pass along my congratulations to Major Beck and his team." beamed the president.

Looks like Captain Beck just got promoted, thought General Parker.

Captain Beck, unaware of his promotion, guided his doubles and Mansour, five hotel porters each wheeling an orange Travelers Choice Maxporter roll-on containing counterfeit money into the freight elevator, did a mic check with his hotel control room to confirm they were live and streaming, pushed the PH floor button, gave a smart salute, said good luck, and watched the elevator door close.

Colonel Robert Axelrod's control room, located 12 floors lower in the sub-basement of The Lux Hotel Sofia and President Burk's Situation Room 5,000 miles away in Washington watched on the monitors as the freight elevator door opened on the PH floor as the al-Baghdadi, al-Anbari, doubles, Mansour and porters walked out into the service corridor, through the double doors and into the PH floor hallway.

They watched as the group stopped in front of presidential suite PH9 and rang the door chime. After a slight hesitation, the door opened, and three security personnel came out into the hallway, closed the door and dismissed the porters. They proceeded to search al-Baghdadi, al-Anbari, and Mansour and opened three of the five roll-ons. The suite door opened and the three were admitted, followed by the security detail pulling the roll-ons.

The three were left waiting in the foyer while the five roll-ons were wheeled into the suite salon. After about ten minutes, al-Baghdadi, al-Anbari, and Mansour were escorted into the salon. All three eye cams focused immediately on the figure seated in a throne-like chair in the 20' x 20' room.

There sat North Korea's Supreme Leader Kim Jong-un. To his right stood General Kim Yong Chol, Director of the Reconnaissance General Bureau, and an interpreter.

In the Situation Room, CoS Nicholas said, "If that's not Kim Jong-un, he's the best double since Hitler's doppelganger, Heinrich Berger."

"Do we know it's not actually the real Kim?" asked the president.

DCI Bader, still trying to recover from losing Cabell the previous day, said, "It's not him..." He was about to add that his assets in North Korea had eyes on the real Kim, but said instead, "The real Kim Jong-un is in...." Just then they heard a loud crashing freight train noise and the eye cams of the two doubles and Mansour looked away from Kim Jong-un and up to the ceiling. The noise grew louder, the room started to shake, a loud boom was heard, and then the streaming a/v connection went squiggly then black.

General Parker was on his phone immediately to find out what happened to the connection but already feared the worst. The phone rang but the connection was dropped. He tried again and again, but the call kept dropping.

"Jesus Christ! What just happened?" shouted the president.

"I think we just witnessed another Pearl Harbor; another 9/11," said Nicholas.

"Yeah, but I don't think it was the Japanese or the Saudis this time," Riley grimaced.

"Those are all wonderful analogies but I think we all know what happened," said the president as he and everyone turned towards DCI Bader.

General Finn, looking directly across the conference table at DCI Bader said, "Director, you may want to check on your MQ-1 Predator and Smart Pyron bomb inventory because I think your deputy Prescott Cabell just sent Kim Jong-un and al-Baghdadi to Hell."

"I thought you got all of Cabell's seven teams?" questioned Riley.

Director Bader felt like shit. His deputy outsmarted him and played him for a fool. He could sense the crosshairs lining up on him now. *Pull the trigger and end it quickly*, he thought.

They continued back and forth for another ten minutes until Kelly heard an IM chirp. She read the message and said, "Turn on *CNN*. They're reporting a big explosion in Bulgaria."

One of the tech aids did just that and a BREAKING NEWS banner filled the bottom of the screen and Wolf Blitzer was in the middle of a sentence. "...turn now to our international reporter Kyung Lah who happens to be in Sophia, Bulgaria reporting on the Association of Southeast Asian Nations, Regional Forum which kicked off today. There seems to have been a rather big hotel explosion. What can you tell us, Kyung?"

"Thank you, Wolf. Kyung Lah here for *CNN* in Sophia, Bulgaria standing in front of what was, until a few minutes ago, The Lux Hotel Sofia. We are being pushed back by the police as they rope off the area around the hotel, but as you can see there are police, first responders, and injured people all over the street. I can see and smell the smoke and hear the cries and screams, but what I can't see is the hotel. It's gone. This just happened less than 20 minutes ago and we are trying to get information from the authorities and witnesses and will bring it to you as soon as we get it. But it's safe to say, from what I'm seeing, there are going to be many hundreds of dead and wounded. I was covering the ASEAN conference at the Sofia Congress Center just eight blocks from the explosion but I can tell you the Lux is, was, a five-star hotel and many ASEAN attendees, diplomats and world leaders including North Korea leader Kim Jong-un were staying in the hotel. I know because I, until twenty minutes ago, had a room there. Back to you, Wolf."

"Kyung, do we know what caused the explosion and if Kim Jong-un was in the hotel and the possible target?" asked Wolf.

"It's too soon to say, Wolf, and I would be just speculating. But I can tell you Supreme Leader Kim Jong-un is scheduled to speak tomorrow and was not in the convention hall today. I can also tell you that this was no truck bomb. This looks like a precision aerial guided bombing similar to what I witnessed in Syria and Iraq. The Grand Sofia Hotel is gone but adjacent buildings, with the exception of some broken windows, seem unaffected. Wolf."

"Thank you, Kyung. Please be careful and check back as soon as you have something. Now to our White House correspondent Jim Acosta outside the White House. Jim. Anything?"

"Wolf, nothing to see here. No one seems to be around. The normal activity you would see after an incident like this, especially involving North Korean Kim Jong-un, including tweets, is eerily silent. I'm standing on West Executive Avenue next to the West Wing of the White House and the only activity I can see are lights coming from the basement Situation Room. Jim Acosta outside the White House for *CNN*. Back to you Wolf."

Turning away from the monitor and looking at the president, Kelly said, "I better get something together and quick. It's going to be a long night."

"Why do we have to say anything? Just say we're finding out about it the same as everyone else; from *CNN*?" suggested Bader.

"Because we were there, John. Because our fingerprints are all over this yesterday and today. Cabell's agents, your agents, Delta. Somebody saw something. We've been set up. Any good reporter, hell, hundreds of good reporters are going to be all over this by tomorrow morning. They are going to speculate on our involvement and then they are going to find something to tie us in; then it's downhill from there. And don't forget our friends across the aisle. I'll bet tomorrow morning's news shows just happened to have already booked Schuster and Bryan. Those two are going to come at us full force, especially if Kim Jong-un or his double and top general have been killed. And let's not forget who signed the operation order to snatch Baghdadi out of the Lux Hotel," added President Burk.

"This is going to get real big real fast. We need to give them something. They're going to be all over me tonight," said Kelly. Her phone was chirping, ringing and pinging. "What do I tell them?"

"Tell them the truth," replied Nicholas.

"They can't handle the truth," said Jack Nicholson, aka Riley.

"I'm not going to be caught in a lie. We need to be transparent. Tell them the truth, not the whole truth but what they can find on their own and verify.

Tell them we were in Sofia and we got Baghdadi and that's it," said President Burk.

"When they find the body of our Baghdadi double how will we explain that? Do you think anyone will believe we just waltzed into Sofia and took Baghdadi but left Kim Jong-un without so much as a 'By-Your-Leave'? We gave the fat kid a pass? We're screwed!" declared Kelly.

"They're not going to find any identifiable bodies in the hotel, not with that explosion and fire. At least not for a long time anyway," deflected Director Bader.

"We have Baghdadi. The weapons buy meeting never occurred and the coup d'etat has begun. Dr. Provenzano, can you please send the jumpers back to Cleveland? I need to know if the attacks on New York and the East Coast have been averted or we've been led down the proverbial garden path," said President Burk.

CHAPTER 42

The White House
December 8

Max, the president's German Shepherd, and Secret Service Director Christian Bounty, the president's old friend, joined the president for a three-mile training run. It was a brisk morning for their easy 30-minute run and still a bit dark. The president had been pushing Max a little more each run hoping to get him up to 8k. This morning with the Secret Service detail in tow, they ran out the south White House exit down the path across Pensylvania Avenue, across Constitution Avenue and west along the reflecting pool towards the Vietnam Veterans Memorial.

As they approached the memorial the president gave a smart salute and said, "To absent Friends."

Director Bounty added, "Till we meet again." And on cue, Max barked.

They continued around the Lincoln Memorial and then started to head back home.

"You know it's gonna start getting rough soon," remarked the president.

"I know and we'll be okay. You do your job and I'll do mine. Let's take it home."

They made it back in just under 30 minutes and walked the final 150 yards to cool down.

"Thanks, Chris, we'll catch up later." The president entered the White House and up the stairs to his bedroom. He had 25 minutes to shower and dress before he had to be down in the Oval Office. He opened his office door at 5:59 and Max scooted in behind him. Kelly, Riley, and Nicholas were all seated drinking coffee and watching TV.

At 6 a.m. *MSNBC's Morning Joe* news talk show came on with Mika Brzezinski saying, "Let's start with. We got three hours. We got all these stories right and we're gonna lay them out, ah in a big way. The leader of the free world is hovering under a 40% approval rating just weeks into his second administration ... Joe."

Joe Scarborough, nicely dressed for a change, appeared on a split screen wearing a red and white checkered shirt (think 50's plastic table cloth), and said, "Mark Halperin, how bad do these numbers impact the president's ability to get anything done, whether it's overseas or at home?"

"It's tough, we talk all the time about how low poll numbers..."

President Burk stood watching with his first of three, possibly four, Diet Cokes. "Poll numbers? Didn't they learn anything about polls this last go around? Everyone got it wrong. They said I didn't have a prayer. They blew it; it's just more biased reporting. Let me know when Schuster comes on," said the president as he walked over to his desk. Max was already ensconced under the desk chewing on what looked like a male femur bone. The president had a smile on his face as he thought of who's leg that might belong.

The show was less than 15 minutes in when Joe Scarborough said, "From inside the Capitol, let's welcome Senate Minority Leader Chuck Schuster, Democrat from New Jersey."

"Tommy, he's on," called Kelly as the president came over to the TV.

"Senator, on Tuesday you accused President Burk of failing to deliver on campaign promises to get tougher on America's relationship with North Korea and China. What do you have to say now since the hotel bombing in Sofia, Bulgaria in which it has been reported that North Korea's Kim Jong-un was staying? I must remind viewers that it has not been confirmed that

Kim Jong-un was in the hotel at the time of the bombing or the intended target, or if it was even a terrorist bombing. No one has of yet come forward and taken credit. North Korean officials are not commenting, and President Burk's White House has yet to release a statement."

"Good morning, Joe. Good morning, Mika, Willie, and Mark. First, I would like to say thank you for inviting me on your show this morning. It just so happens I have some exclusive and extraordinary information which I will share with you, but first. let me answer your question. One of the few hopes we had with President Burk was that he'd finally stand up to North Korea and China. But up to now, when it comes to both countries, he looks like a 98-pound weakling."

"Burk talks a good game and signs a couple of executive orders that mean nothing. Burk's not yet fulfilling a campaign promise to label North Korea a terrorist state and China as a currency manipulator," said Senator Schuster.

"You have us on pins and needles, Senator. You said up until now President Burk was weak. Has something happened to change your opinion, and what's the exclusive and extraordinary news you're going to share with us?" asked Mika.

"Mika, something stinks in Washington. Burk promised to drain the swamp, but I'm afraid all he's done is create a cesspool. You're going to get a press release this morning from the White House that's going to be a game changer. I have seen it and it's shocking. My office has just sent your producer a copy. But let me warn you. What you read in their press release is only the tip of the iceberg and I and Speaker Bryan are calling for hearing to get to the bottom of it."

"The bottom of what, Senator?"

"My sources at the highest levels of the military and intelligence community are telling me President Burk signed a COO Covert Operation Order, sending American operatives into Sophia, Bulgaria yesterday and you can see for yourself the results. Al-Baghdadi, the head of ISIL was in the hotel and so was North Koreas Kim Jong-un. President Burk took them out and everyone else in the hotel." Schuster paused for effect as his eyes teared-up and he began to choke up. It was an award-winning performance. "He's killed hundreds of innocent people: men, women, children and little babies. My god, what have we come to?"

"Do you need a minute Senator?" asked Mika.

"No. But thank you, Mika," the Senator continued, "You'll see nothing about that in their press release. This heinous bombing will set in effect a chain of events which will destroy America's credibility, American security and the American way of life as we know it. President Burk has taken America to the brink of war. The free world will not permit the United States to continue as the world leader. We are going to go through the hearings and find the truth wherever it leads us, but one thing is for sure, President Burk has done the despicable, and when you read his press release on the bombing you will see he also lied to the American people and we have the proof. We are going to begin impeachment proceedings immediately and believe me, this will be a bipartisan impeachment hearing. We have all the votes we need, but more importantly, we will have the American people behind us. What he has done is despicable, but what we and the American people are going to do to him and his 'Live and Let Live Party' is unstoppable."

"The country and the world will be watching. The murder of innocents is not the way America does things. It's not the American way. President Burk has lost his ability to uphold his sworn duty to preserve, protect and defend the Constitution of the United States. God help us, and God bless America."

"Can you believe that pompous son-of-a-bitch, and *MSNBS* for airing that bullshit," said Riley.

"How did he get a copy of the press release draft? I intended to revise it after the morning shows and release it at 9 a.m. We got a leak in my press office," huffed Kelly.

"Et tu, Chuck. The coup d'état has begun," said Nicholas.

"I'll revise it with the whole truth and you can review it before it goes out. We'll still try for a 9 a.m. release. We can't put the genie back in the bottle after Chuckie boy's spiel, but we can put the truth out on our terms and let the people decide," advised Kelly.

President Burk, still standing, sat down and Max came out from under the desk to sit by his side and was rewarded with a head scratch.

"What am I gonna tell them? The whole truth? That I approved a Covert Operation Order to have CIA operatives swoop into a foreign country, in this case, Bulgaria, kidnap a terrorist posing as a Pakistani delegate while he's meeting in a hotel with the leader of another foreign country, in this case, North Korea. Then I change my mind and send in a second CIA team to take out the first CIA team. Then I send in Delta Force to do what the first CIA team was supposed to do, kidnap the terrorist and steal 2.5 billion dollars, of our own money I may add, and replace the real terrorist and the real money with a fake terrorist and fake money so they can still have the meeting with the leader of North Korea whom we also think may be fake. Then I and my team watch it all on TV through embedded contact lenses in our fake terrorist eyeballs as my first CIA team sends in a drone with a smart bomb and blows the fucking hotel to smithereens and everyone in it including most of my second CIA team and my Delta Force who happen to be in the fucking basement?" exploded the president. "And we did all this to prevent a terrorist attack on New York and the East Coast which we know is coming this Christmas because we uncovered it while time traveling into the future? But look at the bright side, we got the real Baghdadi and 2.5 billion in cash. Who's on first!"

"What's on second and I don't know's on third," added Riley.

"Looks like we're fucked, Tonto," said President Burk looking at his old friend Bill Nicholas.

"What do you mean 'we' paleface?"

CHAPTER 43

THE WORLD REACTS

Russia, China, South Korea and most of the world powers have all condemned America's failed attempt to assassinate North Korean Supreme Leader Kim Jong-un.

North Korea sends warning to the U.S. April 8, 2017
Vilgot Anderson *Information Sweden*
The ambassador of North Korea to Moscow has sent a warning to United States President Thomas Dean Burk. He said North Korea is ready to deliver the "most ruthless blow" if further provoked by the United States.

He made this statement after President Burk's attempted assassination of Supreme Leader Kim Jong-un in Sofia, Bulgaria where he was invited to speak before the ASEAN conference.

"Our army has already said that if there is even the smallest provocation from the United States during our upcoming military exercises, we are ready to deliver the most ruthless blow." Interfax news agency quoted ambassador Kim Hyong-Jun as saying, "We have the readiness and ability to counter any challenge from the U.S."

President Burk on Tuesday, one day before the assassination attempt, pledged to Japanese Prime Minister Shinzo Abe that the US would, "continue to strengthen its ability to deter and defend itself and its allies with the full range of its military capabilities," a day after Pyongyang fired a ballistic missile into the Sea of Japan (East Sea).

North Korea's foreign ministry on Wednesday assailed Washington for its tough talk, and for an ongoing joint military exercise with South Korea and Japan which Pyongyang sees as a dress rehearsal for an invasion.

These "reckless actions" of the United States, South Korea and Japan and the attempted assassination against our Supreme Leader Kim Jong-un on Wednesday are driving the tense situation on the Korean peninsula, "to the brink of a war", a ministry spokesman was quoted as saying by the official KCNA news agency.

The idea that the US could deprive Pyongyang of its nuclear deterrent through sanctions, while planning an assassination attempt is, "the wildest dream", said a high-ranking Pyongyang military spokesperson.

The US military said Tuesday that nuclear-armed North Korea had fired a ballistic missile into the Sea of Japan, but that it did not represent a threat to North America.

Pyongyang is on a quest to develop a long-range missile capable of hitting the US mainland with a nuclear warhead and has so far staged five nuclear tests, two of them last year.

U.S. policy on assassinations
CNN

In 1976, President Ford issued executive order 11905 to clarify U.S. foreign intelligence activities. The order was enacted in response to the post-Watergate revelations that the CIA had staged multiple attempts on the life of Cuban President Fidel Castro.

In a section of the order labeled "Restrictions on Intelligence Activities," Ford outlawed political assassination: Section 5(g), entitled "Prohibition on Assassination," which states: "No employee of the United States Government shall engage in, or conspire to engage in, political assassination."

Since 1976, every U.S. president has upheld Ford's prohibition on assassinations. In 1978 President Carter issued an executive order with the chief purpose of reshaping the intelligence structure. In Section 2-305 of that order, Carter reaffirmed the U.S. prohibition on assassination.

In 1981, President Reagan, through executive order 12333, reiterated the assassination prohibition. Reagan was the last president to address the topic of political assassination. Because no subsequent executive order or piece of legislation has repealed the prohibition, it remains in effect.

The ban, however, did not prevent the Reagan administration from dropping bombs on Libyan leader Muammar Gadhafi's home in 1986 in retaliation for the bombing of a Berlin discotheque frequented by U.S. troops.

Additionally, the Clinton administration fired cruise missiles at suspected guerrilla camps in Afghanistan in 1998 after the bombings of two U.S. embassies in Africa.

Following the September 11, 2001, attacks, the White House said the presidential directive banning assassinations would not prevent the United States from acting in self-defense.

According to an October 21, 2001, *Washington Post* article, President Bush in September of 2003 signed an intelligence "finding" instructing the CIA to engage in "lethal covert operations" to destroy Osama bin Laden and his al Qaeda organization.

White House and CIA lawyers believe that the intelligence "finding" is constitutional because the ban on political assassination does not apply during wartime. They also contend that the prohibition does not preclude the United States taking action against terrorists.

President Burk, it seems, is in good company.

NO JOKE

Jon Park, Director of the Korea Working Group at the Harvard Kennedy School.

"North Korea has consistently been treated as a joke, but now the joke has nuclear weapons. If you deem Kim Jong-un to be irrational, then you're implicitly underestimating him. Leaders throughout the centuries have realized it can be advantageous to have your enemies think you're crazy. Machiavelli once wrote that it can be wise to pretend to be mad, while President Richard Nixon wanted the North Vietnamese to think he was unstable and prone to launch a nuclear attack on a whim."

Writing off Kim Jong-un as a lunatic could equally be playing into his hands.

Want proof that he's no senseless madman?

Exhibit A: "He's still in power," said Benjamin Smith, an expert on regime change at the University of Florida. "He and his father and grandfather have stayed in power through a series of American presidents dating back to Truman.

Big Kim to eat Big Apple
NEW YORK POST December 9, 2016
Kim Jong-un has been invited to speak before the United Nations General Assembly.

In an unprecedented move, a majority of the United Nations 15-member Security Council invited DPRK Supreme Leader Kim Jong-un to New York for an emergency meeting of the General Assembly, to express his grievances against the United States and especially President Burk. Nicki Haley, United States permanent representative to the United Nations and current president of the Security Council was the lone dissenting vote.

CHAPTER 44

The White House December 12

"This is getting serious, Tommy. We have to get in front of it and now. All the protest and negative press reports coming in last week and yesterday's morning talk shows, *Meet the Press, Face the Nation, This Week, Fox News Sunday,* and *State of the Union* we're all salivating over your impending impeachment. I swear Matthews wet his pants. Even Wallace has turned on you. Schuster and Bryan were on every show together. How the hell did they pull that off? They had a better routine than Abbot and Costello," declared Kelly.

"Set up a Presidential Address to the Nation for tonight and get as many of the inner circle back in here to the Oval Office after my Cabinet meeting. Have a secure video conference link set up with all our governors, our loyal Senators, and Representatives, and I will be bringing into our inner circle a few more from my Cabinet," directed President Burk.

"I think we need a bigger boat," said Riley.

The members of the president's Cabinet represent, in most cases, his closest and most trusted advisors on critical foreign and domestic policy matters. While each member oversees the day-to-day business of his or her executive department, the president meets regularly with the Cabinet to discuss ongoing strategies to resolve everything from foreign wars to financial crises.

President Burk convened a full Cabinet meeting at least every two months, and today was the day.

If the walls of the Cabinet Room could speak, they would tell of discussions and lively debate over national budgets, the state of the military, domestic and social issues and matters of national security. George W. Bush convened a meeting on September 12, 2001, with his national security team in the Cabinet Room, where he declared that freedom and democracy were under attack. Nearly 40 years earlier, John Kennedy held intense discussions in the Cabinet Room during the days of the Cuban Missile Crisis.

The meeting lasted almost two hours as everyone around the table gave a report on their area of responsibility: Transportation, Commerce, Labor, Interior, Health, & Human Services, Housing & Urban Development, Education, Veterans Affairs, Treasury, and finally Management and Budget. When the last report was filed, Representative of the United States to the United Nations Nikki R. Haley, finally addressed the eight-hundred-pound gorilla in the room. "Mr. President, the United Nations Security Council invited DPRK Supreme Leader Kim Jong-un to New York for an emergency meeting of the General Assembly to express his grievances against the United States and especially you. I was the only dissenting vote. The Security Council is threatening to impose sanctions, and even authorize military intervention against the United States. I need to know..."

"Just a second, Nikki," interrupted the president, "The UK, Israel, Germany, Japan, and most of NATO are still with us but quiet. The rest of the world has always hated us but now have a platform to come out of the closet, so to speak. I'm not worried, nor should any of you be, against sanctions or military intervention against us. What do you imagine they're capable of? Declaring war on the United States? Tried a few times before and how did that work out? This whole thing is a sham, a twisted set-up that would make Niccolò Machiavelli proud."

"Well, it would be nice if you could enlighten us, so I know how to respond. Tell us what Schuster and Bryan are saying is a big lie," said an exasperated Haley.

"What Senator Schuster and Speaker Bryan are saying is the truth, but not the whole truth. We uncovered a nuclear weapon buy between North Korea and ISIL financed by Iran, to be held in Sofia, Bulgaria, on December 7. I approved a COO Covert Operation Order to have CIA operatives go into Bulgaria and snatch ISIL's al-Baghdadi, but not to touch Kim Jong-un, whom we suspected to be a double; a doppelgänger, a body double. The operation became compromised and I had to send in Delta Force to get it back on track. Delta got Baghdadi on December 6, and they never saw or touched Kim Jong-un and were not involved in any assassination attempt or hotel bombing on December 7. I found out about the bombing like the rest of you from *CNN*. Someone else is responsible and trying to pin it on us."

"I must say they have done an excellent job of it," remarked Haley.

"Yes, Nikki. They did but if you all bear with me a bit longer it will all become clear. I have to get back to the Oval Office and prepare for a Presidential Address to the Nation tonight. Vice President Hilton will tell you what I intend to say, what we think happened and what we're going to do about it," advised the president. He stood up and motioned for Secretary of Transportation, Bill Dougherty, Secretary of State Matt Walsh, and Secretary of the Treasury Michael Bloomfield to follow him back to the Oval Office.

President Burk, Riley, Nicholas, and Bounty walked out of the Cabinet Room, some thirty feet from the Oval Office.

Secretaries of: Transportation, State, and Treasury followed the president to the Oval Office. The president asked Nicholas to take the others in, get all the governors, the loyal Senators and Representatives, up on screen-share and finalize the details, while he stayed outside with the three secretaries and proceeded to give them the short story.

Ten minutes later the president and his three new inner circle members entered the Oval Office and joined the others for the podcast to the governors, loyal senators, representatives and the Joint Chiefs.

The president started with an announcement, "Thank you all for being here. The American people are furious. Nothing is getting done. The radical

Democrats and Republicans are doing everything possible to disrupt my administration and my ability to govern, and with the terrorist attacks always looming, we can't let that happen. As most of you are already aware, the collusion between House Speaker Bryan, Senate Minority Leader Schuster, and others within the government and their propaganda wing, the biased news media to overthrow my administration has begun. The American people are so sick of this bullshit. Congress is worthless. The Republicans hate the Democrats. The Democrats hate the Republicans. Both hate me and our Live and Let Live Party. They are not going to stop me, they are not going to stop us. We'll get it done without them. The biased media are clamoring for a press conference that they can control and spin. But tonight I'm going directly to the American people and tell them what's been happening and how I intend to solve it. I want all of you to move forward according to our previously discussed plan. Are there any questions?" No one said anything. Everyone appeared stern and resolved. "Okay, you all know what to do. Be strong and may God guide us and bless us through these troubled times."

After most everyone left the Oval Ofice, President Burk sat on the couch and was joined by Kelly, while Riley and Dr. Provenzano sat on the opposite couch. Nicholas sat in one of the chairs. The president seemed deflated and tired. Kelly got up and went out for a few minutes returning with Max and the steward bearing coffee and tea.

Max jumped up on the couch with the president and rolled over on his back to have his belly scratched. Kelly sat back down beside her husband and imitated Max. That seemed to do the trick; everything seemed to lighten up.

Looking at Dr. Provenzano the president asked, "TP, what did the jumpers find this time?"

"We sent them back again yesterday, as you know, and the situation is still the same. Same attacks, same time, same M.O.," said Dr. Provenzano.

"So the attacks occur regardless of Baghdadi and despite the aborted weapons sale. What does that tell us?" asked Nicholas.

"It tells us everything we need to know," replied Riley.

"And that is?" asked the president.

"That Baghdadi and Kim were a diversion. This whole thing with him and Kim was a sting. While we followed them, Cabell had another plan and that's the one that succeeds," said Riley.

Feeling another Riley moment coming on, the president said, "Okay Ray, let's hear it."

"Look. Cabell brought us the intercepted conference call between Baghdadi and Kim Jong-un: 'the set-up'. Then we took 'the bait' and sent the jumpers to Cleveland. We played 'the wire' in Sofia and it blew up in our face," said Riley.

"So…"

"So? So he's the master of the big con. Cabell is Harry Gondorff. He's Paul Newman."

"Then who are we?" asked the president.

"Not we. You! You're 'the mark'. You're Doyle Lonnegan, 'the Big Mick.'"

"Thanks. So we know who Gondorff is and who Lonnegan is, but who's Hooker, the Redford character?"

"I think we all know who Hooker is," said Kelly.

Ignoring Kelly, the president asked, "Could Cabell be that smart? Or are we just that dumb? Playing both us and his co-conspirators? He sets up this whole weapon buy with Baghdadi and Kim just to get us mired up to our eyeballs in this shit and give Schuster and Bryan the ammunition to impeach me, all the time working the real attack with another terrorist organization."

"Yes. He could be that smart and we could be that dumb, but he doesn't know we know about the real attack. Could he?" asked Kelly.

"Yes. He might know. He knew we time traveled to the past. He was there and whoever he was working with on the inside knows we traveled to the future. So yes he knows."

"This guy is a piece of work. But what are we missing? If we know about the attack then we can stop it. He's just going to allow us to stop it?"

"No. He always seems to be one step ahead of us and somehow knows we can't stop it. And then the final act," said Riley.

"The final act?"

"The Sting," said Riley.

CHAPTER 45

The Oval Office
8 P.M.

Address to the Nation by President Thomas Dean Burk.
8:00 P.M. EST
"5…4…3…"

Good evening. A few days ago, December 7, a date which will, like its predecessor, 72 years ago, live in infamy, the United States of America was suddenly and deliberately attacked not by forces outside our country but by forces from within.

You, the American people reelected me to be your president for the next four years, but a subversive force within our own government feels that they know better than you and they know what's best for America.

This subversive force has conspired to push our country into chaos, in order to discredit your president, have me resign, impeach me, or both, all for their own personal gain and to take control of your government and your country.

Why are they trying to destroy my administration? The country, despite what they are saying, is on the right track. The people gave us four more years; elections have consequences.

There have been no homegrown terrorist attacks in the last two years. We fixed and improved the Affordable Healthcare Act. We solved immigration without mass deportation, our borders are now secure but without a wall. Crime and murder in our cities are down. Schools are much better and producing bright kids for college and trade schools. We're on board with climate change. Jobs are way up, the stock market is up. We instituted college debt forgiveness. The deficit is under control and we are nibbling at the debt. We got rid of the income tax in favor of a universal sales tax. Medicare and Social Security are solvent. We added dental, hearing and vision coverage to Medicare. We sent USA CORP. dividend checks to a quarter of the population. The VA is providing better service for our Vets. Infrastructure improvement projects are many and progressing. Why is this subversive force trying to destroy all these good things?

Because they have to. This subversive force, comprised of members of both Republican and Democratic parties, are like huge dinosaurs with tiny brains. Their survival instincts are keen and have been honed since before the Civil War. If I, we, our Live and Let Live Party are allowed to continue they will perish. We're like the meteor that came out of nowhere, crashed and blocked out their sun. They are incapable of understanding this new world and will only get in the way. But they will try to eat us to survive. It's in their DNA.

My fellow Americans. I cannot and will not allow this. There are too many important projects and policies we as a country need to continue working on together. All the promises of the past administrations both Republican and Democrat were just that: empty, broken promises. And they want you to believe them again, so they can come back into power and fool you all over again.

On Tuesday, December 6, we came one step closer to eliminating radical Islamic terrorism. Delta Force under my operation order abducted Abū Bakr al-Baghdadi, the leader of the Sunni militant terrorist organization known as the Islamic State of Iraq and the Levant (ISIL), which controls territory in western Iraq, Syria, Libya, and Afghanistan. The group has been designated a terrorist organization by the United Nations, as well as by the European Union and many individual states. In June of 2014, he was elected by the majlis al-shura, representing the ahl al-hall wal-aqd of the Islamic State, to be their caliphate and their leader.

Al-Baghdadi was in Sofia, Bulgaria to meet with North Korean Leader Kim Jong-un to discuss a nuclear weapon deal where North Korea would supply nuclear bombs to al-Baghdadi for five billion dollars financed by Iran. These nuclear weapons were to be used against the United States in a horrible, diabolical attack this Christmas. Under interrogation, al-Baghdadi revealed the details of the attack, and because of this information, we will now be able to prevent it.

This subversive force within our government is complicit in this diabolical plot and they will stop at nothing to keep me from my sworn responsibility to preserve, protect, and defend the Constitution of the United States.

This horrible bombing of civilians at the Grand Sofia Hotel in Bulgaria, perpetrated by this clandestine subversive force operating within our government, cost the lives of hundreds and horribly injured scores more, all in an effort to disgrace and embarrass the United States, the American people, and their president by creating an incident intended to bring me and our country down. What this subversive force is attempting is nothing more than a coup d'état to overthrow and force seizure of our country. They want to depose the established regime and replace it with their new ruling body. If they are successful, the usurpers will establish their dominance. If a coup fails, and it will, they will hang for treason.

But now the American people know the truth and their coup will fail. I intend, with your help to expose them, bring them down and try them for treason.

Senate Minority Leader Chuck Schuster, Democrat from New Jersey and House Speaker Paul Bryan, Republican from New York, are the ringleaders. Many radical Republican and Democrats from both the House and Senate, along with members of our intelligence community, the military industrial complex, and most of the mainstream media have all conspired against the United States to overthrow our Constitution and our government. They are a cancer and here is the treatment.

Effective tonight, I have enacted limited martial law through the country until such time as the conspirators can be apprehended and brought to justice. Working with all 50 state governors, the federal District of Washington D.C. and five major self-governing territories, my loyal Cabinet and administration, the Chairman and Joints Chief of Staff: Army, Navy, Air Force, Marines and Coast Guard, loyal and patriotic Congressmen and Congresswomen, will along with the FBI,

Homeland Security, state and local police, protect and uphold our Constitution at home, while our military continues to protect us abroad.

We cannot continue as a country in chaos. We are better than that and I ask all of you, my fellow Americans, to help me bring our great country back and destroy this subversive and evil force festering within our government.

You will not see tanks in the street. You will not see any disruption in your life. What you will see is a vast improvement in how our federal government runs. You are going to start to see things getting done because I'm suspending the legislative branch of our federal government. That's right. I am sending all the House Representatives and all the Senators home until such time as we can determine who was involved in this attempted coup and until such time as they can learn how to get along and work together. I'm shutting down most mainstream media outlets that are part of this subversive force. All other media outlets that profess to be news organizations will be allowed to continue as long as they report the facts and tell the truth. If you are going to continue to report only news that fits your agenda or report fake news, then you must declare yourself a talk show or a tabloid newspaper, not a legitimate news organization. America now more than ever needs someone like Walter Cronkite, "the most trusted man in America". Is there not one journalist with enough integrity to step up and carry his mantle?

What I'm doing to our Congress and the media is what any good parent would do to their children when they are acting like bullies or misbehaving. I'm giving them a time out.

This is a day when all Americans from every walk of life unite in our resolve for justice and peace. America has stood down enemies before, and we will do so this time. None of us will ever forget this day, and let's not forget that freedom is more powerful than fear. I have no doubt America will prevail.

Tonight, I have lifted the sword and have begun the blow to separate the head of the evil snake of embedded subversivism. Help me sever subversivism and move forward to become all that we can be. An America we can all be proud of.

Soon I am going to announce one of the greatest scientific achievements of mankind. It is something which will amaze, excite and benefit America and the world, a dream we have all desired to come true. Until then, I will leave you with this thought inspired and spoken by Robert Kennedy: "There are people in every time and every land who want to stop history in its tracks. They fear the future, mistrust the present, and invoke the security of a comfortable past which, in fact, never existed."

Thank you. God bless you, and may God bless the United States of America.

8:11 P.M. EST

CHAPTER 46

THE WILLARD HOTEL AND THE OVAL OFFICE WASHINGTON, DC 8:13 P.M.

The two lead conspirators were seated in the same private room at the Willard Hotel watching the president's address to the nation on *CNN*. A third member of the conspiracy was on a secure speaker phone, the fourth was absent.

"...and may God bless the United States of America." was the last thing they heard before the TV screen went black.

"Change the channel," demanded Senator Schuster.

Bryan, holding the remote, went to *MSNBC*. Nothing. He tried *CBS*. Nothing. Even *FOX* was black.

"Try *BBC*," suggested Cabell over the speaker.

Bryan searched for it but couldn't find it. "What channel?"

"Bryan, I'm not in Washington. I don't know the channel numbers there," said Cabell.

"Hell, you're the CIA. Can't you call someone?" asked an irritated Bryan.

"Paul, give me the clicker," huffed Schuster.

Schuster started clicking through the channels until he came to something called *i24News* and an anchor person was talking with a picture of President Burk superimposed in the background.

The anchor seemed to be expressing skepticism over President Burk's announcement and seemed to be waiting for direction. She touched her ear and said. "We will be right back after this quick break." The screen went to what seemed to be infomercials promoting Israel.

"Turn it off. We know what Burk said and what he's done. We need to discuss what you're going to do," said Cabell.

Schuster clicked the TV off.

"I can't believe he outed us on live TV. He called us subversive and treasonous without a shred of evidence. At tomorrow's impeachment hearing I will tear him to pieces," promised Speaker Bryan.

"What are you talking about? Evidence? At tomorrow's impeachment hearings, you're going to be the only person there. You two blew it. Everyone will avoid you like the plague. I thought you had this under control but Burk's still alive. We hit 'em with five shots, and he's still alive! Well, that's bad luck for me, and bad luck for you two if you don't take care of your end," warned Cabell and disconnected.

"Was that from the *Godfather*? Doesn't Burk's FBI guy channel movies, too? Do all spooks do that?" asked Bryan.

Ignoring Bryan's analogy Schuster said, "Take care of our end? Burk shut down Congress and all our media. How are we supposed to respond?"

"Twitter," suggested Bryan.

"Twitter? How's that going to help us? I thought only kids use Twitter," said Schuster.

"You'de be surprised who uses it and the power it has," crowed Bryan.

Just then the hotel phone rang and Bryan picked up. "Yes?" asked Bryan.

"Mr. Schuster?" asked the operator.

"One second."

Bryan handed the phone to Schuster, "This is Senator Schuster."

"Please hold for the president."

Schuster turned to Bryan and mouthed, "It's Burk."

"Put it on speaker," said Bryan.

"Good evening, Senator Schuster. How are you and Speaker Bryan tonight?" asked President Burk.

"Spying on us, Mr. President?"

"Have been for some time, actually."

"You won't get away with this, Burk. We have something called a Constitution that prevents someone like you becoming a dictator. The people won't stand for it. Martial law? Please. You're no better than a South American Banana Republic," seethed Schuster.

"Banana Republic. That's a funny analogy, Chuck, and that makes you who, Woody Allen? Keeping with that theme, Chuck, if you and your buddies hadn't attempted a military junta I wouldn't have had to take the actions I did. But, as they say, that's water over the dam and what's done is done. But if you come clean and stop all this nonsense, and permit me to get on with doing the people's business, I might forget about all this. You do know, we have an attack looming against our country and I need to make sure that doesn't happen?"

"Don't know anything about an attack except what I heard from your speech. If you call off your martial law, reconvene Congress and resign, we might forget about all this."

"I wish it were that easy, Chuck. Tomorrow morning when the real unbiased TV, print, and radio news outlets get through with you two and your co-conspirators, you're gonna wish you were dead. But you will be soon because treason is a very serious crime punishable by death."

"You don't have any hard evidence against us, Burk. You only have hearsay and what you have been able to manufacture."

"Don't be so sure about that, Chuckie boy," chortled President Burk as he disconnected.

The Oval Office

"How do you think it went?" asked the president.

"Your speech or the phone call," asked Kelly.

"The speech."

"I think it was over the top. I don't think one American will care that you shut down Congress and the mainstream media. You put all the blame for what's happened in Sofia and the coming terrorist attacks on a subversive force within our government led by Schuster and Bryan. You shut down their only offensive means to fight back and you did it all in under 11 minutes. Brilliant," gushed Kelly.

"I think you had a little something to do with that," said the president.

"Do you think Dumb and Dumber believe you? That you want to work something out with them?" asked Riley.

"Yes. I think they're now desperate. They didn't see martial law coming and will want to believe anything we feed them. Tomorrow the real news will skewer them. Their impeachment hearings will be shut down and they'll have no voice except real news, and they will see right through them," advised Kelly.

CHAPTER 47

Washington, DC December 13

A black Lincoln Navigator came to a stop on First Street directly in front of the Capitol. Two men got out and walked down the arcade towards the Capitol building. The entrance to the Hall of the House of Representatives was on the left and to the right the Senate Chamber. But symbolically today, the two men headed to the main steps in the center of the Capitol, the Great Rotunda.

"I expected to be here this morning holding impeachment hearings against Burk not leading a ten-man march on Washington," bleated a disgusted Senator Schuster.

"We're lucky we have ten people still supporting us after Burk's slap-down speech last night," said Speaker Bryan.

"Who were you able to get to cover this?" asked Senator Schuster.

"All our usual media sources all bailed out because they have either been shut down by Burk's martial law or see us as pariahs. I was able to get the *Pretoria News* from South Africa. Both Stewart and Colbert volunteered but without *Comedy Central* all they could do is stream it on *Facebook*, but now I think that's even been shut down. I did get *RTV* Russia, a couple of *YouTube* channels and a few bloggers," advised Bryan.

"That's just great. We're gonna be on Russian TV and *YouTube*. How the fuck can Burk pull the plug on all our media?" asked Schuster.

"Because he can. His martial law took the Federal Communications Commission away from Congress and put it under Homeland Security," said Bryan.

"All radio, television, print, wire, satellite, and cable in all 50 states shut down. Unimaginable," fumed Schuster. "Unconstitutional."

"Not all. Any media that kisses Burk's ass and his Live and Let Live Party are still open for business," reminded Bryan.

"That's not much but it's a lot more than we got. You couldn't get any big-name TV or press to come out?" asked Schuster.

"O'Reilly had an issue with Burk's wife Kelly Sullivan. I don't know what that was about, but he agreed to help go after Burk, but then he got shit-canned from *FOX*. Besides, *FOX* is also down. I was able to get Al Gore who said he could get *Al Jazeera* to broadcast it tonight. Is that big enough for you?" asked Bryan.

"You stupid fuck. *Al Jazeera*? Are you crazy? Why not have al-Baghdadi do a testimonial for us? Look, in about five minutes we're going to walk up the steps of the Capitol and face a wall of barricades, Capitol Police and a locked down Capitol. I intend to make one of the best performances of my career illuminating Burk's criminal activities and his martial law cover-up. We're getting inside the Capitol and I intend to yell, cry, scream, shed blood, break through the police barricades, and get black jacked. But I'm getting in; and it better be on prime-time TV tonight!" screamed Schuster.

"What about Twitter? We can tweet about the whole thing and get it out to millions," said Bryan.

"Yeah, that and Facebook will help, but most of the people on Facebook and Twitter are young and most don't even know what the US Constitution says about free speech and many don't even know what the Constitution is. We have to get middle America moms and pops everywhere who still tune into the evening news shows. They're the ones who need to turn against Burk. They're the ones who still believe in: mom, baseball, and apple pie."

"Add God, guns, and country to that and you'll get a bingo," suggested Bryan.

"Yeah, and you also get Alabama," said Schuster.

"I thought you had Wolf Blitzer covering this?" asked Bryan.

"He said he might be able to get *BBC* to broadcast it tonight. Wolf has got to be the closest thing this country has to Walter Cronkite so if he can somehow get this on air tonight with *BBC*, tomorrow we could be heroes," said Schuster. "Two brave representatives of the people putting their lives on the line for their country."

Senator Schuster, Speaker Bryan and a small crowd of supporters walked towards the Capitol steps and looked up at the barricade with the Capitol Police behind. There seemed to be plenty of reporters and news crew, but everything would remain in the can unless broadcast outlets could be found. At the bottom of the steps stood Wolf Blitzer, microphone in hand, and a film crew following. It almost seemed like normal except for the absence of satellite broadcasting trucks.

"Senator Schuster, Wolf Blitzer, *CNN*. Would you like to comment on President Burk's allegations of treason made against you and other members of Congress and the military industrial complex last night?"

Speaker Bryan, seeing Al Gore heading his way with an *Al Jazeera* film crew behind, did a quick end run towards a reporter holding an *RTV* sign.

"Yes Wolf, I would," said Senator Schuster. "I categorically deny all those charges made by President Burk. It's a smoke screen he has put out to hide his involvement in the Grand Sofia Hotel kidnapping, bombing, massacre and his attempted assassination of North Korean Supreme Leader Kim Jong-un."

"So, you deny the president's allegations?"

"Categorically. And the president must be impeached, kicked out of office or resign."

"What do you say to the American people who reelected President Burk for four more years? And are you the leader of this subversive force within our government that professes to know what's best for America? President

Burk accused you of trying to destroy his administration. He said the country was on the right track, and that the people gave him four more years and that elections have consequences."

"President Burk has conned everyone. He's not fit to serve and we are going to get to the bottom of it."

"The president seems to disagree with you. He said homegrown terrorist attacks were on the decline. He said his administration fixed the AHA. He solved immigration without mass deportation and didn't have to build a wall. Crime and murder in the inner cities are down. Schools are doing much better and his administration is working on climate change. Jobs numbers are up, the stock market is still positive. He instituted the vice president's pet college debt forgiveness program. The deficit is under control and he has paid down almost a half trillion in debt. Everyone seems to like the new universal sales tax except the IRS. Medicare and Social Security are improving. He sent USA CORP. dividend checks to a large portion of the population. The VA is now providing top-notch service for our vets. What is he doing wrong and what would you do better?" asked Wolf.

"Wolf, he has snookered the American people. He's an opportunist and a carnival barker. Who do you think is going to pay for all that? Do they think it's free? He's the P.T. Barnum of politics and he is making America pay to watch his circus," said Schuster as he started to tremble and tear-up. "I'll tell you who is going to pay: our children and grandchildren and their children." Regaining his composure he continued, "He is digging a deep hole with entitlements and military spending. This martial law is unprecedented and unconstitutional. He has become a dictator no better than Saddam, al-Assad, Stalin, and Hitler. He shut down the only checks and balances that can control him and we can not allow this to continue. I intend to march up these steps with my fellow supporters and fight my way into the hallowed halls of Congress and get on with the people's business," steamed Schuster.

"But for the last four months, Senator, the Senate and Speaker Bryan's House have not been doing the people's business. You had effectively shut Congress down all by yourself. Why are you blaming President Burk for sending you all packing?" asked Wolf.

"That is a flat out lie. We have offered bipartisan support to bills and cooperation requests from Burk's party. It's Dictator Burk's party that has stonewalled," asserted Schuster.

"You deny that al-Baghdadi was in Sofia, Bulgaria to meet with North Korean Leader Kim Jong-un to discuss a nuclear weapon deal where North Korea would supply nuclear bombs to al-Baghdadi for five billion dollars financed by Iran? That these nuclear weapons were going to be used against the United States in a terrorist attack this Christmas?" asked Wolf.

"North Korean Leader Kim Jong-un was in Sofia, Bulgaria to attend and speak at the ASEAN Regional Forum. That I can say for sure. And if Dictator Burk's allegations are correct, what does it matter now? As he said, the weapons buy meeting was bombed out and Baghdadi was captured, so no weapons changed hands and therefore there will be no attack," stated Schuster.

"But isn't that reason enough to hold North Korea and Iran accountable?" asked Wolf.

"Accountable, yes. Sanctions, yes. But war, no."

"Were you at all behind the hotel bombing?"

"Dictator Burk is blaming the horrible bombing of civilians in the Grand Sofia Hotel in Bulgaria on me. Really? Yes, there is a subversive force operating within our government and it's working to disgrace and embarrass the United States and the American people. But it's Dictator Burk, not me who leads this subversive force that is attempting a coup d'état against the Constitution of the United States of America."

"But with your help and the other brave supporters and reporters, the American people will now know the truth and his coup will fail. I intend, with your help, to expose them and bring Dictator Burk and his entire administration down and try them for treason. We'll fight him tooth and nail when he appeals to the baser instincts that diminish America and its greatness that have too often plagued this country and his campaign," said Senator Schuster, as he turned to let Wolf Blitzer know the interview was over.

Senator Schuster started up the steps but turned and whispered to Wolf, "Make sure you get what happens next." Before Wolf could answer, Schuster and Bryan were dashing up the Capitol steps followed by a swelling group of twenty-five supporters and reporters. Guarding the main entrance doors to the Capitol were wooden barricades flanking a retractable belt stanchion, behind which stood a dozen Capitol Police officers. Senator Schuster et al stopped in front of the barricade.

Senator Schuster turned back towards his supporters and the reporters on the steps below, raised his right hand containing a sheet of parchment and said, "My fellow Americans, I hold in my hand the most important foundation, the most sacred document of our great country, the Constitution of the United States of America, signed by George Washington, Alexander Hamilton, Benjamin Franklin, James Madison and other great founding fathers. It was written in the people's blood to protect the rights of all Americans then and now. It begins thusly:

"We the People of the United States, in order to form a more perfect union, establish justice, insure domestic tranquility, provide for the common defense, promote the general welfare, and secure the blessings of liberty to ourselves and our posterity, do ordain and establish this Constitution for the United States of America."

"Article One"

"All legislative Powers herein granted shall be vested in a Congress of the United States, which shall consist of a Senate and House of Representatives."

"The Congress shall have power to, among other things:

Define and punish offences against the law of nations, declare war, raise and support armies, provide and maintain a navy, and to exercise exclusive legislation in all cases whatsoever.

Additionally, the privilege of the writ of habeas corpus shall not be suspended, Congress shall have the authority to remove the president from office because of his inability to discharge the powers and duties of the said office."

"My fellow Americans, our First Amendment rights have been stripped away by Dictator Burk. Dictator Burk can make no law prohibiting the free exercise thereof; or abridging the freedom of speech, or of the press; or the right of the people to peaceably assemble."

"Dictator Burk does not want you to see what is happening here today. He knows you would be outraged and call for his resignation. What House Speaker Bryan and I are about to do may not be seen by you on TV tonight, but we intend to take the first step to reclaim our Constitution. Congress is mandated by the Constitution to legislate the laws of this great country and we intend, if necessary, to shed our blood here today and cross this red line in the sand to reconvene Congress and begin impeachment hearings against Dictator Burk."

With that, Senator Schuster and House Speaker Bryan turned and approached the barricade. In a symbolic gesture of solidarity, they held hands, hollered ohhhh, and charged forward into the barricade and the line of Capitol Police.

At that exact moment, however, the retractable barricade belt was released and sprung back into the opposite stanchion opening a five-foot-wide hole through which Schuster and Bryan dashed through. The enormous Capitol doors flew open and they both continued on through so fast and unimpeded until they lost their balance and toppled forward onto the marble floor of the Capitol Rotunda, seriously scraping both their knees and palms. The last thing viewers saw was Senator Schuster and Speaker Bryan lying on the Rotunda floor holding up, for all the world to see, their scraped palms and knees. Redness and a little blood began to appear on the heel of Schuster's palm as he raised it towards the camera. Suddenly, the doors swung closed and the stanchion belt was pulled out and reattached to the opposite stanchion. The cameras continued to roll as Capitol Police Captain Brian Fitzgerald said, loud enough for all to hear, "All they had to do was ask and I would have let them in."

One reporter later commented that it reminded him of the movie where Butch Cassidy and the Sundance kid jumped off the cliff, only much less inspiring.

CHAPTER 48

The Oval Office 6:30 p.m.

It was now 11:30 p.m. in London, and 6:30 p.m. in Washington when *BBC* broadcast the *CNN* coverage of Wolf Blitzer's earlier interview with New York Senator Chuck Schuster in front of the Capitol.

Inside the Oval Office, President Tommy Burk, Kelly, Nicholas, Riley, Stanton, SecTres Mike Bloomfield, AG Fare, General Mickey Finn, Secret Service Director Bounty and Max watched the broadcast with disdain, shock, amazement and finally with fits of laughter as Senator Schuster and Speaker Bryan ran through the open Capitol doors holding hands, screaming and tumbling to the floor.

"What the hell?" chirped Riley trying to speak while laughing and tearing up.

"Those poor pathetic clowns. They just don't know when to stop," added Kelly, choking back laughter.

"I have to promote Captain Brian Fitzgerald for providing us with all the entertainment. 'All they had to do was ask'. Ha!" howled Bounty.

"Ruff," added Max.

The camera then focused on Wolf Blitzer as he began to sum up what just happened, "Well, there you have it. Senator Chuck Schuster and Speaker Bryan have landed, literally, back on the Capitol floor." He paused for a moment and an uncharacteristic smile appeared for a brief second. "You have it in his own words. He's the victim and President Burk is a dictator, or as he's now calling him, 'Dictator Burk', the one responsible for America's problems. Who's right-who's wrong? You decide. One thing I know for sure, President Burk has declared martial law and not only shut down Congress, but shut down all information to the American public except what he deems acceptable. He has gone against the US Constitution and that is never a good thing. I'm here broadcasting to you tonight through the good graces of the *British Broadcasting Corporation.* I hope to be invited back into your homes tomorrow as *CNN*, but if not, I'll see you on *BBC*. Wolf Blitzer with *CNN*, the most trusted name in news."

"The most trusted name in news? *CNN*? Really, Wolf? I think there is a disconnect between your slogan and your show," mocked Kelly.

"Look. People are already protesting the media shutdown, the whole First Amendment thing and all. They don't seem to mind that we sent Congress packing. Hell, the states are loving having more power to do what they feel is best for their state without Washington meddling. They may not want to go back," SecTres Mike Bloomfield chimed in.

"But the protesting may get worst over the media and free speech thing. If I felt I could trust them not to champion the subversives, stop the fake news and just report the truth, I might let them come back," suggested President Burk.

"Why not do it on a case by case basis? If they say they will be honest and stick to facts, and believe me I don't care if they say bad things about us if they are true, let them back on the air, print or online. Keep their news fair and unbiased and they stay on. Fake it or start towing their party's line and they are out for good, or at least as a 'news organization,'" stated Kelly punctuating news organizations with her fingers for parentheses.

"That's a thought, but we have to be ready in case the protesting turns to rioting," advised the president.

"*Wag the Dog*," said Riley.

"Excuse me?" said President Burk, knowing full well where his partner was heading but played along for the benefit of the others.

"The 1997 movie with Hoffman and DeNiro. It's about a scandal at the White House. The president is accused of fondling a young Girl Scout visiting the Oval Office just a few weeks before election day. That, thank God, is not our problem. Robert DeNiro plays a notorious political spin doctor called to a secret midnight meeting at the White House underground command bunker by Anne Heche's character, the president's adviser, where she asks for his help for a way to divert the news of the scandal when it breaks in the newspapers the next day," Riley explained.

"We also don't have a newspapers problem," added Kelly.

"That's true. Anyway, DeNiro suggests creating an artificial war for television only to distract the American public and let the president get on with the job at hand ... thus protecting the free world. DeNiro and Heche fly to Hollywood where they hire a Hollywood producer, Dustin Hoffman, to help fabricate this non-existent war with the selected country of Albania to divert the public with the real news about the president's problems. All we do is swap out scandal and Albania and insert martial law and NOKO and we have a bingo!" exclaimed Riley.

"Are you suggesting we attack North Korea to take everyone's mind off our troubles here at home?" asked AG Bill Fare.

SecDef Stanton held up his hand for quiet and said, "If we were to strike North Korea, Kim Jong-un's regime would retaliate by unleashing its conventional weaponry lined up on the demilitarized zone. Their weaponry is reliable, unlike their missiles, and would cause major devastation in South Korea. North Korea has a tremendous amount of artillery right opposite Seoul. The Second Corps of the Korean People's Army stationed at Kaesong on the northern side of the DMZ has about 500 artillery pieces, and this is just one army corps. All the artillery pieces in the Second Corps can reach the northern outskirts of Seoul, just 30 miles from the DMZ, but the largest projectiles could fly to the south of the capital. About 25 million people — or half of the South Korean population — live in the greater Seoul metropolitan area…"

Riley tried to lighten it up a bit, "I was just saying…"

But Stanton would not relent, "Moreover, about half of North Korea's artillery pieces are multiple rocket launchers, including 18 to 36 of the huge

300mm launchers that Pyongyang has bragged about. The 300mm guns could probably fire eight rounds every 15 minutes and have a range of about 44 miles. If North Korea were to start unleashing its artillery on the South, it would be able to fire about 4,000 rounds an hour. There would be 2,811 fatalities in the initial volley and 64,000 people could be killed that first day, most them in the first three hours. Some of the victims would be American because we have about 30,000 troops in South Korea. The higher estimates for the 300mm rocket launcher's range — up to 65 miles — would put the U.S. Air Force base at Osan and the new military garrison at Pyeongtaek, the replacement for the huge base in Seoul, within reach."

"But such action would also be devastating for North Korea," countered General Finn, "because our three divisions and South Korean militaries have spent decades developing their counter-battery capability, as well as developing plans for air strikes to take out North Korea's facilities. The U.S. and South Korean response would be immediate. We have assets along the DMZ dedicated for doing this job and counter-battery units trained to conduct these missions."

"Senator Lindsey Graham said this week that he supported striking North Korea to stop it from developing the capability to reach the United States with a missile — even if that came at a huge cost for the region. He said it would be terrible, but the war would be over in Korea, and not here," affirmed Nicholas.

"Yeah, well, Graham is an asshole and now he's back in South Carolina fuckin' with everybody there, and having to attend town hall meetings," said Riley.

"He was a colonel in the Air Force," stated Nicholas.

"He was a judge in the Air Force, a lawyer for God's sake. He didn't have to fight. He never flew a plane," corrected AG Fare.

"Look, said the president, not taking the bait, I believe SecDef Stanton and General Finn are both correct. And of course, it concerns me, but we can't appear weak to our allies. I have something in mind for a show, not unlike *Wag the Dog,* but I've always believed that with good common sense and engagement, cooler heads in both North Korea and the United States will prevail. All right. We have a lot to do and you all know your part. See you all Friday morning at 7 a.m. in the Situation Room to reconvene our defense strategy against the Christmas attacks," said the president.

The December 16th edition of the *Wall Street Journal* (one of the few big print and online papers that hadn't been shut down) front page headlines read;

President Burk Sends Strong Warning To North Korea And Iran: "Your Actions Threaten The World"

Two days ago President Burk authorized a carrier battle group to sail to the Korean Peninsula. To Supreme Leader Kim Jong-un and North Korea, President Burk taunted, "If you want to destroy the United States but were not able to reach us, well here we are! We're right off your coast in the Sea of Japan."

Another battle group is now in the Persian Gulf off the coast of Iran. President Burk said, "Supreme Leader Ali Khamenei, this is no red line in the sand. This is our blue line in the sea and if you want to buy weapons then we have a thousand Tomahawk Missiles pointed at Tehran. Just give us the word and they're yours."

CHAPTER 49

PYONGYANG, NORTH KOREA
DECEMBER 16

Inside the Workers' Party building in Pyongyang, the real Kim Jong-un, Supreme Leader of the Democratic People's Republic of Korea (DPRK) sat around a large table surrounded by his top generals. Kim is also Marshal and Supreme Commander of the Korean People's Army. Also in attendance is 68-year old General Hwang Pyong-so who replaced General Kim Yong Chol (who disappeared along with Kim's doppelganger in the Grand Sofia Hotel explosion), as the new Director of the Reconnaissance General Bureau. General Hwang Pyong-so is now one of the DPRK's most senior intelligence community's managers, and he has been a deputy director of the DPRK intelligence community for the last ten years.

North Korea's Reconnaissance General Bureau (RGB) is responsible for clandestine operations. The RGB includes six bureaus charged with operations, reconnaissance, technology and cyber, overseas intelligence, inter-Korean talks, and service support.

The Korean People's Army (KPA) constitutes the military force of North Korea and Kim Jong-un is the Supreme Commander of the Korean People's Army and Chairman of the Central Military Commission. The KPA defense force consists of five branches: Ground Force, the Navy, the Air Force, the

Strategic Rocket Forces, and the Special Operation Force. The Worker-Peasant Red Guards also come under the control of the KPA.

Ground Force. As of 2013, the US Department of Defense reported the ground forces in number totals 950,000 in strength. 5,500 tanks, 2,200 infantry fighting vehicles, 8,600 artillery pieces, and 4,800 multiple rocket launcher systems. These forces are garrisoned along major north-south lines of communication that provide rapid, easy access to avenues of approach into South Korea. The KPAGF has positioned massive numbers of artillery pieces, including some fakes, especially its longer-range systems, close to the Demilitarized Zone (DMZ) that separates the two Koreas.

The Korean People's Navy (KPN), The KPN strength during the 1990s was centered about 40,000 to 60,000 members enforce. The last projected strength (2008) was at about 60,000. There are some 810 vessels including three frigates and 70 submarines: approximately 20 Romeo class submarines (1,800 tons), 40 Sang-O-class submarines (300 tons) and 10 midget submarines including the Yono-class submarine (130 tons). The North Korean navy is considered a brown water navy and operates mainly within the 50-kilometer exclusion zone. The fleet consists of east and west coast squadrons, which cannot support each other in the event of war with South Korea.

The Korean People's Army Air Force (KPAAF). The KPAF is the second largest branch of the Korean People's Army comprising an estimated 110,000 members. It possesses 940 aircraft of several types; mostly of Soviet and Chinese origin. Its primary task is to defend North Korean airspace.

The Strategic Rocket Forces aka the Missile Guidance Bureau is the strategic missile defense branch of North Korea. The SMF is an important division of the Korean People's Army that oversees North Korea's nuclear and conventional strategic defense missiles. It is mainly armed with surface-to-surface missiles of Soviet and Chinese design, as well as domestically developed long-range missiles. Silo-based launch: South Korean government sources are reported to have stated that a missile silo complex is located south of Paektu Mountain near the Chinese border. The silos are reportedly designed for mid- to long-range missiles, but it is not clear if all of them are operational.

Launch pads: Launching pads are required for the more sophisticated Taepodong-1/2, as their liquid propellant is difficult to store and the missile must be fueled immediately before launch. This launching method poses a significant risk, as the site itself is extremely vulnerable to airstrikes. Launching pads can be used to test different types of SRBM, IRBM, and ICBMs, and to launch space satellites, but they are of little value if any of these missiles are to be deployed as a strategic weapon.

Mobile launcher vehicles: North Korea extensively uses mobile launchers for its missiles, including the Rodong-1 and the Hwasong-10. These are hard to detect and significantly improve survivability.

Submarine/ship-based launch: The Korean People's Navy is not known to have any ballistic missile submarines in its inventory, though has possibly started research and development on a capability to launch ballistic missiles from submarines.

The North Korean Special Operation Force (NKSOF), officially the Korean People's Army Special Operation Force, consists of specially equipped and trained "elite" military units trained to perform military, political, or psychological operations for North Korea. The units are active in testing the defenses of South Korea and have been detected operating in or around South Korea many times in the decades since the end of the Korean War. There are about 180,000 special operations forces soldiers. The missions of Special Operation Forces are to breach the fixed defense of South Korea, to create a "second front" in the enemy's rear area, and to conduct battlefield and strategic reconnaissance.

The Worker-Peasant Red Guards is a paramilitary force in North Korea. It is the largest civil defense force in the DPRK. The Worker-Peasant Red Guard militia, 3.5 million strong, is organized on a provincial/town/city/village level, and structured on a brigade, battalion, company, and platoon basis. The militia maintains infantry small arms, with some mortars, field guns, and anti-aircraft guns and even modernized older equipment such as multiple rocket launchers.

"They're here, my leader. The American carrier fleet is off the coast just 230 kilometers (150 miles) from our southernmost town of Kosong, in the Sea of Japan," said General Hwang Pyong-so, the leader of the North Korea's Reconnaissance General Bureau.

"General. I refer to that body of water as The Sea of Monkeys. Can we reach them?" asked Supreme Leader Kim Jong-un.

All heads turned towards Lt. Gen. Kim Rak-gyom, commander of the Strategic Rocket Forces.

"Yes, my Leader. We can reach them," assured Gen. Kim Rak-gyom.

Kim Jong-un smiled and rubbed his hands together and the others around the table joined in. But just as fast the supreme leader stood, stopped smiling and said, "But can we hit them, general?"

It was the one question General Kim Rak-gyom and the other generals and admirals around the table dreaded: the direct question. As his leader sat down he thought whether to answer truthfully and admit he could not guarantee a direct hit because his missiles were not that accurate. If he told the truth, he would have to say that the American ships were equipped with very accurate defense systems that would destroy any of his missiles that got even close. If he suggested that the American Tomahawk missile retaliation would be devastating, and if he told his leader that the American Block II TLAM had a range of 2,500km (1,500 miles) and a 1,000-lb. class military warhead or a W80 nuclear warhead could destroy Pyongyang he would be asked to leave the room. He would also be embarrassed, asked to resign, asked to relinquish all his wealth, power and property. His family would be relocated, ostracized and disgraced. He would then be lined up against the wall and shot if the leader felt compassion. If not, he would be slowly fed alive feet first into a wood chipper. *If we could only get our SK-17 Scud anti-ship ballistic missile working properly,* he thought.

Consequently, General Kim Rak-gyom replied, "Upon your order my leader, we will destroy the entire American fleet."

Kim Jong-un jumped up again, this time more animated, waving his hands, smiling, laughing and said, "This American fool Burk has now justified to the world why we need to have nuclear weapons: to protect our people and our country from this type of imperial aggression and invasion. Seon'gun!"

All the other generals and admirals joined their leader's exuberance, except General Kim Rak-gyom. He knew that if given the order he and everyone else around the table, his family and tens of thousands more would be dead 15 minutes later. Suddenly, the thought appealed to him.

Tehran, Iran

Approximately 6331 kilometers (3,934 miles) away in the office of The Ministry of Intelligence of the Islamic Republic of Iran (MOIS), sat 62-year-old General Mahmoud Alavi, an Iranian cleric, politician and the minister of intelligence, 77-year-old Sayyed Ali Khamenei, Supreme Leader of Iran and Abu Fatima al-Jaheishi, the leader of ISIL in Iraq. Also around the table sat Major General Mohammad Bagheri, Chief of Staff, Major General Ataollah Salehi Commander of the Army. IRIA, Major General Mohammad Ali Jafari, Commander of the Revolutionary Guard. IRGC, Rear Admiral Habibollah Sayyari Commander of Navy of the Islamic Republic of Iran Army. NEDAJA, Brigadier General Hassan Shah-Safi Commander of the Islamic Republic of Iran Air Force (IRIAF), Brigadier General Farzad Esmaili Commander of the Islamic Republic of Iran Air Defense Force (IRIAF), and Brigadier General Hossein Ashtari, Commander of the Law Enforcement (police) LEF.

"They're here, my Leader. The American carrier fleet is off the coast just 95 kilometers (59 miles) from Bandar Bushehr in the Arabian Gulf," said Mahmoud Alavi, minister of intelligence.

"General. We refer to that holy body of water as the Persian Gulf. We are not Arabs. Can we reach them?" asked Supreme Leader Sayyed Ali Khamenei, speaking modern Persian.

All heads turned towards Brigadier General Farzad Esmaili, Commander of the Islamic Republic of Iran Air Defense Force.

"Yes, my Leader, we can reach them," assured General Farzad Esmaili.

Khamenei smiled and rubbed his hands together and the others around the table joined in. But just as fast the supreme leader stood, he stopped smiling and said, "But can we hit them, general?"

It was the one question General Farzad Esmaili and the other generals and admirals around the table dreaded. The direct question. As his leader sat down he thought if he answered truthfully and said he could not guarantee a direct hit because his missiles are not that accurate. If he told the truth and said the American ships were equipped with a very accurate defense system that would destroy any of his missiles that got even close. If he suggested that the American Tomahawk missile retaliation, would be devastating. If he told his Leader that the American Block II TLAM had a range of 2,500km (1,500 miles) and a 1,000-lb. class military warhead or a W80 nuclear warhead could destroy Tehran he would be asked to leave the room. He would be embarrassed, asked to resign, asked to relinquish all his wealth, power and property. His family would be relocated, ostracized and disgraced. He would then be taken outside, dressed in an orange jumpsuit and beheaded, if the leader felt compassion. If not, he would be put in a cage, doused with gasoline and burned to death. *If only North Korea would sell us their SK-17 Scud anti-ship ballistic missile,* he thought.

Rather, General Farzad Esmaili replied, "Upon your order, my leader, we will destroy their entire fleet."

Supreme Leader Sayyed Ali Khamenei rose up again this time more animated; waving his hands to heaven, smiling, and said, "This Satan Burk has now justified to the world why we need to have nuclear weapons. To protect our people and our country from this type of imperial aggression and invasion. Allah Akbar."

All the other generals and admirals joined their Leaders exuberance, except General Farzad Esmaili. He knew that if he was given the order he and everyone else around the table, his family and tens of thousands more would be dead 15 minutes later. Suddenly, the thought appealed to him.

CHAPTER 50

The Situation Room Washington, DC December 16

Most of the inner circle were already assembled in the situation room when President Burk, Kelly, Nicholas, and Riley entered. President Burk sat at the head of the conference table with Kelly, Riley, and Nicholas close by.

"Good morning. I trust you all saw the *Wall Street Journal* this morning. Any feedback yet, Matt?" asked the president.

Secretary of State Matt Walsh and his staff had been on the phones since 4 a.m. speaking with South Korean President Hwang Kyo-ahn, Japan President Shinzo Abe, China President Xi Jinping, Great Britain Prime Minister Theresa May, German Chancellor Angela Merkel, Israel Prime Minister Benjamin Netanyahu, and Russia President Vladimir Putin. All had received calls from President Burk the previous day giving them a heads up on his decision to send carrier battle groups to the Korean Peninsula and to the Red Sea off the coast of Iran as payback for both Pyongyang's and Tehran's attempt to supply WMD's to al-Baghdadi to attack the United States.

"Want the short or the long?" asked Secretary of State Walsh.

"The short."

"Everyone responded as expected," said Secretary of State Walsh.

President Burk waited and when nothing further came, asked, "How about the long then?"

Secretary of State Walsh placed a piece of paper on the table, adjusted his reading glasses and began, "South Korean President Hwang Kyo-ahn appreciates your support, but warns against taunting Kim Jong-un. "Kim is crazy and may take the bait and attack Seoul." Japan President Shinzo Abe sent two destroyers to join our carrier battle force. China President Xi Jinping wants you to remove the carrier battle group immediately to avoid escalating the situation. He, "Hopes all parties remain restrained instead of intensifying the situation." Great Britain Prime Minister Theresa May is with you no matter what. German Chancellor Angela Merkel said, "Nein!" Israel Prime Minister Benjamin Netanyahu wants us to immediately take out all of Iran's nuclear enrichment and missile sites. North Korea's Rodong Sinmun, the newspaper of the North's ruling workers is threatening that its revolutionary forces are combat-ready to sink a U.S. nuclear-powered aircraft carrier with a single strike. They're also starting to arrest US citizens."

"That's never good. What about Russia?"

"Russia President Vladimir Putin said he will watch closely what the United States does in North Korea and Iran, but cautions us to be very wary of China coming to North Korea's aid and Pakistan coming to both North Korea's and Iran's aid. His parting message probably affirms everyone's position except Great Britain and Israel's. Putin said, and I quote: 'играть курица с петухом и не начать войну земли в Азии.'"

"Matt?"

"Sorry. That translates roughly to: "Don't play chicken with a rooster and don't start a land war in Asia."

"Thank you, Matt. I've always agreed with General MacArthur's advice to JFK and Johnson in 1963: 'Anyone wanting to commit American ground forces to the mainland of Asia should have his head examined.' Looking directly at CIA Director Bader the president added, "Unfortunately, President Johnson didn't take that advice. As far as playing chicken, I agree. Both Kim

Jong-un and Supreme Leader Sayyed Ali Khamenei are both, in my opinion, fuckin' nuts and I have no desire to play chicken with either of them. Besides, our battle groups are out of their effective missile range."

"Then why send the carrier battle groups in the first place?"

"That's a good question, Matt. I was actually sending the message to China and Russia, but it had a residual effect."

"And that is?"

"That I'm also fuckin' nuts."

Everyone around the table became very quiet while contemplating what President Burk just said. Not only was Burk nuts, but so was Riley and now the both were in total control of the country.

Jimmy Cagney and Michael Corleone, thought DCI Bader.

"Okay, said President Burk, turning to Dr. Provenzano, "are the jumpers back?"

"They are, and I have to say they should get the *Ground Hog Day* medal. This is their fifth jump to Cleveland 2017 and it's been the same thing every time. The attacks are still happening and real. If we don't act and act soon we're going to be in a world of shit this time next week."

"We have seven days till lower Manhattan gets hit on Black Friday and fifteen days till we lose the East Coast on New Year's Eve," warned SecDef Stanton. "We have to stop the tunnel bomb sometime between this Tuesday the 20th and Thursday the 22nd. If the bomber doesn't take possession of the suitcase bomb until Friday, it gets real tight. We may not be able to send the jumpers back to see if we succeeded in preventing the tunnel bomb. Nevertheless, we have all been working to that end and we'll be ready to move Tuesday."

"Okay. But you have to take it out before Friday. I want the jumpers back in afterward. We have to know for sure that we got it or we need time to evacuate." Looking at FBI Director Riley, President Burk continued, "Tell me where we are on the lower Manhattan Black Friday tunnel attack."

"Thanks to the jumpers investigation, Assistant Director in Charge, ADC New York City Michael Hoar, and his team have our terrorist driving into Newark, parking and wheeling a large suitcase into the PATH terminal. She goes from New Jersy to the World Trade Center Station and detonates at 6:16 p.m. during rush hour just short of the World Trade Center Station imploding the Hudson Tunnel and river, destroying the station, flooding most of lower Manhattan, and precariously underpinning the Freedom Tower. Thanks to the jumpers, we have film of our bomber and were able to trace her movements back. She's a 22-year-old Berkeley graduate, blond, attractive surfer type, currently living in Santa Monica at her parent's house on 10th Street right off Santa Monica Boulevard," advised FBI Director Riley.

"Who is she?"

"Sheryl Armstrong, the all-American girl. We tracked her car plates; she rented from Hertz, and we were able to get her rental agreement, she isn't trying to hide. We know she flies from LAX this Monday the 19th aboard Jet Blue flight 688 leaving L.A. at 9:10 p.m. to Boston, then on to Newark arriving 9:53 a.m. on Tuesday the 20th. We know she won't have the bomb so we'll wait to pick her up after she takes possession and then we'll also get her accomplice. We know where she is staying in Jersey and what time she leaves for the PATH train to Manhattan. From private and municipal cams we know where she sits and what the suitcase looks like. We'll take her and her accomplices out as soon as they make contact. We have her computer and cell bugged. Everything she has been doing, everyone she has been talking to since last week, we know all about it. We have her motel room and rental car bugged. We have a pretty good idea who her accomplices are and when and where the handoff will occur. That's when we take them down," explained Riley.

"So when do you think that will be?"

"Thursday night, Friday morning."

"Damm! If it's Thursday night we can send the jumpers back. If it's Friday morning it's too late," said Dr. Provenzano.

"Good job Ray. But take her out before Friday; regardless. Okay Director Bader, regarding the EMP over the East Coast, where are we?" asked the president.

"Also, thanks to the jumpers investigation, we have eyes on the Nicole Danial, a 90-foot commercial fishing boat out of Port de Grave,

Newfoundland. We have planted tracking and a/v devices on board and before she sails, we'll plant an explosive device on the hull under the water line. This is the ship that will carry and fire the EMP off Long Island. It's registered out of Newfoundland and will be hijacked December 26th. and not reported missing till the 30th. Somewhere along the 1,000 mile trip to Long Island, the terrorists take her and bring aboard the missile, warhead, and launcher. We have to wait to move till after the ship is hijacked and the missile is on board. We know the seven-man crew will all be killed by the hijackers. Unfortunately, we can't warn them because one or more may be an expendable accomplice," said DCI Bader.

"So what's the outside date for taking them down?"

"Anytime before the ball drops," advised Bader.

"I would argue with you on your choice of words, director. Both you and Director Riley need to take your terrorist out leaving enough time for the doctor to send the jumpers back and get a clean bill or we go to Plan B," said the president.

"What's Plan B?" asked DCI Bader.

"You don't want to know," sighed Riley.

CHAPTER 51

THE OVAL OFFICE WASHINGTON, DC

Back in the Oval Office, Kelly, Riley, and Nicholas, Dr. Provenzano and Max joined President Burk on the two couches.

I didn't want to get into this back there with Director Bader. I'm not sure I trust him, and I'm still pissed off he can't find Cabell."

"Or he doesn't want to."

"Exactly."

"So, what's plan B?" asked Nicholas.

"I haven't the foggiest," said Riley turning to the president. "Sarge?"

"Me neither, but he'll know," said President Burk. How about we take Marine One north to the special place and ask him."

"Tommy, what are you talking about? He's dead. You're so morbid," gasped Kelly.

"You're right. Why don't you stay here? The Captain, Max and I will go?" said the president.

"Ruff," barked Max.

The cabin to which President Burk was looking down upon from Marine One was that special place. It was in Maine, two miles north of a town with the peculiar name of Moscow. The scenic Benedict Arnold Trail, named for Arnold, after his unsuccessful attempt to capture Canada before he became a traitor, winds northward through Moscow on its way to Quebec. In September of 1775, early in the American Revolutionary War, Colonel Benedict Arnold led a force of 1,100 Continental Army troops on an expedition from Cambridge, Massachusetts to the gates of Quebec City. The invasion failed, but passing back through the area, one of his men, Johnathan Colburn, remained. He married and had six children. Johnathan Colburn built a two-room cabin by the lake two miles north of a small town. In November of 1812, a petition was signed to try to incorporate the town. The town was finally given the name Moscow, after the city that was burned by the Russians in 1812 to dislodge the French.

Seven years ago, Tommy Burk (before he became president) and his friend and his friend's German Shepherd refurbished it. The building of the cabin for all three was therapy, pure and simple. His friend had conducted the research and knew the property's history, although the realtor who sold him the property didn't, and his friend didn't feel it necessary to enlighten him.

The cabin was a real cabin that sat on twelve acres, bordered a lake to the west and two thousand acres of reserve north, east, and south, all in the shadow of Wolf Mountain. The nearest neighbors were in Moscow two miles distant. The 650-square foot cabin was one level with two sections, a front section, and back section. The front was a combination kitchen/dining room and library, while the back had the main bedroom, guest bedroom, and a bath. In the wall separating the library and the main bedroom was a double-sided open fireplace. The cabin, despite its isolation, had all the creature comforts: hot and cold running water, a propane gas stove, solar and wind generated DC power which through an inverter was converted to AC. There was no TV, but they did have a direct satellite internet connection. It even had a flushing toilet, hot shower, and a dishwasher. From the outside, Johnathan Colburn might have recognized the cabin, but from the inside, it might as well have been something from outer space.

The president's friend was Israel Colburn. Colburn was a Southie, born in 1949 in the predominantly Irish community of South Boston. His da was

Irish, and his mother was Jewish. He had wavy jet-black hair and amazing turquoise eyes, a solid build, six foot tall and ruggedly handsome.

He had a great life growing up in the 50's but then came Vietnam. By March of 1967, he was six months into his Vietnam tour, as a sergeant and tank commander attached to the 7th Marines. Tanks, especially the 50-ton behemoth, M-48 Patton medium battle tank, and Vietnam didn't go well together. The tank tracks got stuck in the rice paddies or broke-up in the hills. Where most of the ground support was needed, the tanks couldn't go. Sergeant Israel Colburn met Captain Raymond Riley and Sergeant Tommy Burk while accompanying Golf Company 2/7 on a search and destroy mission in Duc Phu. They worked well together and ran more missions until things started heating up 4,500 miles away in the Sinai Desert. The Six Day War was about to begin with the State of Israel fighting for its life against its Arab neighbors. Because Colburn was half Jew and an experienced tank commander, and because he volunteered and was accepted by Israel (the state), and Uncle Sam in its infinite wisdom allowed him to go and fight in the Six Day War. Sergeant Israel Colburn fought well and became one of only a handful of active American servicemen to have participated in tank warfare on this scale. Although he and his crew all sustained injuries, the Israeli Defense Force did not give medals for wounds. They did however, award Sergeant Israel Colburn their second highest award: The Medal of Courage, which his company and platoon commanders, and especially his crew, all agreed he deserved. He was awarded the medal by General Ariel Sharon. Colburn was introduced to Sharon by his Company Commander, Captain Ezar Bitton, as Sergeant Israel Colburn. "We call him Icy," said Captain Bitton. When Sharon asked why they called him by his initials instead of his name, Captain Bitton said, "No, general, not IC, it's Icy. The men and I have seen Israel Colburn in combat, and he has ice cold blood running through his veins. We now call him 'Icy,' because he's cold and fearless in battle, not because of his initials."

After the Six Day War, and Camp Pendleton, California, Colburn received an honorable discharge and left the Marines. Israel traveled to Northern Ireland during the Troubles. He no longer commanded tanks, but every Marine was a basic rifleman first. He helped the IRA in their fight against the Paras and the Ulster Volunteer Force. He then went on as a mercenary to Pakistan, Rhodesia, Cambodia, Lebanon, Laos, Angola, and El Salvador. He fought against China in the Vietnam-China War.

After he solved all the world's problems, he thought it time to let his bones and wounds rest and heal. Israel Colburn then became a partner in the Cambridge law firm of Beston Servienti and Colburn. His clients knew there was no Beston or Servienti, just Colburn, and his assistant. They didn't get any walk-ins; they weren't listed in the phone book; they had no website, Twitter or Facebook accounts. They were strictly referral. Beston Servienti and Colburn, known to the trade as Best Served Cold, didn't handle litigation. Their international clientele came to Beston Servienti and Colburn seeking one thing and one thing only. Revenge. Best Served Cold, or as those really in the know called it, Best Served Icy don't litigate, they eliminate.

Israel Colburn remained friends with Sergeant Tommy Burk, now President Burk, and Captain Riley, now FBI Director Riley. When they were alone or in very close company the three would often revert to their nom de guerre, war names of Icy, Sarge, and Captain. But not recently. President Burk introduced Israel to Faith Knoll, a famous country recording star, and romance blossomed until Faith while doing a USO show in Afghanistan, was kidnaped by someone from Colburn's past. President Burk called Colburn back into service and Israel Colburn, aka Icy, demonstrated to the world what happens when America is forced into the gutter. Icy, an Irish Jew from Boston, and his wonder dog Natasha, both super-predators, taught the world how to deal with terrorists. America and the world held their breath as they went on for a thrill ride past the predictable, towards the unspeakable, and into the deep darkness of the abyss, but unfortunately, both paid the ultimate price. Israel Colburn and Natasha died on Wolf Mountain at the hands of a Russian Spetsnaz hit team.

"I called ahead and had Timmy open the cabin and get a fire going," said Riley.

Timmy was Timmy Logan, the son of Moscow's mayor; he was the boy who befriended Israel Colburn and Natasha, and now at the request of Riley, looked after the cabin. Timmy was now almost 14 and heading for a career in journalism.

Marine One slowed and came in for a soft landing in the open space behind the cabin. Three Secret Service agents exited followed by President Burk, Riley, and Max. The agents were notified about Timmy and allowed him to come forward and greet the president, Riley, and Max.

"Wow, Max you got so big!" said an excited Timmy when he saw Max. Max made a big fuss over Timmy. They hadn't seen each other since he was a puppy, but he still remembered Timmy. Max ran around the cabin and up the steps looking for his old friend Natasha, but she was nowhere to be found. There was about a foot of old snow on the ground and it looked and felt like more was on its way. The four headed into the cabin and the warm fire.

Out on the highway between the cabin and Moscow, Deputy Hinds spoke into his patrol car radio, "Deputy Hinds to Chief Pruitt."

"Go ahead, deputy," responded Police Chief Jim Pruitt.

"They're back."

CHAPTER 52

Moscow, Maine

"How have things been going, Timmy," asked the president as he sat down after stoking the fire.

"Quiet," declared Timmy. "Nothing much happens here, well except when you guys come. We still hear the wolves howling up on the mountain, the town still talks about what happened and I miss Mr. Colburn and Natasha."

"I'll bet you do," said Riley as he gave a wary look towards the president.

"Still want to be a reporter like Mr. Sweeney?" asked the president.

"Oh, yes, but I don't think I'll ever find a story that tops what happened when the Russians came to Moscow," replied Timmy.

"Timmy, you never know what you'll find if you know where to look," said President Burk turning to give Director Riley a grin and a knowing wink.

"I guess, but I still have another couple years left before I can apply to college."

"Any ideas where?"

"Mr. Sweeney said the best school for journalism is Columbia University in New York, but my dad said it's too expensive."

"How are your grades?"

"Straight A's."

"Well, you keep that up and I'll talk to your dad. I know someone at Columbia and if your grades are good and your dad agrees, I think I can get you a scholarship. How's that sound?"

"That would be great, Mr. President. But you know, said Timmy, mimicking the presidents grin and a wink, I might have to do a story on you someday."

"Well, I would welcome that as long as it's the truth and nothing but. Deal?"

"Deal."

"Timmy, thanks for looking after the cabin and opening it up for us. Can I have a State Police drive you home? There's a car close by," said Riley.

"No thanks. I'll just walk home through the woods. My dad doesn't mind now that I'm older."

Timmy got up and President Burk and Max walked him to the door. Timmy knelt, and hugged Max and Max thanked Timmy with a lick. The president shook his hand and Timmy and Max ran down the steps and into the woods. Max did his business and came back up to the president. They both stood there, eyes fixed on where Timmy disappeared into the woods. "Yeah, boy, I see him too. He's got the investigative reporter blood in him and smells a story, and do we have one to give him. Come on boy, let's go inside; we have work to do."

"Are we gonna pull out the Ouija board or what?" asked Riley.

"Why don't we pull out the Jameson, Bushmill, and cigars and see what happens," answered the president.

Riley got up and opened the sideboard and removed a silver tray containing two identical Waterford Diamond Square crystal decanters, each with a silver gorget identifying one as containing Jameson Limited Reserve and the other as Bushmill Old Single Malt. Also on the tray were three Waterford Diamond 7 ounce straight sided crystal tumblers, three Montecristo Cuban cigars, a wedge cutter and an old engraved Zippo lighter.

The president removed both decanter stoppers and poured one finger of Jameson's and one finger of Bushmills into each tumbler. As he was pouring he said, "I am pouring one finger of each into each glass because of an old tale of a widely-accepted Irish-American version that Jameson is Catholic whiskey and Bushmills is Protestant whiskey."

"Though we have never asked nor discussed our spiritual preference, but assuming we are one or the other, I wanted to cover the all the bases."

He picked up his tumbler, handed one to Riley, and left the other on the tray. Max came over and sat between both. "To God," said President Burk.

"To the Queen," replied Riley.

Max alerted. He got up, growled and started to run around the cabin.

"Whoa, boy. What do you got?"

A creaking noise came from behind the wall, then a low deep guttural growl. Max tore over to the bookcase sliding to a halt on the slippery wood floor. Suddenly a three-foot section of the bookcase slid away revealing a narrow stairway. Max backed away as shadows then ghosts appeared. It was them.

Israel Colburn and Natasha entered the room. President Burk, Director Riley, and Max sat there in total silence and stared as the ghosts came closer. Natasha walked over to Max, neither tail was wagging. They were feeling each other out. Israel Colburn aka Icy walked over and picked up the tumbler off the silver tray and said, "To God."

The three men who had been through so much stood together, swirled their glasses, sniffed, then drank. Riley reached for the cigars, as the president and Colburn turned towards the glass doors leading to the deck. Natasha came over and paid her respects to the president and Riley, then Max. Max and Natasha were brother and sister from a different litter and were now roughhousing all over the cabin.

"To survivors," said the president. He then took one last sip from his glass and tossed his crystal tumbler into the fire, as they had done in previous encounters. Riley and Colburn followed suit. The little alcohol left in the three glass tumblers, as they smashed against the metal grate, caused the fire to jump.

"We seem to go through a lot of these," said the president.

They then headed outside to smoke their cigars on the deck overlooking the frozen lake as lightly falling began to stick. They went through the cigar lighting ritual and leaned against the deck railing and watched the snow roll in off the lake.

"I thought you were both dead," said Riley.

"Yeah, well, we are. At least as far as the world is concerned," said Colburn.

"Have you had any contact with Faith?" asked the president.

"Nothing. Being around me was not good for her health. I, we, almost got her killed twice," remarked Colburn.

"Where have you been?" asked Riley.

"Around."

"Can you be a bit more vague?" asked Riley sarcastically.

"I've been around, just not around here. Close enough to know all the shit you guys are in."

"Speaking of shit, we cleaned up the mess you left here on Wolf Mountain. Aside from a lot of blood, we could find no trace of you or Natasha," said Riley.

"My mess? I seem to recall getting drawn into it by you two and I didn't want to be found. I did leave you a message. Didn't you get it?" asked Colburn.

"Yeah. Well, I missed your message. Embarrassing. I had to read about it in Fitzy's book," said Riley.

Natasha and Max came out onto the deck. Max went over to the president and Natasha went between her Da and Riley.

"Well, Icy, you're both here now and alive. That's what counts," said President Burk.

"And if you're here it means you and the Captain want something," said Colburn.

"You got that right," the president fired back as he blew a heavy steady stream of cigar smoke into the falling snow in the direction of a stand of White Birch trees several feet back in the forest. All five were now looking at the trees and what was behind them. "And here is what we need you to do," said the president.

Two hours later Colburn and Natasha watched from the cabin deck as Marine One lifted off, circled the cabin, head over the Wyman Lake and then south back towards Washington. Natasha jumped off the deck and ran to the stand of Birch trees and disappeared. Moments later she emerged followed by Timmy Logan. They walked up to the deck. Timmy looked up at Colburn and asked, "Mr. Colburn, are you all right? Is everything okay?"

Timmy had found Colburn almost two years ago wounded in a deep gorge after Colonel Vova and his Spetsnaz team tried to ambush and assassinate him. A distraught Natasha sought out Timmy and led him to Colburn. Colonel Vova and his Spetsnaz team were all killed by Colburn and Natasha with a little help from the wolf pack that lived on the mountain. FBI Director Riley had a team of agents search for Colburn and Natasha but found only blood and a trail which ended due to new snow cover.

Colburn would have been dead had he not been wearing a Level 5 Nij III Max bulletproof vest under his extended cold weather clothing. A double tap of 9 mm rounds from one of Vova's snipers SR-3 Vikhr assault rifles had penetrated the vest and lodged in his chest causing a great deal of pain and blood but was not death threatening thanks to the vest.

Timmy, at Colburn's urging and direction, managed to get him back to the cabin where ample medical supplies were stored and administered. It didn't hurt that President Burk and FBI Director Riley had second thoughts about Icy's presumed death and sent a medical team to the cabin, just in case. They knew that if Icy survived he would not want his enemies to know, so, they played along.

Timmy, Colburn, and Natasha had become good friends while Timmy came to the cabin daily, under the guise of the property caretaker, to nurse Colburn back to health.

Colburn didn't answer and seemed to be in a daze, so Timmy asked again, "Are you okay? What did they want, Mr. Colburn?"

Colburn snapped out of it and answered Timmy this time. "I'm okay, Timmy, but you won't believe what they want me to do," said Colburn. "Come on up and I'll tell you."

CHAPTER 53

WHITE HOUSE AND NEW JERSEY DECEMBER 21, 10 A.M.

Noreen came in the Oval Office and said, "FBI Director Riley needs you down on the Situation Room ASAP."

The president jumped up from behind his desk and told Noreen to get Kelly to join him. He left the office at a fast pace and took the stairs down one flight to the Situation Room with Kelly right behind. When they got there, some but not all of the inner circle were huddled in the middle of the conference table looking at a bank of monitors on the opposite wall.

"What's up, Ray," said the president to Riley.

"She's on the move. We've been on her since she landed yesterday at Newark and picked up the rental car we had Hertz put aside for us. She's in the silver Toyota Corolla just leaving her hotel at the Hampton Inn right next to the airport. On the monitor there, you can see we have her on drone-cam driving south on Spring Street," advised Riley.

"Where is she heading?"

"I think she is going to take us for a ride first but pretty sure she intends to rendezvous with her accomplice and take delivery of the suitcase bomb. If she does, we'll take them down. If not, we'll just sit back and wait. We have her boxed in but are giving her plenty of room. The drone is on her tail. SAC Hoar is in one of the dozen chase cars behind her."

"What are you going to do if it's the actual handover?" asked the president.

"Depends on where and the field conditions. We know Ms. Armstrong was recruited by and is a martyr for ISIL, so we have to assume she will detonate the bomb if she suspects we're on her. If the handoff takes place in a heavily populated area, we may have to let them go and take them out separately. SAC Hoar will make that call," said Riley.

"I understand all that. What I'm asking is, if you decide to take her down, how will you do it?"

"We have two Apache attack helicopters out of McGuire Air Force Base op/coned to us at Newark. One in the air now. Both are armed with multiple Global Defender Blast Mitigation System Rockets. When she gets the bomb in her possession and we have a positive ID that both she and the bomb are in her car, we'll light her up."

"What exactly does blast mitigation mean?"

"We worked with Global Defender, the company that invented it to take their spray foam system which contains a foaming agent that significantly mitigates the effects of dispersed chemical, biological, and radiological and explosive threats from dynamite, ammonium nitrate, C4, smokeless powder, dispersal devices, package bombs and suitcase bombs, or as in this case a car bomb. It's designed for rapid, remote, non-contact deployment, and the system provides for superior operator safety and effectiveness."

"English."

"We fire the rockets at the car and it explodes into a self-forming foam which completely encapsulates the vehicle. Then we fire another which covers the first shot. If she detonates the bomb it will go off, but nothing will escape the foam coffin. The force of the explosion will be contained within the car and after twelve hours the foam and whatever it is covering will begin to biodegrade and all that will be left if a foamy brown puddle on the highway. Kind of like tossing a grenade into a tank and closing the hatch," said Riley.

"So, the dirty bomb radiation won't get into the air when the foam dissolves?"

"Negative. We go in afterward and suck it all up into a lead container and it goes into another concrete transportation container ready for deep borehole disposal. I think I'm gonna put Baghdadi in with it and bury them together in some shithole."

"Where?"

"I'llthinkaboutit," said Riley.

Armstrong's car had gone almost two miles down Spring Street and made a quick U-turn then went all the way back to the hotel area before it made another U-turn, drove back south on Spring again, then slowed and turned onto Bond Street, her attempt at 'tradecraft'. She then drove down to Catherine St. and left onto the Magnolia Avenue overpass and took a left on Henry St. to Julia St. into what appeared to be a deserted container storage yard.

"This is the perfect location. If this is where it goes down we'll take her here," said SAC Hoar. He was live streaming the drone a/v and told his forward observer to bring the Apache online and lock onto the target but hold for the fire order.

They watched the silver Toyota slow next to a container. Armstrong stopped but did not get out. Two men came from behind the container and approached the car. They were neither believers nor radicalized. They were just part of New Jersey's bad element who needed another payday. The hidden microphone, planted by Hoar's team, picked up the audio.

"Did you make sure you weren't followed?" asked the older, smaller man.

"I wasn't followed," said Armstrong. "Do you have it?"

"Yes."

"Can you put it in the trunk or in the backseat?"

"Yes, but don't you want to see it first, so I can explain how it works?"

"Yes, of course. But I just push the button. Right?"

"Yes, but you have to arm it first. Just turn it on is all." He looked up and down the yard and up to the sky then motioned for the younger, bigger man to get the suitcase. The younger man went into a container and wheeled out a large black carry-on suitcase. He pulled it over to the car window.

The older man repeated the instructions he was given by the Algerian who hired him, "Right now, it's not armed. All you do is reach in here." He opened a side flap. "Lift this plastic cover and throw the switch, then it's armed." He handed her a small wireless remote control. "When you're close to the target arm it. A red light will go on in the suitcase and on the remote. When you're ready, push the on button on the remote. That's it." The Algerian didn't tell the older man what the bomb was for, but the older man was paid well and that was enough.

"Put it in the car, please," instructed Armstrong.

The older man nodded and the younger went to the back and lifted the rear hatch and lifted the heavy suitcase into the trunk.

They didn't hear it first, just felt a vibration, then they saw it about three football fields away. The Apache was stationary, hovering about fifty yards above the ground. The older man noticed it first then the younger man and then Armstrong.

"You were," said the older man.

"I was what?' asked Armstrong.

"Followed."

A whoosh sound came from the helicopter and a bright light. That was the last thing all three saw before a mild explosion enveloped them in a dark haze. They couldn't see or hear. *Oh shit,* thought Armstrong. She had time for one last gulp of air as she pushed the power window button to close her off from the thickening cloud. Time for one final breath; only what entered her lungs wasn't air.

The Algerian watching from his third-floor room in the Royal Motel two blocks away saw his operation dissolving before his eyes. He pulled out his burner phone and pressed *666. This override app armed the suitcase bomb and detonated it at the same time. But as fast as the Algerian reacted he was too late. The car was already completely enveloped. The bomb detonated with nothing more than a snap, crackle, and pop.

Everyone in the situation room cheered. The president said, "Outstanding," and turned to Dr. Provenzano, "Are the jumpers ready?"

"They are."

"Okay. Send them back into January 3rd and let's see if we nailed it this time."

CHAPTER 54

Oval Office
December 21, 6 p.m.

Most of the inner circle were back in the Situation Room waiting for the a/v report from the Cleveland jumpers. The president, Riley, Kelly, and Max were in the Oval Office with Dr. Provensano also waiting to hear if the jumpers were successfully back to January 3.

Dr. Provensano had a live link on his laptop with Cleveland Control and looked at the president and nodded. All four turned to the monitor and held their breath as they watched the now familiar *Al Jazeera London* BREAKING NEWS banner appear and the now familiar anchor Sandy Burden say, "While the U.S. continues its martial law, we are one of the few media outlets able to continue broadcasting live. More on that later. But first, we have two live reports from New Jersey and New York. First, Tracy Borman live in Elizabeth, New Jersey."

The Oval Office broke out into a cheer and they could almost feel the vibration from the cheers coming from the Situation Room below them who were watching the same feed.

The shot switched to Tracy Borman standing in a deserted lot that looked like a container storage yard.

"Right. Tracy Borman here, *Al Jazeera London* live in Elizabeth, New Jersey, Tuesday January 3, in a storage lot just south of Newark Airport. We have an update to the strange terrorist car bomb explosion that we reported on December 21st. This is the first time we have been permitted into the lot where the car bomb supposedly prematurely detonated. U.S. Homeland Security is giving us little information as to what happened, but as you can see there is little evidence of any major or minor damage one would associate with a terrorist car bomb. A witness, however, has now come forward and told us a different story. He is afraid to speak on camera but claims that an Army helicopter fired a rocket at the car and that the explosion came from the rocket and not a car bomb. The witness went on to say that the rocket was something out of the future; it exploded but there was no big bang, smoke or fire, but rather only a big ball of foam like they spray on planes when they have an emergency runway landing. Local authorities and Homeland Security are refusing comment. This seems to be a developing story and we will keep on it."

"In another seemingly related incident, Elizabeth, New Jersey authorities have reported a very strange double murder. Two men, who I'm told were members of the DeCavalcante crime family, were found yesterday just two miles from here floating off Shooters Island in the Newark Bay. Both were covered by what authorities are calling an oven cleaner foam like substance and the autopsy reports show the foam was ingested. A spokesperson for the New Jersey State Police is telling *Al Jazeera* that this double homicide is not related to the car bomb, but just a wise guy message to other rats. 'Keep your mouth shut'. More as it develops. Back to you, Sandy."

The screen switched back to the *Al Jazeera* anchor in London who said, "Now to Rupert Stone in front of the Trump Tower on Fifth Avenue."

The screen flashed to Rupert standing in front of a dark Trump Tower on Fifth Avenue. He was wearing his familiar blue North Face jacket and no Haz-Mat suit. The floodlights lit up the tower and Rupert while the police sirens began to wailed on cue.

"Good Morning, Rupert Stone, *Al Jazeera London*, live in New York City in front of a deserted Trump Tower. If fact, I am standing in an almost deserted part of Manhattan. The lights went out in the Big Apple at midnight New Year's Eve and most of the east coast from Boston to..."

Another cheer and sigh of relief came from the Oval Office as they realized they prevented the tunnel bomb and that what they had accomplished would change the world forever. They now knew it was also possible to prevent the attack over the East Coast. Half the room thought with time travel now possible they could now prevent bad things from happening. The other half knew that with time travel they could now change the future, similar but possibly very different aspirations.

Now all they had to do was stop the High Altitude Electromagnetic Pulse Bomb (HEMP) from exploding over the East Coast on New Year's Eve.

CHAPTER 55

United Nations NY and the Oval Office Washington, DC December 26

North Korean Supreme Leader Kim Jong-un addressed the U.N. General Assembly on Monday.

Here is the full text of his remarks. Due to his education in Switzerland at a private English-language international school, he addressed the assembly in English but with a thick Korean accent.

> *Your Excellency, Mr. President, your Excellency Mr. Secretary General, distinguished heads of state and government, ladies and gentlemen, the 71st anniversary of the United Nations is a good occasion to both take stock of history and talk about our common future.*
>
> *In 1950, the Fatherland Liberation War began when we were invaded by South Korea on May 23. They invaded north across the 38th parallel and captured then destroyed our western town of Haeju. We defended ourselves and on May 25, we advanced south and conquered the aggressors. The United Nations, duped by the United States to be the principal aggressor force, came to the aid of South Korea.*

China came to our aid and together we crushed the United States, the United Nation contingents, and Syngman Rhee's puppet South Korean Government.

President Burk, before you do something stupid, remember those who cannot learn from history are doomed to repeat it.

The US has made more than 50 attempts to assassinate world political party leaders. Many succeeded. All such assassinations are illegal, performed for undisclosed reasons by American operatives, and rarely if ever a clear humanitarian benefit is identifiable. They do this because they want all the world's countries to pay homage and because they can.

In 1949, you assassinated Kim Koo, president of the Provisional Government of the Republic of Korea.

In the 50's you made several attempts to kill China's Chou En-Lia, Indonesia's President Sukarno, Philippines Opposition Leader Claro Recto, and Cambodia's Norodom Sihanouk. You even sent a Cherokee Indian to try and assassinate my grandfather Kim Il Sung. Operation Buffalo you called it, but it failed.

In 1963, you killed South Vietnam President Ngo Dinh Diem and his brother Ngo Dinh Nhu, and a few days later you even killed your own President John Kennedy. You assassinated the great civil rights leader Martin Luther King Jr. and Killed Robert Kennedy to prevent him from becoming president. You tried many times to kill Cuban President Fidel Castro and his brother Raul, Qaddafi, Khomeini, Fadlallah, Saddam Hussein, Bin Laden and the list goes on and on. And now you have tried to kill me.

Why do Burk and his Washington policymakers trumpet their strategies, their victories and their power so? It is because the demise of the communist enemy has left the M-I-I-C, the Military Industrial Intelligence Community, thrashing about for a new mission, a new raison d'etre. The American M-I-I-C has been meddling in the affairs and searching for new enemies in many countries through the world: China, Italy, Greece, the Philippines, Korea, Albania, Iran, Guatemala, Costa Rica, Syria, Indonesia, Guiana, the Soviet Union, Vietnam, Cambodia, Laos, Haiti, the Congo, Algeria, and Cuba. And that was all before the mid-60's. Then they started again against many of those same countries but also against many new targets: Bolivia, Iraq, Angola, Zaire, Grenada, Libya,

Panama, Afghanistan, and El Salvador. And that only brings us to the end of the 90's. From then till now many, many more countries have been targeted by the CIA. And now they want to start a war with Iran and the DPRK, The Democratic People's Republic of Korea. But President Burk knows we have nuclear defensive capabilities and is afraid.

We are a peace-loving country and I believe the American people are peace-loving people, but President Burk wants war. He is planning to invade my country as President Truman did in 1950. When are you ever going to learn?

But for our ability to defend ourselves, and our loyal friends and allies China and our development of a nuclear bomb, we would surely have gone the way of Vietnam, Panama, Iraq, Afghanistan, Libya, and the list of American aggression goes on.

President Burk and his CIA Gestapo have long had a policy of assassinating individuals for a mixture of reasons. Formerly, these attacks were covert, but increasingly, the US government is open about assassinating anyone whom it pleases. The official narrative, however, avoids the word assassination, preferring instead the euphemism "targeted terminations". Attacks are being made on individuals or leaders of small groups who are post hoc designated "terrorists". Since 2011 there have been killings of nuclear technicians in Iran. Drones are proving increasingly effective at killing targets, and are even being programmed to make autonomous decisions about whom to kill.

This is not the America of John F Kennedy, the America that wanted to win the peace. This is the America under President Burk that wants to win the war.

The great countries of the world, assembled here together in the United Nations, cannot let President Burk continue his imperialism. He condemns and topples dictators, yet he becomes one himself. I, we, cannot let him destroy my great country. Let South Korea and North Korea solve our differences and unite in due time.

On December, 14, President Burk authorized a carrier battle group to sail to the Korean Peninsula. He has threatened me, North Korea and world peace. President Burk taunted, "If you want to destroy the United States but were not able to reach us, well here we are! We're right off your coast in the Sea of Japan."

And now I say to you, President Burk, if you want to assassinate me, well here I am! I'm right here in New York City.

Ladies and gentlemen, colleagues, it was on the 10th of January 1946, in London, that the U.N. General Assembly gathered for its first session. Mr. Suleta a Colombian diplomat and the chairman of the Preparatory Commission opened the session by giving, I believe, a concise definition of the basic principles that the U.N. should follow in its activities, which are free will, defiance of scheming and trickery and a spirit of cooperation.

Today, his words sound as a guidance for all of us. The Democratic People's Republic of Korea believes in the huge potential of the United Nations, which should help us avoid a new global confrontation and engage in strategic cooperation. Together with other countries, we will consistently work towards strengthening the central coordinating role of the U.N. I'm confident that by working together, we will make the world stable and safe, as well as provide conditions for the development of all states and nations.

Thank you.

(Huge applause and standing ovation)

The Oval Office

The usual suspects were seated watching *CNN*, which on probation was allowed to broadcast.

"Wow, didn't see that one coming. So much for McCain's "Crazy fat kid" comment," said Kelly.

"He's got a really good speech writer," said the president.

"Did he just call you out, Sarge?" taunted Riley.

"He made a good case for the United Nations to vote for sanctions against us and possibly more," remarked Nicholas.

"Like I said before, what are they gonna do, invade us?" said President Burk. "Canada down from the north. Mexico up from the South. Japan attacks Hawaii. England and Spain sail their armadas west?"

CHAPTER 56

Oval Office
December 26, 5 p.m.

Things were getting somewhat back to normal for the Senators and Representatives who had been returning to Washington in droves. After being sent home by the president and having to deal with constituents, especially at town hall meetings, it was a lot harder than hiding out in Washington pretending to do the people's work. The cafeteria in the Hart Senate Office Building was serving as the temporary Senate for Schuster and the other Senators while the Cannon House Office Building's gym became the temporary House for Bryan the other Representatives.

"Turn on *CNN*," said Noreen Ward, walking into the Oval Office.

Kelly picked up the clicker and turned on the TV.

Senator Schuster and Speaker Bryan appeared on the screen in what looked like a gym and then the camera panned around to show about forty men and women and a host of TV film crews and anchorpersons.

"Give them an inch and they take a yard," spat Nicholas.

"Who, *CNN* or Bryan and Schuster?" asked Kelly.

"Both," answered Nicholas.

"Kelly, can you please turn it up," asked Riley.

Most Senators were off doing Senator things but the bipartisan House was engaged in an informal impeachment proceeding session of about forty members headed by Bryan. Speaker Bryan sitting behind a long card table leaned over to his invited guests, Senator Schuster and said, "I never thought I would say this, but I now love North Korea and Mr. Kim."

"That fat kid really handed it to Burk," said Schuster with a chuckle, not realizing his mic was hot.

The president just shook his head at the amazing gaffe.

"Wonder if the new-improved media will run with that?" asked Kelly.

A director or producer came over and informed Schuster his microphone was live. He quickly turned it off and pushed it away.

"Look, said Bryan after checking to make sure his microphone was off, I thought we wanted Burk to get tougher with Korea. Do we want a war or not?"

"Of course we do, but that can't be our position. Now that he's got the whole fucking navy off Kim's coast, we need to urge caution and restraint. Diplomacy is the answer. Let the United Nations lead and we'll follow," whispered Schuster holding a sheet of paper to cover his mouth the way a football coach would when he called a play.

"People are starting to riot but it's not getting televised. *CNN* covered it yesterday but didn't sensationalize as usual. I guess they're playing by Burk's rules," said Bryan.

"Yes, and I hear *Fox News* is coming back on," added Schuster.

"We need to start the impeachment proceedings now. Burk thinks he can suspend Congress and shut us up. He suspended Congress but he can't stop us from meeting and proceeding," said Bryan as he pounded his gavel on the tabletop. When quiet returned to the gym, Speaker Bryan said, "Mr. Hyde, from the Committee on the Judiciary, submitted the following report together with additional, minority, and dissenting views. Mr. Hyde, please proceed."

Mr. Hyde walked to the podium, adjusted the microphones, placed the report on the ledge, and turned on the PowerPoint which immediately proclaimed to all that serious business was at hand. Following the text of the projected report, he began to read to the assembled Representatives and assembled foreign and domestically approved news organizations the following:

IMPEACHMENT OF THOMAS DEAN BURK,
PRESIDENT OF THE UNITED STATES
REPORT OF THE COMMITTEE ON THE JUDICIARY
HOUSE OF REPRESENTATIVES
TOGETHER WITH ADDITIONAL, MINORITY, AND
DISSENTING VIEWS TO ACCOMPANY
H. RES. 711

The Committee on the Judiciary, to whom was referred the consideration of recommendations concerning the exercise of the constitutional power to impeach Thomas Dean Burk, President of the United States, having considered the same, reports thereon pursuant to H. Res. 711 as follows and recommends that the House exercise its constitutional power to impeach Thomas Dean Burk, President of the United States, and that articles of impeachment be exhibited to the Senate as follows: Resolution impeaching Thomas Dean Burk, President of the United States, for high crimes and misdemeanors. Resolved, that Thomas Dean Burk, President of the United States, is impeached for high crimes and misdemeanors, and that the following articles of impeachment be exhibited to the United States Senate: Articles of impeachment exhibited by the House of Representatives of the United States of America in the name of itself and of the people of the United States of America, against Thomas Dean Burk, President of the United States of America, in maintenance and support of its impeachment against him for high crimes and misdemeanors.

ARTICLE I In his conduct while President of the United States, Thomas Dean Burk, in violation of his constitutional oath faithfully to execute the office of President of the United States and, to the best of his ability, preserve, protect, and defend the Constitution of the United States, and in violation of his constitutional duty to take care that the laws be faithfully executed, has willfully corrupted and manipulated the judicial process of the United States for his personal gain and exoneration, impeding the administration of justice, in that: On December 12th, 2016, Thomas Dean Burk did: (1) name Congress as a subversive force without any proof whatsoever; (2) declare martial law without cause; (3) attack a foreign country and attempt the assassination of a foreign leader; (4) suspend Congress; (5) suspend free speech and suspend the right of the mainstream media to report to the American people the truth. In doing this, Thomas Dean Burk has undermined the integrity of his office, has brought disrepute on the presidency, has betrayed his trust as president, and has acted in a manner subversive of the rule of law and justice, to the manifest injury of the people of the United States. Wherefore, Thomas Dean Burk, by such conduct, warrants impeachment and trial, and removal from office and disqualification to hold and enjoy any office of honor, trust, or profit under the United States.

ARTICLE II *In his conduct while President of the United States, Thomas Dean Burk, in violation of his constitutional oath faithfully to execute the office of President of the United States and, to the best of his ability, preserve, protect, and defend the Constitution of the United States, and in violation of his constitutional duty to take care that the laws be faithfully executed, has willfully corrupted and manipulated the judicial process of the United States for his personal gain and exoneration, impeding the administration of justice, in that: (1) On December 12th, 2016, Thomas Dean Burk, sent two carrier battle groups off the coast of Korea and Iran without Congressional consent or approval and threatened Supreme Leader Kim Jong-un of North Korea and Supreme Leader Sayyed Ali Khamenei of Iran. Thomas Dean Burk has undermined the integrity of his office, has brought disrepute on the presidency, has betrayed his trust as president, and has acted in a manner subversive of the rule of law and justice, to the manifest injury of the people of the United States. Wherefore, Thomas Dean Burk, by such conduct, warrants impeachment and trial, and removal from office and disqualification to hold and enjoy any office of honor, trust, or profit under the United States.*

ARTICLE III *In his conduct while President of the United States, Thomas Dean Burk, in violation of his constitutional oath faithfully to execute the office of President of the United States and, to the best of his ability, preserve, protect, and defend the Constitution of the United States, and in violation of his constitutional duty to take care that the laws be faithfully executed, has prevented, obstructed, and impeded the administration of justice, and prohibited the removal of offensive statues, monuments and flags honoring the Confederacy. By honoring these slave-holders and desiring to perpetuate the glory of the South, President Burk has shown his racist colors and...*

I've heard enough. Turn it off," ordered President Burk. "Racist? Are they accusing me of being a racist?

"So, it's okay that you're a dictator?" asked Nicholas.

"Yes. But I'm not a racist."

CHAPTER 57

Oval Office
December 26, 5:30 p.m.

"I'll tell you who's racist, Schuster, and Bryan, that's who. Racism is not racist. It's not just for whites. Every nationality, religion, and culture can be and are racist," stated President Burk.

"Koreans hate Japanese. Japanese hate Chinese. Chinese hate Vietnamese.

Whites and Blacks in Vietnam were racist. we all fought well together in the bush. Whites, Blacks, Chicanos, Indians. But when we came in from the bush the racism showed its ugly side. The Blacks went to one tent, the Whites, Chicanos and Indians to another. From one tent, you would hear Percy Sledge and Otis Redding, from the other you would hear Dylan, the Beatles or Johnny Cash and Marty Robbins," said Riley.

"The Chicanos listened to Dylan and Buck Owens?" asked Kelly, somewhat surprised.

"This was pre-Santana and pre-Los Lobos. You would hear La Bamba occasionally. But hey, everyone loved Valens," advised Riley.

"Which tent did you go to?" asked Nicholas.

"Neither, said the president, Riley was an officer and a gentleman, and he didn't fraternize."

"Right. I was not allowed to fraternize with the unwashed. That was hard to do since we were all unwashed, weren't we?" asked Riley.

"Which tent did you go to, Tommy?" asked Kelly.

"The soul brothers probably would have let me in, but I just stood outside and listened. Dylan and the Beatles were good, but Percy Sledge and Otis Redding, come on," said the president. He waited a moment before continuing. "People are people. I usually don't like someone until I do, if that makes any sense. I like people who like me. That's just a common emotion. I always showed respect to everyone until they proved me wrong," said the president.

"Tommy, you're ethnocentric," said Kelly.

"English, please?"

"You favor your own ethnic group."

I'm nice to everyone and expect the same. I show respect and expect the same in return. I like to be around people who I feel comfortable being around. If that makes me ethnocentric, then I guess I am. There are plenty of Whites, Blacks, Chicanos, American Indians and Asians I like and like being around. There is an equal number I don't. Does that make me a racist?"

"Yes," said Riley.

Ignoring Riley the president continued, "I'm against changing history? Really? I'll rewrite history if it was recorded incorrectly, or purposely misleading; but not because it offends someone, or it isn't politically correct. I'm not against taking down statues of Confederate generals or politicians in towns and city. Most soldiers then, as now, didn't care much for their generals anyway. Stonewall Jackson was shot and killed by his own men. They said it was an accident; I might send jumpers back to fact check that. Robert E. Lee was one general worshiped by his men and supported and revered by both the North and South after the war. But in the end, the South lost, and the North won. To the victors and all that."

"What I am against is tearing down of monuments on the battlefields; and that makes me a racist how? Pretend the war never happened or at least take away any sense that the South fought admirably? For most Confederate soldiers, it had nothing to do with slavery. The South was an agrarian economy while the North was industrialized. Diverse cultures. Different political beliefs. Not too different than today. The Civil War was about: taxes, tariffs, state rights versus federal rights, secession and slavery. Ninety-five percent of those fighting for the South never owned a slave and they weren't fighting for slavery. There are 500 Confederate soldiers buried in Arlington; are we going to dig them up and pretend they never died?"

"No," said Riley.

"If you want to rewrite history, why not tear down Mount Rushmore? We stole the land and the whole fuckin' mountain from the Sioux. It was their sacred land and still is. The Sioux called it "The Six Grandfathers" but we put four dead white presidents up there instead, two of which, by the way, were slaveholders. Should we tear it down?"

"We should have put Chief Gall, Sitting Bull and Crazy Horse up there," said Nicholas.

"If it were up to me, I would put John, Martin, and Bobby up there.

"It is up to you. You're the president," said Nicholas.

"Right. And the mainstream media would spin it that the president was a sending subliminal racist message," remarked Riley.

"What message?" asked Kelly.

"That President Burk put the 'KKK' on Mount Rushmore," replied Riley.

"Ray, you're funny," said the president, knowing his friend would take the bait and lighten things up a little and channel Joe Pesci from *Goodfellas.*

"What do you mean, I'm funny?" asked Riley.

"It's funny, you know. It's a good story, it's funny, you're a funny guy," said President Burk.

"What do you mean, you mean the way I talk? What?"

"It's just, you know. You're just funny, it's ... funny, you know the way you tell the story and everything."

"Funny how? What's funny about it? What did ya say? Funny how?"

"Jus..."

"What?"

"Just ... ya know ... you're funny."

"You mean, let me understand this cause, ya know maybe it's me, I'm a little fucked up maybe, but I'm funny how? I mean, funny like I'm a clown, I amuse you? I make you laugh, I'm here to fuckin' amuse you? What do you mean, funny, funny how? How am I funny?"

"Just ... you know, how you tell the story, what?"

"No, no, I don't know, you said it. How do I know? You said I'm funny. How the fuck am I funny? What the fuck is so funny about me? Tell me, tell me what's funny!"

"Get the fuck out of here, Ray!"

"Ya motherfucker! I almost had him, I almost had him. Ya stuttering prick, ya. Nickels, was he shaking? I wonder about you sometimes, Tommy. You may fold under questioning."

"Are you two done? Do you practice these routines at night after I go to bed? Look. We need to get off all this unpleasantness: impeachment, racism, riots, what we need to get the country moving forward," said Kelly.

"What we need is to get the country moving forward into a good war," suggested Riley.

"I think we need to see what 'you know who' has come up with," said President Burk. "But first I want an update on the New Year's Eve attack."

CHAPTER 58

The Oval Office December 27, 7:30 a.m.

Inside the Oval Office, President Tommy Burk, Riley, Kelly, Nicholas, SecDef Stanton, DCI Bader, AG Fare, General Finn, and Secret Service Director Bounty were finishing up domestic issues when the president turned the subject to the imminent Electromagnetic Pulse Bomb attack on New Year's Eve over the East Coast. Looking at CIA Director Bader, he said, "Director, where are we and it better be good."

"Mr. President, the Nicole Danial, the 90-foot commercial fishing boat out of Port de Grave, Newfoundland sailed yesterday, December 26, as we anticipated. We have tracking and a/v devices on board and have planted several large explosive devices on the hull under the water line. She is currently in the Canso Bank off St. Peters, Nova Scotia. This is the ship that will carry and fire the EMP off Long Island," informed Bader.

"That's not going to happen, is it director?" asked the president.

"No, sir. Somewhere along the 900 mile trip to Long Island the terrorists take her and bring aboard the missile, warhead, and launcher. We have been tracking and following a Russian Kilo-class diesel-electric submarine, the Noor 902, heading for Nova Scotia."

"Russia is supplying the Electromagnetic Pulse Bomb?" asked the president.

"Negative. Russia sold three Kilo-class diesel-electric submarines to Iran in 2014: the Tareq 901, Noor 902, and the Yunes 903. The Tareq is currently operating in the Gulf of Oman and we have not been able to locate the Yunes.

"Could this be another trick?"

"No sir. The Nicole Danial and the Noor have been in communications with each other for the last 12 hours."

"So it's not a highjacking. One or more of the crew is in collusion."

"Right."

"When and where will they rendezvous?"

"Just south of Halifax in about five hours. They will make the transfer then it's just a little over 400 miles to the coast of Long Island."

"Why make the transfer so far from the launch site?"

"We think it's because of the subs range and inexperience. They don't want to get any closer to the U.S. than they have to. If they suspect anything or feel us closing in they can set up quickly and launch from the southernmost tip of Nova Scotia and still knock out Bangor, Boston, and Providence."

"So why not take both the ship and sub out now?"

"We can and will if that's what you want, but then there goes all the visual proof. We'll get condemned for sinking a fishing boat 350 miles off our coast and a foreign submarine even further away. Besides, we need to be sure. We need to witness the Noor offloading the bomb and launcher. Then we hit them both in about six or so hours from now and have film to back us up. We must wait till then in case…"

"In case what?"

"In case the whole thing is a faint? We take them out now and think we nailed it and the Yunes 903 sneaks by us."

"You mean there could be another fishing vessel and sub out there?"

"Yes, but it could also mean that the Yunes is one of the Russian subs sold with a SAM system."

"Surface-to-air missile tube launch capabilities?"

"Correct. Eight 9K34 Strela-3 (SA-N-8 Gremlin) surface-to-air missiles, which have the range and are capable of carrying the PULSE warhead."

"Oh, shit," blurted the president. Looking at Director Riley he then said, "Get Israel on a secure line."

Everyone around the table thought President Burk was reaching out to Benjamin Netanyahu, but President Burk and FBI Director Riley were not thinking state.

After everyone left the office, Riley's secure phone chirped, and he answered, "Icy, I'm here in the Oval Office with Sarge. Thanks for getting back so fast. I'll put us on speaker."

"Good morning, Captain, Sarge. Your nickel," said Colburn.

"We need to know what you found out and what you're going to do about it," said President Burk.

"Whoa! replied Colburn, I agreed to do some snooping and come up with a plan but I'm dead and I want to stay that way."

"Right. What do you have?" asked Riley.

"So, you both understand there are only seven souls who know I'm alive. You two clowns, Timmy and Smith & Wesson. You remember those two from your last fuck-up. I trust all with my life."

"I'm thinking the other two are Natasha and Max," said Riley.

"Roger that, Captain. Working through Smith & Wesson I was able to find out a lot more than your CIA. First off, that Cabell guy is a piece of work. He snookered you guys and I think you need to get rid of Bader because he's lost all confidence within the agency."

"You want the job?"

Colburn didn't respond to the offer, "You got the how, when and where correct. It was the who that he played you for. You know it wasn't al-Baghdadi and Kim Jong-un. Those two were the smoke and mirrors. It was Pakistan that supplied the bombs."

"Pakistan? Motherfucker!"

"Yeah, but it was still Iran that paid the bill and ISIL is still the delivery boy. Cabell was playing father against son. Chesmis Bakr, Baghdadi's 16-year-old son is the guy now running the show for ISIL."

"So young. Can he hold ISIL together?"

"ISIL is hurting. They had the shit kicked out of them in Syria. But here's the rub. ISIL has taken on a partner. While ISIL has been coming back down the ladder, al-Qaeda passed them going back up. Hamza bin Osama bin Mohammed bin Awad bin Laden, aka Hamza bin Laden, is a son of Osama bin Laden. Hamza's dad and his brother Khalid were killed in the SEAL raid back in 2011. Ham is now 28 years old, full of piss and vinegar, and now the leader of al-Qaeda. Al-Qaeda and ISIL have been competing for many of the same resources, mostly money, and recruits, and they have different views on the establishment of a caliphate, but hard times makes for strange bedfellows. Hamza made an offer to Chesmis that he couldn't refuse and "abracadabra" we now have al-QISIL."

"How the fuck do you know all this and we don't?" asked President Burk.

"Cabell saw the future and it's with the young guard Hamza and Chesmis," replied Colburn.

"Ham & Cheese?" quipped Riley.

"Cabell bet that Kim and al-Baghdadi would throw you off your mark and it worked. He wanted to draw you into a war with North Korea that would not end well for you and the country. He knew you could go back and forward in time but didn't think you could change the future."

"I don't get that. Why would he think we couldn't change the future?"

"Beats me, but after you took the tunnel bomber out he knew he underestimated you. He's done the Houdini," advised Colburn.

"So, what do we do about North Korea and Iran?"

"Nothing," said Colburn.

"Nothing?"

"Well, almost nothing. Pull your carrier battle group out of North Korea," suggested Colburn.

"What about Iran?"

"Screw Iran. Let's stick with Korea," said Colburn.

"Okay. But CIA Director Bader put through a "Wag the Dog" plan that we approved. We intend to put it into effect tomorrow. Like you said, I pull my battle group out of the Sea of Japan but with his plan, I'm not running away."

"Enlighten me," coaxed Colburn.

"Who do the North Korean's, South Korean's, Chinese, Taiwanese, Vietnamese, Laotians, Cambodians, Thais and most of Asia hate more than the United States?" asked Riley.

"Japan," breathed Colburn.

"Right," answered the President.

In 1895, Japan won the Sino-Japanese against China, but it was fought in Korea. Japan then killed the Queen of Korea. Afterward, the people of Korea, desperate for allies, made friends with the people from Russia. In 1905, Japan won the Russo-Japanese War. In 1910, the Emperor of Japan made Korea a colony of Japan.

Korea had been occupied by Japan from 1910 to 1945. The Japanese, sure of their imperial mission and their superiority as a race, had set out to destroy almost all vestiges of Korean independence. What they wanted was nothing less than to obliterate Korean culture. The Japanese colonization of Korea was an unusually cruel one.

When Japan lost World War II, the United States occupied the south of Korea and the Soviet Union occupied the north of Korea. But soon the United States and the Soviet Union were no longer allies and the Cold War started. In 1948 the people in the south made a country called South Korea with the help of the United States and the people in the North also made a country called North Korea with the help of the Soviet Union.

In 1950 a war started in Korea. China came to the aid of North Korea and the United States aided South Korea. Truman called it a police action. However, five million soldiers and civilians were killed and wounded, and Truman called it a police action. The war ended in in a stalemate in 1953. The borderline between North and South was the same in the end as it was before the war. No land was lost or gained.

"And Japan still feels Korea lies like a dagger, ever pointed towards its heart," said Riley.

"So, in Bader's plan, Japan is what, going to attack North Korea? Japan's army, on paper, is supposed to be strictly defensive, remember," reminded Colburn.

"Japan's Self-Defense Forces, the SDF is a full-fledged military, with army, navy, and air force branches. You're correct. Technically, the SDF is not allowed to conduct offensive operations or to deploy outside Japan, but Bader's plan allows for this," said Riley.

"So where is all this going?" asked Colburn.

"We wanted to 'Wag the Dog', right? Well, North Korea is going to launch another mid-range ballistic missile. This time towards Japan," said Riley.

"But their missiles only go a little over 300 miles and can't reach Japan," replied Colburn.

"Correct. But our satellites just yesterday, picked up new launch site 30 miles north of their 38th parallel. Near their port city of Kosong. So, from there they could theoretically hit hundreds of cities in Japan including Hiroshima," claimed Riley.

"Bader's plan is to have North Korea nuke Hiroshima again?" asked Colburn.

"Not exactly. Later today we bow to international pressure and pull our carrier battle group away from the Korean Peninsula towards Japan's international waters. North Korea is scheduled to launch a solid-fuel Pukguksong-2 missile tomorrow towards Japan, we assume to spite us, but it will land short as it always does. We keep one of our subs back and when North Korea launches its missile towards Japan our sub launches a Tomahawk towards our carrier battle group. Their missile splashes down somewhere in the Sea of Japan, ours hits and obliterates one of our destroyers, the USS Spruance, which we will abandoned of all personnel tonight. Within 24 hours we'll have all 27 of our NATO allies, including Germany, Great Britain, and France, coming to our aid and upholding their oath to defend a fellow NATO member, not to mention our major non-NATO allies, South Korea, Japan, and Israel. You know what NATO Article 5 stipulates?" asked Riley.

"An attack on one is an attack on all," replied Colburn. "But our Tomahawk missiles and their Pukguksong missiles are not the same. Someone will know the difference?"

"Possibly. But it's our ship and it will not be salvaged. She'll stay where she lay, a memorial grave like Pearl Harbor," said Riley.

"What about that whole thing of never fighting a land war in Asia? And what about China? They'll intercede and come swarming across the border like they did the last time," stated Colburn.

"Ah! Good points. First of all, we don't see this as a boots on the ground war, at least not for us and NATO. We'll surround them and hit them from the air and sea. South Korea can then move north and unite the country. As far as China is concerned, for 100 years now she has been landlocked from access into the Sea of Japan, but Bader's sources say that President Xi Jinping, if given access to the Sea of Japan between Korea and Russia, right where North Korea and Russia meet, would be a very happy sailor. Plus, he would be rid of Kim Jong-un. So, this time tomorrow the world will be with us and against North Korea. We'll have our war and I can continue as a dictator or abdicate my throne and go back to being just plain old President Burk."

"This is the worst plan I ever heard of and you two guys are buying into it? And Bader thought this up all by himself?" asked Colburn.

"If you got a better plan to eliminate North Korea, let's hear it," pressured President Burk.

"No! How could anyone possibly top that? When you two come to your senses, and I hope it's soon, call me. In the meantime, I'll give it some thought."

CHAPTER 59

The Situation Room
Washington, DC
December 27, 12:30 p.m.

The usual suspects, aka the president's inner circle, were all seated around the conference room table, eyes fixed on the many wall-mounted monitors, when the president entered and took his seat at the head of the table. The subject was the imminent Electromagnetic Pulse Bomb Attack on New Year's Eve over the East Coast. Looking at CIA Director Bader, the president asked, "Everything set?"

"Affirmative," answered Director Bader and continued. "Mr. President, the commercial fishing boat, the Nicole Danial and the Russian Kilo-class diesel-electric submarine, the Noor 902, now operated by Iran, have linked up as suspected 48 miles south of Halifax along the Sambro Bank. What you're looking at is a live video feed from one of two MQ-9 Reapers aka Predators. On the monitor to the left, you're seeing real-time video at deck level from a slew of Cicada, Covert Autonomous Disposable Aircraft. They were dropped from the Reapers and look like Sea Gulls. We're recording everything. If anything goes wrong with our embedded explosives, we have the USS Zumwalt guided missile destroyer close and we have two Virginia-class submarines, the USS Delaware and the USS John Warner closer. As you can see in the video the submarine is in the process of unloading the missile components now."

"Are we sure it's the Electromagnetic Pulse Bomb there're unloading?" asked the president.

"Affirmative," replied Director Bader.

The president looked around the table for confirmation and he got it from Stanton, Finn, Michaels, and Chairman of the Joint Chief of Staff, General (Chief) Ely Parker.

"Have you been able to locate the Yunes 903, her sister sub?" asked the president.

"We think it's around but not around here," said Bader.

"That's ambiguous," cautioned Chief Parker.

"Yes. Well, we don't have to worry about her," said Bader.

Just as Bader said that an aide came into the Situation Room and leaned over Chief Parker's shoulder and handed him a note. The Chief conferred with SecDef Stanton for a moment then said, "The Delaware's sonar is picking up a shadow behind the Noor."

"A shadow?" asked the president.

"Another sub following directly behind the Noor. These Kilo-class diesel-electric submarines run silent," advised Chief Parker.

"I guess we just found the Yunes," said General Finn.

"Are the explosives attached to the Nicole Danial powerful enough to take her out and both subs?" asked the president.

"It looks like the Yunes is up in the Noors ass and the Noor is tethered to the Nicole Danial. The hull explosives we attached before she left port are so powerful they will disintegrate her and the Noor. It's probable the underwater concussion will also implode the Yunes. You give the order Mr. President and all three and their payloads will be on the bottom before you can say 'Davy Jones Locker,'" promised Chief Parker.

"Take all three ships out now," ordered President Burk.

Chief Parker spoke into his secure phone then stowed it. Everyone watched the monitor for what seemed an eternity but was in reality just 30 seconds. There was no sound, just a bright light followed by a shaky picture, shock waves then smoke. After a few seconds, the smoked cleared and the Nicole Danial and Noor were gone. Just ocean waves and some debris rippling away from the detonation point.

"How can we be sure we got the Yunes?" asked the president.

Just then a submarine bow chin followed by its forward planes and sail broke the surface like a whale breaching from the depths. The submarine seemed to be intact until a tremendous amount of air came blowing out of her forward ballast tanks. She started to dive and her stern planes, rudder, and propeller came fluking out of the water. Her skin ballooned then deflated while the water and air seemed to go into shock. The implosion was fast and final.

"Thar she blows!" shouted Chief Parker and the Situation Room erupted in applause.

The president picked up the conference room phone and said, "Get me, Dr. Provenzano, please." After a few seconds, the president spoke again, "Doctor, please send the jumpers in one more time."

Dr. Provensano was in Cleveland with the jump team waiting for the president's call.

In the adjoining control room, Russell Randazza and his NASA technicians and engineers watched the wall mounted a/v monitors in each room and via Bluetooth monitored each jumper's vital signs. At 1 p.m. Randazza started the countdown.

"On 5-4-3-2-..."

Just like the dozen previous jumps, the house began to shake, rattle and roll, but as quickly as it begun it subsided. Then there was complete quiet.

The rooms visible on the monitors showed three empty beds. "They're gone," confirmed Randazza. Randazza repeated his now traditional farewell, "Have a good trip guys, I wish I could be there with you."

For the umpteenth time, Sweeney felt himself being pulled back into his body. Before he knew it he was awake and sitting up in the bed. It was 1:01 p.m. He lunged up and forward and reached for his Recon glasses on the nightstand and put them on. The glasses, motion activated Cleveland Command and President Burk's Situation Room with a live feed on their wall mounted monitors. He reached for the remote and swung himself to the end of the bed and pushed the TV on button. The TV came to life. It was set for *Al Jazeera English* as had been established from the previous jumps, but instead of seeing the now familiar *Al Jazeera London* BREAKING NEWS banner appear and the now familiar anchor Sandy Burden or one of the other *Al Jazeera* anchors, the screen was black. Not black-black but fuzzy black with an irritating audio squelch.

Almost simultaneously Felton's *BBC* and Ceretti's *CNN* live feeds came up on the Cleveland and Washington monitors. All were black.

"Jesus," said the president.

"Keep switching channels until you get something," demanded SecDef Stanton.

But all the channels were the same, black nothingness.

"Dr. Provenzano, please tell me you have a technical problem," said the president.

After several minutes of muted conversation between the doctor, Randazza and the NASA technicians, engineers, and jumpers, Dr. Provenzano came back online. "Negative. The problem is not on our end or the jumpers end Mr. President. It seems that on January 3, 2017, no one is broadcasting."

Everyone around the tables in the Washington and Cleveland of 2016, and the jumpers in Cleveland 2017, immediately grasped the implications of Dr. Provenzano's statement. Only the president verbalized it, "Oh, shit."

CHAPTER 60

The Situation Room Washington, DC December 27, 1:30 p.m.

"Send the jumpers out into the field now. We need to find out if a mouse chewed the TV wires or we started World War III," said President Burk to Dr. Provenzano.

Tom Sweeney would head out to see if he could find out what happened from his contacts at the *Cleveland Plain Dealer.*

Agent Ceretti would chase down Special Agent in Charge of the Cleveland office, SAC Ross and the local offices of Homeland, CIA, State Police and the Cleveland PD.

A/V Tech, Felton would head to the different international civilian and military communication outlets, offices and bases. But her top priority would be connecting with all the many Shortwave-Ham-Radio enthusiasts outside the Cleveland area.

Sweeney and his teammates Felton and Ceretti knew that the now *'fait accompli'* by Washington to 'Wag the Dog' and start a war with North Korea had created an impediment to their original task of finding out if the sinking of the Nicole Danial, Noor and Yunes prevented the PULSE attack over the

East Coast or not. They also knew that their time travel into the future just got a whole lot more interesting.

Thirty minutes later back in the Situation Room, the president and his inner circle all came to the same conclusion without waiting to hear back from the jumpers. And that is that Bader's or Cabell's CIA plan to eliminate North Korea backfired or succeeded, depending on how you looked at it, and that prevented them from finding out about the Nicole Danial, Noor, and the Yunes. If they didn't send the jumpers they would have gone through with Bader's plan, but now the plan was on heading for the cutting room floor along with CIA Director Bader head.

"John, what the fuck were you thinking?" asked the president. He then looked around the table at the others and continued, "and more importantly, what were we all thinking, and why did we all go along with it?"

"Everything's falling apart according to plan," answered Riley.

Dr. Provenzano was listening to the conversation on the live-feed monitor from Cleveland and said, Mr. President, we…"

The president interrupted him. "Doc, bring the jumpers back home now then send them off again as soon as they're ready and you can reset the vortex."

"Will do. But to confirm your gut feelings, all three jumpers have just reported in and we are very close to WW III. When you decided today to go ahead with your fake attack and sinking of the USS Spruance stunt, you set in motion events which have become reality in January 3, 2017. NATO attacked North Korea, China came to their aid, and Russia is threatening to join them. South Korea and North Korea are in the middle of a catastrophic meat grinder on the 38th parallel. It's a real clusterfuck out there."

"Like I said, bring the jumpers back and then send them out again. There will be no dog wagging tomorrow. We got sidetracked. The only thing I want to know now is, did we stop the PULSE attack over the East Coast or not?"

"On it, Mr. President," assured Dr. Provenzano and disconnected.

"You guys hold the fort," said the president as he nodded to Kelly, Riley, and Nicholas to join him as he got up and left the Situation Room.

Back in the Oval Office, the president asked Noreen to send the steward in with a late lunch.

"Whether it's Bader or Cabell or both, I swear I'm gonna do what Kennedy said he would do but never got the chance. "I will splinter the CIA into a thousand pieces and scatter it into the wind," boasted President Burk.

"Just don't make his mistake and announce it to the world beforehand," suggested Nicholas.

"Do you think that was 'the Sting', Captain? Was this 'Wag the Dog' Cabell's final sting?" asked the president.

"I would like to think so, but they broke the mold with this guy Cabell. I think this attack on North Korea comes from Bader's brain. We asked for a distraction and he gave us one," said Riley.

"I wanted a distraction, not World War III. Just like the Bay of Pigs, they knew it would escalate and we'd be sucked in."

"I still think 'the Sting' is out there," said Riley.

"Oh, merde," said Nicholas.

"When will this all stop?" asked Kelly.

"It has stopped. We're not going to go through with Bader's plan and we sunk the Nicole Danial, Noor, and Yunes. When the jumpers go back and report in we'll get the real skinny," said Riley.

"You two get back down to the Situation Room and make sure Stanton and Parker put the kibosh on Bader's plan," demanded the president.

After Kelly and Nicholas left, the president ordered, "Captain, get Icy back on the horn."

After a minute Riley put his secure phone on speaker. "What took you so long?" asked Colburn.

"How did you know it was me and what do you mean what took me so long?" asked Riley.

"You're the only one with this number and what took you so long to come to your senses? I assume you're calling because you decided that Bader's plan to attack North Korea was bullshit. Nothing good would come of it unless you were going for World War III."

President Burk looked at Riley, shook his head and asked, "Do we have a leak here or are you really that good?"

Colburn didn't answer. The president continued, "Let's just say we've seen the future and it is not ours."

"Alright, guys lets cut to the chase. Like I said before, pull your carrier battle group out of North Korea."

"And?"

"And let me take care of Mr. Kim."

"Can you share with the rest of the class?"

"Kim's younger sister is Kim Yo-jong. She and her older brother Kim both studied together in Berne, Switzerland. She's 29 and currently in charge of North Korea's Propaganda and Agitation Department (PAD). As the vice director of the country's propaganda arm, she oversees developing her brother's cult of personality. She's already a power player in North Korea and recently married Choe Song. Choe is in his early 30's and is the son of powerful party official Choe Ryong Hae.

"So, this is North Korea's new power couple?"

"Could be, or maybe North Korea's new supreme leaders."

"Kim's going to abdicate to his sister?"

"The elder Choe has held several top positions under Kim Jong-un and previously under his father, Kim Jong-il, and Choe's family has long ties with the ruling dynasty. He took part in a rare delegation to South Korea recently where his sympathies to the South and to Moon Jae-in surfaced. I believe those sympathies filtered down to the newlyweds. When Kim Jong-un became incapacitated two years ago with gout, diabetes, and ankle problems, his sister Kim Yo-jong ran the country while he recuperated."

"So, you're planning a coup d'état?" asked Riley.

"Hardly. She loves her brother. But if her brother's health declines and he goes into diabetic shock and dies, she and the country will mourn, then she will take his place."

"And, as the new supreme leader she begins unification talks with South Korea and Moon Jae-in, and soon there's no North, no South, just one Korea?" asked the president.

"Something like that."

"No muss, no fuss. I like it. But how do we know Kim Jong-un will go into shock and die?" asked Riley.

"Because he goes to Switzerland to Le Centre Hospitalier Universitaire Vaudois every year for a checkup, and he's due there next week."

"How do you know?"

"There is this doctor who is in residence. He's German and very sympathetic to the plight of the Korean people."

"So, he's going to inject Kim with something?"

"Once in the clinic, Kim will redevelop symptoms of diabetic hypoglycemia: clumsiness, muscle weakness, slurred speech, and blurry vision, which are all easily hypnotically induced. He will be diagnosed, treated and immediately bounce back after he is administered a one-time delayed released capsule. He will feel 100% better. The capsule overcoat and membrane will begin to dissolve eight hours later when he is back in Wonsan. Drug compartment one will begin to release followed minutes later by the release of drug compartment two."

"What's behind door number one?" asked Riley.

"VX, the same poison chemical he used in the Kuala Lumpur airport to murder his half-brother. Immediately after ingesting the .001 milligrams, Kim's pupils will begin to constrict. He will experience reduced vision, drooling, sweating, diarrhea, nausea, vomiting, and abdominal pain. His tongue will swell, and he will choke to death."

"What's behind door number two?" asked President Burk.

"HI-6 and Atropine. HI-6 restores the function of the enzyme acetylcholinesterase. Atropine repairs the nerve receptors."

"Autopsy results?" asked Riley.

"It will appear as though Kim died of severe diabetic hypoglycemia. No trace of the VX will be found."

"You're putting a great deal of faith in this German doctor. How can you be so sure he'll deliver?" asked Riley.

"Habe ich noch nie enttäuscht," said Colburn.

"No, mein freund, you never have," declared President Burk.

CHAPTER 61

The Situation Room
Washington, DC
December 27, 2:25 p.m.

Vice President Hilton joined Riley and the president as they returned to the Situation Room and took their seats. CoS Nicholas got up and offered his seat to the vice president and moved to the end of the conference table.

"Where are we?" asked the president.

SecDef Stanton, looking at DCI Bader answered, "The clusterfuck ... the event planned for tomorrow has been terminated. Press Secretary Sullivan has put out a press release stating your reasons, the primary being your respect for the international community's appeal for restraint."

"On the other matter, your timing is good. Doctor Provenzano just put us on standby. He is about to launch the jumpers, so we should hear something any minute." The monitor came to life with Randazza starting the countdown.

"On 5-4-3-2-..."

The house shook and then there was complete quiet.

The rooms visible on the monitors showed three empty beds. "They're gone. Have good trip guys, I wish I could be there with you," said Randazza.

For what he hoped would be the final time, Sweeney felt himself being pulled back into his body. Before he knew it he was awake and sitting up in the bed. It was 2:31 p.m.. He jumped up and reached for his Recon glasses on the nightstand and put them on. The glasses gave Cleveland Command and President Burk's Situation Room an immediate live feed of Sweeney's room TV on their wall mounted monitor. He mechanically reached for the remote and swung himself to the end of the bed and pushed the TV on button. The TV came to life. His TV was, as always, set for *Al Jazeera English*. On the screen appeared *Al Jazeera London's* BREAKING NEWS banner and the now familiar anchor Sandy Burden.

Everyone in the Situation Room and the Cleveland control room held their breath. The breaking news banner had become almost boilerplate for all the news shows. Sandy Burden was in the middle of a story,

"...and tonight the world is applauding President Burk's decision to remove the carrier battle group away from the Korean Peninsula..."

Everyone in the Situation Room and Cleveland's control room immediately reacted. Some cheered, some pounded the table and some bowed their heads and uttered a silent prayer. "We dodged the bullet. Congratulations, Mr. President," said Stanton.

Sandy Burden continued, "On December 28, just six days ago, no one thought it possible for President Burk's armada to leave the Sea of Japan, but he did and the world's tension level has gone from DEFCON 1, a cocked pistol, war is imminent, to DEFCON 5, a fade out, lowest state of readiness. I never thought I would say this about President Burk, but well done Mr. President." Meanwhile, on the Peninsula, both North and South Korea are standing down with..."

"Switch to Ceretti's *CNN*," ordered Kelly.

CNN appeared on the main wall monitor with Wolf Blitzer standing in front of a huge monitor displaying the shows name: *The Situation Room With Wolf Blitzer.* Wolf was in the middle of the story, "...and if you haven't seen it yet, let me show you a clip of a portion of yesterday's speech."

A film clip came up with President Burk standing in front of the United Nations assembly with a green marble wall in the background.

> *"...To all Terrorists: Radical Islamist, Fear Mongers, Terrorist States, Lone Wolves and Home Wolves, I offer you an opportunity to present your grievance here in the United Nations and before the World. We will listen, learn, and try*

and understand you and your ideology. We may not accept your views as you may not accept ours, but we must learn to, we must want to, live together in peace. The world must come together and decide to continue this unwinnable war or accept an honorable peace. We either triumph together or accept world subjugation together, for this war against terror can never end. There will be no armistice, no surrender, no treaty, no ceasefire, no white flag."

I speak of peace because of this new face of war. With such a peace, there will still be quarrels and conflicting interests, as there are within families and nations. World peace, like community peace, does not require that each man love his neighbor--it requires only that they live together in mutual tolerance, submitting their disputes to a just and peaceful settlement. And history teaches us that enmities between nations, as between individuals, do not last forever. However, fixed our likes and dislikes may seem, the tide of time and events will often bring surprising changes in the relations between nations and neighbors.

No government or social system is so evil that its people must be considered as lacking in virtue. As Americans, we find radical Islamic terrorism profoundly repugnant as a negation of personal freedom and dignity. But we can still hail Muslims for their many achievements--in science, in economics, in culture and in acts of courage.

So, let us not be blind to our differences--but let us also direct attention to our common interests and to the means by which those differences can be resolved. And if we cannot end now our differences, at least we can help make the world safe for diversity. For, in the final analysis, our most basic common link is that we all inhabit this small planet. We all breathe the same air. We all cherish our children's future. And we are all mortal.

The United States, as the world knows, will never start a war. We do not want a war. We do not now expect a war. This generation of Americans has already had enough--more than enough--of war and hate and oppression. We shall be prepared if others wish it. We shall be alert to try to stop it. But we shall also do our part to build a world of peace where the weak are safe and the strong are just. We are not helpless before that task or hopeless of its success. Confident and unafraid, we labor on--not toward a strategy of annihilation but toward a strategy of peace.

Applause rang out from the assembly as general members from 193 countries stood and gave President Burk a standing ovation.

The screen flipped back to Wolf Blitzer in the *CNN* studio. "That was President Burk yesterday addressing the United Nations and he is getting very high marks for…"

President Burk, in his Situation Room, said, "I can't believe I said all that."

"I can't believe I wrote that," said Kelly, "That was good."

"Well, actually some of it sounds a bit familiar. I'm thinking JFK's commencement address at American University in 1963," offered Nicholas.

"Turn to *MSMBC*," said Kelly.

Kathleen Felton who had been watching her TV and monitoring the chatter between the president and his staff switched from *BBC* to *MSMBC*.

Felton's feed came up on the monitor. Stephanie Ruhle, an *MSNBC* anchor appeared with a Breaking News banner, and sitting across from her were both Senator Schuster and Speaker Bryan.

"Jesus. If we let *MSMBC* back on we must have lifted the ban for everyone," said Nicholas.

Stephanie was saying, " …to make sure I understand you correctly, Speaker Bryan, you feel that President Burk has sold out the country by removing the carrier battle group from the Korean Peninsula last week and by yesterday's address to the United Nations asking for peace with the terrorists. Do I have that right, Speaker Bryan?"

"The world is laughing at us. He could have taken a world threat off center stage by eliminating North Korea and he could have taken out Iran's nuclear capabilities. The world would have been a much safer place today, I can assure you. What did he do? He ran away. NATO now knows that they can no longer depend on the United States to be the leader of the free world. I'm not alone on this. Germany's Merkel on Sunday declared a new chapter in U.S.- European relations after contentious meetings with President Burk last week, saying that Europe 'really must take our fate into our own hands.'"

"But isn't it true that Merkel went on to say that President Burk deserves high praise for reaching out to terrorists and offering peace? I am hearing

President Burk has authored a new peace initiative. It is being called the Audacity of Peace. The president has rescinded martial law and the American people were marching in the streets last night supporting the president. There was a front-page editorial in today's *Washington Post* recommending President Burk for the Nobel Peace Prize. Don't you think both of you should rethink your positions and feel the pulse of America?"

"I don't buy any…"

Senator Schuster interrupted Speaker Bryan, "You're absolutely right, Stephanie. I think Congress needs to stop all this bickering and get behind the president. We need to ratchet down all this hateful rhetoric being slung from all sides. I will, however, make the time to follow and scrutinize the president's every move."

Speaker Bryan turned from Senator Schuster into the camera with the look of a deer caught in the headlights. Senator Schuster continued, "I will ask my friends in the Senate, both Democrats and Republicans, to give peace a chance."

"It sounds like you two are in different camps, but Senator I think you have just given tomorrow morning's *Post* a banner headline and tonight's prime time news their sound bite. Senator Schuster wants Congress to 'Give Peace a Chance'. On that note, we'll be right back after a commercial break."

"Turn it off. I think I've seen enough," said the president.

"Schuster just threw Bryan under the bus and I think you have a new bestest friend, Mr. President," said SecDef Stanton.

"That's right, Senator, replied Riley talking to the black monitor screen, you go ahead and 'make the time', and you're going to have plenty of time real soon," mocked Riley.

Everyone listening, except the president, missed the significance of Riley's comment. Instead, everyone in the Situation Room and both Cleveland's, current and future, stood and started to applaud.

There was no mention of or 'Breaking News' banner announcing the sinking the Nicole Danial, Noor and Yunes. Unless you were looking for an oil slick or a debris field 50 miles off the coast of Halifax, or you reported your subs missing, why would there be?

CHAPTER 62

WONSAN, KOREA
JANUARY 6, 2017

"Wife, get me some water. I am very thirsty after my trip," said Kim Jong-un to his wife Ri Sol-ju.

Supreme Leader Kim Jong-un had just returned from his yearly physical in Switzerland an hour previous aboard his private jet the Chammae 1, to his family's private compound and palace in the resort town of Wonsan. The compound had a staff of 50 plus military staff and other regular hangers-on.

For his convivence, Kim had recently completed a private airstrip and private train station adjacent to his palace. Wonsan had been converted into a world-class tourist beach town and resort for Kim's family, friends and the privileged few.

Director of the Reconnaissance General Bureau, General Hwang Pyong-so was also in Wonsan awaiting the arrival of Kim's younger sister, Kim Yo-jong, her husband Choe Song and her father-in-law, Choe Ryong Hae, who were due in from Pyongyang any minute.

After they arrived they headed together to the palace to see their leader. The mood was light, and they expected a wonderful family weekend of jet-skiing and moonlight cruises aboard his Princess 95MY yacht, especially since the Le Centre Hospitalier Universitaire Vaudois had given their leader such a clean bill of health.

After he quenched his thirst, Kim laid down in his bed, "Is my sister here yet?" he asked his wife.

"She is outside with her husband and his father."

"Ask only my sister to come in."

A few seconds later the door to his bedroom opened and Kim Yo-jong entered. She never stood on ceremony when she was in private with her brother.

"You don't look well, brother."

"I feel dizzy. It must be from all the travel and pressure."

"You are sweating. I will turn up the air-conditioning and summon your physician. My husband, father and the general want to see you."

Kim did not answer as his sister left the room only to return a moment later with her husband, father-in-law and General Hwang Pyong-so.

"What is that smell?" asked Choe Song.

Kim Jong-un was breathing hard now and holding his stomach and grimacing.

Kim Yo-jong ran out of the room to see what was keeping the doctor. She returned after a few minutes with Doctor O Kuk-mu in tow.

Kim was mumbling, "My stomach hurts. I am having trouble breathing" He began to cough as the doctor rushed to his side and began to examine him.

The coughing began to get worst as the doctor attempted to take his temperature. Kim's hands were now grasping his throat and his head was thrashing about. Everyone instinctively began to move back away from the bed.

Kim's eyes were now bulging, and his face was turning from red to blue. He tried to stand but stumbled. General Hwang Pyong-so was able to catch him before he fell and pushed him back into the bed. His face was blue, his lips were bright red, and his tongue was twice the size and hanging out of his mouth. He looked all the world like the Rolling Stones logo. His tongue retreated inside his mouth, his hands grabbed at his throat, while his eyes rolled back into his head. If his agony was overwhelming and unattainable, his death throes were almost comedic. Like a chicken without a head, the supreme leader was dead. He was dead, but his body, legs, and arms continued to shake. The convulsions continued until the doctor threw himself on Kim's corpse in an attempt to do something.

After a minute, the doctor stood up and held his stethoscope to his dead leader's chest to confirm what everyone knew. Kim Jong-un, Chairman of the Workers' Party of Korea, and Supreme Leader of the Democratic People's Republic of Korea, and Supreme Commander of the Korean People's Army was dead. He choked to death on his vomit, swallowed his tongue and pooped his pants. It was not a very pleasant or dignified way to pass.

All heads turned towards Kim Yo-jong, his young sister. She was crying but held her hands over her eyes and mouth, so no one could see her emotion. They all knew; they all hoped she would have the stamina and determination to follow her brother as supreme leader. For if not, they would all be dead in a military coup which would surely follow. Everything would be gone in an instant.

January 6, 2017

Korean Central Broadcasting System announced this morning the peaceful passing of Supreme Leader Kim Jong-un and the ascension of Kim Yo-jong, his sister, to Supreme Leader of North Korea.

Supreme Leader Kim Jong-un died peacefully in his sleep. No further details are available at this time.

Kim is dead. Long live Kim. The Dynasty continues...

CHAPTER 63

Oval Office January 7, 2017

"Wow, Kim Jong-un dead? Is it true? What was he, 33?" asked Kelly.

"He would have been 34 tomorrow," said Nicholas.

"Too young to die and too young to die in his sleep. This morning's *Washington Post* is speculating we're somehow behind it," declared Kelly.

"I think he was a diabetic. He probably died of diabetes. Diabetic hypoglycemia is a possibility," hinted Nicholas.

"Tell me Tommy you had nothing to do with this." mouthed Kelly. Then she decided to have some fun of her own. Walking over towards her husband she stopped and said, "Michael is it true?"

Riley was about to answer but the president couldn't resist the invitation. He walked slowly from behind his desk towards Kelly and stopped. In his best Michael Corleone said, "Don't ask me about my business Kate."

"Is it true?"

"Don't ask me about my business," yelled the president. Then slammed his hand down hard on the desk.

After a moment reflection, the president said, "All right. This one time, this one time I'll let you ask me about my affairs."

Kelly knew that her husband, Riley, and Nicholas were enjoying this. After all, they were all still just little boys. "Is it true?" demanded Kelly.

"No!" said the president.

Kelly smiled and walked into the president's arms and keeping on script added, "I guess we both need a drink huh? Come on." But then pushed away and looked her husband, the President of the United States in the eye and threatened, "If I find out you're lying to me Tommy, tonight you'll sleep with the fishes."

Noreen Ward knocked and then came in and told the president that AG Fare and Treasury Secretary Bloomfield were outside and that Dr. Provenzano and his team were 15 minutes out.

"Thanks, Noreen, have the attorney general and the secretary come in."

Kelly and Riley excused themselves and left to go down and greet Dr. Provenzano and his team when they arrived.

AG Bill Fare and Treasury Secretary Michael Bloomfield came in and sat on the couch opposite the president and CoS Bill Nicholas.

"Tell me again why the banks don't need any more regulation?" asked President Burk.

"Honestly, Mr. President, I didn't see this coming. They just got hammered in their retail banking division. That sales scandal last year involving the creation of as many as 2.1 million phony accounts in customers' names without their permission should have put the fear of God in them," stated Treasury Secretary Bloomfield.

"It obviously didn't, but this new scam is too much. What is it called again?" asked the president.

"It's their new retail product they're selling to retirees on Social Security. They call it LCRM's."

"How does it work?"

"They have boiler rooms cold call seniors and get them to direct deposit at least 25% of their Social Security checks into these LCRM's. It's a potential multi-billion a year product."

"What do they say to the seniors to get them to give up part of their Social Security checks?"

"These guys are good. First, they tell them that it's a government program to help seniors get into the booming stock market. They tell them that's why the Social Security Administration allows them to do direct deposit. They say their money is 100% secure and FDIC guaranteed. Here's the closer. They say the certificates earn 12% tax-free interest, and if you leave the money in until you die, it goes tax-free to their grandchildren. They say some seniors are amassing huge sums to pass on their grandchildren tax-free. They play on grandma and grandpa's heart strings."

"Is any of that true?"

"Almost none of it, and after the seniors die and the bank fees are deducted, there's little to nothing left for the grandkids."

"And we allow direct deposit out of their Social Security checks into First Fargo?"

"The seniors have to sign a Social Security direct deposit authorization. The banks have good lobbyists. The money goes offshore somewhere, bounces around a while, then goes into one of First Fargo's holding companies for investments. They're making a killing. They send monthly statements to the retirees showing them how well their accounts are doing, all exaggerated. They are even offering free vacations for referrals that are anything but free."

"Is First Fargo still headquartered in Indiana?" asked Nicholas.

"Correct."

Looking at the Attorney General, the president said, "Bill, I want this shut down immediately. Plus, I want all the money plus penalties and the promised 12% returned to these senior's, and no more deductions from Social Security accounts for any reason." Turning to his Chief of Staff, Bill Nicholas, he said, "Bill I want this out there. Have Kelly put the entire scam over the wire. Hold a press conference. If we don't get tough on First Fargo now the other banks will smell easy money and think of another senior scam," said the president.

"By the way, said Nicholas, what does LCRM stand for?"

"Leverage Certificates Rate Modifications. But the guys in the First Fargo boiler rooms say it stands for 'Last Chance to get Retirees Money,'" said Treasury Secretary Bloomfield.

After the secretary and attorney general left, Noreen ushered in: Kelly, Riley, Project Christopher's Dr. Provenzano, Project Director Russell Randazza, Cleveland jumpers Tom Sweeney, Kathleen Felton, Rob Ceretti, and special guest, Dallas jumper Bob Scales and his wife Nancy.

"Dr. Provenzano, Mr. Randazza, jumpers, and guests, thank you all for coming. Normally we would be meeting with you in the Rose Garden with the rest of our inner circle and the press, but until we are ready to make our time travel public I'm afraid we'll have to continue our clandestine meetings within the confines of the White House," said the president.

With that said, two stewards entered the office carrying trays holding flute glasses of Cristal Champagne. The stewards offered a glass to everyone.

"We salute you who have made possible the most amazing achievement since our landing on the moon. Your special talents, your bravery, and your pioneering spirit not only accomplished the impossible and solved the crime of the 20th century, your efforts also saved America from a terrorist attack and prevented World War III. We salute you all," praised the president as he and everyone raised their glasses for a toast.

"On behalf of the entire Project Christopher team, we thank you, Mr. President. Scientists and adventurers are we, but without Queen Isabella, there would have been no Columbus. Without Kennedy, there would have been no Moon landing, and without you, President Burk, there would have been no time travel," stated Dr. Provenzano.

"Thank you doctor. Director Randazza, outstanding job. I understand your send-off to the jumpers always ended with, 'I wish I could be there with you.' We might be able to accommodate your wish and arrange a special trip for you. How does that sound?"

"That sounds wonderful, Mr. President," said Randazza. *Or ominous, Mr. President*, thought Randazza.

"Mr. Sweeney, Ms. Felton, Mr. Ceretti, we have special plans for you three and I guarantee it will set the bar for time travel. And I can guarantee it will not be another groundhog day trip.

Mr. Sweeney, so good to see you again. It's unfortunate what happened to Mr. Todd, is it not?"

"Mr. President, knowing Ron as I do, did, I'm sure he made the most of it and enjoyed a full and exciting life."

Agent Ceretti, you have come through again for your country and I have asked Director Riley to find you a more exciting position while you're waiting for your next jump assignment.

"What could be more exciting than Bangor Maine?" joked Ceretti.

"Ms. Felton, I understand we have been interrupting your wedding plans. Who is the lucky guy?"

"It's been a little harrowing, Mr. President but he's worth the wait. We are getting married this spring and his name is Bucky. Bucky Rozniakowski. He's a pretty special guy."

"I would love to meet him. How about having your wedding here in Washington? We could have the reception right here in the White House. The Rose Garden will be lovely this spring and we would be honored."

"The honor would be ours, Mr. President."

"Dr. Provenzano has assembled more jump teams but I promised you three another jump, this time back in history. We have three mid to late 19th-century historical destinations we think need a history book rewrite: Lincoln's assassination, Custer's Last Stand and The Great Chicago Fire of 1871. Did Mrs. O'Leary's cow really kicked over a kerosene lantern and start the Great Chicago Fire? What do you guys think?" asked President Burk.

"Whoa," cautioned Tom Swenny with a smile. I think you would do better with re-enactors as jumpers. I can't see the three of us blending very well at the Little Big Horn as Indians or dressed as troopers with Custer. We all know how that ends."

" I'm for the Lincoln's assassination. But we need to be careful and not end up 'well hung' with the conspirators," offered Ceretti.

"I'm thinking poor Mrs. O'Leary and her cow had a bad rap and need a break," said Felton.

"Think about it," said the president, turning to the oldest jumper and his wife. "Agent Scales, or should I say Mr. and Mrs. Scales, I must say I'm in awe of you both. I just can't believe I'm standing here with you. You were there. You saw Oswald and two of Kennedy's shooters. And Nancy, you were among them all in the Carousel Club: Ruby, Oswald, Tippit. I just can't believe it but here you are."

Tammi True, aka Nancy Myers, aka Nancy Scales, in a black sequin gown with a red boa and large hooped earrings looked at the president and cooed, "Honey, you can call me Tammi, and everything you just said is true. But you know, here I am almost 54 years later in this beautiful office talking to the President of the United States. I have to tell you, honey, you are much better looking in person. That TV adds 20 pounds to your face," teased Tammi. Turning to Kelly, she added, "He's a keeper, darling, but I suspect you know that."

Kelly couldn't contain herself. She burst out laughing and moved to give Tammi a hug. "Honey, we need someone like you around here who doesn't hold back."

"I'll tell you what we need. We need you all to line up over here for a couple of pictures for prosperity," insisted the president.

"Will what we did in Dallas ever come out Mr. President?" asked Scales as he managed to get a moment alone with the president.

"Sooner than you think, Bob. Sooner than you think."

"That's good to hear, Mr. President. I made an exception and flew up here hoping to hear just that. I'm 83 you know, and sooner is good."

CHAPTER 64

MOSCOW, MAINE
JANUARY 8, 2017

Timmy Logan had been to the cabin every day after school to feed and take Natasha out for walks. Mr. Colburn had to go away but was due back from Switzerland that night. Timmy, Mr. Colburn, and Natasha had grown close over the last couple of years, they were 'pack' now. A pack of three. It was cold and snowing as he and Natasha climbed Wolf Mountain looking for their old friends.

"Are we getting close, girl?" asked Timmy.

Natasha acknowledged the question with a sharp bark and by dashing up ahead and around the bend. Timmy ran to catch up and noticed Natasha had led him to the spot where they first found the wolf lair.

This was the same spot where he first met Faith Knoll. She was with Mr. Colburn and she was beautiful and so nice. After the Russians came to try and kill Mr. Colburn, Timmy tried to console Ms. Knoll, but she was so sad. Mr. Colburn asked Timmy not to tell anyone he was alive, including Ms. Knoll. He said it was for her own good. But Timmy knew Mr. Colburn and Natasha missed her badly.

A howl brought Timmy out of his reverie and it wasn't from Natasha. Another howl from down lower on the mountain and another came from the east.

All were getting closer as if they were being stalked. Natasha alerted. Eight wolves closed in around them. Timmy knelt in the snow as the wolves circled closer and closer. Two wolves broke from the pack and came running at Natasha and Timmy as the others continued to circle. One Alpha male came and sat on his haunches and began to feverishly lick Timmy's face. The wolf then stood and put his front legs around Timmy's shoulders and neck and continued kissing and licking Timmy's mouth while moaning in ecstasy. Another dominate male rushed to Natasha and both bared their teeth and growled, but soon tails were wagging until a dominate female came over and attacked Natasha's mate. The male reacted by tossing the female to the ground, applying a sort of headlock until she assumed a submissive position, while he viciously straddled her, growling and baring his teeth.

Timmy was faring better, as several young wolves playfully jumped on his back. This went on for several minutes until Timmy and Natasha realized they were now surrounded by over 15 wolves all vying for their attention. This pack could have easily dispatched both Timmy and Natasha, but they were old allies and friends. Several of the older wolves were present on the mountain when the Russians came. The encounter didn't fare well for the Russians. Natasha, now surrounded, solved the problem by aggressively asserting herself towards the Alpha male. This unexpected challenge momentarily scattered the pack and gave Timmy and Natasha the opportunity to make a break.

"No one's going to believe that, are they girl," said Timmy as they ran down the mountain towards the cabin.

Later Timmy said goodbye to Natasha and locked the cabin but made sure the doggy door was open. With Natasha inside, no animal, two or four legged would dare attempt to climb through.

"I'll be back tomorrow and your Da tonight." Da was the term Mr. Colburn used to identify himself to Natasha.

Natasha was at the window looking at Timmy as he ran through the woods. She wanted to follow but her Da would not want that, so she stayed and protected their laird.

Timmy had to get home quickly because he promised his dad he would help him sort through his grandmom's old farm house. She had died a few weeks ago and Timmy missed her so. He loved her so much and she was the first person he ever knew who had died, that is, not counting the Russians, and of course Mr. Colburn and Natasha that did but didn't.

"Timmy Logan, what kept you boy? You know what we must do this afternoon. Your mom and I have a church meeting back here in a little over an hour and I have a good mind to leave you there by yourself," said Timmy's father who was the mayor of Moscow. Timmy's mother was already at the farmhouse sorting out this and that.

Ten minutes later they drove up to an old Victorian farmhouse. It belonged to his mom and dad now and Timmy supposed someday it would belong to him. It was not a grand Victorian, just a two-floor house with a cross gable roof, with three bedrooms and one bath and a small attic. The bath was added just before Timmy was born but the outhouse was still out behind the house at the end of a grapevine trellised pathway with an open culvert that guided kitchen waste water to flush out the outhouse. Ingenious for the time.

"What do you want me to do, dad?" asked Timmy as they walked from the porch into the front parlor.

"Ask your mother. Up to me, we would just leave things as they are. It's not as though we have room for any of this stuff in our house and Lord knows she's never going to sell any of it."

"Timmy, go up to the attic and find grandmom's secretary. See if there are any letters or pictures. Look for any hidden secret drawers and pull-outs; I remember there being some," said Timmy's mom.

"Secretary, mom?"

"It's a tall piece of furniture with a ledge that lowers down so you can write on it."

Timmy walked towards the back parlor, past the old upright piano, past grandpa's old banjo and his bottle lens glasses that grandmom refused to move, and past all the memories of the off-key piano, accompanied by all the off-key singing. Past all the wonderful times. He climbed the rickety wood steps to the second-floor hallway beyond which were the bedrooms that still had the porcelain chamber pots on the bedside tables.

Timmy opened what looked like a small closet door, bent low and walked up the stairs that spiraled for four treads before straightening out to ascend the attic. The plaster walls were cracked, exposing wood laths and globs of plaster that made the walk up the steps both scary and sad.

I don't think anyone's been up here for years, thought Timmy.

At the top of the stairs, he found the light chain, gave it a pull and a single light bulb that looked like one of Edison's originals dimly lit the room. Old pieces of furniture lined the walls and boxes, and chests were neatly stacked on the floor. Everything seemed orderly, but dust was thick and dead yellow jackets and flies were on the floor and window sills. The attic smelled old and the floors creaked as he began to walk around the room. He stopped by the window and tugged the old shade pull but held on, so it wouldn't sputter up too fast. Sunlight filled the room, and dust particles caught in the movement began to dance.

He found what looked like a writing desk in front of the brick chimney. It was tall and wonderful and made of a strange wood that Timmy had never seen before, not a dark wood but not too light either. The grain was like a flowering pattern with borders of a lighter wood inlay. The top part had two wood doors with glass panes revealing many old books in different shapes and colors. The bottom of the piece had two large drawers, but the middle of the secretary is what drew Timmy's attention. He pulled it towards him and lowered it. It was a writing surface with hinges on either side, and pull-out supports to keep it in position. More drawers, some straight and some curved faced with little silver pulls, and several cubbies filled the back space. There seemed to be something in every drawer and cubby: letters, coins, pictures, a skeleton key, and some things he didn't recognize. At either end, there were panels that that looked like columns. Thinking these might be the secret pull-outs his mom said to look for, he pulled one out. It was filled with money. Lots of money.

Mom really needs to come up here and see this, thought Timmy.

He pushed the panel back in and closed the writing surface and turned to leave but noticed what looked like a pirate chest hidden in the corner. Timmy couldn't resist. He walked over and knelt down in front of the chest. Its top was curved with brass trim and round rivets. It had big handles on either side for lifting; it looked very old. It was locked and had a dark metal plate on the top with the initials MTL engraved. The L, he assumed, was for Logan, but neither his parents nor his grandparent's names started with M. He got up and returned to the secretary, lowered the ledge and removed the skeleton key and went back to the chest. He inserted the key, turned it and the lock opened. He removed the lock, lifted the latch and pushed the chest top open. A lift out tray with cubbies contained: a pipe, watch, coins, keys, cufflinks, and other things one collects during a lifetime. He lifted the tray to reveal more men's stuff. Under an old sweater was a bag. It looked like a shopping bag with an unfamiliar name of Neiman Marcus in script across the front. It looked old and fragile, so he carefully removed its contents. It was a box containing, according to the box label, a Bell & Howell 414PD Director Series Double 8mm Zoomatic home-movie camera. He opened the box, and everything was neatly in its place including a paper handwritten Neiman Marcus Dallas receipt to Michael Logan for $89.00, dated November 22, 1963.

CHAPTER 65

Oval Office January 16, 2017

Kelly came in, reached for the clicker and said, "It's breaking. Lester Holt just went to commercial and will open with it in the next segment."

President Burk, Riley, Nicholas and Dr. Provenzano moved over to the TV monitor and took seats next to Kelly.

"Fifty-four years and the truth will finally set us free," observed the president.

"Let's see how they spin it. Mainstream media has been part of the 53-year cover-up and lie and I don't see them doing a complete mea culpa unless you really did put the fear of God in them Tommy," noted Kelly.

Lester Holt came back with what would become one of the biggest news stories of the year, if not the century. And of course, below his image was the ever present 'Breaking News' banner, which in this case was true. As Lester began to report the story, stock footage of the JFK assassination appeared on the screen. "A little over fifty-three years ago, Friday, November 22, 1963, Lee Harvey Oswald shot and killed President Kennedy from a sixth-floor window of the Texas School Book Depository on Elm Street in Dallas. But a recent discovery of an old 8mm film found in a locked chest may change all that. NBC correspondent Peter Alexander has this breaking story."

"Thank you, Lester. I am standing here in Moscow, Maine in front of a farmhouse that has held a treasure for over 50 years. It was hidden in a locked pirate chest, but the treasure was not a pirate map or gold doubloons; it was a Bell & Howell 414PD Director Series Double 8mm Zoomatic home-movie camera just like the one Abraham Zapruder used to capture the amazing footage of President Kennedy's assassination. I was shown the short film this camera contained this morning and I must say it's a game changer."

Alexander walked over to a porch where a man and a boy were sitting on the front steps. "I have with me today *Hedgehampton Press* investigative reporter Tom Sweeney and the young man who discovered the film, Timmy Logan. Tom, if I may start with you; what is your involvement in this discovery, as Moscow, Maine is about as far away from the Hamptons as you can get."

"Peter, first, let me say that Timmy called me as soon as he found the camera. He is somewhat of an investigative reporter himself and we met a couple years ago when my partner, *New York Post* reporter Ron Todd and I came up here to investigate some wolf sightings…"

"Let me stop you there, Tom. Isn't that the same Ron Todd who disappeared last month? Have you heard from him?"

"Yes, I have, and he hasn't disappeared. He's around, just not around here. He decided to take a sabbatical and live a quieter, simple life, like the one he had growing up in the 60's. But as I was saying, Timmy and I became aquatinted a couple of years ago. He wants to be a reporter, so we have stayed in touch and that's why Timmy called me."

"So, Timmy, any seasoned reporter would die for a scoop like this. How did a budding cub reporter such as yourself, stumble upon it?"

"Well, Mr. Alexander, that's exactly what happened. I stumbled on it. My grandmom passed away recently and my mom, dad and I were looking for old photos, important papers and such, and I was sent to the attic to see what I could find. That's when I found my great-grandfather, Michael Logan's chest. I opened it and found the camera and undeveloped film."

"But what made this camera so special?"

"When I took it out of the bag there was a receipt for the camera. It was made out to my great grandfather, Michael Logan from Neiman Marcus and was dated November 22, 1963. That's when I called Mr. Sweeney."

"You put two and two together that fast? I bet you're going to get an 'A' in history, Timmy."

"Well, this story is not about me, it's about the film my great-grandfather recorded and the lie that has been told to the country and the world for the last 53 years. You saw the film, Mr. Alexander. You saw that Lee Harvey Oswald did not shoot President Kennedy from the sixth-floor window."

Having just been schooled by a kid, Alexander turned to Sweeney and asked, "Mr. Sweeney, is any of this being investigated by the authorities? I mean, there have been so many hoaxes and conspiracies, and this could be just another."

"Peter, last week the FBI took the camera, original film, and all the evidence and opened an investigation. But the preliminary report back from the FBI states that this is, to use your term, 'a game changer'. Michael Timothy Logan, Timmy's great-grandfather was in Dallas on November 22, 1963 and registered at the Adolphus in hotel room 1405; they have copies of the hotel registry. Neiman Marcus did sell a Bell & Howell 414PD Director Series Double 8mm Zoomatic home-movie camera to a Michael Logan on November 22, 1963; the receipt has been authenticated. Michael Logan did move to this farmhouse with his wife and children in 1964 upon discharge from the Air Force and took a job here in Moscow. He raised his family right in this house. What he captured on film almost 54 years ago in Dallas, and has been hidden away here in Moscow, Maine is, we believe, the most important piece of evidence to surface proving without a doubt that the "Lone Nut Gunman", Lee Harvey Oswald, did not shoot President Kennedy."

"Thank you, Tom and Timmy. I have to agree. I think Timmy has found the "Smoking Gun" and it wasn't in Oswald's hands. I'll have more on this breaking story and will show you the actual film tonight on my 9 p.m. prime time special, "The Patsy." Peter Alexander, *NBC News*, Moscow, Maine. Back to you in New York, Lester."

"We did it!" exclaimed President Burk. "Congratulations to everyone. By tonight this story will go viral and by next week Senator Angie Kling of Maine will announce a reopening of the assassination and the formation of a new JFK Assassination Commission. With this film, we'll excoriate Lee Oswald, blow the lid off the conspiracy and "splinter the CIA into a thousand pieces and scatter it into the winds"."

"I thought you just wanted to prove Oswald didn't take the shot," reminded Kelly.

"I changed my mind. I want to get rid of Bader, Cabell and the CIA forever."

"You think that's possible? You think that's the answer?" posed Nicholas.

"Yes, I do. It is possible and 'The answer my friend is blowing in the wind, the answer is blowing in the wind'," sang President Burk in a Dylan sing-song nasal voice.

"Mr. President, Senator Schuster, and Speaker Bryan are here for your 7 p.m.," said Noreen.

"Give us a minute then send them in."

Kelly, Riley and Dr. Provenzano left by the side door while Schuster and Bryan were escorted in by Noreen. They both walked in with assurance and smiles on their faces, as though they never intended to destroy and impeach the president. Such are politics and politicians.

"Mr. President, began Senator Schuster, what a pleasure to see you again."

President Burk walked from behind his desk and warmly shook the Senator's hand, "Senator. Nice to see you again, then grasped Bryan's hand; Speaker Bryan always a pleasure."

"Good to see you, Mr. President," said Speaker Bryan.

"Sit down, fellows and I'll tell you why I asked you both here tonight. Thanks to your help we have finally gotten the country moving forward together and I want to show the country, the world, that we're united. I want to do a victory tour celebrating Congress and my administration's cooperation and our successful peace brokering deal between North and South Korea, and our, so far successful, olive branch offering to al-QISIL and all terrorists. I'm calling it the 'Give Peace a Chance' tour," stated President Burk.

"I love it," said Senator Schuster.

"I thought you would, Chuck. I'm announcing it today in honor of Martin Luther King Jr. day and I want to kick it off this Monday the 23rd in Dallas. I want you two to be my special guests. I arranged a private jet to bring you both down on the 22nd. I booked you into the Adolphus Hotel and reserved the entire 14th floor for you."

CHAPTER 66

The Hay-Adams Washington DC January 16, 2017

The Hay-Adams Hotel is located at 800 16th Street NW directly across the street from the White House. The hotel occupies the site where the 1885 homes of John Hay, private secretary and assistant to Abraham Lincoln, and Henry Adams secretary to his father, Charles Francis Adams, Abraham Lincoln's ambassador in London, once stood. In 1927, Harry Wardman bought the property and razed the homes. The hotel, designed by Mihran Mesrobian, was built on the site in 1928 in Italian Renaissance style.

The president liked the classic restaurant and sometimes he and Kelly would unceremoniously slip across the street for dinner. Tonight though, he wanted to have some private time with his friend, Dr. Provenzano.

At a private corner table, with no Secret Service agent's visible, executive chef Nicolas Legret and staff served the president cold water Atlantic cod in a white wine, butter and lemon sauce and melt-in-your-mouth pork chops from Colorado to Dr. Provenzano. More wine was poured then the chef and staff departed leaving their guests to discuss whatever important people discuss.

"TP, you and your NASA team did an outstanding job and someday your country and the world will honor and reward you. Soon we will announce your accomplishments and the residual effects of saving the United States from the attacks and saving us from World War III," advised President Burk.

"Tommy, you and I go back a while and you know I don't care about accolades. A pat on the back for NASA would be nice. All you hear about nowadays are the great things Elon Musk's SpaceX and Jeff Bezos's Blue Origin are going to do. It would be nice to tell the world what NASA has already done."

"Well, when Musk and Bezos hear what you guys pulled off they're going to shit moon rocks."

The president was done with small talk and got to the point for the private dinner. "TP, can you take someone back in time to when they were young? You know, like we did in Dallas but arrive age appropriate?" asked the president.

"You mean could a man go back to his childhood and become himself as a boy of say ten years old?" asked Dr. Provenzano.

"Yes."

"The answer is a simple yes, but the process is not. It's similar to what we did in Dallas with the vortex, but we don't send the actual person back; only his mind, so to speak. Like Dallas, we need to set the mood, location and time and prepare the traveler for an OBE. It's more akin to mind travel than time travel," clarified Dr. Provenzano.

"So, you don't send the person back, but you send his mind?"

"Unlike ReKall, Inc., in the film *Total Recall*, we don't implant fake memories for ideal vacations. We can, however, stimulate the brain in such a way as to awaken latent memories and experiences to the point of reality. We don't send the brain back, we send the brain waves."

"Once there can you stay or is it a short visit?"

"Either can be realized but there are paradoxes one must consider. You can go back in mind and become a boy again, live in your boyhood house, see your mom and dad again and live your life over for a few days or forever."

"You can do that?"

"Yes, but you'll never know it, at least not as President Burk. It will be just like you fell off today's boat on the river and got back on 60 or so years back. If each boat equals a day that would be over 21,000 boats behind where we are today. You may experience déjà vu from time to time but that's about it."

"But that would be like it never happened. I wouldn't remember the future?"

"That's right."

"But I mean going back like in Francis Ford Coppola's *Peggy Sue Got Married.* You know, where Peggy Sue, a middle age mother is thrust back in time to when she was in high school. She gets to live her life all over again, but because she remembers her future she really appreciates her family, school, friends, and all the experiences that she took for granted the first time around."

"Ah. You want to bring your future consciousness along with you."

"Exactly."

"Tommy, if that were possible then this ten-year-old boy would never get the chance to live his own life. You're going back and hijacking it would negate you in the future. You today would not be you. You would be someone else."

"So, it's not possible?" asked the president.

"I didn't say that, Tommy. Remember what I said to you all in the Oval Office about astral projection being the technique of the spirit leaving the body and traveling any distance? It's called astral time travel. How astral time travel works is like focusing on a memory. It is a practice that should be done very carefully. By the theory, time is like that river, it flows down but with the aid of astral projection you can go back to certain times in that river and look at a memory. Out of Body Experience or OBE and the vortex will get you there, but we need to be careful. Do you believe in life after death?"

"Yes."

"Well, you could do it the way you want but you would have to die first, and we would have to keep your brain alive. You must die so we don't usurp your original life. But if you change anything besides appreciating a second chance we might not be here today having this discussion," cautioned Dr. Provenzano.

CHAPTER 67

THE SITUATION ROOM JANUARY 17, 2017

The usual suspects were around the Situation Room conference table including Director of National Intelligence, Dan Core. The vice president was also present.

"What was the original purpose of the CIA? I know Truman morphed the OSS into the CIA, but I thought it was supposed to be intelligence gathering only and to report unfiltered intelligence directly to the president," stated Dr. Provenzano.

Attorney General Bill Fare answered, "Exactly. The CIA was established to prevent unanticipated disasters, such as the Japanese attack on Pearl Harbor, but it has repeatedly failed to warn the White House of looming threats. Unlike Project Christopher, it missed many important events. It missed the North Korean invasion of the South in 1950, and the Chinese entry into the war that fall; Israel, France, and Great Britain's attack on the Suez Canal and Egypt in 1956; the Soviet invasion of Czechoslovakia in 1968; the Shah of Iran's ouster in 1979; the Soviet invasion of Afghanistan that year; the Iraqi invasion of Kuwait in 1990; the Indian nuclear tests in 1998. 'We didn't have a clue,' confessed CIA Director George Tenet about the attack on the World Trade Center in 1993; the bombing of American military barracks in Saudi Arabia in 1996 and of U.S. embassies in Africa in 1998; the attack on the USS Cole in 2000; and of course, the attack on the World Trade Center and Pentagon in September of 2001; and finally, most if not all of the terrorist attacks on the United States since 2001, including the Beltway Snipers, Fort Hood and the Boston Marathon bombings."

"Yes, but they did warn us recently of impending attacks from North Korea, Iran, and ISIL," chirped Nicholas sarcastically.

"You got that right. That was purposely bad intelligence to keep us from sorting out the real threat from Pakistan, Iran, and al-QISIL," said Riley. "And I have to take some responsibility for Fort Hood and Boston. Both were 'Home Wolves."

Attorney General Fare continued, "In his memoir, present at the creation, former Secretary of State Dean Acheson expressed his misgivings about the creation of the CIA in 1947. He said he had the gravest forebodings about the organization and warned the president that as set up neither he, the National Security Council, nor anyone else would be in a position to know what it was doing or how to control it. In 1991 and again in 1995, Senator Daniel Patrick Moynihan introduced bills to abolish the CIA and assign its functions to the State Department, which is what Acheson and his predecessor, George Marshall, had advocated. But Moynihan's proposal was treated as evidence of his eccentricity rather than of his wisdom and the bills never came to a vote."

"Yes, but what do we do now?" asked the president.

Moynihan proposed moving the CIA's functions into the State Department, where they would be more subject to international law and congressional oversight. But questions about this proposal abound. Would the State Department also perform covert operations, and not simply spying, overseas? Who would oversee them? The answers to these questions are unclear," admitted Fare.

"What is clear is that the CIA is broken. And to repair it, we may have to start from scratch," concluded Director of National Intelligence, Dan Core. The CIA along with 15 other IC agencies report to his office, the DNI.

"Like I said before, let's take 'em outside and shoot 'em," threatened Riley.

"We still can't find Cabell," reminded Nicholas.

"Look, let's fire Bader, shut down their operational arm and turn their intelligence gathering over to State. Eventually, we'll 'splinter the CIA into a thousand pieces, and scatter it into the winds.' You okay with that, Dan?" asked President Burk.

"I am," replied Dan Core.

"Matt?"

"Do I have a choice?" asked Secretary of State Matt Walsh.

"Not really." confessed the president.

"Eventually Project Christopher will go live and then we'll announce it to the world. And if one ounce of its technology leaks I will personally hand the leaker over to Riley. We'll then spin off an intelligence gathering wing for you, Dan. Our time travel technology should be able to replace the CIA in intelligence gathering and do a hell of a better job. We'll need a department name and an acronym," observed the president knowing Riley would come through.

"We could call the spin off, the department of Time Intelligence Technology," offered Riley and waited for the reaction.

President Burk had a word with Vice President Hilton and she took over the meeting. Then the president, SecDef Stanton, General Mickey Finn, CoS Nicholas, FBI Director Riley and Dr. Provenzano left the Situation Room and took the stairs up to the Oval Office.

"You two are like Rowan and Martin," Nicholas jested.

"What?" asked Riley.

"The new agency acronym will be TIT? Tell me you two didn't rehearse that?" asked Nicholas.

"What?" asked the president.

Kelly was waiting for them in the Oval Office and their discussion on acronyms terminated.

"Any fires we need to put out now or tonight?" asked Kelly.

"Nothing that can't wait," assured the president. "Vice President Hilton is still down there sorting some other things out. Let's wait for her take," suggested the president.

"I'll bet she is," mocked Kelly as she scrunched her lips to show concern.

They all took seats while the steward served coffee and tea.

Looking at General Finn, the president inquired, "Everything good with Korea, Mickey?"

"Never thought I would ever hear it called Korea without a North or a South in front of it. But yes, so far so good. Moon Jae-in and Kim Yo-jong are working it out one day at a time. The border started coming down and we started lifting sanctions accordingly. Kim Yo-jong is allowing her people to go south to search for relatives and Moon Jae-in is allowing families north. No further missile tests or cyber-attacks. Looks like it's gonna work," said Finn.

"Outstanding!" burst the president. "What about Pakistan and Iran?"

"I thought you offered all the terrorists an olive branch. Give peace a chance and all that. We are planning a "Give Peace a Chance" rally in Dallas six days from now on the 23rd," advised Kelly.

"I did and will, but Pakistan and Iran are not terrorists, they are terrorist states. That makes all the difference and they attacked us in New York on Black Friday and the East Coast on New Year's Eve. Had we not sent jumpers into the future and not witnessed the diabolical attacks, we, the United States, would now be gravely, possibly mortally wounded. We would now be a failed state with sharks circling. Only by the knowledge we gained were we able to prevent the attacks. We cannot let this go unanswered," maintained the president.

"Mr. President, if we were now to retaliate against Pakistan and Iran we could find ourselves right back in the same World War III scenario we faced if we had attacked North Korea," suggested Stanton. "Why don't you send the jumpers to a future date and have them witness any possible fallout?" imparted Stanton.

"We already have," divulged the president.

CHAPTER 68

The Oval Office January 17, 2017

Later that night President Burk, Riley and Max sat alone by the fire enjoying their whiskey and Cubans. "Are we ready, Sarge?" asked Director Riley.

"Make the call."

Director Riley pulled out his secure phone and pushed speed dial #1. After three rings Israel Colburn answered and Riley pushed speaker.

"Gentleman, it's late. You're probably sitting around the fire, with Max, sipping your Jameson and Bushmills while enjoying your Montecristo's."

"Should I have the Oval Office swept?" asked Riley.

"To paraphrase Lao Tzu, knowing others is intelligence; knowing what they're up to is true wisdom."

"Speaking of intelligence, we're going to turn the CIA intelligence gathering over to State, shut down their operational end and fire Bader."

"Good start. But finish it. Don't let it fester," admonished Colburn.

Finally recognizing Colburn's voice Max said, "Ruff."

"Hi Max. Let me put you on speaker and you can say hi to Natasha."

"Ruff," barked Max again and was greeted by an equally strong reply from Natasha.

"You done good, Icy. Nice, clean job with your patient," praised Riley.

"I have been told that I have good bed manners."

"You take care of that other thing we talked about?" asked Riley.

"What thing?"

You know. The thing. The other thing?" asked Riley.

"I thought you squashed that with your 'Give Peace a Chance' thing."

"'Give Peace a Chance' is a slogan for the appeasers? The window dressing. Does anyone really think terrorist and their Arab state supporters, Ayatollah's, and Lone Wolves are going to sit down and play nice? The only thing they want is total world domination and nothing short. They will not stop until there is a Quran in every hotel room, a scraggly beard on every man's face and a burqa covering every woman from head to toe. I offered an olive branch to buy time, they took it for the same reason. I want to win the war on terror, but we can't win with conventional forces," contended the president.

"My thoughts exactly," Colburn chimed in.

"So, what have you come up with?" asked President Burk.

"Look, when we first talked at the cabin we still thought it was North Korea and Iran planning the subway and East Coast attacks. We found out later it was Pakistan and Iran. We can take both out the conventional way with bullets, bombs, and boots or with strategic Tomahawk missile strikes, but that will, most likely, get us into World War III faster than the scenario Bader intended to use on North Korea," said Colburn.

"So, what do you suggest?" asked Riley.

"I suggest we get our newest bestest friend Korea, both Moon Jae-in and Kim Yo-jong owe me one, and our next best friend India to put all their cyber warfare assets on to Iran and Pakistan. After all, they set North Korea up as the fall guy, so revenge is plausible, and India would love nothing more than to see Pakistan knocked down a peg or two. We will of course assist, but it will be their fingerprints. The world won't care if Pakistan and Iran lose their nuclear weapons or nuclear capabilities. Korea and India can have some additional fun fucking with their dams, banks, and outing Sharif and Khamenei's finances and love life."

"I like that; let's do it, but what about the terrorist's groups?" asked the president.

"As for the terrorist groups: al-QISIL; al-Badr; al-Shabaab; Boko Haram; Hamas; Hezbollah; Muslim Brotherhood; PLF; Taliban; Lone Wolves and all the rest, you will never beat them with bombs, bullets and boots on the ground. You can't blow-up or shoot an ideology. You can't trample a dream. You can try, look how well it worked after 17 years in Afghanistan. Right now, there are political leaders of terrorist sponsored states and radical spiritual leaders: preaching, fostering and supporting Islamic radical ideology. Until that stops nothing will change. We can't round up all their leaders' family's and ship them to 'Catch 22' at Bagram Air Base in Afghanistan like we did Baghdadi's et-al family's. The way I see it we have two options. The right way and the wrong way."

"What's the right way?" asked President Burk.

"The right way is to break the chain of radical ideological thought. To accomplish that we would need the total support and dedication of all good Muslims everywhere. They must condemn 'Radical Islamic Terrorism' and refute the broken ideology fostering it. The Mosques need to preach and teach the holy Quran not holy war. 'Radical Islamic Terrorist' to good Muslims need to become pariahs as Neo Nazis are to good Christians and Jews."

"That's not gonna happen." said Riley.

"Wait. Why don't we give that a chance? Incorporate it into my 'Give Peace a Chance' tour. Let's invite Muslim: families, political leaders, spiritual leaders, community organizers, law enforcement, artist, educators, and athletes to be part of the rally's. Invite the local Muslim community to every city on the tour. Make them part of the solution instead of part of the problem."

"Right," said Riley, "Good luck with that. They are more scared of the terrorist than they are of us. The Germans loved Hitler and the Iraqis loved Sadam until both countries realized they were losing."

What's the wrong way?"

"Start recruiting and radicalizing a force of terrorists with an equally powerful ideology as a counter force. One that has been around as long as Islam."

"Who?"

"Christians."

"Christians? There are 'Radical Christians Terrorists?'" asked the president.

"One man's freedom fighter is another's terrorist. Just as there are plenty of Radical Islamic Terrorist who want to cleanse the world of non-believers, there are just as many Radical Christian Terrorist who would be glad to return the favor."

"Who?" asked the president.

"The Lord's Resistance Army (LRA) is a Christian Fundamentalist terrorist group originally from Uganda; National Liberation Front of Tripura, out of India; Antibalaka in Central Africa; Tzar Lazar Guard from Serbia; Group in Poso, Indonesia; Sons of Freedom, Canada; Guardians of the Cedars, Lebanon; The Alexander Verkhovsky Whites in Russia; and the Russian National Unity. Hell, we could even get the IRA to partner with the Ulster Volunteer Force."

"We can drive a wedge further between Shia and Sunni and further exasperate tensions between Iraqi against Iran. The possibilities are endless. All the Christians need is a little push, a little help, direction, financing, and PR. They're looking for a mission, but we can give them a crusade," intimated Colburn.

"How do you want to proceed?" asked Riley.

"It has to stay black and the CIA is out. Op/con me General Troy's operations out of Bagram. The whole thing, including Colonel Robert Axelrod and Captain Beck. We all worked well together last time getting Faith out."

"Captain Beck is now Major Beck," corrected Riley.

"Well deserved. You give me Troy's crew and give him everything he asks for including SecDef Stanton and Chief Parker's full support and we'll destroy the Islamic terrorists once and for all."

"And give us Radical Christian Terrorists," declared President Burk.

"Possibly, but Christian's don't want to put you to death if you won't accept their God. The worst they'll do is send Jehovah's Witnesses to your door and talk you to death," Colburn jested.

"Let's go with what's behind door number one first. The right way. Let's invite the Muslim community into our Give Peace a Chance tour. Let's start the dialog. If it doesn't work or they don't want to be part of the solution we'll revisit what's behind door number two," said President Burk.

"What about the homegrown Islamic terrorist organizations and 'Home Wolves'? How do you want to handle them?" quizzed Riley.

"Same way. We'll handle it, but you need to be prepared for fallout. We've got home-grown Christian groups that would also gladly ethnically cleanse our country of all Radical Islamic Terrorist. The Ku Klux Klan; Neo Nazis, the Aryan Nations; the Christian Identity Movement; Phineas Priesthood; Army of God, and a few more."

"Right, but most of those groups would also gladly ethnically cleanse the country of all blacks and Jews. Like I said, let's open door number one to start then will reevaluate," said the president and disconnected.

It was late when Chief of Staff Bill Nicholas knocked and entered with Press Secretary Kelly Sullivan, accompanied by Attorney General Bill Fare, Secretary of State Matt Walsh and Treasury Secretary Mike Bloomfield; all five took seats on the sofas.

Max went over and sat by Kelly and was rewarded with head and neck scratches. When Kelly stopped to speak, Max returned to President Burk's side. "We're all set for the Give Peace a Chance kick off tour in Dallas on the 23rd," assured Kelly.

Looking at the attorney general, President Burk asked, "Is everything back to normal, Bill?"

"The impeachment proceedings have been dropped; martial law has been suspended, and all the media outlets are back. You made a great speech at the UN; you're going to get the Nobel Peace Prize and the market's up. I'd say the country is in pretty good shape. Your administration is in good shape. We may not be back to normal but we're in what is now the new normal."

Looking at his old friend SecTres Mike Bloomfield the president probed, "Mike?"

Bloomfield turned to Bill Fare and said, "Bill, with all due respect this is not normal. At least not in the financial markets. You remember back in '96 when Greenspan used the term 'Irrational Exuberance'? That infamous term he threw out during a speech he gave at the American Enterprise Institute during the Dot-Com bubble? The phrase was interpreted as a warning that the market might be somewhat overvalued. Well, that term is more relevant today than ever. Only this time it's the entire stock market that's the bubble. The entire world's stock markets are experiencing 'Irrational Exuberance'. It's like a Ponzi Scheme and now even the little guys are it up to their necks. Don't they remember economics 101; buy low and sell high? They're always the last in and the last out. When it goes south, and it will, the big guys always get out first and fast. There are dark clouds on the horizon."

"That sounds a bit ominous. When?"

"Later this year or the beginning of next. Some municipality will go bankrupt, then pension funds will start to implode, then some banks will go under, then Greece, Spain. Then it will all spiral down from there and turn to shit."

"I have to agree with Mike," said Secretary of State Matt Walsh. "I just came back from Russia and ever since we increased sanctions their economy is booming. We suspended credit that encourages exports to Russia and financing for economic development projects, so now Russia has been forced to develop their own agriculture and it's booming. They can't sell enough crops to China. Their oil is in demand. China is struggling in debt and if the market collapses she along with most of Asia will fall hard and fast. For Europe and the US, it will be a catastrophe. Worse than '08. But Russia, because of our and UN sanctions, has become an Island unto itself. They will be impervious to a market crash."

Why?"

"They take payment in Norwegian krone's only, reinvest in their own infrastructure and are shorting the market."

"Then we better lift sanctions on Russia and place some on ourselves. We can't let Russia be the last man standing," proposed President Burk.

CHAPTER 69

Dallas, Texas
January 23, 2017, 11:10 a.m.

Their private jet landed at Love Field where a trio of black Secret Service Suburban's met it. Secret Service Agent Bill Wells had one of his agents grab Senator Schuster's and Speaker Bryan's overnight bags and put them in the middle Suburban and led the two congressmen to the back seats while he rode shotgun. He spoke into his mic and the small caravan proceeded towards Dallas and the Adolphus Hotel.

"Gentlemen, welcome to Dallas. There's a chilled bottle of Aquafina in your armrest and we'll be at the hotel in about 20 minutes," informed Agent Wells.

It was almost a straight shot from Love Field down Lemmon Avenue to the Dallas North Tollway merging into Stemmons Freeway through the underpass onto Commerce St. and straight to the Adolphus. But at Griffin Street, the three Suburban's turned left and came up to the newer Adolphus Tower back entrance on Main Street. January in Dallas can be warm and congested. The 6-mile drive took almost 40 minutes, enough time for both the Senator and Speaker to finish their bottled water.

"Why are we going around back?" asked Senator Schuster.

"Those are my instructions, Senator. It's for your own protection. The hotel is very crowded and there are some anti - 'Give Peace a Chance' protesters forming in front of the hotel's main entrance. We have you all checked in and we just want to get you up to the 14th floor with as little fuss as possible," reassured Agent Wells.

They were met at the back entrance by other agents who had sealed off any prying eyes as they led Schuster and Bryan through the new hotel addition into the original hotel where an elevator was waiting to take them straight up to 14.

"I thought we were supposed to meet the president for lunch?" asked Speaker Bryan as the elevator doors closed and the ascent began.

Secret Service Agent Wells did not respond as the doors opened to the 14th floor. Schuster and Bryan got out followed by Wells and another agent.

More agents were already stationed at rooms 1404 and 1405. Both doors were opened as Senator Schuster was guided towards 1404 and Speaker Bryan to 1405.

"Why don't you both freshen up?" suggested Agent Wells as their overnights followed the two into their rooms. "The president has just arrived and requested you meet him in the main floor dining room for lunch in about 20 minutes at 12:15 p.m.," informed Agent Wells as he turned and left.

Schuster and Bryan closed their doors but noticed their adjoining room door was open allowing Bryan to wander into Schuster's room. "What a dump. I stayed here many times and the rooms were very nice. My room has Zenith TV with rabbit ears. So does yours. What the hell?" fumed Bryan.

Agent Wells, Dr. Provenzano, and Russell Randazza watched on the monitors in the control room as both Schuster and Bryan tried to understand what was happening. Both began to show signs of disorientation and slurred speech.

"What time zit?" asked Schuster.

"Now time or lunch time?" answered a light-headed Bryan.

"What? Both I think. I'm just gonna lie down for a min..," said a now confused and tired Schuster.

Bryan followed almost immediately and in the same bed next to Schuster. In less than a minute they were both out cold. The Aquafina spiked with Avinal had done its trick.

Randazza, always alert, also began to feel a bit strange. He turned to look at Dr. Provenzano. "I don't feel so well, doc," as he dropped his bottled water on the floor.

"You have to answer for Santino, Carlo," said Dr. Provenzano following Director Riley's suggestion to channel Michael Corleone.

Randazza stared in silence for a moment before asking, "What?"

"You sold us out to Cabell and you have to answer for it."

Randazza started to say, "Doc, you got it all wrong. I never..." then headed towards the bathroom but stopped short, went down on one knee, then slid prone on the floor.

Ten minutes later all three were in their own beds in rooms 1404, 05 and 06. No effort was made to change them into period clothes but each had their wallets switched out to their new legends.

Dr. Provenzano, Agent Wells and a room full of NASA technicians and engineers watched the wall mounted a/v monitors in each room, and via Bluetooth monitored each jumper's vital signs.

"Are all three showing signs of chemically induced vibration and ringing?"

"Check."

"Have all three achieved OBE?"

"Check."

"Open the vortex on my count."

"Check."

"On 5-4-3-2-..."

The 14th floor started to shake, rattle and roll but as quickly as it begun it subsided. Then there was complete quiet.

The rooms visible on the monitors showed three empty beds. "They're gone," said Dr. Provenzano. "Have a good trip guys, and Razz, be careful what you wish for."

Schuster felt himself being pulled out of a dream. He was shaking and sweating. He got up and looked around. The radio clock on the table read 12:15 p.m. He climbed out of bed and noticed the open door to the adjacent room, went in and saw Paul Bryan sitting on the edge of the bed watching TV. "I must have fallen asleep but I don't remember. We're supposed to be down with the president now for lunch. Let's get a move on it," said Schuster.

"I thought we had Zenith TVs? Now their Philcos? What's with all these old re-runs," remarked Bryan as he got up and turned off the TV and looked towards Schuster. "You look like shit, Chuck."

"So do you, Paul," said Schuster and went back into his own room and into the bathroom. He splashed some water on his face, combed his hair, straightened his tie, took a piss, washed his hands, and went back in to join Bryan who was just coming out of the bathroom drying his hands.

"Let's go," said Schuster. He opened the room door, entered the hallway and pressed the elevator down button. Bryan followed and together they waited for the elevator. The door of the next room opened and Randazza came out and stood with them, nodded and said, "Senator. Mr. Speaker."

Thinking Randazza was part of their security detail, Schuster said, "We're late, agent. We were supposed to meet the president at 12:15. We have to hurry. We don't have much time."

Randazza accepting his fate said, "Senator, you have no idea how much time you have."

The elevator arrived, the three got in and they began their descent to November 23, 1963.

CHAPTER 70

Dallas, Texas
November 23, 1963, 12:25 P.M.

Schuster and Bryan rushed out of the elevator looking for the dining room. The lobby was grand, almost overwhelming, but not as Schuster remembered it from his recent visits.

Not being able to locate the restaurant Bryan turned to the agent for help but he was gone.

"What the hell?" said Bryan, turning back towards the lobby and seeing a bellboy. "Excuse me, where's the restaurant?"

The bellboy pointed and said, "Follow me, sir."

Randazza hung back and watched the two follow the bellboy to what he knew would become an event. He wanted to see what happened but not be associated or get involved. But he knew it was gonna be good.

"What is this, some kind of a theme hotel? Everyone looks the same, like an old 70's TV show," stated a confused Bryan.

"More like the 60's. They all have hats on and are smoking and reading newspapers. It's like the hotel is in color but the people are in black and white," remarked Schuster.

"Are these the protesters the agent warned us about, and where's that Secret Service agent who came down with us?" asked Bryan.

"Here we are, sir," said the bellboy, opening the restaurant glass door. "Will there be anything else?"

Neither Bryan and Schuster responded, they just walked past him and into the restaurant as if he wasn't there.

"May I help you, gentlemen?" asked the maitre d' from behind the podium.

"Yes, we're here with the president. He's expecting us," said Senator Schuster.

"And you are?" asked the maitre d'.

"Honestly, you don't know?" asked Senator Schuster.

"I'm sure I don't," replied the maitre d'.

"I'm Senator Schuster and this is Speaker Bryan, and we have a 12:15 lunch with the president. Now, will you please take us to him?"

"Gentlemen, the president was shot yesterday…"

Schuster and Bryan weren't listening as they pushed past him and started to look for the president in the restaurant. Not finding President Burk, they raced out of the restaurant past the maitre d', who was now on the phone with hotel security and the Dallas PD, and over to the crowded check-in desk, and pushed their way to the front on the line.

"Get me the manager immediately!" yelled Bryan.

The startled clerk, who was in the middle of assisting customers, picked up the phone to dial the manager's office. The same newlywed couple, encountered by Todd and Scales two days previous, were checking out, and with what just happened to their president, were in no mood to be pushed aside. The husband, a house painter from Philadelphia, stepped forward and got between the check-in clerk and the two interlopers and demanded the clerk finish checking them out first.

Speaker Bryan, not one to be put off, ignored the man and exclaimed loudly, "Excuse me, but this is an emergency. I'm House Speaker Bryan. We have a meeting here with the President of the United States and we demand to see him immediately." Turning to Schuster he added, "You think the president stiffed us?"

Without waiting for an answer Speaker Bryan spat, "If that son-of-a-bitch is playing games with us, he's done. I'll personally put a bullet in his head."

Feeling intrusive and hoping to defuse the situation Schuster added, "It's Okay. The Speaker's from New York."

The newlywed husband turned to Schuster and said, "Been hearing that a lot lately." Turning back to Bryan he said, "House Speaker Bryan, I'm House Painter Murphy and I loved President Kennedy." He then punched Bryan in the face.

Bryan hands flew up to his face as he fell backward. Two hotel security personnel came up and grabbed Murphy and restrained him before he could do any more damage to Bryan. Mrs. Murphy, the others in line along with the check-in clerk all pointed to Bryan and Schuster saying they started it by butting the line and saying bad things about President Kennedy. Two Dallas police officers entered the fray and pulled Schuster and Bryan aside, offering Bryan a handkerchief to stop the blood pouring from what now looked to be a broken nose.

A Dallas homicide detective following up on the assassination with two Secret Service agents happened to be at the hotel having lunch when the commotion began, intervened and started pulling people and hotel employees aside for questioning. The detective and senior Secret Service agent eventually made their way over to the two Dallas police officers holding Schuster and Bryan, spoke to them briefly and then sent them off to check to see if Schuster and Bryan were registered guests.

Reading from his note book Detective James Leavelle asked, "It's Senator Schuster and House Speaker Bryan, is it? You recognize these boys, Agent Betts?"

"Never saw them before, detective. What's more, John McCormack is our Speaker of the House and Ken Keating and Jacob Javits are the only two New Jersey or New York Senators I know of," said Secret Service Agent Betts.

"You boys have any ID?" asked Detective Leavelle.

Russell Randazza, now sitting in a chair pretending to read the newspaper, watched as Schuster and Bryan reached for their wallets.

"And you are?" asked Schuster.

"James Leavelle. Detective. Homicide division. Dallas PD."

"This is ridiculous," said Schuster, opening his wallet and pulling out what he thought was his congressional ID.

Secret Service Agent Betts took the ID but also took the wallet.

"Is this some sort of joke? Are you making a movie? Why are you dressed in a cowboy hat?" asked Bryan through his bloody handkerchief as he handed his wallet to Detective Leavelle.

They studied the ID's and content of both wallets then they compared I.D's. "Jesus, this can't be right," said Agent Betts.

"No shit. Why don't you run them and see what you get?"

Secret Service Agent Betts took both wallets and headed to the checkout desk phone.

Detective Leavelle motioned the two Dallas police officers back.

"They're not registered," said one of the officers. Detective Leavelle pulled his revolver and said, "Put the bracelets on these two clowns."

"For what? What's wrong with you people? Were United States Congressmen. The Speaker has been assaulted and you're arresting us?" fumed Schuster.

"Your ID says you're someone named Sy Sperling, president of something called Hair Club for Men, and you, looking at Bryan, you're Eddie Munster, a gravedigger for the Gateman Goodbury and Graves Funeral parlor. Is that some sort of joke? You big city boys have a real funny sense of humor; but tell me, why do you both have Lee Harvey Oswald's name in your address books?"

"You're making a big mistake here Detective Leavelle. Oswald? What's the fuck does he have to do with any of this? If you don't remove these handcuffs immediately, I will have you transferred to the Canadian Mounties. You will never be heard from again," promised Schuster.

"Oswald murdered the president yesterday, and you boys have his name in your address books, that's what. That little shit murdered Kennedy and normally I would treat that no different than a South Dallas nigger killing, but now you two boys just made it a whole lot more interesting," said Detective Leavelle.

Randazza watched as Senator Schuster, aka Sy Sperling, and House Speaker Bryan, aka, Eddie Munster, were led away by the Dallas police and the Secret Service. He knew both Schuster and Bryan were in for a couple of horrible days and a confusing uncertain future, and that 43-year-old Detective Jim Leavelle would be known forever as the detective who was handcuffed to Oswald when Ruby took his shot. Uncertain about his own future, Randazza reached in his pocket to see if he had any money and a wallet and found a note from Dr. Provenzano.

Razz, you were always a loyal friend and good partner, so I convinced the president and Director Riley to allow you time exile instead of being accused of treason. There is a $25,000-dollar time sensitive bank check payable to you from the Dallas Republic National Bank in your wallet. Not a fortune today but plenty to get you started in '63. Your new legend has been set so you will have no problem getting a job with NASA and being part of the Apollo Space Program. Who knows, you might help put Armstrong on the Moon. Now wouldn't that be something? Goodbye, old friend, have a good life and be careful what you wish for.

Tony

CHAPTER 71

Dallas, Texas
January 23, 2017, 1:25 p.m.

President Burk and his team chose Dallas for the kick-off tour primarily to coincide with the discovery of the controversial JFK assassination film now being called 'The Logan Film'.

President Tommy Dean Burk and First Lady Kelly Sullivan Burk aboard Air Force One touched down onto Love Field, waved to the small crowd and assembled press and walked over to the presidential limo. Designed from the ground up by the Secret Service, President Burk's $1.5 million Cadillac One, aka The Beast, is a moving fortress impenetrable to bullets and bombs. The president and first lady got in and drove off for the start of the 'Give Peace a Chance' kickoff rally to be held in Dealey Plaza.

The motorcade consisted of: three Dallas police patrol cars setting the route, followed by two Cadillac Ones both flying the presidential seal, but only one carrying the president and first lady (codenamed Stagecoach). The other carried VIP's and staff. More Suburbans and vans were carrying: electronics, control, support, CAT (Counter Assault Team), hazardous material mitigation, press, White House communications (codenamed Roadrunner) and an ambulance. Several DPD motorcycles ran interference.

From Love Field, the presidential motorcade followed the same route that President Kennedy took on that fateful November day 53 years previous. The motorcade turned onto Mockingbird Lane, along Mockingbird Lane to Lemmon, then Lemmon to Turtle Creek, from Turtle Creek to Cedar Springs, Cedar Springs to Harwood, Harwood to Main, Main to Houston, Huston to Elm and finally Dealey Plaza and the rally.

"Tommy, do you think this is a good idea?" asked Kelly.

"What? The rally?"

"You know exactly what I'm talking about. You did this on purpose, didn't you? We're following Kennedy's route and going right past the Texas School Book Depository and adjacent to the 'Grassy Knoll'. Is this some sort of macho Marine bullshit?"

"Kelly, nothing is going to happen. We're in a bullet and bomb-proof limo."

"More like we're in a bullet and bomb magnet. Besides, we're gonna get out in Dealey Plaza in a minute and you're gonna give a speech about making peace with the terrorists. Not exactly what Texans believe or want to hear."

"I could wear a bulletproof vest."

"A lot of good that did Kennedy and his brother Bobby. Both head shots. And what about John Kearney who stood next to you at the Dallas Trade Mart debate? The assassin took his head off. And Martin Luther King Jr.? Shot in the neck. A lot of good a bulletproof vest would have done them."

"Look. I have lots of security, and a back-screen behind me flanked by stone columns and a podium and Teleprompters in front. To hit me would be like threading a needle or they would have to get real close or real lucky."

The crowds lining the route, from Love Field to Dealey Plaza were sparse, to say the least, but Dealey Plaza was starting to fill up. Except for the cars, and the way people dressed, Dealey Plaza hadn't really changed much since 1963. The Texas School Book Depository, Dal-Tex Building, County Records Building, County Criminal Courts (Jail) Building were all the same. The Old Court House, Post Office, Peristyles and Reflecting Pools, Triple Underpass were all still there. The only exception was the Dallas County Government

Center, under construction in 1963, was now complete. It almost felt like time stood still in Dealey Plaza when the Beast pulled to a stop on Houston and Main. Unlike November 22, 1963, there were no snipers in the TSBD, the Dal-Tex Building or on the Grassy Knoll. But in the steeple of the Western Heights Church of our Lord across Stemmons Freeway, a killer waited.

TrackingPoint is a precision-guided, comprehensive, purpose-built weapon system for rifles.

It incorporates the same tracking and fire-control capabilities found in advanced fighter jets. Shooters of any skill level can now shoot better than the best shooters who ever lived.

A TrackingPoint Precision-Guided Firearm system ensures never-before-seen precision at extreme distances and high target velocities. TriggerLink connects the tracking optic with a guided trigger. Tag-and-Shoot technology lets a person designate an exact target impact point. The tracking system then guides the trigger release. Press the tag button to designate an impact point.

Align the reticle with the tag, then squeeze and hold the trigger. The Precision-Guided Firearm does the rest. When attached to a Barrett XM500 gas-operated, semi-automatic 50-caliber sniper anti-material rifle it is a deadly accurate weapon.

Basically, when you acquire a target the system will lock on the target and fire automatically when all the conditions are perfect: wind, distance, deflections, temperature, and curvature of the Earth. It's like automatically threading a needle. This is the weapon that former DDCI Charles Cabell had mounted on a bipod in the fifty-foot-high steeple of the Western Heights Church of our Lord.

"I agree with Kelly. This whole thing is nuts. We don't know where Cabell is and there are too many Home Wolves, RIT's and Neo-Nazis, who would love nothing more than to take your head off. We have counter sniper teams watching every building, but anyone with a cell phone looking gun could shoot you while taking a selfie," intimated Secret Service Director Chris

Bounty from the jump seat across from the president. Bounty went way back with President Burk and didn't hesitate to say what he felt.

FBI Director Riley was handling a potentially explosive situation in Philadelphia from within the FBI's massive SIOC Strategic Information and Operation Center at FBI headquarters in Washington. FBI AIC Michael Hoar, head of the New York Office, was in Dallas representing his boss Director Riley, and assisting Bounty. Hoar had plenty of experience with snipers and sniping so he was a natural to have around as an extra pair of eyes. He was riding shotgun.

Cabell was in the church steeple preparing for the shot. It was a beautiful church with a steeple spire topped with a ball and cross, that towered 50 feet above the two-story church. Monday's services celebrating Martin Luther King Jr. Day were over and the church was now empty. Cabell worked his way up to the steeple tower. Spiral stairs led through the belfry and trap-door into the steeple lantern room. The lantern room was a six-sided glass-enclosed structure, each with fifteen small lites of glass separated by wood mullions and muntins. With the trap-door closed there were almost 64 square feet of interior space, plenty of room for Cabell to set up and snap in. The first thing Cabell did was check his site line and distance to the target. The site line was clear with a slightly downward angle, but even with his Vortex Fury HD Range Finding Binoculars, the distance seemed daunting. The church was old and the individual glass lites were each eight inches square. The lantern room was vented but the windows didn't open, and the small room was hot. From a soft case, he removed a fully charged electric drill with a 2.5-inch diameter carbide tip glass cutting round saw. The saw was modified with a built-in suction cup to grab and retain the glass once the hole was cut. He carefully applied a clear 5" x 5" film over the lower middle lite or what some might call a window pane, and soaked the round carbide saw with oil. He then pressed the drill against the glass and quietly and slowly began to grind. When about half way through, he applied more oil and engaged the suction cup. He finished the cut, then removed the saw with the round piece of glass.

From another soft case, he removed a Barrett XM500, a gas-operated, .50-caliber semi-automatic sniper/anti-material rifle. He attached the TrackingPoint system and bipod and placed the rifle on the floor.

He went behind the rifle, assumed the prone position and began snapping in. The suppressor end was just through the hole and Cabell was back from the window about three feet. It was tight for his tall frame as he looked through the scope and waited.

Participation by the Muslim community was overwhelming. Several speakers, including a Dallas Imam, preceded the president but now it was his turn. President Burk walked up onto the stage and over to the podium. He received a good reception from the assembled and the rally was adequately covered by the mainstream media outlets including many internationals like *BBC* and *Al Jazeera.*

> *"My fellow Americans, thank you all for joining me here in beautiful Dallas for the first of many Give Peace a Chance rallies. I would like to thank Governor ..."*

The president continued speaking but Secret Service Director Bounty and his agents and counter sniper teams were not listening. They were looking for anything out of place including profiling the crowd. In addition to several hundred Dallas police officers, some with dogs, he had over a hundred agents watching buildings and the assembled crowd. He had two-man counter sniper teams consisting of a spotter aka wind reader and a shooter, in buildings behind the president looking for open windows in the buildings to the president's front and side. They scanned the overpass and parking garages for cars or vans that looked suspicious and building roofs. He had response teams ready to move in and secure the slightest offender.

"Alpha six. Alpha six, this is Sierra Tango two" said Enrique Montalvo speaking into his collar mic. Enrique was one of the best, if not the best, shooter of the twenty counter sniper teams assigned to protect the president. Based out of Miami, Montalvo was specifically op/coned to Dallas by Secret Service Director Bounty.

Enrique Montalvo was 38 years old, athletic and chiseled face handsome. Think a Latin Gene Kelly. The ladies loved him. He was intelligent, fun, attentive, respectful and a bit of a momma's boy. His guy friends knew him as a smooth operator who could cross over to the dark side when pushed. Just under six-foot-tall, Enrique spent his days in the gym and the shooting range, his nights with his friends experiencing all that Miami had to offer.

Montalvo and his wind reader, agent Brian Harrigan were on the second floor of the Old Court House on Houston Street just behind and slightly above the president. Montalvo was prone on a sandbagged secured table allowing his rifle barrel a 3-inch clearance over the open window sill. He was behind the ultimate sniper weapon: the McMillan TAC-50. The TAC-50 fires .50-caliber match grade bullet 2,600 feet per second and weigh just 26 pounds including a scope, mount, and bipod. For his optics, Montalvo chose a Premier Reticles Heritage 3-15 x 50mm Tactical Scope. This rifle, this ammo, this scope and this shooter are the ultimate killing machine.

"This is Alpha six," responded Director Bounty, "go ahead, Suave." (Montalvo's war name)

"Across Stemmons I got something," cautioned Montalvo.

Both Bounty and Hoar swung their binoculars towards the Frank Crowley Courts Building directly across Stemmons Freeway, thinking the 639-yard distance building could be a sniper's nest.

"The Court Building?" asked Bounty.

"A little further out," replied Montalvo.

Bounty tolerated Montalvo's vagueness because that was how Montalvo's brain worked and because he was that good. "How much further out?" asked Bounty.

"We register 3,678-yards."

"What the fuck? That's almost two miles. Why are you wasting your time looking that far out? Nobody would take a shot from there."

"Boss, it's 2.09 miles and let the other teams look inside the box. I'm looking out and I tell you I got something."

"Okay, what do you have?"

"It's right out of a movie, boss, a church with a steeple. A big white steeple with the cross on top. Straight ahead at 12 o'clock, 3,678-yards."

Both Bounty and Hoar adjusted their Leica HD-B Rangefinder Binoculars, found the church but the Leica could not read range past 2000-yards.

"Got it," said Bounty.

"Big glass window near the top of the steeple. Three rows of glass panes across and five high."

"Got it. What am I looking for?"

"Bottom row, middle glass pane."

"Got it, but what am I looking for?"

"See the little hole in the glass and the little thing in the hole?"

"Jesus, Enrique, how the fuck did you find that?"

"Cause I'm looking for where I would take the shot."

"A little hole with a little thing in the hole? It looks like a decal. I can't see anyone in there, can you?"

"The little thing in the hole just moved."

Hoar was looking through his binoculars and saw what Montalvo saw and immediately understood what was about to happen.

"Montalvo. This is FBI AIC Hoar. Take the shot."

Montalvo hesitated. "Boss?"

Bounty looked at Hoar and saw something in his demeanor, in his eyes that told him not to question his call.

"Suave. Take the shot," commanded Bounty.

If the sniper is the gas pedal and the spotter is the steering wheel, this means that a good spotter will locate the target, talk the shooter onto the target and help him obtain a hit.

"Ready," said Montalvo as he applied more pressure on the trigger and took a last deep breath.

"Wind left .4 and that's all I got, buddy. Nobody's ever done one this far. You're on your own. Send it," coached Harrington.

Montalvo released his breath, applied a little more pressure and BOOM!

One second. Two seconds. Three seconds.

Everyone heard the shot. It wasn't a bang or a crack. It could not be mistaken for a backfire or a firecracker. This was a heavy, throaty explosive boom. Montalvo occasionally suppressed his shots but never one this far. Even President Burk flinched but his security detail had been listening and knew what was coming and signaled the president it was outgoing. The president continued, "*...and I say again, we must give peace a chance...*"

Four seconds, Five seconds. Six seconds.

Montalvo, Harrington, and Hoar took the time lap in stride. A shot this far would greatly reduce the projectiles speed. Bounty, not a sniper, was getting nervous as he focused on the steeple window.

Seven seconds. Eight Seconds. Nine Seconds. It seemed as though the ultrasonic projectile was traveling in slow motion. Through their scopes and binoculars, their vigil was finally rewarded when the steeple lantern room's second-row middle glass window pane exploded, and all the remaining 14 glass panes turned red. Sadly, the four completely missed President Burk grab his chest as he was blown backward off the stage. It took just under 10 seconds for both rounds to travel the 3,678-yards. Both rounds crossed paths at 1825-yards where a sonic boom occurred causing shock waves to slightly alter both projectiles paths. Cabell's shot fell while Montalvo's rose. Cabell's head shot became a body shot. Montalvo's little black thing in the little hole shot went a bit higher. His .50 Caliber match grade round passed through the glass pane, through the TrackingPoint System scope, through Cabell's right eye bursting his head like an exploded watermelon and continuing down his throat and tumbling through his chest cavity ripping out his stomach and intestines.

It didn't take long for a response team to access the church and steeple. They attempted to lift the trap door but were only able to open it but a crack before blood and gore began pouring down all over them. They commandeered a Dallas City electric truck with a lift basket which enabled them to observe the lantern room from the outside. What they saw was sickening. The .50 caliber round, even after two miles, had done horrible damage to Cabell. But the talk around the water cooler for the foreseeable future would be about Enrique Suave Montalvo making the longest confirmed kill shot in history.

CHAPTER 72

DALLAS, TEXAS
JANUARY 18, 2017, 2:15 P.M.

President Burk was rushed the three miles from Dealey Plaza to Parkland Hospital and admitted to Trauma Room 1. He was in critical condition with a chest wound from a .50 caliber round that entered clean and left dirty. He suffered a hole the size of a quarter through his right pectoralis, just missing his heart but shattering his clavicle, taking out two ribs, piercing a vein and artery, puncturing his lung, severing his diaphragm, and taking a chunk of his liver before splattering on the pavement and causing injuries to bystanders from jagged missiles of copper and cement. But for an ambulance standing by with a veteran Army medic who dealt with trauma in Afghanistan in attendance, the president would be dead.

The assassination attempt was covered live, and many people would forever remember where they were when President Burk was shot. Many were sad, or in disbelief or in shock. Some were happy and hoped he would die. A few immediately realized the potential downside and began dumping stock before Asia and Europe woke up. Get out now in case he dies; then it will be too late.

One would think President Burk was the most beloved president in recent history the way the mainstream media and Congress sang his praises.

"Who would shoot our beloved president?" said one talking head. "He was a good man with a good agenda battling a tough Congress." said another. "Why haven't we heard from Senator Schuster or Speaker Bryan?"

The Secret Service would release no details about the shooter, so speculation and blame became the news. "Has any terrorist organization claimed responsibility yet?" asked one reporter. "We need to reinstate the travel ban." opined another. "We need stricter gun laws," voiced yet another.

Each news program had its own military parade of retired generals, colonels, CIA and Delta analysts who orated with great authority why the assassination occurred and who was responsible. The list of culprits included Kim Jung-un loyalists, Iran, and al-QISIL.

The president was in and out of surgery constantly. When one problem seemed fixed or at least stabilized, another would flare up. He had been badly hurt and lost a lot of blood.

Las Vegas odds were 20-1 he wouldn't pull through. Because the president had to go under anesthetic so often, Vice President Hilton was sworn in and out as the president lost and regained consciousness.

Kelly and Riley never left the hospital and were by his side constantly when permitted. Bounty came and went and Dr. Provenzano had an opportunity to have some private time with his old friend. Even Israel Colburn in disguise visited with Riley's help.

A week passed before the president started showing some progress. It wasn't much but he was cognizant and able to have brief conversations. The president was in no condition to be moved so top specialists were flown in as needed.

Riley had been down in the press area giving an update when he came back up to the president's hospital suite. There was one room, and an adjacent family room that Kelly, Riley and special guests could stay and maintain visual contact with the president.

"Who's that in there with Tommy?" asked Riley.

"It's that writer, Fitzpatrick, the one who has been chronicling Tommy's presidency in *Fear Itself* and *Best Served Icy*."

"What the hell? I leave for 20 minutes and that prick gets in? How did he get in?"

"Relax, Ray. Tommy asked for him and wanted to talk to him alone. He just got here."

"I'll be damned. The president was Fitzy's source all along. I didn't see that coming," admitted Riley.

"I guess they're working on the third installment, a trilogy. I really hope it's not the last, Ray. I love that guy," said Kelly as tears started to flow for the umpteenth time that day.

Riley took Kelly in his arms and they held each other. "I love him, too. I should have been there."

Fifteen minutes later the president's personal physician, Dr. Tyner, Dr. Provenzano and the head surgeons from both Parkland and Bethesda went in with the president and asked Fitzpatrick to leave. Fitzpatrick considered protesting but when an attending nurse made a move towards him he said his goodbye and left.

Dr. Provenzano came out about twenty minutes later and joined Kelly and Riley in the adjacent family room.

"It's not good. He's developed congestion and water in his left lung. It's looking like pneumonia. His immune system has been battling it but he's losing," said a grave Dr. Provenzano.

"I want to go in," begged Kelly.

After Kelly left the family room and went in with her husband, Riley looked at Dr. Provenzano and said, "Tell me, Tony."

"If he makes it through the night we have a chance."

He didn't.

The New York Times

New York Saturday, March 4, 2017

President Dead

Nation Mourns

Vice President Hilton to take oath upon return to Washington.

First Lady Kelly Sullivan Burk wanted the president's body flown immediately to Washington. The Dallas County Sheriff's office was claiming jurisdiction and the Secret Service was going ape shit. The sheriff's office was calling the president's death a homicide and wanted to perform an autopsy before they would release the body.

Secret Service Director Bounty and FBI Director Riley were threatening to remove the body by force. "Where did I hear this before?" asked Bounty.

"Autopsy? Do they need to cut him open after just sewing him back together? They have Cat Scans, X-Rays, and MRI's, what more do they need?" fumed Riley.

The Secret Service prevailed and with Dr. Provenzano constantly at his side the president's body was flown back to Washington.

CHAPTER 73

MOSCOW, MAINE MARCH 29, 2017

President Burk had been laid to rest March 8th with full honors adjacent to JFK in Arlington Cemetery. Former First Lady Kelly Sullivan Burk, President Burk's family, cabinet, close friends, president's, prime ministers, ambassadors and people from around the world joined America to mourn and celebrate the life of Thomas Dean Burk. All major media outlets throughout the world covered the funeral and there was an absolute heartfelt sadness expressed followed by accolades and respect for President Burk's vision and accomplishments.

When they met in the cabin in Moscow, Maine three weeks later the country was finally getting back to normal. President Chelsey Hilton reinstated Director Bader as head of the CIA and together they were initiating a commission, to be headed by the president's mother, former President Hillary Hilton, to investigate President Burk's assassination.

The stock market was beginning to show signs of recovery. The media was allowing President Hilton a few weeks grace while consumed by the disappearance of Senator Schuster and Speaker Bryan. The *New York Post* had them married and honeymooning in Tahiti. *The National Enquirer* had them abducted by aliens, but Hilton and Bader suspected that Burk sent them on a one-way trip. Regardless, as far as they were concerned, good riddance.

Kelly was no longer first lady and Riley, Bounty, and Nicholas resigned as did most of the Cabinet and other members of the inner circle. Still, others stayed on until a suitable replacement could be nominated and confirmed.

Riley, Max and Dr. Tony Provenzano flew up to Bangor on one of Mike Bloomfield's private jets and arranged for a helicopter service to shuttle them back and forth to Israel Colburn's cabin. Kelly was home with her family and asked Riley if he wouldn't mind looking after Max until she got back and settled in. This was Dr. Provenzano's first trip to the cabin. He and Natasha sat next to each other, by the fire, getting acquainted. Dr. Provenzano missed his own friend at home, Pandemonium; his 130-pound Rottweiler. Max was playing with Timmy when Riley and Colburn came in and took seats by the fireplace.

Snow was beginning to fall and if they stayed too long they would be grounded for the night.

Riley and President Burk had trusted Dr. Provenzano, but Colburn didn't trust anyone, except Riley, Natasha, and Timmy, and there were some things Riley and Colburn couldn't discuss in front of Timmy and Dr. Provenzano.

It was getting late and the snow was beginning to accumulate so Timmy said his goodbyes and made his way home through the woods. His dad would be worried, especially after hearing a helicopter pass over town.

Around 8 p.m., Riley, Colburn, Natasha, Max and Dr. Provenzano sat around the fire discussing events. They were all sort of unemployed now and while strange it also felt kind of good. Colburn was introduced to Dr. Provenzano as an old friend, but the doc knew there was more to it and let it go.

Looking suspiciously at Dr. Provenzano, Riley said, "I can't believe he's gone."

Dr. Provenzano shook his head in agreement but took the conversation in a different direction. "So, this is it? Cabell came back for the final con, assassinates Tommy. 'The Sting' I believe you called it."

"'The Sting'. Yeah, it's the sting all right. But remember what Paul Newman said, 'You have to keep the con even after you take his money. He can't know you took him.' It was the sting all right but not the way you think."

"Why?" asked Dr. Provenzano.

"That's the real question isn't it: why? The how and the who is just scenery for the public. Cabell, Bader, the CIA, and North Korea keeps 'em guessing like some kind of parlor game, prevents 'em from asking the most important question: why? Why was President Burk killed? Who benefited? Who has the power to cover it up? Who?"

"Cabell?"

"Cabell was just the patsy. It was Vice President Hilton who planned the whole thing. She had CIA Director Bader create the chaos then ordered President Burk's assassination. They're the ones who benefit. They're the ones who have the power to cover it up," said Ryley.

"Jesus. We trusted her. Tommy trusted her. I know he had his doubts and so did Kelly. We should have listened. He brought her into his inner circle. How could anyone be so cunning, so scheming, and unscrupulous? Talk about advancing one's political career. Devious is the word," confided Dr. Provenzano.

"Machiavellian," proposed Riley.

"So, Cabell wasn't Harry Gondorff after all. It was the vice president behind the entire thing. She created 'The Sting,'" said Dr. Provenzano adding, "She wants to meet with me about Project Christopher."

"And?" asked Riley.

"And I'm not sure I can refuse a request from the president. But God only knows what Project Christopher would become in the hands of Chelsey Machiavelli."

"My advice is to play along. If you try and duck her they'll send for you and that may not work out too well. Don't give them anything. Just see what they want then get back to me," advised Riley.

"This Project Christopher, this time travel thing, you can really go back and forth in time?" asked Colburn.

"Yes, we can and have," assured Dr. Provenzano.

"Then why don't we go back and save President Burk?" asked Colburn.

"President Burk never wanted to change history just history books. We swore an oath never to try and change the past," replied Dr. Provenzano.

"But we did change the past, doc. Just by sending the jumpers: Todd, Flatly and Scales back and leaving them stranded changed the past," protested Riley.

"We didn't try to change the past. We only proved that Oswald didn't take the shot. We're here, and nothing has changed." said Dr. Provenzano.

"You don't know that for sure. Remember when Todd walked into an MG dealership and paid cash for the sports car? Suppose the salesman celebrated his good fortune with a few drinks at one of Ruby's clubs. One thing then led to another and the next morning his wife found lipstick on his collar. They get a divorce and never have the son or daughter who might have grown up to be president or a serial killer. Get my drift?" asked Riley.

"Yes, but you don't understand," continued Dr. Provenzano.

"What's to understand, you could send me back and I could have Montalvo take the shot 10 seconds sooner. We get Cabell and he never gets his shot off. Both Tommy and Project Christopher get to live a good long life and the vice president loses," said Riley.

"Tommy said you wouldn't let it go. He said you both would persist," observed Dr. Provenzano as he scratched Natasha's neck.

"What's that supposed to mean?" asked Riley.

"Nothing. Tommy's gone; dead and buried. He's home and that's exactly where I need to be. We need to leave now, or we'll be stuck the night."

"You take the chopper back, doc. I'm gonna stay the night. Ask the pilot to come back and get me tomorrow morning if he can."

Around midnight, Riley, Colburn, Natasha, and Max were sitting around the fire when it started. Natasha and Max heard it first then Riley and Colburn. The howling of the Wolf Mountain wolf pack. First, it was just a lonely haunting howl from the top of the mountain. It was answered by a chorus of three or more wolves' closer to the cabin.

Natasha and Max were getting uncontrollably excited wanting to get out of the cabin. Natasha started to groan, eventually morphing into something resembling a broken howl. She could have just bolted out the doggy door, but she waited until her Da gave her the okay.

"You're not going to let her out, are you?" asked Riley.

"Why not? She's a big girl and can take care of herself. Besides, she knows them, and neither is a threat to the other."

"I can't let Max go. If anything happened Kelly would kill me."

"You sound like an old lady, Captain. They'll be okay." Turning to Natasha he said, "Stay near girl and take care of Max. Now go."

Natasha let out a loud, sharp bark of acknowledgment followed equally by one from Max before they both bolted through the doggy door and into the snowy night.

Colburn stood up and mimicked Natasha's howl and excitement and headed towards the deck and opened the door. Riley followed Colburn onto the snow-covered deck. They watched together as Natasha and Max rounded the clearing before disappearing into the forest. More howls and more chorusing came from the mountain until it all blended together about a half mile north of the cabin.

"They'll be back in a half-hour or so. Don't worry, they're all kin. Let's go back in and do what we have to do," said Colburn.

On the mantel over the fireplace were three new Waterford Diamond 7 ounce straight sided crystal tumblers, three Montecristo Cuban cigars, a wedge cutter and Burk's old Zippo lighter. On the sideboard was a bottle each of Jameson Limited Reserve and Bushmill Old Single Malt.

"The last time I did this here in the cabin, Sarge and I were mourning you. Whoda thunk? Do you think he knew this was going to happen? Could he have known Cabell would come for him in Dallas?" asked Riley.

"No. If he did he wouldn't have put himself and Kelly in harm's way," said Colburn. "No. We all missed it."

"But what about the doc's vagueness and all that stuff about Tommy knowing we wouldn't let it go and would persist? He's dead and buried for sure. I was at the wake and never left his side till after he was in the ground.

But the doc's comment about Tommy being home. What was that?" asked Riley.

Colburn shrugged then got up and poured some Jameson and Bushmill into the three crystal tumblers and handed one to Riley, kept one for himself and placed Burk's on the table between them. As before, in the White House and the cabin, what seemed like a long time ago, Colburn said, "To God."

Riley replied, "To the Queen."

They both gave a little sigh, swirled the glass, sniffed, then drank.

They turned towards a rumbling from outside just as Natasha and Max came barreling through the doggy door. Both ran over to the fire where they decided was the best place to vigorously shake off the wet snow. This went on a couple of times before both laid down on the carpet to warm by the fire.

"That was fast, girl. You two thought you were missing something?"

Colburn reached for the cigars, as Riley, Natasha, and Max got up and headed towards the glass doors leading to the deck. Riley hesitated and said, "How does this end?"

"I guess we'll have to wait for Fitzy's book," advised Colburn.

"Don't get me started on that SOB."

"Why? His books are a bit too sarcastic and tongue and cheek for me, but he seems to get it right," reasoned Colburn.

"Well, he just lost his source, and let me know if you want to revise your review when he outs you," said Riley.

"What do you want to do with Sarge's tumbler? asked Colburn.

Riley thought a moment then said, "Just place it on the mantel like we did last time. Who knows?"

"To survivors," toasted Colburn.

"And to absent friends and payback," added Riley.

Colburn took one last sip from his glass and tossed his crystal tumbler into the fire, as they had done before. Riley followed suit. The little alcohol left in the glasses caused the fire to jump. Colburn picked up Sarge's crystal tumbler, careful not to spill any, and placed it on the mantel.

The Captain and Icy, and their two best buddies, Natasha and Max, walked out on the snowy deck to smoke their cigars and commiserate the loss of their leader and best friend Tommy Dean Burk aka Sarge, and to contemplate their acceptance or their revenge.

Da safe, Captain safe, Max safe, Natasha safe, pack safe, thought Natasha, but then she remembered the kind man her Da called Sarge, the nice female her Da called Faith, and her friend Timmy. *They should be here with us*, thought Natasha.

Natasha began to howl. She needed to bring them back to the pack. Max quickly joined in and was followed by a couple of wolves near the cabin.

The snow was falling harder under a full high Moon. The branches of the pine and spruce trees were bending down under the weight of the heavy wet snow. The howling was getting louder. Beautiful, eerie and haunting, it was almost like a chorus in harmony. Then from the top of Wolf Mountain came a stronger reply. A larger chorus but just as haunting. Closer and closer they seemed to be coming together until at last, they seemed to be singing as one pack.

The hypotonic mood unraveled quickly when local town dogs, two miles away joined in. The mood deteriorated quickly from mystical to more like a parody of Pongo and the Great Dane from a Disney movie.

EPILOGUE

Southwest Philadelphia, 1957

Everything's seems a bit foggy. My chest is killing me. Something hit me. Wait, something did hit me. A bullet and it killed me but I'm still alive, thought Tommy.

He looked at his hands. They were familiar but smaller. He had on a white dress shirt, dress trousers, and dress shoes. Everything was smaller including his perspective. *I wish I had a mirror,* he thought.

He was standing across the street from his boyhood home. Before he could stop himself, he unbuckled his belt, unzipped his trousers and tugged on the waist band of his Jockeys and looked down and thought, *Jesus. He did it. He made me young again.*

Looking at the house and the neighborhood Tommy thought, *My God, nothing's changed. It's exactly as I remember it.* A tingling sensation began to envelop his body, like a chill up his spine. He was about to experience what he had been thinking about for so many years. Would she be there?

It was 1957 and Tommy Burk was back home in Southwest Philly and just ten years old, just as Dr. Provenzano promised. He walked up the steps and opened the front door. "Mom? Dad? It's me, Tommy, I'm home."

There she was in the kitchen. The tingling sensation increased. His mom turned and smiled. *She's so young, so beautiful,* thought Tommy.

He ran up to his mother and threw his arms around her waist and started to cry, "Mom, I missed you so much."

"Tommy, that's so sweet, but you only had a half-day of school today. Now go upstairs to your room, change your clothes and do your homework before your father gets home."

All Tommy could think about was seeing his dad, sister, brothers and friends again.

Homework? Baseball, baseball cards and summers down the shore. What a wonderful time to be alive. Homework? I have a feeling I'll never have to study for a test again, thought Tommy.

"Okay, mom, but can I do something I have been waiting a long time to do?"

"And what's that young man?"

His mom was much taller than he, so he gestured with his index finger for his mom to bend down to his level. He put his arms around her neck, gave her a kiss on the cheek and said, "I love you so much mom and I never thought I would ever get the chance to tell you again. I won't make that mistake this time around."

THE END

Made in the USA
Middletown, DE
04 June 2022

66674176R00195